Frayed

"Angst-filled and compulsively readable.... Karr's world is filled with imperfect yet relatable characters, a familiar but well-written story, and hotter-than-hot sex scenes."   —*Publishers Weekly*

"Filled with passion, heart, and emotion.... Kim Karr did an amazing job with this story."   —Debbie's Book Bag

"This series is absolutely amazing: from the rich and colorful cast of characters, to the crazy and surprising plot twists, and the all-consuming blazing-hot passion.... [Karr] is at the very top of my autobuy list."   —A Bookish Escape

"Kim Karr is an amazing storyteller.... [*Frayed*] is dramatic, intense, and realistic."   —The Reading Cafe

Mended

"Kim Karr is one of my few autobuys! Romantic, sexy, and downright gripping! I read it in one sitting because I just couldn't put it down!"
                            —*New York Times* bestselling author Vi Keeland

"Prepare to have your heart stolen by another Wilde brother. Fans of the first two titles in the series will surely fall in love with Xander Wilde and *Mended*... scorching hot."   —*Romantic Times*

continued ...

"A stunning new romance that has it all . . . tension, heartbreak, passion, and love. . . . [*Mended*] showcases the best aspects of what these stories can give us emotionally."   —Harlequin Junkie

"Incredibly sweet. [Xander and Ivy] are a great couple."
—Book Binge

Torn

"I was riveted from the first line and couldn't put it down until the last word was read."   —*New York Times* bestselling author A. L. Jackson

"After an edge-of-your-seat cliff-hanger, Kim Karr returns to beloved characters Dahlia and River. . . . Their passion is intense."
—Fresh Fiction

"The story is fabulous, the characters are rich and full of emotion, and the romance, passion, and sexy are wonderfully balanced with the angst and heartbreak."   —Bookish Temptations

Connected

"I was pulled in from the first word and felt every emotion . . . an incredibly emotional, romantic, sexy, and addictive read."
—Samantha Young, *New York Times* bestselling author of *Hero*

"Emotional, unpredictable, and downright hot."
—K. A. Tucker, author of *Ten Tiny Breaths*

"This book had all my favorite things. This was one of those holy-smokes kind of books!"
—Shelly Crane, *New York Times* bestselling author of *Significance*

THE 27 CLUB

KIM KARR

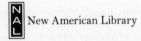 New American Library

New American Library
Published by the Penguin Group
Penguin Group (USA) LLC, 375 Hudson Street,
New York, New York 10014

USA | Canada | UK | Ireland | Australia | New Zealand | India | South Africa | China
penguin.com
A Penguin Random House Company

First published by New American Library,
a division of Penguin Group (USA) LLC

First Printing, March 2015

 REGISTERED TRADEMARK—MARCA REGISTRADA

LIBRARY OF CONGRESS CATALOGING-IN-PUBLICATION DATA:
Karr, Kim.
The 27 club/Kim Karr.
p. cm.
ISBN 978-0-451-47566-4 (softcover)
I. Title. II. Title: The twenty-seven club.
PS3611.A78464A614 2015
813'.6—dc23   2014041824

Printed in the United States of America
10 9 8 7 6 5 4 3 2 1

Set in Bell MT
Designed by Spring Hoteling

For my mother . . . who lost her life
young and tragically.

And to everyone else who has also
lost someone young and tragically.

No matter the cause.

We don't meet people by accident.
They are meant to cross our path for a reason.

—Unknown

THE 27 CLUB

PROLOGUE
Happy 27th Birthday to Me

Zachary Flowers | August

Let's be honest.

Nightclubs aren't about dancing. They're not about drinking. They're about the chase—about scoring.

So any guy volunteering to wait in line and sweat his balls off to be given the privilege to pay a ridiculous cover, squeeze his way through a jam-packed bar, spend twenty-five dollars on a Red Bull and vodka, and scream over the blaring music—all with no guarantee of getting laid—is out of his fucking mind.

I mean, come on!

The corner joint has just as much potential as any fancy-ass club, if not more, with its far less discriminating patrons and cheaper drinks.

Nate's mouth stretches into a huge-ass grin. "We've arrived."

"No shit." If Nate's a-little-too-excited announcement hasn't alerted me, the flashing lights of the neon sign that read THE BALLROOM certainly has. Fucking A, the sign nearly blinds me. One glance out the window and I'm ready to turn around and go home. The line is just as I expected—miles and miles long. I consider making a quick exit with a more than friendly "Peace out," but something makes me stick around.

Nate slows the car to wait in traffic and grips my shoulder. "I almost forgot. Happy birthday, my friend."

I shrug his hand off me. "Fuck birthdays. I still can't believe I let you talk me into this."

The CEO of Skyline Holdings, who also happens to be my best friend, pulls his decked-out Range Rover up to the curb. "Come on, man—it's not every day that a guy turns a year older."

Yeah, twenty-seven—what a great fucking year to look forward to.

Generation after generation, several members of my family have died—not all of them, but enough of them to warrant concern—at the age of twenty-seven.

My great-great-great uncle jumped from the roof of a building during the depression; my great-great aunt's daughter drowned in a lake; my grandfather died in the Vietnam War; and my mother overdosed.

All were twenty-seven.

All died tragically.

Based on those odds, there's a very good chance I could be next.

So yeah, like I said—great fucking year.

"You know what they say, don't you, Z?" Nate's enthusiastic voice brings me out of my sullen disposition.

"I think I do, Nate, but please tell me again." I try to suppress the sarcastic tone oozing through my words, but it isn't easy.

Some douche bag wearing a red jacket pulls Nate's door open and Nate practically howls at the moon, "Live life in the fast lane!"

My door swings wide seconds later. I step out while reaching into my pocket to retrieve a pack of Marlboros, needing a quick one before we enter the nonsmoking zone. "I hope that's just what you've been doing, because I might just kill you after I wait in this line."

Nate hands the valet a wad of cash and waits for a ticket. "Please, you know me better than that."

I can't stop my lips from tilting upward. "I should have guessed you'd have an in," I mumble while sticking a cig between my lips. "How'd you swing something like this?"

He shrugs. "A friend of mine works close by, and she wanted to introduce me to someone."

"She?" My brows wiggle in excitement.

Nate just shakes his head at me.

Whatever.

Typically, Nate's an all business or all play kind of guy; so coming to a club doesn't fit his MO. Skydiving, the track, a quick trip to the casinos in the Bahamas—that's more his speed. I was wondering what brought this outing about, and now I know.

A girl.

Nate and a girl.

My curiosity is piqued. For the five years I've known him, I've never seen him with the same girl twice. In fact, he's a love-'em-and-leave-'em kind of guy.

Over the flare of the lighter, I study my friend as he circles around the car. Nate Hanson, a freak of nature—a geek and a god all in one. A guy who gets what he wants without even trying. And oddly enough, he just doesn't take advantage of all the beautiful women at his feet like he should.

I couldn't even tell you the last time he got laid.

Mind-boggling.

Me—I'm the complete opposite. I take what I can get whenever it's offered.

With a deep inhale, I let the smoke slowly slide from my lungs. Nate meets up with me on the sidewalk and I can't help but tell him, "You know, I'm actually looking forward to tonight."

He looks over at me. "Glad to hear it. Now let's go inside so we can start celebrating."

I roll my eyes at that.

Enjoy the beginning of the year I might die?

Hard to do.

The thought of new beginnings strikes a chord somewhere deep within me. I look right at him. "Starting tonight, I have a new motto to try out."

He raises a brow. "Oh yeah? Let's hear it."

"Screw living life in the fast lane. How about: Live like you're dying?"

I haven't told Nate what this year means, but I will soon.

Seemingly unfazed by my changing our long-adhered-to motto, he grins at me. "Sounds like a great plan. Let's get started."

That's the problem—I don't have a plan, but I need one for the first time in my life.

Nate walks toward the entrance, ignoring the fact that the back of the line is miles in the other direction.

Horns blow as a pack of chicks with banging bodies walk by, taking my head with them.

I love women—every single one of them.

God knew what he was doing when he created them.

In fact, I think fucking would be the thing I'd miss the most if something happened to me—if you can actually miss anything after you die, that is.

Nate looks over at me. "What's the smirk for?"

My head snaps back, and I point behind us. "Didn't you just see them?"

He raises his shoulders as if he doesn't have a fucking clue what I'm talking about.

"Never mind. I've been thinking a lot lately, and I think this might be the year I finally settle down."

"You're fucking nuts. You know that?"

I can't help but laugh. "Never said I wasn't."

"Who knows, Prince Charming? Maybe you'll meet the love of your life inside."

My mood having lifted with my outlook on life, I respond, "That's the problem. How to pick just one when I love them all?"

He picks up the pace. "Come on. Keep up with me, will you?"

I exhale my last puff, looking for a place to put my cig out before catching up to him. A skirt walks by with legs longer than any supermodel. "Fuck, she's hot."

Nate shakes his head. "You're one horny motherfucker. Screw finding your Cinderella. Face it, you could never settle for just one."

"Yeah, you're probably right. I can't help it though—there's nothing like the touch of a woman. And at least I take the time to admire what this beautiful city has to offer, unlike some people I know."

He shoots me a glance. "Waste of time, man."

I grab my chest and stumble backwards. "Yeah, so you've said many times. Your philosophy on romance always breaks my heart."

"Well, get used to it. You should just stop searching now because if you do find someone, she'll only end up breaking your heart in the end."

The truth is, I'll only break hers if my fucking legacy ends up fulfilling itself. But I already decided that I can't live this year thinking that way. Instead of crying the blues, I tell him how I feel about his outlook on love. "You kill me, man, you really do."

"Gives you something to talk about."

My cell vibrates, and I pull it out of my pocket. I glance at the screen and can't hide my grin. It's a text with a picture attached of my sister next to a chocolate birthday cake. Chocolate because it's her favorite, and she'll be the only one eating it.

Nate glances over. "Your booty call for the night?"

I glare at him. "No, it's my sister wishing me happy birthday."

Zoey has called me about five times today. I usually go home for my birthday, but running the gallery full-time means I just can't swing it this year.

He grabs my phone to look at the photo. "Why is it she's never come to visit in all the years I've known you?"

I shrug. "Mimi was sick most of the time, so it was just easier for me to go home."

Zoey is the single most important person in my life. She's the ray of sunshine you can see through the clouds. She's the light at the end of the tunnel. She has always believed in me when no one else has. She has also always kept me moving forward when there were times I thought I might not be able to.

I owe her everything.

All I want is for her to be happy.

She deserves it.

I'm hoping she'll find happiness as soon as all the shit she's had to worry about is taken care of; then she can finish her schooling. I need to find a way to help her—soon. No matter what, her name will have the abbreviation "Dr." before it.

I'll make sure of it—no matter what. I've let her down too many times already in my life not to come through this time.

"The birthday cake is sweet, but it's time to put sweet away and celebrate for real," Nate says.

I fire back with a little sarcasm. "The anticipation is fucking killing me."

"You know what, Flowers? You're a piece of work," he laughs.

I laugh along and allow my gaze to wander. Nate patiently waits for the chick in front of him wearing a very short skirt and sky-high heels to pay her fifty-dollar cover. I give her a once-over; but when she turns around and I see her buttoned-up blouse, I look elsewhere.

She's hot but not my type.

We're in the heart of South Beach on Miami's colorful Washington Avenue. The Ballroom has to be the most insane club around. This crowd is unreal. There are hundreds of people anxiously waiting outside to get in, and we get to walk right in. But the chicks here, they might not be for me. Pretentious, bitchy women are the only type I can't stand. And I can spot them a mile away.

When we finally reach the front, the velvet rope blocks us from going any farther. "Tell Jeremy McQueen I'm here," Nate says in a stern and even voice.

The giant muscled man looks him up and down. "Your name would be?"

"Nathaniel Hanson."

The man's head snaps up. "Sir, nice to meet you."

Sir? I'm impressed.

Nate pulls out his wallet.

The bouncer dismisses him with the wave of his hand. "Your money isn't welcome here."

Sweet.

Nate's chin dips. "Appreciated, but not necessary."

Before the bouncer unhooks the velvet rope, he looks right at me and grunts, "Next time wear a tie."

I ignore him. Do I look like I've ever worn a tie? When he doesn't let us pass, I give in and nod.

The dude finally opens the rope and I quickly move inside. I look over to Nate, who's dressed in a black button-down and expensive black slacks. "You're not wearing a fucking tie."

He shrugs. "Just forget it and have fun."

I let it go and look around, actually feeling like coming here is just what I need to kick off this new year of mine—the one that just might be my last.

The vibe inside is nothing like I've ever seen. There's a lobby of sorts, with an old-fashioned, huge-ass chandelier. The archways into the bar area are covered in mirrored glass panels with LED lights. There's a towering ceiling over the dance floor and the area beside it is filled with leather couches and ornate fireplaces.

"Nice! Right?" Nate scans the crowd.

"Yeah. This place is swarming with chicks, and not just pretentious ones." The club is wall-to-wall tits and legs. Deep-cut dresses, short skirts, and high heels surround me.

It's fucking heaven.

He lifts a brow. "Knew you'd like it. I'll grab us a drink. What are you feeling?"

"Beer for now. Thanks, man. I'll just be here checking out the scene, waiting for my chance to blow out a candle or two."

He shakes his head before walking away. His stride is full of confidence and, as always, he's in no hurry. We both stand over six feet but I'm much bulkier. However, don't let that fool you. I might lift weights, but Nate has trained in martial arts his whole life. Although I'd never admit it, he could kick the shit out of me.

The music booms as I take in the competition—guys in suits, most of them clean-cut like Nate. I stick out like a sore thumb in my jeans, work boots, and black T-shirt.

Like I care.

A group of cute girls are standing together. I zero in on them until I notice one is wearing a crown or some shit like that.

Way too girly for me.

My gaze shifts to a trio of chicks.

One is dressed in leather.

More my speed.

I'm just establishing eye contact when a raspy feminine voice whispers in my ear, "You new here?"

My neck whips around. A vision of utter splendor is standing next to me—an exotic woman with dark hair, dark eyes, and an olive complexion that practically glows. She has ruby red lips and high cheekbones and looks like Elizabeth Taylor in *Cleopatra*. Mimi made me watch that movie at least fifty times—it was her favorite.

I can't move.

I can't talk.

I'm completely taken—bewitched.

"Ummm . . . yeah, it's my first time," I manage to say.

"I can always tell a new face."

The knockout that I can't believe is still talking to me is wearing a low-cut blouse and a hip-hugging skirt.

Hot. Totally fucking hot.

Pulsing, searing heat goes straight to my cock.

Fuck me.

My dick is throbbing and my heart is beating at double speed.

"Do you come here often?"

Holy shit! Did I just use the oldest line in the book?

She laughs. "I'm here a lot and I've never seen anyone quite like you in here before."

My headshake is subtle. If she were anybody else I'd have responded by talking shit or walking away.

"I didn't mean that how it came out."

I shrug. "I get it."

She pulls her hair to one side.

It's then I notice her nametag.

It has THE STYLIST printed on it.

"So tell me—do you work here?"

Her smile wanes as she fumbles to remove the name tag. "No, but I work close by. I forgot I was wearing this."

"Oh yeah? What do you do?"

Her eyes catch mine. "It's complicated."

My brows draw together. "Mysterious."

"It can be."

"Do tell."

She bites her lip in contemplation, but before she can respond a beer is shoved in my face and the person holding that beer wraps his arm around my girl's shoulder and kisses her.

Every instinct in my body goes live wire and the urge to punch, to kill the motherfucker, roars loud in my ears until I hear a deep, familiar voice.

"I see you've met Gisele." Nate grins at me.

Fuck, he knows her!

"Z, this is Gisele. Gisele, this is my friend Z, and tonight is his birthday."

"Happy birthday." She smiles at me, and I know immediately what I want for my wish.

Gisele better not be Nate's girl.

I extend my hand, but when she places hers in mine, I have an urge to kiss it rather than shake it. So I do.

My lips against her skin ignite a fire within me.

Gisele gives Nate a knowing glance. "Jeremy is at the bar. Over there." She points. "Leather jacket. Tall."

He looks over his shoulder. "Thanks. Excuse me a minute."

I take a sip of my beer. "Let's grab a table."

She nods. "Follow me. It's quieter in the back."

Her walk is just as captivating as everything else about her.

Through the crowd of people, she makes her way easily to a high-top table over in the corner. When we sit, she crosses her stocking-covered legs in such a way that I catch a glimpse of her bare skin and the garter just above it.

My eyes widen.

I have an urge to reach over and stroke her there.

I can barely stop myself.

I redirect my gaze up to her face. "You were saying?"

She laughs, obviously having noticed my distraction. "How about we start with you?"

"Okay. What do you want to know?"

"What's your real name?"

"Zachary Flowers, but my friends call me Z."

"Z? Not Zach?"

I nod.

She giggles. "I like Zach better. Do you mind if I call you that?"

"Nope. Call me whatever you want. Only my sister has ever called me Zach."

She smiles. "So, Zach, what do you do for a living?"

I smile back, loving the shape of her lips and the sound of her voice. "Right now I'm managing Nate's father's gallery."

She takes a sip of her drink, then licks her lips, allowing her tongue to slip out and lick off the alcohol. "So, are you an artist?"

I nod, too absorbed in what she's doing to speak.

I'm staring—I know I am.

But once again, I can't help it. Her lips are like a perfect kiss left on a napkin—heart shaped, red, and beautiful. Her body moves with a confidence I've never seen in a woman.

The cocktail waitress arrives with a tray of shots and sets them in the center of the table.

"We didn't order these," I let the waitress know.

She shrugs. "That guy did." She points to Nate. "So do you want them or not?"

"Yes," Gisele answers before I can. The cocktail waitress scurries away, and Gisele picks up one of the shots.

I do the same. "To new friends."

She holds a finger up. "No, wait."

I pause my glass in midair.

She clinks my glass. "Happy birthday."

I give her a slow nod, drinking her in, every inch of her, and slam my shot back, realizing that when she said happy birthday, I didn't think about my legacy, my destiny, or the club.

All I thought about was her.

"It's your turn. Tell me what your name tag means," I insist.

"Hmmm. . . . That's not easy."

"Well, try."

"Let me put it this way. If you worked with me, a good name for you would be the Artist."

The Artist. I like the sound of that.

I move closer. "Tell me more."

"What do you want to know?"

My new motto rings in my ears—*live like you're dying.*

And I decide to do just that.

"Everything," I whisper.

A Word, First

Dr. Julia Raymond | Late May of the following year

Try not to be naive.

In terms of phobia development, we know that phobias are either caught or taught.

If caught, it's typically due to something happening that the person couldn't cope with at the time. Whatever it was plants itself into the subconscious.

If taught, it's usually due to conditioning or receiving misinformation. For example a child may be told, "Stay away from dogs. They can bite and kill you." If the child already has a tendency to be fearful or anxious, the child will more than likely be afraid of dogs.

Zoey Flowers suffers from thanatophobia—the fear of death—or at least, that was my initial diagnosis when she came to see me five weeks ago.

I'm not so sure anymore.

From the minute she stepped into my office, I was intrigued. Something was different about her. I'd seen her as a patient years ago when she was trying to work out her feelings for her mother.

Now a woman, she is still polite, intelligent, and nicely dressed, but when she came in, she wore the type of sadness on her face that only evolves from despair.

"So, Zoey, what brings you to see me today?" I asked once she'd settled into her seat.

She didn't fidget or make excuses like most of my patients. She looked me in the eye and said, "There's a very good chance I'm going to die within the next year, and I'm scared. Some days I'm so angry about it, but others I just feel lost. I'm here because I want you to help me accept my destiny so I can find some direction."

I settled into my seat, selected a pen from the holder on my desk, and set it next to my pad of paper. In my head I had already diagnosed her—classic case of thanatophobia. "What makes you think you're going to die?"

"My brother died a few weeks ago."

I said nothing and waited patiently.

"Before you think I have thanatophobia, I want to tell you my fear is not irrational."

Typical response, I thought. "Go ahead."

A tear leaked from her eye, and I handed her a Kleenex. "Years ago my great-aunt told my brother and me that our family was cursed, that generation after generation of family members have died young and tragically at the age of twenty-seven. She called it the Twenty-Seven Club and she told us her daughter had joined it along with many other relatives. My brother and I thought she was crazy. Although we were aware that our grandfather had died at twenty-seven—he died in the line of duty—and our mother had died at twenty-seven—she overdosed—we didn't give much credence to her statement. It just sounded absurd."

Phobia—taught, I thought to myself.

I scribbled on my notepad the number—*27*.

"You said your brother recently passed. How old was he?"

She averted her gaze this time. "He was twenty-seven."

Phobia—caught, I jotted down.

"And last week was my birthday—I turned twenty-seven."

This got my attention.

"Well, it certainly does seem very coincidental. Let's back up a little. You said your great-aunt first brought your attention to this . . . phenomenon. Did she give you any more information— family history, mental health issues, anything that could shed some light?"

A small frown presented on her face as she thought back. "No, I was just a teenager then. And like I said, I thought she was crazy. In fact, I never paid any attention to what she had told us until my brother died."

Not a classic case by any definition.

Since Zoey's return to my office, I've spent session after session discussing this incapacitating syndrome that has prevented her from completing the simplest of tasks, like planning what to make for dinner the next day, to the more complex ones like completing her application for her doctorate or even going to Miami to clean out her brother's things.

She's lost.

On my own, I've spent countless hours researching her condition and discussing it with my colleagues in roundtable discussions. From everything she's told me, we all agree—her fear is not irrational.

As crazy as it sounds, based on predictability, her fear is logical.

The prescribed courses of treatment were not working though.

She continued to remain adrift.

Her dreams were also getting worse. She dreamed of dying in the simplest of ways. They were always a product of what she did the previous day. This was one of the obstacles preventing her from planning. I'd given her exercises to relax her body and free her mind from getting trapped in her thoughts. Yet, after three weeks, her dreams were still occurring.

I had to change my treatment plan and use unconventional methods.

Rather than focus on what might occur in the future, I decided to go with the accept-your-destiny route. Not in terms of dying, but rather in terms of living.

I fear all this did was manifest resoluteness within this young woman though. Her fear seems to have subsided, and what has evolved is resignation.

Not what I had hoped.

My course of treatment changed yet again when I realized this, and we went to work on getting her life back on track. We started by setting small goals—what she wants to accomplish tomorrow, next week, and even in the fall. Daily sessions did get her to the point where she's now planning her meals, agreeing to appointments beyond the next day, and returning to her job at the summer's end.

That was a stride worth celebrating.

Yet, there is a darkness in her I can't seem to get to. A sadness that has manifested itself so deep, she won't let it come to the surface. I fear this is a combination of events that occurred in her childhood and her most recent tragedies.

She's fragile.

Still, yesterday we had our most significant breakthrough.

"I booked my ticket to Miami this morning," she said.

I clasped my hands together. "How do you feel about that?"

She took a deep breath. "I feel good about it. I want to see where my brother lived and what his life was like."

"Let's discuss your trip. What do you hope to accomplish while you're there?"

"This might sound weird, but I want to prove to myself that what he lived of his life was worth it. I think it will help me move forward."

Pride shone through in my smile. I couldn't help it. "So do I," I told her.

However, at the same time, I was fearful that taking on too much at once might threaten her emotional state. She's not delusional, but she is fragile. She feels she has nothing to live for, and that concerns me the most. Unless she latches on to a reason to live, her fear concerning the Twenty-Seven Club might just become a self-fulfilling prophecy.

"Thank you, Dr. Raymond, for everything."

She pulled me from my dark thoughts. "You don't have to thank me, but please call me if you should need me for anything. I have you scheduled to be back in my office in ten days."

This beautiful young girl had somehow become very special to me, and I was hopeful this next step would be the breakthrough she needed to look past what might be and concentrate on the present. She needed to live her life and not dwell on the maybes.

"Don't forget to focus on your inner voice," I reminded her as she opened the door.

She smiled. "I won't."

Your inner voice—it can be a source of amazing strength, wisdom, and guidance if you can hear it.

Luckily for Zoey, she can.

1
Pandora's Box

Zoey Flowers

In the darkness, it looks more like Pandora's Box than a place where an artist once lived. Nestled between two houses, each the size of an arena and both lit up like football fields, this much smaller home sits dark and alone—no movement from within, no cars in the driveway, no one living inside.

The picture that appears through the rain doesn't seem to reflect any part of him. But something of my brother has to be here. Even just a small piece left behind for me to catch a glimpse of.

A rush of melancholy hits fast.

My throat tightens.

I can't breathe.

Sweat forms on my brow, even though the car is cool.

This isn't one of my asthma attacks—this is grief rearing its ugly head. The grief I tried to deal with at home in all those therapy sessions. The grief I know I have to accept. But just like accepting my destiny—I'm having a hard time doing this.

Destiny—that hidden power that controls fate. Even though it's a path I don't want to be on, I'm not certain I can stray from it.

It owns me—I don't own it.

My fate might very well be inevitable, just as my brother's was. I've almost come to accept that.

Almost.

Taking a deep, calming breath, I close my eyes, demanding my fear stay at bay.

I'm stronger than this.

Yet in the darkness, I don't feel stronger.

My mind swirls with sadness and I quickly snap my eyes open, hoping to eradicate this feeling of dread. My eyes flutter for a moment before I'm finally able to lean forward and take a closer look.

With the illumination of the car's headlights, I stare through the windshield at the house I've stayed away from for far too long.

And in this moment, everything about the property comes to life. It's a work of art—as if my brother painted the picture for me to help ease my fears, like he did when we were kids.

It's there, the small part of him left behind for me to see. Not his body turned to ash, not the marker at the cemetery bearing his name, but a piece of who he was during the life he led here.

The green bricks of the driveway show his funky edge; the triangle-shaped sailcloth carport demonstrates his love for the abstract; and the house's tropical-modern design with its Spanish-style roof is in itself a work of art worthy of being hung on a gallery wall.

Yes, I can see it now.

I can see him living here.

Happy with the life he led before he died.

Just what I was hoping for.

As I sink back down, the worn leather seat seems to swallow me whole as sorrow mixes with relief and rivets through every vein in my body.

Not what I imagined, but the longer I look, the more I can see him living here.

It's perfect.

It's him.

Suddenly, I'm stuck between the dreamlike state I've been in, refusing to accept the truth, and the reality of my situation. The finality renders me immobile—I'm here but he's not, and all I can do is sit motionless.

"You did say 302 South Coconut Lane?" the driver asks over his shoulder.

My eyes meet his in the mirror. "Yes, this is the right place. Just give me a moment, please."

With trembling fingers, I reach for the handle and attempt to gather the courage to at least open the door. I just don't know if I can do this. I'd have thought the passing of time would have made it easier, but maybe it hasn't been long enough.

The driver clears his throat, sensing my apprehension. "Do you want me to take you somewhere else?"

I hand him my credit card. "No, this is what I came to Miami for."

With a signature on the driver's iPhone, I'm ready. I pull the strap of my overnight bag onto my shoulder and step out. Water sloshes everywhere, but I stop for a minute and look up to the heavens.

Moments pass.

Seconds.

Minutes.

I have no idea.

Once I've gathered my courage and strength, I shift my gaze back down and notice the balcony. It's too dark for me to tell, but I can't imagine it wasn't built for framing some kind of beautiful picture, something worth looking at.

Water fills my eyes and my tears mix with the rain, as the idea of Zach sketching from there comes to mind.

The driver hands me my suitcase and shuts my door before hopping back in the car.

At that moment, the sky seems to open up, and before I can button my coat, I'm soaked.

Hurrying forward, I stop at the white metal gate. With a slight push, I'm walking into a tropical paradise. Trees line the walkway and a natural stone wall protects the area. The pathway leads to a few stairs with a glass door at the top of them.

Walking slowly, very slowly now that I've shielded myself from the rain, I'm at the bottom of the stairs way too soon.

I'm not ready for this.

Feeling like a lost girl, one who is waiting for her brother to take her hand and guide her to the playground to swing, I can't help but wish that he were here beside me.

With a breath in and out, the smell of salt in the air assaults my senses. The ocean must be very close. I wonder if the sand that surrounds it is anything like the sand at the beach Mimi took Zach and me to every summer.

God, how we loved going there.

We'd walk on the pier, swim in the lake, ride the carousel, and eat Abbott's famous custard. There was a beach closer to where we lived in Canandaigua, New York, but it didn't have an Abbott's. Zach loved the black raspberry ice cream so much that he'd get two.

"I need to stock up until next year," he'd say.

It was so rare that anything made him happy, and I bet Mimi would have bought him a hundred ice-cream cones if only his happiness would have lasted.

Tires squealing onto the main road jar me from my memories.

On shaky legs, I take the stairs slowly. I reach for the keys Zach accidentally left at home when he visited at Christmas. He left his whole keychain. I would have mailed it, but I didn't find it for months and by then he had had new keys made.

I remember the day Zach told me he had bought a house. I was so glad he was doing well, that he was happy.

Finally, I had thought.

It takes me a few more seconds to gather the courage to unlock the door. The first key I insert doesn't work; neither does the second, nor the third.

A gust of warm wind whips around my black raincoat and blows up the nylon like a tent—a sign of the impending tropical storm that the driver mentioned before I tuned everything else out.

Nervousness and impatience blend as I wonder who I'll call if I can't get in. Zach's friend Nate would be a good start. Over the years, we've talked on the phone if he was around when I'd call my brother. He also called me right after Zach's death. He told me he would take care of everything until I could make it down here. And we've e-mailed quite a few times over the past seven weeks. In fact, I e-mailed him just before I boarded the plane this afternoon, telling him I was coming. But last I checked he hadn't responded yet.

I'm surprised.

He's always responded immediately to my previous messages. It may seem odd, but I feel like I know him well, even though we've never met.

The rain comes down harder and I look around for where my brother might have hidden a spare.

The terra cotta planter off to the right seems like the perfect location, but when I try to lift it, I can't. The palm tree inside is much heavier than I thought.

With nowhere else popping out as a place to hide an extra, I wonder if I should call and ask the driver to return. But before I do, I try the keys again—this time turning a few of them the other way.

To my shock and surprise one finally works. My stomach flips as the door easily swings open and I'm launched into darkness and the loud sound of beeping.

Shit, the alarm. I hadn't thought of that.

Should I try the same code Zach used on all his accounts?

That should work.

With the flip of a switch, a long narrow hallway presents itself. I find the alarm pad behind the door and press 0515, my birthday.

It doesn't work.

I press 0815, his birthday.

It doesn't work either.

What else?

The name of the gallery he worked for maybe? Nate's father's gallery.

What was it? Yes, Wanderlust.

I type the numbers corresponding to the letters and holy shit, the beeping ceases. I can't believe it. After all this drama, my nerves are finally starting to settle.

Once my bags are tucked inside the door, I glance down the hall.

Hardwood floors seem to run for miles until they end at the underside of an open-air staircase. With small steps I walk until I've reached the end and I'm standing at the perimeter of a large living room. My attention goes immediately to the windows and doors—they are everywhere. The entire back of the house is sliding doors with windows above them.

The night and the rain don't allow me to see anything beyond five feet, but I can make out palm trees, lots and lots of them. They sway back and forth through all the glass.

A beautiful picture.

Looking up, the high ceilings and large glass windows make the palms feel like they are part of the room. The two sparkling crystal chandeliers catch my eye—they are beautiful, but so unlike my brother. He always went for the shabby chic look. Modernism was never his thing.

Another hallway across the way mimics the one I'm standing in, and a fireplace sits in the corner. A large black leather couch, glass coffee table, and giant TV complete the room. I'm actually surprised by the sparse décor. It doesn't seem to be Zach's style at all, but maybe it came furnished.

I circle around the stairs to the landing and come face-to-face with a black plaster, life-size statue of a woman. It's definitely something Zach would have been drawn to—mysterious, sad.

It seems out of place in this space.

Surveying the rest of the room, I see a square kitchen in the center of the living area that separates the two hallways. The high-gloss black countertops match the stairs. Walking around them, I notice the kitchen looks perfect—like it's never been used. I quickly walk in and open the refrigerator—water, beer, wine, and nothing else. I guess Nate cleaned it out.

Following the hallway of windows that ends with a closed door, I turn the knob and squeeze my eyes shut, not opening them for what seems like hours. When I do, I'm standing in the entrance of what must have been his office. Computers, printers, and papers cover a large desk. Odd—I would have expected an easel and art supplies. And the walls should be covered with his sketches, not watercolors in ornate frames.

His studio must be elsewhere in the house.

I shut the door knowing I'll be spending time in there later going through all his papers.

Another door opens into the garage. I glance around—a few fishing poles, a basketball, football, and Frisbee, nothing else. The thought of Zach fishing or playing ball makes me smile, because aside from our yearly beach trip, he very rarely spent time outdoors—it just wasn't his thing.

Across from the garage is another door. When I open it, the switch on the wall does nothing. The brightness of the hall casts a sliver of light, and all I can see is an empty room with a bed in the middle of it.

With a turn of my flip-flops, I head back to the living area and the stairs. The entire space lacks anything personal, except the statue. Something about the statue speaks to me, but why I have no idea. It doesn't feel like it belongs, but it does—like the way Zach always felt.

With each step, I increasingly start to wonder if I should have just hired someone to do this and had the boxes shipped home.

This is so much harder than I imagined.

The stairs are sleek, so I take them slowly. When I reach the top, I pause and look around. It's an empty loft with two doors; one must go to the balcony, the other is open and leads to a huge bedroom. It too is white, no color at all.

So strange.

In the middle of the room is a large mattress with a wooden bedframe and metal bars inset in the headboard. The sheets are rumpled—the only evidence in the entire house that someone lives here—no, *lived* here.

With my hands clenched to my heart, I draw in a breath and attempt to push away my tears. I've cried for far too many weeks already. I'm trying to be strong. That is what he would have wanted.

I find myself once more searching for a piece of my brother, but again there's nothing. But then a small crystal dish on the dresser draws my attention.

Once I see what it holds, I can't stop the flow of tears from my eyes as I approach it. With wavy vision I pinch the small diamond that Zach wore so proudly in his ear.

Memories flood me once again.

"Please, Mimi, please. I really want one," Zach begged over and over.

"No, Zachary. There's nothing but trouble that can come out of that," Mimi would say.

It felt like the conversation took place every day for almost a year. But Zach didn't let up. He begged our grandmother to let him get an earring. She always refused. Over and over and over he asked and she said no. Then on his fifteenth birthday he came home from being out with Mimi sporting this very diamond. My grandmother finally gave in, probably feeling it was better than the fights, the drugs, and his all-encompassing need to rebel against everything.

The other metal in the bowl belonged to him as well—all his forms of self-expression. His lip ring, ear gauges, the circles with a ball hanging from them, most of which he acquired after he turned eighteen and no longer needed Mimi's permission.

These things in my hand were all a part of my brother.

He was a rebel.

Funny thing is that I always thought he was a rebel without a cause. I used to laugh about that, but today it makes me sad.

I remove my wet coat and shoes, circling around the rest of the room looking for pieces of him.

Nothing.

Nothing that was any part of him, not anything to define who he was.

But I know who he was.

He was my older brother.

He was my best friend.

He was a good man who didn't always make the right choices but had the best intentions.

Sadness lingers, as I think that I no longer have to wonder about him or worry about him. Now all that's left is for me to miss him, but I already miss him so much.

I'm alone.

Growing up, we only had each other—and our grandmother too. Our grandfather died before my grandmother gave birth to our mother, so Mimi knew single parenting well. She was amazing. She taught us everything she could, told us anything we wanted to know, but she refused to talk about the club. Mimi said she didn't believe in that old family legend.

Too bad destiny isn't something you can choose to believe in—it just happens.

Now, it's become more than a legend. It took him dying for me to believe. My constant reminder is the fact that Zach is also dead—he, like my grandfather and my mother, will forever be twenty-seven.

The question is: will I be joining my ancestors at the same young age?

Is that my destiny?

I hope not—but how could it not be?

I set the dish down and emotion overtakes me, the magnitude of my losses and my short life becoming all too real.

I collapse on the bed.

If I die at twenty-seven, will I have even lived a small part of my life?

Did my grandfather? Did my mother? Did my brother?

My head spins and I find myself back at that place I can't seem to crawl out of—I feel like screaming, but I can't because the idea of yelling seems like too much work when all I can think about is myself being next.

I yank off my wet T-shirt and shorts and bury my head under his pillow, wanting to block out that small voice telling me to push through this. I thought coming here would give me hope that life is worth the chance of what might or might not happen, but the sterility of my brother's home, the lack of anything he was surrounding me, stirs an uneasiness I can't seem to shake.

I feel like I'm already dying.

I've felt like this for many weeks.

Validation of a life worth living and dying young for was what I hoped to find by coming here. But instead all there is is a reflection of what I see when I look in the mirror—emptiness.

I close my eyes, wishing for all of this to be nothing more than a dream. But I know my first impression was right—I've opened Pandora's box.

2
Coffee Beans

The wind howls and the palm trees whip against the windows as the storm seems to make its way closer to landfall. Thunder booms and lightning lights up the room, startling me. No, not lightning—a lamp.

"Hello, Zoey." The voice is deep and husky.

As the sound registers, I scream. I quickly sit up and scan my unfamiliar surroundings. My eyes immediately land on the silhouette of a man standing beside me, and I scream again, this time scrambling off the bed in terror.

In this moment, my heart stops beating, my lungs stop breathing, and my brain stops thinking. I'm petrified.

The man raises his palms up in surrender. "Zoey, I'm Nate, Z's friend. You don't have to be scared. I'm not going to hurt you."

My fear must be evident. I stare at him for a few long moments, both alarmed and trembling. Only once realization sets in, that yes, this is Nate, my brother's best friend, do I attempt to calm my ragged breaths.

He takes a cautious step back. "Just cover up with something so we can talk."

Oh my God, my clothes.

Tangled sheets catch on my limbs as I climb back onto the bed and unsuccessfully try to pull the covers over my practically naked body. Before humiliation grabs complete hold of me, I give up and dive for my soaking wet shirt lying on the floor.

Sliding the cold fabric over my head, I pull it down to cover my panties and stand up, quickly crossing my arms over my chest to shield any signs of the chill I'm feeling.

Not great, but better. At least I can look at him with a little dignity.

Finally, I glance up and my gaze catches his. As soon as it does, he drops his eyes.

The photos I've seen of him over the years, when my brother would text me a funny shot—a selfie of him and Nate at some top chef restaurant, at the beach, or at a coffee house—didn't nearly do him justice. Those shots were goofy poses with baseball caps turned backwards and funny faces. Not that I didn't think he was good looking in them, because I did, but there's just something different about him.

I blink and focus on the matter at hand. "You scared the shit out of me. What are you doing here?"

Staring at the ground, he leans against the doorjamb. "You beat me to the punch. I was just about to ask you the same question."

"Why would you ask me that?"

He raises a brow. "I guess I'm just curious."

I sigh, feeling confused.

His gaze lifts, and those eyes, those bewitching emerald green eyes, stare back at me. "Not that I mind that you're here. It's just— a little warning would have been nice. That's all."

His tone is more bemused than apologetic.

I'm not sure what to think.

With a straight and confident stance, I clear my throat. "I e-mailed you earlier today to let you know that I was coming for the weekend. I'm really sorry about the late notice, but I decided at the last minute."

He reaches into the pocket of his low-slung jeans and pulls out his phone. After a few taps and scrolls he looks up at me. "I guess you did. Here it is. I'm usually on top of my e-mails but today my . . . schedule was full. Had I seen your message, I would have tried to rearrange my plans."

"That's fine really. I managed. It's not a big deal."

I steal a glance at my reliable Timex—just after midnight. What is he doing in my brother's house in the middle of the night? Just as I'm about to ask him, my eyes catch sight of the way he predatorily walks around the room and I'm momentarily distracted. He moves like a panther—slowly circling his prey, keeping his distance, not too close, but close enough to pounce if he feels the urge. He settles back against the wall, just a little closer now. "Zoey, did you hear me?"

I swallow. "Sorry, what?"

His tone grows more insistent. "I said I would have at least sent a car for you. You shouldn't be out in this weather on your own."

My brow furrows. Why is he still talking about the airport?

When I don't respond, he crosses his arms over his chest like he owns the place.

It's then that reality sinks in. And as cliché as this sounds, I am not going to let Mr. Tall, Dark, and Handsome intimidate me. It's time to take charge. "There was no need. I managed just fine. But if you didn't know I was coming, can I ask what you're doing here?"

Confusion seems to have taken over his thoughts as he steps even closer—moving with a lethal grace that makes my body start to hum. I can't help but study him as his features come into clear focus. His body is long and lean. His hair is dark, the most unusual shade of brown, maybe like the color of expensive chocolate, but not exactly. His eyes are languid, watchful, and the most beautiful shade I've ever seen—darker than emeralds or the deepest of forest greens. His lips look full and soft. He is handsome in a way that is unlike anyone I've ever seen.

My mind is going haywire.

"Nate, why are you at my brother's house in the middle of the night?" I ask him again.

A look of realization seems to cross his face as he stares at me. With a smirk, he ignores my question. Instead of answering me, he opens the door beside him. It's a closet, Zach's closet to be exact, and he steps right in, again like he owns the place.

"What are you doing?" I ask impatiently.

He comes back into the bedroom with a pair of sweatpants and a T-shirt in his hand. "You're trembling. How about you get changed and we sit down to talk?"

The audacity of this man is beyond comprehension. From his e-mails he seemed nice, but then again, you never can tell what lurks behind the words on a computer screen.

He stares and his small smirk really irritates me. "Take these, they're mine. I'll wait downstairs while you get changed."

If I weren't standing here, chilled and in my underwear, I might just tell him to go to hell.

But instead I reach for the clothes, and as I do, I start to wonder if he's been squatting in my brother's house. Once the clothes are in my hands, his mouth spreads into a slow, easy grin.

Annoyance grabs hold of me as I pivot on my bare feet and head toward the bathroom, making sure not to glance over my shoulder. When I hear heavy footsteps, I let my body fall back and shut everything out of my mind for a few short seconds.

What is going on?

When I've gathered my composure, I quickly strip out of my wet clothes and redress. Then I make the mistake of looking in the mirror. A wet dog would look better than I do right now. In an effort to improve the image, I grab a towel and wipe the black mascara from under my eyes. Then I use my fingers to comb through my mass of curls and try to calm them, but that's nearly impossible.

Okay, better—but not great.

Who cares anyway?

It's not like I'm trying to impress him. In fact, I've never tried to impress a man.

Ever.

Time to get down to business. I stomp out of the bedroom and down the stairs. The TV is on and I can hear the weatherman announcing the same info the driver relayed to me. "Tropical Storm Angela seemingly having stalled out once it passed over Cuba is picking up wind speed as it makes its way toward the Florida Keys."

The rain is still beating down, but there are no calls for evacuations so I can only assume I am fine staying here.

Determined to get this conversation over with, I'm stopped dead in my own tracks.

Nate is standing in front of a built-in coffeemaker, waving his hand frantically up and down, cursing under his breath, "Motherfucking piece of shit."

"What happened? Did the Miele not do what you told her to do?" He turns.

I feel like I'm watching him in slow motion.

Without warning, the air crackles.

He's momentarily taken aback, but then a look of amusement crosses his face. "Zoey Flowers, you are . . ."

Words pop into my head—sexy, beautiful, hot as hell, fuckable.

Where did those come from?

That grin lingers on his mouth. "Your brother's sister, without a fucking doubt."

Tears prick my eyes. Not the words I hoped to hear, but so much more meaningful.

His face contorts, the glow of amusement gone from his eyes, shadowed by something darker. He sets two cups of coffee on the counter that separates us. "Hey, I'm really not good at this stuff. I didn't mean to make you cry."

I swipe the drops away. "No, really, it's okay. I just miss him. That's all."

Nate's hands grip the counter and his head falls. "Yeah, me too."

Silence sweeps the vastness of the space, but strangely it's not uncomfortable.

His gaze lifts. "Zoey, it's nice to finally meet you."

I can't help but be charmed. "It's nice to finally meet you too, Nate."

He clears his throat and a bit of shyness seems to cross his face.

I fear I might be staring, so I avert my gaze to look down at the counter and it lands on the two cups. "Are those lattés?"

His head lifts at the same time mine does. The connection is immediate—a jolt of electricity travels between us and I swear I see a little smile—not a smirk, but an actual smile on his face.

The most adorable boyish grin.

My belly flutters and I can't help but return the smile, feeling a little shy myself.

"Yeah, well, that's what they're supposed to be. I didn't know what you drank, but thought I'd try these."

I move closer, close enough that my hipbones nudge the edge of the counter. "Lucky for you, I'll drink anything made with coffee beans."

Then it hits me that his hair is the color of the finest imported coffee beans.

"Yeah, lucky for me," he repeats.

Taking a seat on one of the barstools, I blow on the top of the latté. The froth is not exactly froth-like, more like big soap bubbles or maybe clumps of soured whipped cream.

"You're a schoolteacher, right?" he asks.

"Something like that," I say. "I'm employed by the University of Rochester. You're a landlord, right?"

His lips tip up a fraction. "Something like that."

I laugh. "Just kidding. I know all about you—big successful CEO of an up-and-coming development company, who buys un-profitable businesses, turns them around, and then sells them. Zach said you are very business savvy."

This is true, but what I fail to mention is Zach told me so much more about him.

He raises one brow in the sexiest way. "You're going to make me blush if you keep talking like that. But it sounds to me like you're leaving some crucial things out. I'm sure your brother must have given you some dirt on me."

How does he know Zach told me all about his inability to commit, his obsession with work, and his need to always be in control? He never spoke of him in a demeaning way though. No, rather Zach seemed to idolize this man. The words *integrity, hard working,* and *respectful* always followed anything that might have been construed as negative. Zach once mentioned that he thought something must have happened that triggered Nate's extreme behavior.

He could understand that.

Honestly, so could I.

"Z never could give a compliment without making sure to put a little bite in it. My guess is he would have said something like this: "Big-shot asshole of some rising development company."

I shrug. He did have my brother pegged. "Maybe it did go more like that."

He smirks, and God help me, I have to look away.

I try to tuck my emotion aside by sipping on my latté. It tastes more like water, but the coffee lover in me is far too distracted by the trouble that's watching me to care.

His eyes seem to darken as they follow the liquid into my mouth and then down my throat. His breath seemingly goes shallow as if he's picturing my mouth on something else.

My imagination must be in overdrive. I shake it off and point to my cup. "Not bad."

He takes a sip of his and practically spits it out. "Not bad! It tastes like shit."

I can feel my lips turning upward again. I swear I haven't smiled in so long that I snap and just let the laughter roll through me—my body quaking, my hair bouncing like a lion's mane.

Nate stares flabbergasted, and I can see his body tensing.

Once I'm finally able to speak, I manage to say, "Really, it doesn't taste terrible. You just have your timing and ratios off, that's all. Steam the milk a little longer, and add more beans."

He sets his cup down and gives me a skeptical look.

"I used to work at a coffee shop when I was in college. I can show you if you like?"

Our gazes lock.

When he doesn't respond, reality crashes down around me. I can't let this become flirtatious.

I clear my throat. "Well, anyway, can we get back to why you're here in the middle of the night? You can be honest with me—have you been staying here?"

A muscle twitches along Nate's jaw, but he doesn't answer me. Instead, he picks up his cup and turns to the sink, dumps his full latté down the drain, and then walks to the back of the house in the darkness.

My head twists so my eyes can track him.

He flicks a light switch on and twists his own head.

I know he must have caught my stare, and God knows what possessed look I might have had on my face. I quickly turn back.

"Zoey, I think we need to talk."

"I know we do. And Nate, it's okay. Really. I don't mind that you've been staying here," I reassure him as I turn back around.

He opens one of the many sliding glass doors and the sound of the storm gets louder. "Come over here. I want to show you something."

Something draws me toward him.

He's a man of authority. I can tell he's used to getting his way, but I'm not usually one to submit to dominance. I've been around it enough at work—male professors are the poster children for authoritative personalities.

But still I move forward, approaching him with caution.

The sound of the waves crashing against the shore is beautiful. With the door open the smell in the air is pungent in the most delicious way, or maybe that's Nate—clean, fresh, manly.

Without realizing it, I'm standing right in front of him. I get lost in the wind, the air, the sound—and him. I tilt my head back to look at him. I'm tall, but he's almost a head taller than I am—he must be six-two. Something about his proximity makes my body feel possessed.

It's nothing like I've felt before.

He steps out the door and onto a covered deck, scrubbing his stubbled jaw. "I told you I'm shit at this kind of stuff so I'm just going to get this over with."

Relief takes over.

Here it comes.

He's finally going to admit he's been crashing here. God, what if he has nowhere else to go? I never thought of that. Maybe he's not as successful as my brother thought he was. What am I going to do if that's the case? It's not like I'd throw him out of my bed—shit, I mean out on the street.

I move forward and stand beside him. "Yes, that would probably be best."

"Look, Zoey, I think there's been a misunderstanding. Can you see over there?"

I take a step out even further, and the force of the wind travels underneath my thin T-shirt. "Just barely."

He points to something, but I can't make out what it is. "It's a boathouse that sits on the edge of the property. Zoey, Z lived there, not here."

I twirl around and my words come out as forceful as the storm. "That's not true. He told me he lived here, in a house, that he owned."

"It is true, Zoey. Are you sure he told you he lived here?"

"Yes, I'm sure. I wouldn't be here otherwise."

His face seems to pale. "Maybe you misunderstood him?"

"No!" I shake my head.

"I'm sorry. I had no idea he told you that. I just thought you got the locations confused."

"No, I'm not confused. God, I wouldn't have fallen asleep in your bed! Zach told me he bought a house that he lived in on the water."

"He did live in a house on the water. But he didn't own it, and it isn't this one."

I can feel the blood rush to my face. I swallow hard. "No! That can't be true. I'm not sure what kind of game you're playing, but don't try to take advantage of my brother now that he's dead. Tell me the truth—you've been living here since he died. Haven't you? I'm going to find out anyway."

He grabs my arms, stepping closer. "Zoey, I'm telling you the truth. I wouldn't lie about something like that. I wouldn't do that to my friend."

I push him away. "So you're saying that my brother lied to me? He wouldn't have done that. We told each other the truth. Always."

"He moved in when I did. I had an empty place back there, and he needed a cheaper place to live."

I shake my head, still finding it hard to believe him.

"Why does it matter which house he fucking lived in? The address is the same." His voice rises, his control now lost as his anger comes to the surface.

The floor seems to tilt—my world spinning on its axis. "It does matter. It matters that he lied. He just wouldn't do that."

Tears stream down my cheeks as I realize that Zach did lie.

The look in Nate's eyes tells me so.

This is his house—not Zach's.

I know it is; now the space makes sense.

And with that sudden realization, I seem to lose my mind. With my world crashing down around me even more than it already has, I run out into the rain, across the wet grass, toward the dark boathouse.

Nate shouts, "Zoey, come back inside! We're in the middle of a fucking storm."

The thunder is so loud my ears are ringing. The lightning is so bright that I can see the boathouse with its solid wooden door right in front of me.

Ignoring his plea, I turn the knob and jerk on it.

It's locked, but I keep twisting it over and over.

When I can't get it open, I pound on the door. I pound until I swear my knuckles are bleeding. I don't even know what I'm doing.

Suddenly, the wind picks up and I can feel the forcefulness as it rocks the boathouse.

I lift my head toward the rain.

"Why did you have to die?" I yell.

"Why did destiny take you?" I scream.

"Why did you lie?" I whisper.

Big, strong hands grip me and turn me around. "Shhh . . . it's okay, Zoey. We'll figure this out."

I look at him. "No, no, we won't."

"We will. Let's just go back inside."

"Why would he lie?" I yell.

"I don't know!" he shouts back. "I don't know," he repeats more quietly.

"I have to see for myself," I scream over the noise of the storm.

"Not now. We have to get back inside. You can see tomorrow."

Tree branches tumble to the ground. I can't see the water but I can hear it slamming into the shore.

"Why did he have to die?" I cry. They're the same words I've been crying for weeks.

"I don't know," Nate whispers in my ear and it's the first time someone has answered my cries.

"He was all I had left," I mumble.

The sky lights up, flashing over and over, but I don't move. Then a long boom, another flash, and suddenly complete darkness. Gone are the lights from the house that allowed me to see Nate's face. Everything is gone.

"Fuck! The power went out."

A tree branch smashes against the side of the boathouse.

Nate looks at me. "We have to get back inside . . . now."

A moment of sheer fear strikes me as I search for the stars, the moon; anything to shed light on the darkness. But my quest is fruitless. I feel completely lost, and my sobs grow louder.

Shock.

Fear.

Sorrow.

They're all I can feel, and I can't move.

I'm helpless.

I'm empty.

Lost.

Strong arms scoop me up and carry me across the grass. In those arms, I allow myself to find comfort—a comfort I never expected to feel in the arms of my brother's best friend and a comfort I didn't realize I needed so very much.

3

The Warrior

The wind fights against his long strides but he moves like a warrior during battle—swiftly and in precise movements. His boots don't even sink into the wet, soaked grass that my bare feet must have left pocked.

His body is covering mine. When I try to lift my head from the safety of his neck, his head tucks down to force mine back in place. If I didn't know better, I'd say he's trying to protect me from the harsh rain. But after the accusations I just threw at him, I can't imagine that to be the case.

My mind is filled with scattered thoughts, blown apart by the bomb he dropped, and yet the panting sound coming from his mouth oddly eases the destruction I'm feeling.

The wind and rain stop their assault the minute he crosses the threshold into the house. Both of us soaked to the bone, he sets me down. His hands on my hips steady me while I find my footing, but they linger in place even after I've gained my stability.

Again I find comfort in his touch.

I tilt my head to try to see him, but I can't. It's just too dark.

The feel of his touch and the sound of his breath are the only evidence that he's standing there in front of me.

When his grasp is suddenly gone, my sense of direction seems to go with it. "Nate?" I reach out terrified and grab onto him—his biceps, I think. "Don't leave me alone."

"Stay right here. Just give me a minute to secure the windows."

The house is so dark.

I can't see a thing.

My teeth are chattering and my mind is spinning.

All of a sudden images of my brother are all I can see. Images painted with his lies. I want to know why he would have told me something that wasn't true. I would never have cared where he lived—so why did he feel he had to lie to me?

I just don't understand.

The sound of Nate's boots on the floor weakens—he's moving further away. I reach out for something to hold on to as a feeling of panic begins to overtake me, but I find nothing except air.

Is this it?

Will tonight's storm end with me dying?

I never used to think that way until Zach died.

Now confusion clouds me daily.

Since the day I turned twenty-seven, fear of dying has sucked out my will to live.

I'm alone.

Adrift.

Lost.

Every time I slam on my brakes, I think: *Maybe this will be it.* Every night when I fall asleep, I think: *Maybe I won't wake up.* And every day when I do, I think: *Will today be my last day?*

I don't know how to move forward, or even if I should be trying.

Nate's phone sheds a small halo of light, pulling me from my reverie. I watch him, feeling relieved that I can see and relieved that my mind has something else to focus on. He slides open one side of the bank of glass doors and steps outside. The sounds seeping in don't do anything to mute the foreboding silence within these walls.

Needing to escape it, I step toward him cautiously, on my bare feet, making sure not to slip. The storm seems more severe in the pitch black of the night, and a slight twinge of fear strikes me again.

Nate looks up just as I step outside. "Goddamn it, Zoey. Didn't you hear what I said?" His stern voice snaps me out of the tailspin I was headed into.

The sounds of the storm are as fierce as his tone, and I take a step back. "I heard you. I just wanted to see what you were doing." I try to sound just as stern, but I'm pretty sure the squeal that accompanied my tone took the edge off.

The light fades as he tucks the phone into the front pocket of his jeans.

"Can I hold your phone for you?"

The wall perpendicular to the glass houses a panel, and he opens it. "Just stay there," he says and then pulls out something that looks like a metal curtain.

Curious, I lean forward but keep my feet planted on the wet floor inside. "Do you need help?"

His hands go to his hips and his head drops. After a moment he looks toward me and over the howling of the wind he shouts, "No! I told you to stay inside."

I sigh, not surprised his patience with me is wearing thin. In fact, I'm shocked he's even allowed me back in his house, but I guess leaving me out in the storm wasn't really an option.

He drags the accordion-looking sheet toward me, and the pleats begin to flatten as they cover the glass doors. He moves with a competence that I can't turn away from.

When the metallic shutter is completely stretched across one side, he does the same on the other. The shutters are tall enough to protect the windows above us as well. Once both sides meet in the middle, he steps back into the house and latches them together, then he closes and locks the glass doors.

"We're going to have to stay in this room tonight. It's the safest spot. I never activated the storm shutters before the power went out so these are the only ones in place. I've been meaning to get a generator. I just haven't gotten around to it."

Wondering just how bad the storm is going to get, I ask, "Are we going to be all right staying here?"

He runs a hand through his wet hair. "We'll be fine. Don't be scared. The storm isn't that bad."

My teeth are chattering. "I'm not scared."

But I am.

I always seem to be scared lately.

His eyes lock on mine, and water drips down his body. "I'm going to grab some towels and see if I can find a flashlight. I'll be right back."

"Are you sure there isn't anything I can do?"

"No. Just sit down."

I nod, and with the slight glow of his phone I move toward the couch. The squeaking of his boots fades and I'm alone in the room. I've never been afraid of storms, but this one petrifies me. The wind whistles so loud and the rain pounds down like a jackhammer. A loud shattering noise makes me jump, but Nate's curse tells me he must have run into something.

"Nate, are you okay?" I call out.

"Yeah, but that was the only flashlight in the whole fucking house."

"Don't you have any candles?"

A moment later, the glow is back and Nate reaches me carrying a pile of towels and blankets under his arm. "If I had some, I wouldn't be pissed that I dropped the flashlight," he snaps, clearly frustrated.

I stand up. "I guess not. Sorry."

He sets the stack on the coffee table and steps toward me. "You don't have to apologize. My temper has nothing to do with you. I'm just pissed that I'm so ill equipped for this weather when hurricane preparation has been drilled into me my whole life."

"What do you do to prepare for a hurricane besides put shutters over your windows?"

He laughs dryly. "A lot. Water and supplies would be a good start."

"I've never been in a hurricane before."

"Well, you still haven't. Trust me, this isn't one."

"Has one ever hit close to where you lived?"

"Yeah," he sighs.

My hand flies to my mouth. "That must have been awful."

"I don't like to think about it."

"I can understand that."

"No, I don't think you can," he mutters.

Something about the way he says it makes me shiver.

"Zach told me about a few that hit close, but never anything too bad."

"No, we haven't had a bad storm in years."

Able to talk much more calmly now, I ask him, "Why do you think my brother told me he owned this house?"

He takes a step closer. "I wish I could answer that for you."

A flash of lightning and the crashing sound of thunder startle me.

His hands gentle but firm, Nate squeezes my shoulders. "There is nothing to be afraid of."

Although his words are comforting, it's his unexpected touch that causes tingles to explode under my skin, covering me in goose bumps. My reaction catches me off guard, and I slip a little, grabbing onto him for support. His grip on me tightens but I continue to slide. He moves quickly. His hands shift to my hips and he steadies me, pulling me back up—closer to him.

We breathe each other in. Flesh to flesh, my fingers remain wrapped around his upper arms and his hands stay firm at my waist. Our touches linger, even after I'm anchored. The contact between us feels like more than just the aftermath of him catching me.

All I know is that my pulse is racing.

The light on his phone fades, but he doesn't turn it back on.

We're in the dark.

My senses intensify. The sound of his breathing continues to mix with mine. The dripping of the water from his clothes, and mine, hits the floor. Neither of us speaks, but we seem to naturally move even closer—a strange mutual draw.

Moments pass as we stand like this, and with each passing one, I can feel the heat between us growing. I can also feel just how close his lips are—I'd say his mouth is hovering very close to mine. The pull between us seems to escalate.

Somewhere deep within me, the flicker of want erupts.

It surprises me.

It makes me feel alive.

Even after everything that's happened today, my body seems to react on its own to this man.

The silence is intoxicating.

I become hyperaware of his every breath, each slight body movement, even the blink of his lashes. Drifting closer, our bodies brush against each other. Immediately, I feel like a bolt of electricity is zapping through me.

Suddenly, my teeth chatter.

Nate steps back. He sucks in a deep breath and then hands me a towel. "Here, take this. I'll grab us both something dry to put on."

"Okay," I whisper, my voice raspy.

My heart is pounding.

My pulse is racing.

What was that?

His phone guides his way up the stairs.

My mind wanders, but strangely I'm not thinking about the uncertainty of what my life holds—I'm thinking about Nate. I hadn't really given him much consideration before. Had never even tried to put a personality to the man who was my brother's best friend, but if I had, I'm not sure I would have gotten it right. He's intense but kind, unassuming but demanding, confident but not arrogant. He's everything I would have swooned over in a man before I lost my way. Before my life became so uncertain.

The towel being pulled from my hands alerts me that he's returned. "You were supposed to put this around yourself, not hold onto it." Then he laughs.

His chuckle is a welcome relief among all the stress.

"Sorry." It's all I can say. I feel like it's the only word I've used all night.

My emotional state is so mixed up right now.

His phone is in one hand and dry clothes are in the other, yet his gaze still pins me.

I stare back and feel like I'm drowning in his eyes.

My eyes flutter and I pull myself from his depths and catch sight of all of him. He's long and lean and competent as he stands before me. He's changed into a pair of sweatpants, plain gray ones like the ones I'm wearing, and a white T-shirt, again like the one I'm wearing. "We're going to look like twins."

He drops his stare. "Yeah, I guess we are."

I reach for the clothes in his hands and our fingers touch.

He sets his phone on the table. "You're shivering."

"I'm fine—really."

He unfolds the towel and wraps it around my shoulders.

My body tingles in the strangest way.

His touch electrifies me.

With the gentlest of touches he lifts the corner of the towel. Water trickles down my nose, my cheek, my chin, and he gently pats them away, and then moves to my hair and does the same.

His kindness eases into my soul.

His concern makes my heart flutter.

The glow of his phone fades, and again we're in darkness.

But I can still feel his eyes on me.

He leaves us in the dark—and I'm fine with that.

"Do you want me to take you to the bathroom to change? There's one at the end of the hall."

"No, I'm good here." He's already seen me practically naked, and it's so dark, it's not like he's going to see anything anyway.

A flash of lightning illuminates the room from the windows in the hall and for a brief second I can see the expression on his face—he looks deep in thought. As I watch the water drip from his wet hair, I wonder if the seemingly worsening weather has him concerned. Or is he stuck in the present—working out my brother's deceit, or on the strange pull between us?

Even though we've just met, I know my brother trusted him. And I feel like I can too.

He once again seems to move closer—that pull still strong between us.

My breathing picks up.

My hands move on their own as I strip the T-shirt from my body and then remove the sweatpants clinging to my legs, before I re-dress.

He can't see me, but the shadows surely paint the image. I don't have to see his eyes to know he's watching—I can hear his own loud breathing.

And I know he's feeling what I'm feeling.

Once I'm finished, I take the towel in my hands and on tiptoes pat his wet hair, getting close enough that I can almost taste the salty rain on his skin.

My heart beats faster as a strange nervousness overcomes me.

With clumsy fingers, I drop the towel but instead of picking it up, I smooth his wet hair with only my hands. "I'm sorry. I should have never run outside in the rain."

Silence.

More heavy breathing—both of ours.

Our bodies are so close they're practically touching.

I look up through the darkness to the loft I know is up there, and wonder if I kissed him, whether he'd bring me up to his bed, or if he'd take me with an urgency that doesn't allow for time to change locations.

I shake the crazy notion off and repeat myself. "I said I'm sorry."

"I heard you." His breathing intensifies, to almost a panting, like it was when we were outside.

He grabs my wrists and stops my lazy caress of his hair. "Look, Zoey, I can't fucking think right now. I'm not sure what I'm supposed to say. I can't figure out what to do to make you feel any better about your brother. And to be honest, I'm not even sure if there is anything I can do."

I shake myself free, wondering what caused him to pull away and overreact.

The darkness, the sudden feeling of loneliness, coupled with the truth about my brother, seems to engulf me—I came here to help myself move forward, but I fear all I'm doing is taking a step back.

"Hey, I didn't mean to sound so harsh."

Another flash follows another rumble and my scream is not intentional as I'm jolted from my own thoughts. I stumble back onto the couch and now sitting, I wrap my arms around my knees. My body is wrought with tension and my stomach is in knots.

Why did my brother lie?

My weeping isn't intentional.

Nate sits next to me and pulls me to him. "Shhh . . . don't cry. I'm sorry I'm acting like such an asshole," he whispers in my ear.

His arms are around my body and the comfort he's providing me can't be denied. I take a breath trying to stop my sobbing. "No, you're not."

His laugh changes the mood between us.

The tears stop on their own, and my breathing steadies as my emotions shift from sorrow to something else.

When he leans back against the couch, he takes me with him. He pulls a blanket from the pile he had set on the table along with the towels and covers us, cocooning me in a balm of safety that for some reason pushes all my fears away.

I'm so mentally and physically spent, I can hardly keep my eyes open.

With my face resting over his beating heart and his fingers caressing my head, the only thing I think about before exhaustion cripples me is, *You, Nate Hanson, are anything but an asshole.*

4

Unsigned Notes

A sense of horror rips my eyes open.

But instead of seeing darkness, a hazy blue sky and giant skyscrapers present themselves.

My body is drenched in cold sweat.

My breathing is labored.

But I'm alive.

I didn't drown in a torrential downpour or get sucked up into the ferocious hurricane-speed winds—that was just a dream.

My death seems to lodge itself into my dreams so easily lately that I'm starting to question whether it could only be a matter of time before it happens.

I hope not.

I pull the blanket tighter to me, absorbing the comfort it provides. Once my nerves settle, I sit up. The power is back on—the air-conditioning is going full blast. With a toss of the blanket, I stand up and walk toward the bank of sliding glass doors. The shutters have been pulled back, and even through the drizzle, the Miami skyline is breathtaking.

With my arms cradled around myself, I step outside to get a better view to assure myself this is real. As soon as I reach the end of the lanai, there it is.

The boathouse—the house where my brother lived.

What I came here for.

I have a week to go through his belongings and try to discover what his life was like before I pack everything up and return home. One week to see that Zach loved his life and maybe make myself believe that every minute is worth living, regardless of how many minutes are left.

Because really—do any of us know how much time we have left?

I try to force myself to focus on what I see before me and not the finite, not the narrowing of time, but my mind wanders to Zach's life and how he was taken way too soon. A sudden mind shift has me thinking about last night—to the fact that he didn't tell me the truth about that life.

What other lies were there?

But I can't think that way.

No.

He was my brother and I loved him.

The tragedy of his death overpowers everything.

The lie, the betrayal—how much do they really matter?

The only thing that matters is that he died.

He died at twenty-seven.

He died before he even had a chance to live.

He never got to find the girl of his dreams and start a family. For a man who rebelled against just about everything in life— school, rules, walking the line—the one thing he didn't rebel against was love.

He was a romantic.

I blame Mimi and all those old movies she made us watch when we were little. He wanted to woo a woman. It was a dream of his to be some girl's knight in shining armor. I wanted that more than anything for him.

But it will never be.

A stray tear falls and I wipe it away.

With a deep breath, I refocus my gaze to my surroundings. The kidney-shaped pool with palm trees scattered around it looks so inviting in the light of day, and the ocean's water is incredibly turquoise. It looks so calming. When I spot a triangle-shaped sail-cloth cover, what I see beneath it makes me smile.

It's a cherry red boat sitting on top of a hoist.

Red.

Bright shiny red.

My brother's favorite color.

The sun peeks through the gray clouds and my eyes dart to the name scripted across the boat—THE FAST LANE.

A smirk crosses my lips.

Boys and their toys.

With a shake of my head, I pivot around and decide to try to find Nate. I think I need to apologize for my reaction last night and for breaking into his house. A feeling creeps through me— it's not the foreboding unease I've had shadowing me for weeks— it's excitement, a thrill, a rush of adrenaline at the thought of seeing him.

As I walk through the large living room, it becomes more than clear that what surrounds me wouldn't have been Zach's style at all. And after the desolation I felt when I first entered, the realization releases some of my apprehension. I push aside the revelations of yesterday for now, deciding on Nate and coffee first.

When I reach the kitchen, I spot a note on the counter:

> In the middle of a big deal at work. Had to take care of a
> few things. Here's a key to the boathouse. Help yourself to
> anything else you need.

The lack of any personal touch reminds me that we are strangers, and any closeness I may have felt toward him last night was a result of the trauma I had experienced. I shouldn't have expected a *Morning, Zoey,* or a *Later, Nate.*

But I would have liked one.

I turn on the Miele, and one perfectly crafted latté later, I head for the door where I dropped my luggage last night.

When I get there my suitcases are gone, but a note is taped to the glass door.

> I put your bags upstairs, outside the bathroom door. I
> assume you'll stay here for the duration of your trip. Check
> your e-mail. My office number and my cell, in case you
> don't have them, are in the reply to your message. If you
> can't reach me, leave a message with the answering service.

This stupid note, along with his kindness toward me, makes my heart beat faster and I run up the stairs to grab my phone.

The e-mail response is simple, like his other notes.

> Here are my numbers...

I practically skip into the shower only stopping to pull out my toiletry bag filled with my travel-sized items.

Part of me isn't surprised by my actions.

It's a piece of the old me.

The other part is shocked by my giddiness but that doesn't stop me from enjoying myself. While luxuriating in the coma-inducing spray, I take my time, allowing the water to cascade over me. It's then that I realize I haven't felt like this in a very long time. It's been too long since I paid attention to any small detail in my life—like the way the water feels pebbling against my skin or the delicious smell of my lavender-scented wash.

As the jets massage my body with the steamy warm water from almost every angle, it feels soothing, relaxing, and I take the time to enjoy it. When I massage my head, the memory of Nate's long fingers stroking my hair as I fell asleep last night comes rushing back. The spray touches me with an intimacy I wouldn't think water could, and a sensuality blooms from beneath my skin.

I try to push the feeling aside.

Shampooed, conditioned, shaved, and clean, I emerge from the shower feeling more than ready to face the day—a welcome change from the past weeks.

The mirror is covered in steam and I use a towel to wipe some of it away. A quick comb through my curls, add some frizz control, and I'm done. I'm not going to fuss too much because I'm certain the humidity of the Florida heat will do nothing but expand the volume. My curly hair has a life all its own and no matter what I do, there's no preventing the fact that as soon as I set foot outside, I'll be looking like a throwback from the eighties.

Oh well.

I pull out one of many dresses Zach sent me last summer. He said Lilly Pulitzer was all the rage in Miami and he thought I'd like them, and I do. I had trouble packing so I threw in everything he sent into my suitcase.

The one I select has a slight V in the front and back with a navy and white umbrella pattern all over it. The humidity in the bathroom alone is stifling, even with the air conditioner blowing.

I open the door and decide to finish getting ready in the bedroom. The room is similar to the rest of the house—walls painted white, nice modern but sparse furniture, and black accessories. Even the lampshades are black.

With a push of my hair to the side, I pop my small silver hoops in and clasp my silver heart locket around my neck.

Next, I use the mirror above the dresser to swipe a little makeup on.

I don't get far.

My eyes land on the crystal bowl on Nate's dresser. I pick it up and stare at its contents—it contains everything that Zach wore to make himself different—to make himself stand out from everyone else. Yet, the ironic thing was he was always unique; he didn't need any of that stuff to be noticed.

I always knew who he was, and I loved him for it.

So why the lies? I can't stop wondering.

"Those belong to you." The sexy, deep voice I recognize surprises me.

With a slight jump, I set the dish down.

"The police released them to me when I went to identify his body." His voice falters.

I stare at the silver in the dish and choke back my emotion.

He clears his throat. "The rest of his items are in the top drawer of my dresser. Like I said, they belong to you. I was going to mail everything, but then you said you'd be coming, so I figured I'd wait. The bag broke, and Rosie put the smaller things in that bowl."

I spin around with the words *who is Rosie* on my tongue, but then I catch sight of Nate standing in the doorway, and my heart, my body, and my mind instantly seem to perk up. He's wearing a white T-shirt, another pair of low-slung jeans, and a pair of Ray-Bans. It takes me a moment to refocus and even longer to notice the two cups of Starbucks and a pastry bag in his hands.

"Thank you. I don't think I ever said thank you. For everything."

"You don't have to thank me." His voice is raspy and laced with a sadness I know all too well.

"Can I ask you something?"

He nods.

"I know I asked this before, but are you sure the police didn't give any more information about what happened? I mean besides it being a motorcycle crash."

Nate drops his eyes with a wince. "No, like I said, all they told me was that he was going too fast and lost control when he turned and hit some debris in the road."

Moments of silence pass.

I dab my eyes.

I have to stop crying.

"Is one of those for me?" I point to the cups in his hand.

He nods. "Can I come in?"

"It's your room. Of course you can."

He strides toward me and my heart goes *thump-thump*. "A latté and a scone. And I guarantee this latté is much better than the one I made yesterday."

I smile at him.

His grin in return is breathtaking.

As I take the cup and the bag our fingers collide and a spark flickers between us. "I made one this morning and Miele managed to do her job just fine. But I'd never turn away a second cup."

He raises a brow. "Coffee lover, huh?"

I nod and take a sip of my latté.

"Just like your brother."

"Well, not to the same extreme."

"You mean you aren't always on the hunt for the best?"

"No." I raise my cup. "Starbucks works for me."

"Ahh, I bet you've never had Cuban coffee then."

"You'd be right, I haven't." I start to get a little excited. "But Zach used to send me pictures all the time from various coffee-houses he'd stumble across. I remember one time he sent a photo of this little dive with a walk-up window. He'd texted along with the photo, *Best* café con leche *this side of Havana.*"

Nate sips from the white lid of his cup, his eyes watching me intently.

The way he looks at me gives me butterflies.

"Las Olas Cafe. It's in South Beach and they have the absolute best *coladas*, hands down."

"*Colada*? What's that?"

His excitement matches mine. "Hmmm, I'm not sure words can do it justice, but it's when Cuban coffee is made on the stove. Once the coffee boils, you pour a small bit into a glass with a lot of sugar, stirring it until it's pastelike, and then you add the rest of the coffee. Z and I used to drink them like shots."

Come to think of it—I think Nate was in that picture.

"Sounds delicious."

"I'll take you there in the morning. You can't leave Miami without trying one."

"I'd love that. I'd really like to see the places my brother liked to go."

He leans against the dresser and his eyes seem to simmer.

My free hand flutters to my hair—with the curls drying and the volume expanding, it feels like a wild mess. I tuck a few strands behind my ear and sigh, not even aware that the sound was audible.

"You look . . ." He mumbles a word that I swear sounds like *beautiful*, and out of nowhere there is a shyness in his eyes that makes my stomach flutter.

Blood rushes to my cheeks.

He clears his throat. "You look . . . ready to start your day."

My eyes drop and my blush instantly fades. "I am. I have a lot to accomplish."

"I know. That's why I came back."

"I appreciate it, but I thought you had to work."

"I did. I had a property to check out and I'm waiting on a call, but everything else can wait. My assistant—"

I stare up at him.

He stops talking the minute his gaze catches mine.

His eyes are so green, I get lost in them.

He reaches toward me.

My breath catches.

His thumb brushes across my lower lip.

I swallow, the heat between us consuming me.

His touch. His words. They're unexpected. They're warm. They make me feel alive.

The movement is soft and gentle. I want to reach into it, to grasp his hand and pull him to me.

But he's my brother's best friend. I can't do that.

Can I?

Yet, when he steps forward, his stare rocks me with an intensity that makes my heart stop.

The moment is broken when his phone rings. He glances at the screen and puts a finger up. "Harper, did you get in touch with him?"

Silence.

"Keep trying. I want that property bought by the end of the day. And at the price we originally agreed upon, not the one he thinks it's suddenly worth. He must have caught wind of the upcoming announcement for the improvement project."

Nate creases his brow.

"I understand that. But he's been shit with details. This doesn't make sense."

More silence.

"It's simple, call Holden and postpone the announcement."

He hangs up and looks back over at me. "Sorry about that. Some douche bag is trying to pull out of a deal we've been working on for months because he thinks the property is miraculously worth double."

"But if you had a deal, how can he do that?"

"No transfer of ownership has been made. He can try to do

anything. Greedy son of a bitch." He shakes his head. "But anyway I was saying . . ."

I look at him, a cocky businessman with such confidence; I can see why he's successful. I refocus on the conversation.

"I realized you didn't have a car and knew I had no food in the house."

"I probably should have rented one, but I was trying to minimize my expenses. Had I known the house was on an actual island, I would have splurged."

"How long are you planning on staying?"

"A week. But I can get a room if that's too long."

"No. I told you already—you are staying here."

I had drifted back toward the bed without realizing it until I stumble into the footboard. "Thank you for letting me stay."

He looks at me and pushes his hair from his forehead. "What did I already say?"

"I know, but still it's really very nice of you."

His laugh is dry.

"What?"

He shakes his head. "It's just been a long time since anyone called me *nice*."

The intensity in his eyes doesn't mimic the slight laugh I've heard a few times from him—it's a disapproving laugh.

I walk back over to the dresser.

Closer to him.

"Well, you *are* nice. I'm not sure I would have responded as kindly if some stranger showed up at my house, slept in my bed, and basically called me a liar."

He shrugs. "Don't worry about it. And I want you to know, I'll do what I can to help you. But look, I have somewhere I want to take you first. Have some time?"

I grab my clear gloss and open it. "Really? Where?"

"There's something I think you should see before you leave. You'll like it."

I manage a slight smile and roll the gloss over my lips. "I'd love to go. And if you don't mind, I'd like to see the gallery too."

"Sure, if we have time." He seems hesitant.

I walk over to my suitcase and pull out my sandals, tossing them to the ground before sliding into the flat silver thongs and grabbing my purse. "Yes, of course. I have to get back anyway and go over to the boathouse. I can always go on my own this week."

"That won't be possible."

I twist to look over at him, thinking he must be joking, but I can see he's not.

"It's not open. It hasn't been since . . ." He seems unable to complete the sentence.

"Since my brother died," I finish for him.

"Yeah. I'll wait for you downstairs. Take your time."

"Nate."

He pauses at the door, grabbing at the jams.

I want to tell him I'm sorry. I never thought about how much Zach's death must have changed his life too.

I want to tell him I know how he feels.

I want to comfort him, like he comforted me last night. But I say or do none of those things. Instead I settle on, "I won't be long."

He nods and disappears.

Tossing a few things back into my suitcase, I zip it up along with my other bag, sip my latté, take a quick bite of scone, and then attempt to carry my luggage down the stairs.

Nate's standing at the windows that look out over the water. The pounding sound of my suitcase makes him twist as it hits each of the steps. "What are you doing?"

"Just cleaning up my stuff. After yesterday I think I've taken up enough of your personal space."

My eyes follow his every movement as he rushes toward me.

God, the way he moves.

I study the lean lines of his body and appreciate the way his muscles flex with each step.

He stops so close to me, I can feel the whisper of his labored breath on my neck.

I shouldn't be thinking that way.

I haven't thought about today being my last day alive since I woke up.

Is it because of him?

Maybe he is exactly what I should be thinking about.

I shake the thought away.

That's not how I should be thinking.

Then his hand covers mine over the handle of the suitcase and the thought becomes even stronger as a sudden shot of arousal shoots right through me.

I stare at him.

He stares back. His hand stays right where it is and he grabs the other bag off my shoulder. "I thought you agreed to stay here."

Warmth swirls inside me. "I did."

"Then where do you plan on sleeping tonight?"

"I thought I'd stay in the boathouse, if that's okay with you of course?"

He takes my suitcases back upstairs, breaking our connection.

I remain where I am, watching as he sets the bags down.

The entirety of his body is in my view as he inches back toward me. I feel like he's taking the steps much slower than he had mounted them. And the closer he gets, the more I can feel myself tremble, especially when his gaze travels along my body and the heat of it sinks all the way to my core. He finally stops on the step before mine, and this time stands taller than me.

His hand splays against the wall. "Another storm is coming

tonight. I'd rather you stay over here. You can stay in my room. I'll take the couch."

I try to focus on him. To steady my breath. "If it's not safe, why would my brother have lived there?"

He eases forward just enough that I have to tip my head to see him. "I didn't say it wasn't safe. It is. It's just during storms, Z would crash in the spare room, if the winds got too high."

I drop my chin under his fiery gaze. "Okay then, I can sleep there."

"No, you can't. There's no bedding, and I don't have any."

Knowing it was completely vacant when I saw it last night, I want to ask why, but I feel like I shouldn't push. I look back into his eyes. "Fine, I'll sleep on the couch then."

A whisper of a smile curls his lips. "For a teacher, you don't listen very well."

With a laugh, I pivot around and walk down the stairs. "I'm employed by a college to teach; listening isn't part of my job description."

He scoffs. "You're a smartass, just like your brother."

Pride swells within me and under my breath I say, "If only that were true," so only I can hear it.

Zach and I were so different.

He was fearless. I'm fearful.

He was wild. I'm tame.

He did what he wanted. I do what's expected of me.

He was fun. And I'm boring.

The truth stings even though it never used to. Lost in my thoughts, I take the steps slowly and feel my pulse accelerate when Nate follows right behind me. Once I reach the hardwood floor, I come face to face with the statue and quickly turn. Something about it makes me feel uncomfortable.

Nate passes by me, not even giving it a second glance. "Come on. Let's get out of here before the storm moves in. We have time to argue about sleeping arrangements later."

I trail behind him out into the garage, trying not to watch the muscles ripple across his back when he reaches for the passenger door to his black Range Rover.

He offers his hand to assist me.

"I can do it."

He bows a little extending his arm. "After you."

My breath catches from his charm and as gracefully as I can, I lift the hem of my dress, grab the roof handle inside the car, and hop up and into the seat. Before I settle, I steal a glance over at him.

He's watching me.

"All set?" His shy grin is all knowing.

Knowing he just got caught staring.

And now I can hardly breathe.

5

Say Anything

The storm damage appears minimal—a few downed tree limbs here and there but not much more than that. The clouds haven't completely cleared, but the sun is peeking through. The splashing fountains and sparkling waterfalls that mark the entrance and exit of Palm Island are functioning perfectly.

As we turn off Fountain Street and onto the MacArthur Causeway, I can't believe how beautiful everything is. The view from the bridge that spans Miami to Miami Beach is breathtaking—the shoreline meets the skyline in the most mesmerizing way.

I could stare at it all day.

It gives me an inner peace I haven't felt since my brother's death.

"What made you buy a house on Palm Island?" I ask Nate, breaking the silence that's lasted for the past ten minutes.

"The fishing," he says without hesitation.

My head cocks to the side as I consider his answer. Then turning to look at him with a hand shading my eyes, I remember the poles I saw in his garage, the ones that I couldn't see my brother owning. "You don't look like a fisherman."

He takes off his sunglasses and offers them to me. "Here, put these on so you don't have to squint."

"What about you? You're driving. You need them more than I do."

He pushes them toward me. "I'm used to the sun."

Giving in, I take them and slide them on.

Sunshine streaks his face, but he doesn't squint as he looks forward, pulling the visor down. "So tell me—what does a fisherman look like?"

I consider his question. "I don't know. Older, gray hair, beard, overalls, yellow boots maybe."

He laughs. "Classic *Old Man and the Sea* look. Funny, I had the very same image in my head when you said that. But to be honest, I'm not the fisherman. My father is. I fish because my father loves it. I bought that house because of the location. Palm Island affords me the ease of hopping in a boat and trolling Biscayne Bay whenever I want. The bay has miles of grass flats along with a shallow hard bottom—a fisherman's dream, or my father's anyway."

"I saw your boat this morning. It looks fast."

"That's not just any boat. She's a Scarab Jet with twin Rotax engines. That's five-hundred horsepower of pure adrenaline," he scoffs.

I refrain from rolling my eyes. "I have to say, I'm surprised by your color choice—you strike me as more of a black-and-white kind of guy."

He raises a brow. "If you're trying to say I'm boring, I promise you I'm not."

"No, that's not what I meant at all."

With a smirk he looks over at me. "Just so we're clear."

Silence.

"Can I be honest?" he asks.

"Yes, of course."

"You're not too far off."

My heart is pounding.

"Sleek black was what I planned on getting, but I made the mistake of taking your brother to the track with me the night before I went to buy the boat."

His face is a bit strained.

"Go on. You can talk about the things you did with my brother—they won't make me sad. In fact, I really want to hear everything you want to tell me."

"Are you sure?"

"Yes. I obviously didn't know my brother as well as I thought. Maybe you can help me know him a little better."

A look of mischievousness crosses his face.

It warms my heart to know my brother had such a close friendship with someone.

He was always so closed off.

So much like me.

"Like I said, we were at the track. We'd had our fair share of beers before the last race of the night came around. But imagine my surprise when Z takes all his winnings and bets on a horse because of his name."

"What was it?"

He shrugs. "Something like *Just Talk*, I think."

My nose scrunches in thought. "That doesn't mean anything to me."

"I tried to stop him. The horse's odds were shit. But he was insistent that horse was going to win. He said the movie ending was classic and there was no way he was going to lose."

"Did he tell you how it ended?"

He seems to be thinking for a moment. "With some dude holding a boom box over his head."

"Oh my God, do you mean *Say Anything*?"

"Yeah, that's it."

"You've never seen that movie?"

He shakes his head.

"We loved that movie. We went through an eighties classic marathon one year when Zach came home for Christmas and Mimi was too sick for us to go anywhere. We alternated with Elizabeth Taylor movies when she felt up to it. Mimi loved her. Okay, sorry, tangent—go on."

His smirk widens. "That's okay, I'm sure you see where this is headed. I scoffed that he picked a horse on name and not stats. He bet me the color of my boat that his horse would win. I looked at the tip sheet and took him up on his bet. I then spent a good ten minutes picking my horse before placing my own bet. And wouldn't you fucking know it—his horse won."

I let out a big laugh. "Classic Zach move all the way."

"Yeah, that's for damn sure."

"What did he have to do if he lost?"

"Ah, some things aren't meant to be shared with friends' sisters."

"Excuse me, but that's not fair."

He shrugs. "Sorry, but no can do."

"Well, at least finish the story."

"That I can do. So, the next day he came with me to the marina and picked out the shiniest, reddest boat available. I rolled my eyes, but I never renege on a bet. Red or not, she still rides like a dream."

"Boys and their toys. How *Miami Vice* of you."

"You know what they say?"

I scrunch my face. "No, what do they say?"

"Live life in the fast lane."

I suck in a deep, shuddering breath. "I think my brother may have used that line a few times. And he did love his toys too. Just don't drive yours too fast."

"Shit, I'm sorry. I shouldn't have said that. I don't know why I did."

"No, it's okay. Isn't that what my brother was doing—taking a curve way too fast?"

"It wasn't that simple. I already told you debris in the road caused him to lose control."

I drop my head. "Yes, at eighty miles an hour, without a helmet."

"Hey, look at me."

When I don't, he reaches toward me and takes my chin. "He lived his life the way he wanted to live his life—we have to accept that."

"I do. I always have. You just don't understand."

"I do understand. He was important to me. I feel like I lost my brother in that accident too. And Zoey, even after you leave, if you ever just want to talk about the accident, or him, or anything—I'm here."

I clutch his hand. "Thank you. I can see in the way you talk about him that he is just as important to you as you were to him."

His warm touch is suddenly gone.

I close my eyes to hold in my tears.

The silence that seems to keep finding its way to us fills the SUV.

Once I'm able to dispel the sadness, I open my eyes.

He looks lost in thought. Something has drawn his attention, something that seems almost painful.

"So where are we going?" I ask, hoping to breach the barrier that seems to have fallen between us.

Nate quirks a brow. "Someplace Z couldn't stay away from."

"Where?" I ask again.

His grin is endearing. "Just sit tight. We're almost there."

"Has anyone ever told you you're kind of bossy?"

"Never," he responds quickly, his grin shifting into an all-knowing smirk.

I roll my eyes. "I doubt that."

"Well, one person did all the time."

My brother would be the only one I can see doing that. Nate can be intimidating, and I bet the majority of people he comes into contact with would never come out and say anything like that.

Except he doesn't intimidate me. I can't explain why. Maybe it's because I feel like I know him through Zach. Or maybe it's because I feel comfortable with him. Or maybe it's simply because he's the only link to my brother that I have left.

"We've arrived," he says, pulling into a gravel-covered parking lot.

High on a colorful wall overlooking a row of restaurants and bars is a mural of a man in a cowboy hat and tie, hands held up in delight. And behind it are miles and miles of similar graffitilike works of art.

"Where are we?"

"Wynwood Walls, but we just call it the Walls."

"What is this place?" I ask in awe.

He opens his door and looks over at me. "It's kind of like an outdoor gallery."

"It's amazing."

"I know." He smiles.

I open my door.

"Stay there. I'll help you down."

"I can do it." But before I even pull up the hem of my dress, he's at my door extending a hand.

Butterflies catch in my stomach as I step down from the car.

He averts his eyes when I smile at him, but I see the shyness in them.

Standing so close to him, my pulse races. It reminds me that I'm still alive.

I like the feeling.

He shoves his hands in his pockets as if he's considering grabbing mine but tucking his fingers inside the denim is a better choice.

I walk beside him as we cross under a blue metal sign that reads WYNWOOD WALLS, and painted images emerge everywhere. They cover large warehouse buildings for blocks—hieroglyphics, the Dalai Lama, the Planters Peanut, *Chipmunk* cartoons, and what look like happy blobs of bacteria.

"Hey, Nate, my man, how the fuck have you been?"

I look at the man walking toward us with an extended arm, and his eyes widen when he takes notice of me.

"Santiago, how's it going?" Nate grasps his palm and they come together in what I can only define as a guy hug—thumbs locked, a quick embrace, and an even quicker disengage.

"The shop is coming along pretty good. If all goes well, I should have it open by the fall—mechanics and all."

Nate nods and swings his eyes over toward me, noticing Santiago's are already there. "Good for you man. Glad it worked out."

"I couldn't have done it without you."

"Don't sell yourself short."

"Never," he says and then raises his eyebrows. "Handsome, are you going to introduce me?"

Handsome?

Nate's hand goes to my back and a shiver runs down my spine. I thought he might have forgotten I was standing next to him. I look over at him.

His gaze lowers.

I swear I see that shyness again.

"Yeah, sure. This is Z's sister," he says.

"No shit."

I extend my hand. "Hi, I'm Zoey."

Santiago takes my hand and shakes it, smiling with a kindness that seems too soft for his gruff look.

"You should have told me she was in town."

Nate drops his hand from my lower back and I mourn the loss. "I talked to your wife this morning. Don't you two ever talk?"

Santiago shrugs. "Too much. That's why I end up tuning her out."

Nate laughs.

The sound melts me.

I look over at him and mumble, "Handsome?"

"Ignore him," Nate mutters, moving a little closer to me.

I give him a blatant once-over. "I can see it," I say with a laugh.

His body stiffens.

That may have been too flirty.

Santiago looks around and then cups his hands over his mouth. "Hey, Speedy, come over here. There's someone you've got to meet."

The distinctive scents of wet paint and dried sweat assault my nose. Before I can figure out where the smell is coming from a lanky skater scrapes up behind Nate and flips the end of his board to stop. "What's up?" he says to Santiago.

"You're never going to guess who this is."

He can't be any older than twenty-one, but his eyes look me over like I'm a girl he just might be interested in.

I try not to laugh.

Nate moves even closer and gives Skater Boy a shove but then extends his arm and pulls him around the neck, knuckling him in the head. "How's the summer treating you?"

Skater Boy pulls back and tries to redeem himself, obviously not liking the fact that he was just made to look like a kid. He looks back at me and drops the facade, letting out a loud whistle. "You're Z's sister."

"I am."

"Come with me. I've got something to show you."

Before I can answer, Nate says, "We're only here for a quick walk through. Zoey has a lot to do today."

"Relax, Nate, Z was my man too. I'm not going to do anything. I just want to show her something."

Nate raises his fist to cover his mouth and seems to be snickering

"Sure," I say, avoiding Nate's bemused gaze focused on the kid in front of us.

Santiago slaps a hand on Nate's shoulder. "Look, there's something I've been meaning to talk to you about."

Their conversation fades as I walk beside Skater Boy, who is now carrying his board under his arm. We walk down wide blocks of warehouses diced with smaller alleyways. One in particular grabs my attention when I see a bright dragon mural on an abandoned building with the fronds of a palm rising over it.

"I'm really sorry about what happened to your brother. He was a great guy, and we miss him around here."

Skater Boy's voice breaks through my thoughts. Sincerity bleeds through his words and I can tell he must have respected my brother. "Did you know him well?"

He rocks his head. "Pretty well. I saw him every weekend when he used to come to the community center with Nate. While Nate was teaching, he'd sit around and show some of us how to sketch cartoon characters. He was pretty cool, but then about a year ago he stopped coming around."

"Why?"

He shrugs. "No idea, but that dude should have been an artist."

"He was an artist."

"Yeah, I know he was—but I mean he had so much more potential."

I look at him questioningly. From what Zach told me, he was selling his pieces, so I'm not sure what Skater Boy is talking about. "He was doing very well." I try not to sound defensive.

"Oh, I had no idea. I just never heard him talk about moving any of his pieces like all the guys that hang out here."

Just another mystery to uncover.

We turn a corner and color blazes from building to building. "You said Nate teaches at the community center?"

"Yeah, BJJ. He volunteered every Sunday morning. I've been taking lessons from him since I learned to walk."

"BJJ?"

"Brazilian jiujitsu. He's a black belt."

"That's something I'd love to see. Will you be meeting tomorrow morning?"

"The center closed down last week."

"Why?"

"Lack of funding."

"That's too bad."

"It is. A lot of kids went there instead of hanging out on the streets."

I come to an abrupt stop and stare in awe at a crackling black-and-white border that contains a rainbow burst. Over the rainbow are gold block letters that say I REMEMBER PARADISE.

"Cool, right?"

"Yes, it is." I have no idea if he's talking about Nate or the painting, but both are cool.

"Come on before Nate hunts me down," Skater Boy quips from under his cap pulled low.

I shake my head. "We're just friends."

"Right, because every dude looks at a chick the way he looked at you," Skater Boy says, dropping his board and pushing off on it.

"Hey, wait up!" I call, chasing him. "What do you mean?"

He stops at the end of the block and points to the wall.

Practically out of breath I stop as well. "Oh my God." My hand flies to my mouth.

"See how I knew who you were?"

Tears leak from my eyes as I stare at the image of two children around ten years old—one boy, one girl—who look very much alike. The boy has short hair. The girl has long curly hair. Their hair is auburn. The boy is holding two dark pink ice-cream cones in his hands. The girl is holding one chocolate one. The words *My favorite memory* are written above it in red.

"He didn't want anyone to know this was his. He said it was just for him."

"But you knew about it?" My voice is shaky.

"I was hanging down here one Sunday morning and saw him painting it."

I fumble through my purse to find my phone and snap a picture of it. Once I drop my phone back into my bag, I look over at Skater Boy. "Are there any others my brother painted that you can show me?"

He shakes his head. "The walls are repainted every year to allow for more artists to showcase their talents. As far as I know, this is the only one he painted this year."

"There's one more," Nate's raw voice says from behind me.

"You knew about this?"

"No, not this one."

He stares at it.

The same sadness that fills his eyes has already overflowed mine. He looks shaken.

"Everything okay?" I ask.

He nods his head. I wonder if Santiago had some bad news.

But before I can ask, Nate swings his head in the other direction. "Come with me. There's something else you need to see."

Skater Boy gets on his board. "It was great meeting you. And I told you he'd hunt me down."

With a laugh I yell, "Thank you," before he turns the corner.

We both watch him go. "This place is amazing."

"I know. There are so many talented artists."

"Do they transfer their work and sell it?"

"Some, not many."

"Why?"

"It's hard to make a living selling over here."

"What do you mean?"

"Since the whole South Beach resurgence, art sales barely register on this side of the bridge. If you're an artist, you want to be selling across the causeway, but getting into those galleries isn't easy—it's a completely different culture."

"How so?"

"Miami Beach is trendy, so more of the people buying want artists with an established name. They'll pay a million for one provenanced piece, but won't pay a hundred for an unknown. Makes it hard for the little ones to survive. So instead, they spend their time at festivals and markets. But it works for them. They're happy."

"Why? Why wouldn't anyone buy these? Everything is so breathtaking."

He shrugs. "The way of the world, I guess. The thing is, this started as a neighborhood revitalization project, a way to keep everyone busy and off the streets. And as you can see, it worked. There's a lot of hidden talent being found, crime is down, and the neighborhood has had life breathed into it—so by all measures, it's been really successful."

"Well, you were right—I really love it here despite the heat." I fan myself a little with my clutch.

A satisfied grin crosses his face and I have an urge to throw my arms around him.

I don't.

Instead, I walk beside him as he takes us through a maze of buildings and across a street where we enter a park with big beautiful trees and boulders with some kids sitting around and talking on them.

"What is this place? It looks different," I ask.

"This is Wynwood Doors. Tony Gold was the local developer who was partially responsible for transforming South Beach into the mecca it is today. Then about twelve years ago he had a vision for what I call his Eliza Doolittle of neighborhoods. He master-minded this entire area's neighborhood renovation project as a tribute to inner-city life. It had a few phases—this is the second. In the Walls he wanted change. Here he wanted continuity. So he installed metal roll-down gates for graffiti use. They don't get wiped away every year; instead they stay painted and anyone can put their mark on it if they want, wherever they want. You see that one over there?" He points to the roll-down door in the middle. There's a man's larger-than-life face on it, painted so true to life, it could be a photograph.

"Yes, it's the only door without any graffiti on it."

"Z was asked by the city to paint the portrait shortly after Gold's death. It was a really big honor, but true to form he never told anyone. I knew because I was on the committee."

I turn toward Nate, and this time I do throw my arms around him. "Thank you. Thank you for bringing me here. This is just how I imagined my brother's life."

Nate's return embrace is tentative, but I don't care. This isn't about lust, or need, or want—this is for gratitude. His warm breath cascades down my neck. "Come on, let me take you through El Barrio."

"Do you speak Spanish?"

"Enough to get by."

I purse my lips together with a raise of my brows.

I'm impressed, even if he's acting nonchalant.

We walk over toward the sidewalk and down the street. I know when we've reached El Barrio right away. Booths line the square. It's utter chaos with wall-to-wall people. To the left are vendors selling their wares. To the right is a barrage of food choices.

Nate heads that way, rubbing his stomach. "What do you say we eat? I'm starving."

My eyes go to those amazing chiseled abs. "Sure."

With my gaze fixed on Nate, I don't even notice when he stops and I bump right into him. The moment he twists around, our mouths practically meet.

His body stiffens and he jerks his head back.

Feeling a little flushed from the contact, I quickly turn around and start looking at the sunglasses offered for sale at the booth beside me.

Fumbling through them, a pair of navy and white checked Wayfarer knockoffs catches my eye. "What do you think?"

"They look nice."

"Maybe you need to see them on?" I take his off my face and slide on the blue checked ones. "What do you think now?"

He gives me a quick glance. "They're fine . . . nice, I mean," he says again.

Okay, so he's either not a shopper or not one to comment. I turn back to the merchant and when I do I spot a red pair and a pink pair too. I pick them up too—they'll match some of the other dresses I brought with me. "How much for all three of these?"

"Two hundred dollars."

My eyes grow a little wide. Maybe these aren't knockoffs. I take the blue ones off my face. "How much for just these?"

Nate's husky voice cuts in and he starts speaking in Spanish to the older woman behind the table. *"Cuál es tu mejor precio . . ."*

The words jumble together as the speed of the conversation between the merchant and Nate picks up. *Seems like much more than just enough to get by, if you ask me.*

"Nate, it's fine. I really don't need the sunglasses," I say over the two of them.

He ignores me, still conversing in that hotter-than-hell Spanish language and then all of a sudden the woman smiles at him. *"Sí, señor, estamos de acuerdo."*

Nate pulls out his wallet and hands the woman five twenties.

I grab his wrist just as she takes the money. "No, let me pay her." I set my purse on the table and fumble for my wallet. "Do they take credit cards?"

"No." His hand covers mine with the gentlest of touches.

All I can do is stare at him.

"I got it," he says.

The woman hands me a small plastic bag, and I take it. "I'll pay you back."

I feel like an idiot.

He shrugs. "I just wanted my sunglasses back."

"Oh, right. Here you go."

I slide them onto his face.

He quickly takes them from me before I even push them up his nose. I try to ignore his reaction and instead of dwelling on it, I remove the blue ones from the bag and slide them on and then strike a pose.

"Beautiful," he says, almost inaudibly.

"You think?"

A soft, sexy laugh slides from his lips.

I pull a Marilyn Monroe and blow him a kiss.

Where did that come from?

So very much unlike me.

His stare locks on me.

My cheeks start to flush, and I look away.

"Yeah, beautiful," he says again.

He walks toward the row of delicious-smelling food vendors and I try to keep up, but those damn butterflies decide to take flight and slow me down.

He stops and waits for me.

With everything from empanadas, churros, cheap wine, flan, and meat kabobs, it's hard to decide what to choose—so we stop and eat something at practically every booth.

"Try this," Nate insists.

"I can't. I'm so full."

"You have to. You can't go back to New York without trying one of these."

"Okay." I open my mouth without thinking.

And he steps forward to feed it to me.

His eyes lock on my lips.

My breathing picks up, and suddenly he freezes.

We stare at each other with our eyes connecting, as once again our bodies seem to naturally drift closer to each other.

I cover his hand with mine and bite down.

He quickly withdraws his hand, but his body remains close.

I chew slowly.

Our gazes stay locked.

When the taste registers in my mouth, I blurt out, "What is this?"

The moment is broken.

He steps back and laughs. "A *tortica de guayaba.*"

"Oh." I cover my mouth.

"You can only get them here."

I try not to make a face, but my dislike for the taste must be apparent.

"Don't tell me you don't like it."

I shake my head. "I think I need to spit this out."

"Are you kidding me?"

"No. It tastes like peanut butter mixed with something I don't care for."

"It is peanut butter. It's peanut butter mixed with guava."

I swallow what's in my mouth and hand him back the rest of the cookie. "It's all yours."

He smirks at me in that adorable way that makes my heart skip a beat. "You'll drink my coffee, but not eat the best cookies ever."

I laugh. "Sorry."

He takes a bite of the cookie looking prouder than ever. His eyes are gentle and teasing as he finishes the last bite. We stare into each other's eyes, a strange feeling of lust whipping around me. Someone bumps into Nate.

He seems to blink his thoughts away. "Come on, we should get back."

We walk side by side back to his Range Rover while admiring our surroundings.

I look over and stare at him. I feel drawn to everything about him. His business savvy, his kind heart, the way he looks at me—the way he makes me feel.

He turns as if he's been doing the same thing.

I quickly avert my stare and look up at the sky. "It looks like rain."

"Yeah, it does. Don't worry, I'll have you back before the storm hits."

"I'm not worried."

He steps in front of me and turns around, continuing to walk backwards. Hair blows in my face, and he tenderly brushes it away.

I close my eyes and feel my heart race.

"You seem fearless," he says.

I open my eyes and try to keep the sadness out of my voice. "I'm anything but."

He shakes his head. "Oh, I disagree. I think you're selling yourself short."

I smile at him and let him believe that I am. "And what are you?" I ask with a flirtatious tone that comes out of nowhere.

He glances over his shoulder and then turns back around to walk beside me. "Hmmm . . . good question. What am I? I was born Milo Nathaniel Hanson, son of Milo Hanson, given his name but never called by it. I grew up believing Transformers were real, thought the Power Rangers went to school with me, and could never watch *Star Wars* enough. Does that help you out?"

I laugh. "Yes, it does. Now I know what kind of movies you like to watch."

"Well, you never know when that tidbit might come in handy."

As we get closer to the entrance, the crowd seems to thicken and Nate takes my hand to lead me through it. When he comes to an abrupt stop, I run into him. My front crashes to his back. He turns. "Sorry. Are you okay?"

"I'm fine."

The minute he notices how close our faces are he drops his hold and keeps walking. I increase my pace to keep up with him. Something's going on. He's drawn to me, I can tell—but the minute we become physically close, he pulls away.

I'm not sure why.

We reach the edge of the parking lot and I can't stop admiring him. His body is long and lean, not big and bulky. He's smart and funny. He's kind and charming, and I'm having a much harder time than he is ignoring the pull.

"Ready?" he asks, opening the car door. This time he doesn't offer a hand.

I look at him. "What? You're not going to help me up?"

"You're fearless. You got this. But if you fall, don't worry, I'm here to catch you."

I quickly hop in, trying to calm my racing heart.

As we drive out of the parking lot, I stare behind me, thinking today is the happiest I've been in a long time.

I got to see a piece of my brother.

And spend time with someone I hadn't thought would help me along this journey. I look over toward him. "Thank you for taking me there."

That green-eyed stare is strikingly powerful, but a gentleness seems to present itself when he looks at me. "I thought you'd like it."

Nate's fingers tap the steering wheel as he handles the Rover with ease, passing cars weaving through traffic—he's always in control and full of confidence. Silence fills the space as my mind churns. When he veers off the causeway, I finally look over at him. "Can I ask you something?"

"Sure," he says as he pulls onto Fountain Road.

"Why do you think my brother told me he owned a house if he didn't? It doesn't make sense."

Nate's grip tightens on the steering wheel. "I wish I could answer that for you, but I think you'll be able to figure that out better than me."

With a sigh, I clutch the locket. "That's what I was afraid you'd say. I've been racking my brain all day but I can't come up with any valid reason. I thought he was just looking for a safe investment for his money when he told me he'd purchased a house on the water."

Nate's body visibly stiffens.

"What is it?"

He comes to a stop at the iron gate that opens onto his street and looks over at me. "What kind of cash do you think he had?"

"I'm not sure. I know he'd been selling his sketches for quite a bit of money. Enough that he was able to help me pay off Mimi's house and all of her doctor bills. I told him it wasn't necessary. I had already consolidated all the bills into one loan and was teaching private art lessons to pay them down, but he insisted he had more than enough money to take care of it."

"How much money are you talking?"

"Mimi had taken a second mortgage on the house, so that was one hundred and seven thousand. And her medical bills were just over two hundred thousand."

Nate coughs, or maybe chokes. "He paid both those off in one year?"

I nod.

He pulls into the driveway but doesn't take the keys from the ignition. "Zoey, it's not like I knew that much about his finances, but I do know what he made at the gallery and it was nowhere near that. I paid him what I could, but the gallery just wasn't doing that great."

"He said he was selling his sketches to pay off the loans. He said he had plenty of extra money."

He hesitates before speaking.

"What are you thinking? Tell me."

"As far as I know, he hadn't sold anything in years."

The words catch in my throat and my voice doesn't sound like mine. "Then where could he have gotten that kind of money?"

Nate shakes his head. "I honestly don't know."

From the driveway I can see the neighbors' houses. Finely manicured lawns, circle drives, and both with fountains in front of them. Then I look at Nate's house, much smaller, although still much bigger than my own. "Do you think your father could have loaned it to him?"

He looks forward. "No. No way."

"Are you sure?"

"Yeah, my dad just doesn't have that kind of cash."

"Well, he got it from somewhere, but where?"

Nate glances over at me with the same shocked look I'm wearing. "I have no fucking idea, but my guess is he told you he owned this house and that he was selling his sketches so you'd believe he had enough money to pay off all that debt."

My stomach lurches.

Nate's phone rings. He glances at his screen. "I have to take this."

I nod.

"Did you get ahold of him?"

Pause.

"I'll be there in twenty."

Nate looks over at me and takes my hand. "I have to run into the office. I'll be back as soon as I can and we'll try to figure this out."

An ache grips my chest. Images of guns, getaway cars, robberies, theft, and drug deals pass through my mind. I push them away. I don't want to believe Zach would do anything illegal. But where in the world did he get the money?

6

They Say

They say the dead don't speak. They say the dead will never leave you. They say a lot of things about the dead. What they don't tell you is what you're supposed to do when they weren't who you thought they were.

I guess you start by trying to figure them out—or settle for always wondering.

The alarm pings when I enter in through the garage door. I turn it off and look around. The house feels so quiet. And even though the sun bleeds through the clouds and the light is everywhere, the starkness of my surroundings hits me hard.

Nate lives here, but the place looks anything but lived in. There is nothing of any personal nature anywhere. It's as if he just sleeps here. Uncertain why the sparseness affects me so much, I hurry through the vast space and up the stairs. A quick change into shorts and a tank top and I'm back downstairs in a matter of minutes, coming to a dead stop at the statue. The woman looking out at the water seems lost and alone. Yesterday I thought it was the only thing that didn't belong but today, as I stare at the desolation in her eyes, I think it does—it belongs perfectly.

It mimics my own feelings, to a tee.

The keys to the boathouse are still on the counter.

Uncertain, I pause before grabbing them. Trepidation consumes me.

What if I don't find anything?

Or what if I find something I'm not looking for?

You're searching for a reason to move forward. My inner voice reminds me what this trip is all about.

And for some odd reason Nate comes to mind.

With a slight jog out through the back lanai, I'm standing at the wooden door in seconds. Funny, it seemed much farther last night in the rain.

The green paint is peeling in sections and the wood looks weathered, battered even, but the key slips easily into the lock.

I pull open the door and find that what's before me is not what I expected. A rickety old fishing boat sits snug in a slip barely wobbling from the ebbs and flows of the waves. I thought Nate's fishing boat was the Scarab. I look around some more. A massive amount of fishing gear is pegged on hooks to one of the walls, with tackle boxes and nets on the floor beneath it. On the other wall a number of brown boxes are stacked up, and a staircase is to the right of them. Old wooden paneling leads the way up with photos of different men at various stages in their lives all holding their catches with pride.

Oh my God. There's a photo of Ernest Hemingway next to a man that has to be Nate's grandfather, holding a marlin.

As I make my way up each step, I study the photos.

A man, whom I'm assuming is Nate's grandfather, and a boy both smile with their catches. Another photo, this time the young boy has aged into a man, again both smiling with their catches.

And next another small boy appears in the photos—Nate. The older man is gone, replaced by a man that must be his dad.

My hand flies to my heart as I reach the top of the stairs—a photo of Zach and Nate with that man between them, each holding a fish; my brother's is the biggest.

My brother a fisherman. Who would have thought?

I swipe away the tears from my eyes and open the door.

Stale air and the smell of garbage tell me no one has been in here. I take a step further with my hand over my nose. Wooden floors, a haggard-looking checked sofa, a TV, a gaming console on the floor, a small wooden kitchen table, and pictures of Mimi and me everywhere. The place is disheveled—actually a complete mess, but even so, I tear up again as I enter the house my brother used to live in. It looks like Mimi's family room, and I recognize his presence here.

The smell in the air is pungent, and I quickly move toward the kitchen. Suppressing my gag reflex I take the garbage bag from the can and then decide to open the refrigerator. Expired milk and some Chinese containers go into the bag, which I promptly take to the large green trashcan I saw at the side of the garage earlier.

Once I return, I look under the sink and since there is no air freshener, I pick up the Windex and spray it in the sink just to help relieve the foul air.

With my hands on my hips I scan the room, my eyes landing on the sliding glass doors toward the back. They need to be opened immediately. With force, I manage to pry them apart. The doors are heavy and seem to stick, but I finally open them.

The view is amazing.

It's one of the most beautiful I have ever seen. Drawn to the tranquility of the water, I step out on the deck and lean over the railing smelling the fresh, clean ocean breeze.

Surrounded by land, sea, and sky, what could be more perfect?

Then I see it, his easel tucked away in the corner. Yes, seeing Zach sketching out here is the only thing that could make this scene more perfect. And then I sense that he must have been happy here.

This place is paradise.

The sun ducks behind the clouds as I sit out on the deck in one of the two yellow striped chairs and pick up a sketch pad tucked behind the easel.

It's gotten wet.

The pages are crinkled and some of the papers are stuck together, but I'm able to open it.

A scene of the sea—boats speeding by and birds flying. This one had to be sketched from right where I'm sitting. It's labeled *Paradise*, and I smile. My first thoughts were correct.

I flip the page to a colorful sketch of the face of a beautiful woman with dark hair, enchanting dark eyes, and an olive complexion. There is a heart just above the title, which is smeared so I can't read it.

Is this someone he had a crush on?

The next few pages are stuck together. I flip until I come to a sketch of a couple, the man looking up with a grin, the woman above him and looking down at him. Both are naked. The title reads, *Never Look Back*.

I'm not sure who the couple is.

Turning the page, I flip to a portrait of a woman. Her breasts are the focal point of the sketch. It's titled *Always Remember Me*.

The last sketch is of a different naked couple. The man is beneath the woman. He is looking forward with a smirk. She is above him with her hand grasping his chin. The title reads, *Wildly in Love*.

Again, I have no idea who the couple is or why he'd be sketching nudes of couples. These sketches are true to life, not in cartoon form. He hadn't sketched anything realistic since the day our mother died. What brought about the change?

Unease strikes me.

What changed?

Time passes and the light rain turns into heavier drops. I watch the way it disappears into the water at a relentless pace, and my mind wanders.

Where did he get the money?

Who are the people in the sketches?

Why was he sketching couples in sexual positions?

The wind picks up speed and the rain pelts against my skin. I don't move; instead I let darker thoughts consume me.

Was he happy?

Am I?

My grandmother, my schooling, my job, and my brother had always kept me happy, at least kept me from being unhappy. I didn't have a lot of friends. I never had time for socializing. Mimi was sick so much of the time.

And just like men, sex was never important to me.

With my one serious boyfriend in college, the sex had stalled out and become so routine, it left me staring at the ceiling bored out of my mind. After three years, I finally ended that relationship. Ever since, casual lovers and a vibrator for the occasional release were all I've needed.

But I feel a strange shift within me.

Lustful thoughts have crept into my mind all day, replacing the adrift ones that have plagued me for weeks. No longer am I worrying about how soon I'm going to die. Instead, my thoughts are of Nate.

I can't seem to shake them.

I stand and ease my body against the glass. Pressing my thighs together, I try to tame the ache between my legs and instantly feel the wetness through my panties that isn't from the rain.

When I step inside, a sad thought strikes me. If what I think might happen does, and I die before I turn twenty-eight, I will have missed something extraordinary. I've never thought of my life as lacking anything, but I do now.

For the first time in my life, I really want someone with a deep yearning.

A boat goes flying by at warp speed, and the waves left in its wake look like angels' wings. I glance up into the heavens, and guilt reminds me I came to Miami for my brother.

I came to find a way to move forward.

My inner voice is drowned out by my sorrow.

I set the sketchpad down and glance around. My stare locks on the two doors sandwiching the television. I open the first one—a bathroom. A simple room with a sink, shower-with-tub combination, and mirror. All beige tiles, nothing fancy, but red towels in all shapes and sizes are stacked in a cubby under the sink.

That makes me smile.

I open the cabinet above the sink—a razor, shaving cream, toothpaste, toothbrush, a box of condoms. Shampoo and a bar of soap are in the shower.

That's it.

Nothing more.

Totally Zach.

Back in the living room, I open the second door and stare into his bedroom. The bed is unmade—a blue comforter is thrown over lighter blue sheets. There are piles of clothes in a basket in the corner. Once again, photos of Mimi and myself are on his dresser; and sketches, the type of sketches I remember, cover the walls—a cartoonish marlin lying in a lounge, a dolphin in a chair having a cigarette, seashells with faces, a fishing boat on wheels.

Humorous illustrations—"Zach style" is what I used to call it—and it's everywhere. It's how he escaped from life when we were little. It was the one thing he was really good at. Sketching kept him from making poor choices he might have never come back from.

I don't know how long I stand there looking at the walls, but the dimming of the natural light has me reaching for a light switch. The overhead fan starts turning, alerting me to just how warm it is in here. Feeling exhausted and knowing tomorrow is another day, I decide that's enough for tonight. I can't bear the thought of leaving, but all my energy seems to have been zapped from my body.

I turn the air down to help cool the place for tomorrow, and then I lock up. I jet across the wet grass and back into Nate's house where the cool air assaults me. Wet clothes and air-conditioning are not the best combination. Once I take a shower, I change into a dry tank and yoga pants and head downstairs. I fall to the couch and glance at the time. It's almost eight o'clock.

Where did the time go?

A strange shiver of loneliness hits me.

Outside the storm is in full force—thunder and lightning alternating between blasts of power and light—but the wind is nowhere as fierce as last night.

I reach for the blanket, still thrown where I left it this morning, and lean back. Closing my eyes I think, *Another day done.* Another day destiny hasn't called on me yet.

The sound of a door closing wakes me what seems like moments later, but the clock tells me I've been asleep for an hour.

"Nate?" I call into the darkness.

The kitchen light flicks on. "Zoey, what are you doing down here in the dark?"

I squint at the brightness. "I don't know. I must have fallen asleep."

"Are you okay? You sound a little strange."

"Can I ask you something?"

"Yeah, sure." He drops his keys on the counter.

"How often did my brother go fishing with you? I can't remember any specific conversations with Zach about fishing, but I can recall a faint memory about a trip to Key West."

The faucet runs and he fills a glass with water. "He went with my dad and me pretty frequently, short trips around the bay usually. And once a couple of years ago, we took the boat down to Key West."

The friendship these two shared fills my heart with a warmth I am having trouble understanding. It's like a missing piece of his childhood, and maybe mine, was found. I sit up straighter. "When we were little, he used to want so much to be able to fish. My grandmother would take us to the pier and he'd watch the boats go back and forth with their poles in the water and ask Mimi if we could do that. It used to make my grandmother cry, because if she could have made it happen for him she would have. One time she bought us a pole and took us to the pier. Zach was so proud when he put the worms on the hooks. Then we put our poles in the water and sat for what seemed like hours. When we finally took the poles out of the water the worms were gone but we never felt a bite. We tried all day and couldn't catch anything. After that he never wanted to go again."

The kitchen light turns off. "He always caught the biggest fish when we went."

The thought makes me smile, but at the same time something inside me breaks.

Loneliness.

Fear.

Lies.

They all come at me together and I can't stop myself from crying.

Nate rushes toward me. "Hey, I'm sorry I wasn't here when you went over to the boathouse. I tried to get back earlier."

I fall against him. "It's okay. I needed to do it alone."

"I'm sorry," he repeats.

I enfold myself in his arms.

He holds me.

And I cry.

Cry for everything I've lost. Cry for everything I don't know. Cry for everything I'll never have.

I want to run. I want to hide. I want to escape the destiny that awaits me.

"Let it out," he whispers, kissing my forehead.

It's a soft and gentle gesture meant to ease my tears.

He does it again and this time his mouth lingers a little longer. The feel of his lips against my skin unleashes a savage need in me that I don't want to suppress any longer.

I drag my fingertips down his chest.

He shudders.

I lift my chin, and his mouth hovers just over mine.

I move forward and allow my hands to creep under his shirt. He's fast and grabs them. "We can't do this."

I pull away and look at him. "We can."

Nate shakes his head no but his body language isn't saying no.

I part my lips for him.

"Fuck," he hisses and crashes his mouth to mine. But he quickly pulls away.

"Stop thinking," I whisper.

He buries his head in my neck. "I can't."

"Yes, you can." I thread my fingers in his hair.

His tongue licks the sensitive skin behind my ear.

"That's it. Let's not think about anything right now."

"Zoey." His voice is pained.

"Shhh... I don't want to talk. I just want to feel. Help me. Help me just feel. Can you do that?"

When he doesn't answer, I reach for the button of his jeans. He doesn't stop me.

A slight tug of his zipper and suddenly the air shifts—there's a current crackling in the silence. No, it's a growl unlike anything I've heard from a man before—wild and guttural.

The sound ripples through me as arousal overtakes my entire body. Never have I felt like this before.

In the next moment his lips glide over mine and our mouths fit together perfectly. I'm not really sure who kissed whom first, but I really don't care.

Quick as a flash, our mouths seek each other—licking, sucking, tasting. There's an urgency I can feel with each stroke of his tongue against mine. His lips taste of salty rain but feel velvety soft—a delicious combination.

In the next moment he rips his shirt off.

I do the same.

His hand grips my neck to hold me to him.

Flesh to flesh—the feeling is so good.

I wrap my arms around his back. The feel of his skin is smoother than I ever imagined but it's the bunching of his muscles beneath my fingertips that sends my body into a frenzied need—a need to know if he feels the same way I do.

With a press of my hips against his, it's there—an erection that tells me just how much he wants me. Finally, I feel all of him. Strong and defined. He's just how I imagined he'd be—hard, chiseled, primal—all male.

He pushes into me and we meld closer and closer together—our bodies uniting in a need for more than warmth or comfort. My bare chest pushes into his until there is absolutely no space between us. At this moment I'm pretty sure that if we could have become one, we would have.

Urgency presents itself as he pulls my yoga pants off. The light is dim, I can barely see him, but the minute he rises I know it's to take his clothes off—not walk away.

He settles between my legs and his hips thrust forward. His kisses are just as powerful as the swivel of his hips. His body and his mouth are just like his stride—fearless and fierce. His kiss takes away everything bad I'm feeling, and the movement of his body solidifies my need for him to take me. I don't have enough air to breathe and I don't even care. I just want to get lost in him.

And then it happens—I do.

His free hand reaches down between my legs and his fingertips press against my already hot and swollen sex.

I gasp at the contact.

There is no talking between us, as right now there is nothing that needs to be said.

He circles my clit, rubbing, stroking, and it feels incredible. As soon as he slips his finger inside me, sensations rivet through my body.

I try to stifle my moans but I can't stop my body from shaking in pleasure. In this moment of utter ecstasy, where the world around me ceases to exist, I know this man owns me. Never in my life has anyone's touch made me feel like this.

"Oh God, don't stop!" I scream out.

His groan of satisfaction is unmistakable.

In the darkness, my senses seem heightened. I reach my hand out and find his throbbing cock. I'm glad I can't see his face and he can't see mine—it gives me the freedom to move without restraint and feeling him is what I need the most. I stroke up his shaft—it's long and thick, but the skin is so soft. With a quick swirl around his blunt head, I stroke back down—going all the way down and then beneath his cock, where the skin is even softer.

"Oh fuck." A loud guttural groan escapes his throat as my fingers stroke him.

Suddenly, the contact is gone.

There's a slight shifting, fumbling on the floor, and then a rip of a package echoes in the air.

His fingers push my reaching hands aside as he rolls on the condom. "Zoey," he breathes.

"Nate," I answer back into the darkness.

"Sit up," he demands.

Wanting to obey him, I do so without thought. His bold command unleashes a need in me, and all I can think about is how much I want this man to fuck me.

Not make love to me or have sex with me, but fuck me.

Nate shifts, as if sensing my needs, and pulls me onto his lap. With my knees on either side of his thighs, his hands grip my hips. Mine automatically reach for his shoulders. With no further foreplay needed, he lifts me higher and then lowers me onto him.

In the next moment Nate groans, "Fuck, you're so tight."

The feel of him inside me is like nothing I've ever felt.

He moves me slowly at first; up and down with steady strokes as if he knows I needed to adjust to his size. As his quickening thrusts rub against my clit, the pressure I'm feeling starts to rise. His thumb moves to my most sensitive flesh and the slightest of pressure causes a powerful sensation to slam into me so fast, I have to squeeze Nate's shoulders to stop from screaming things I shouldn't be saying out loud. He stops the caressing only to let me ride out the aftershocks of my orgasm, and then he mercilessly starts to circle my clit again.

"You're so wet," he whispers into the darkness in a low, raspy voice.

The sound thrills me.

Out of nowhere, a quaking warmth ripples through me in waves and this time I can't stop from crying out and praying to God, to Nate, to the heavens. My head falls back, my body arches, and his hips swivel into me with a tantalizing pressure.

None of it can ground me though, and I can feel my fingers gripping his shoulders so tightly, there's no doubt I must be drawing blood. The pleasure is insurmountable, and I can't stop myself.

In a quick motion, both of his hands plant firmly on my hips with a grip so tight that I'm sure I'll have bruises tomorrow, but couldn't care less. He moves me at a quicker pace, as his thrusts increase with equal vigor.

The only sound in the room is the slapping of our skin and our heavy breathing.

Then suddenly something shifts, I can feel it all happening—the arch of his back, the swiveling of his hips, the stilling inside me.

The sexual pull is explosive.

I wouldn't say I've had tons of experience with sex, but I wouldn't say I'm inexperienced either, and without a doubt, this is unlike anything I've ever felt. Another release erupts from within me—it makes me want to believe the only thing coming for me is pleasure.

Ever.

"Fuck," he mutters in a hoarse, thick voice filled with sexual satisfaction.

He falls back with labored breaths, taking me with him, pressing my head into his chest and attempting to run his fingers through my tangled curls.

It feels good to be in his arms.

It makes me feel alive.

I feel safe from the world outside. It almost makes me believe things might not happen the way I know they will.

Almost.

But the feeling won't last—if only I could stay in his arms forever.

Just as my eyes close he lifts me from his body and my cocoon of safety is gone.

I hear a snapping sound, knotting the condom would be my

guess, and then feel the cushions of the couch dip. He drags me on top of him and covers us with the blanket.

I feel safe again.

His hands weave through my hair and then he tugs it back, placing a chaste kiss on my forehead.

I like the gesture.

And then I lay my head on his chest, listening to the soothing sound of his heartbeat.

7

Miami Vice

The thumping soundtrack of *Miami Vice* plays in my head while Colin Farrell and Jamie Foxx pursue criminals on the streets of the city. Palm trees, flamingos, racing greyhounds, bikinis, fancy cars, sleek apartments, drugs, and of course, money—it all plays on a slideshow reel. When the camera zooms in on the criminal's face, it's not just anyone's face—it's my brother's.

With a start, I bolt upright and cradle my head in my hands. My dreams have shifted—one nightmare to another.

I can't leave here always wondering what he did to pay off my debt and make my life easier.

I have to know.

I squeeze my eyes shut, but quickly reopen them when I realize I'm in Nate's bed. He must have brought me up here after I fell asleep last night.

But he's not beside me.

I fall back down onto the pillows and stare at the ceiling.

"Hey, you're awake." Nate stands in the bathroom doorway wearing only a towel.

My pulse races at the sight of him.

In return, his gaze roams my body.

"Yes." I sit up and pull the sheet up, feeling a little shy.

He steps forward and sits on the bed, twisting to look at me.

"Nate," I begin.

At the same time he says, "Zoey."

Our eyes lock, and both of us stop talking—lust sparks the moment our eyes connect.

"You first," he finally says.

"About last night . . ." My voice is hoarse. I want to look away, but I don't. I encouraged what happened; who knows—maybe I even instigated it.

"That can't happen again," he finishes for me.

I flinch without intending to. I would have said something more along the lines of, *It was amazing and helped me forget everything, but we probably shouldn't do that again.* But he puts so much finality into his statement that it stuns me. "Why?"

His audible intake of breath is the only response.

I inch forward, taking the sheet with me. "Why?"

He twists back around and leans over, resting his arms on his thighs and dropping his head.

I stare at the ripped strength before me and wait. Not really sure why it even matters—I shouldn't be thinking about getting involved with anyone.

He does something to me that I'm not sure I want to let go.

A heavy sigh. "You're my best friend's sister. I shouldn't have taken advantage of you like that."

My feet hit the floor, and I wrap the sheet around myself. Before I know what I'm doing, I walk around the bed and crouch in front of him.

He lifts his eyes, and I see guilt swimming in the green depths.

I drop to my knees. "Look, I'm not looking for anything more than what happened last night, but I want you to know: not, for one second, do I think you took advantage of me."

He shakes his head and stares at me. "There's so much more to it."

My hands go to his thighs. "Then tell me."

Ding-dong. The doorbell rings.

He runs a hand through his hair, messing it up even more. "Fuck."

I stand up. "Are you expecting someone?"

He rises and strides into his closet. "Get dressed, and come meet me downstairs. My attorney is here to meet you."

"Why do I need to talk to your attorney?"

The doorbell rings again.

He comes out in jeans and a T-shirt. "Could you just do as I ask?" he snaps.

I blink. "Sure."

He heads for the door, then grabs the jamb. "I'm sorry," he says and then closes the door.

I stand there, staring at the closed door, openmouthed.

Sorry for what? Sorry for snapping? Sorry for sleeping with me?

I need someone to talk to, so I call the only person I can—my shrink. When I get her voice mail, I leave her a message.

Voices travel from downstairs, and I wonder why Nate wants me to meet with an attorney. Maybe he knows something about my brother. The thought gets me moving and I bolt into the bathroom.

After a quick shower, I pull out another one of the dresses Zach sent me. This one is a short aqua tank dress with pink jelly-fish all over it. I dry my hair with my diffuser as fast as I can and let it fly wild to save time. Mascara, a quick dab of blush, and a swipe of gloss, and then I finally slide into my sandals before putting my necklace and earrings on.

Ready, not bad, in less than twenty minutes.

When I open the door, I can hear voices down below. As soon as I reach the staircase, both men stand up from the sofa. I give Nate a smile as he stares back at me.

God, just looking at him makes my body tingle.

When I reach the halfway point, he walks over to the stairs and meets me at the bottom. The look he's giving me is not the look of a man who doesn't want to sleep with me again—it's a look of want, lust, and need all mixed together.

I'm sure my look mimics his.

"You look beautiful," he murmurs in my ear.

A thrill whirls through me.

Now I *know* he said that yesterday when he first saw me. And I swear, just like yesterday, his eyes drop, and a shyness presents itself.

It makes my heart stop.

"Thank you," I whisper back, thinking that swipe of blush wasn't needed as my cheeks flame.

"Zoey, this is my attorney."

I look across the room. The man, like Nate, is tall, dark, handsome, and very well dressed in a gray pinstriped suit, white shirt, and red tie.

We walk toward each other and meet in the middle.

"Hi," I say.

"Miss Flowers, Oliver Martinez." He extends his hand.

"Zoey." I smile and shake his hand in return.

"Zoey." He rubs his hands together. "Nate here tells me we don't have much time. So if you could follow me, I have some papers for you to sign."

"Papers for what?" I ask.

He glances to Nate, who is right beside me. "I was going to explain earlier; I just hadn't gotten to it. Oliver is going to help you with everything you need. I wanted you to be able to access all of your brother's records; and to do that, you need proof of his death and proof that you're his next of kin. Oliver will take care of that for you."

My hand flies to my locket. "Yes, of course I do. Thank you for taking care of this."

I follow Oliver over to the counter and sign the papers, my hands shaking as the reality of Zach's death haunts me once again.

"Zoey," Oliver says, "do you know if your brother designated you as a payable-on-death beneficiary?"

I squeeze my locket tightly. "I honestly have no idea."

"Was your brother's name on the deed to the house you currently live in? Nate mentioned your deceased grandmother owned it. I assume she left it to you in her will."

"I don't know." I take a deep breath, finding this much harder than I would have expected. Talking to a complete stranger about my brother's death and looking like an idiot, because I don't know anything, isn't easy.

Nate's hand grazes my back and it surprises me. "It's okay, Zoey. That's why I thought you should meet with Oliver."

I look at him, grateful not only for his help, but that he's here with me.

"Okay, one last question. Are you interested in looking into any liability as it applies to your brother's death?"

"Oliver!" Nate hisses.

"Nate, I know you said that wasn't necessary, but not all accidents are accidents, especially when debris in the road was the cause. I could look into what he hit and how it got there."

"Z had a motorcycle accident going way too fast. Why make Zoey live through it again?" Nate's tone is dismissive.

"Nate's right," I confirm.

"Yes, of course. I understand. Let me pull together the required documents. I'll get you what I can before you leave. The rest I'll have to mail."

"That will be fine. Thank you."

"What you can get done before she leaves would be appreciated," Nate interjects.

Oliver grins at Nate. "I'll be as expedient as I can. And, Zoey"—he turns to me—"here's my card. If you need anything else, don't hesitate to call me."

"Thank you."

"Nate." Oliver shakes his hand. "Good to see you."

Nate claps him on the shoulder. "Thank you for doing this on a Sunday."

He nods. "Anytime, you know that. I'll see myself out."

Oliver has obviously been here before, since he heads for the garage door.

Nate turns his attention to me before the door even closes. "I know I told you I'd take you to get that coffee, but can I get a rain check? My assistant called and told me there's some issues with the deal I'm working on. I have to drive to Tampa to iron out the details in person."

I nod. "Sure, of course. I understand."

His hands go to his hips. "Look, Zoey, I know that conversation between us earlier didn't go well. But I really do think it's for the best."

I lift my chin. "I don't disagree."

And I don't. Do I?

He hesitates for a moment before walking down the hall toward the garage.

I follow him, feeling the need to clarify. "My reasons are just different than yours."

He steps into his office and emerges, dropping a pair of boots to the ground, and then shoving his feet into them. When he's done, he looks up. "I'm sure they are."

"But you're right—it's for the best."

He nods.

Silence.

We stare at each other.

My heart beats a little faster from the look in his eyes.

He blinks as if blinking away his thoughts. "Hey, I almost forgot. I'm going to have my dad's car dropped off today. He doesn't use it, and I don't like the idea of you being stuck here without a way to get off the island. The spare key is on the counter."

"That's nice of you, but really I'm fine. I don't have anywhere I need to go."

"It will be in the driveway later today," he insists.

And then just like that, he closes the door.

I stand there, trying to stop myself from running after him. I steady myself against the wall, trying to stop myself from falling back.

It's for the best.

The door opens again and he leans in.

My breath catches.

When he sees me still standing here he looks surprised. "Hey," his voice is soft, gentle. "I forgot to tell you to help yourself to whatever you want to eat. Rosie left the refrigerator full."

He closes the door one final time.

"Rosie?" I ask, but it's too late.

He mentioned her yesterday as well.

A girlfriend?

A friend?

I have no idea.

It's not my business.

My head drops.

This is not a fantasy. This is reality. I try to get the facts straight—last night I had sex with my brother's best friend.

Sex.

That's all.

But it's the only thing since my brother died that has breathed any life into me. Well, actually being with Nate is the only thing that has taken my mind off my destiny. If I want to be honest—I don't want things with him to end. But at the same time, I know it's not fair to him. He has a life of his own.

But it's not that I'm using him, because I absolutely am not.

I feel a connection to this man that I should not be feeling.

Allowing anyone in my life is a mistake. My uncertainty about how much time I have left should be reason enough to stay away.

I blow my hair out of my eyes.

I need to stop this.

My gaze rises. The spare room door is open. I walk to the end of the hallway and peek in. The night I arrived, I glimpsed in but didn't really see anything except a bed. In the light of day it doesn't look any different—just a bare mattress on a bed frame and nothing else. Nate must have cleaned it out sometime after my brother died. And then I remember the boxes in the boathouse. I planned on spending the day over there, so I might as well start now. I make my way through the living room and I hear my cell phone ringing. I hurry up the stairs to answer it.

"Hello."

"Zoey, it's Dr. Raymond. I'm just returning your call. It sounded urgent."

"I'm sorry to have bothered you. I just needed someone to talk to."

"Are you okay? You sound out of breath."

I smile. "I'm better now, Dr. Raymond. I just left my phone in Nate's room, and ran up the stairs to get it. But my call might have been premature. I'm feeling better."

"Nate? As in your brother's best friend Nate?"

"Yes, that Nate."

"Would you like to tell me what you're doing in his bedroom?"

I sigh and plop on the bed. "Well, things aren't going exactly how I thought they would."

"What do you mean?"

Dr. Julia Raymond is my shrink. I've known her for a long time. Although before my brother's death, I hadn't seen her for years. But since his death, I've gone back to her—she's not only my therapist; she's also the only person besides my brother who knows everything about me.

When I called earlier, I needed someone to talk to about Zach and Nate. Even though the desperation to talk is gone, I still tell her everything that's been going on, from this not being Zach's house to my feelings for Nate. Thirty minutes later, we're still on the phone.

"Zoey, I think you're experiencing what I'd call a sexual awakening. It makes sense with the recent trauma in your life that you're seeking an outlet for your emotions. But I want to caution you not to confuse love with lust."

"Dr. Raymond." I clear my throat. "I never said the word *love*."

"No, but it's clear that you have feelings for him."

"Yes, feelings—feelings of desire."

I have always talked openly and honestly with Dr. Raymond, but for some reason I leave out this morning's conversation—it seems somehow unfinished. I also don't bare the fact that I like Nate's domineering side. When I was with him, I didn't have to make decisions or think about what was next. He took care of that.

It felt freeing.

"Well, if Nate is how you've described him, it sounds like he might not be looking for any more than you say you are. But, Zoey, I want you to proceed with caution. I'm all for exploring your feelings. I just don't want you to get hurt in the process."

"I won't. You know having a relationship isn't anything I'm interested in."

"I know, but perhaps it's time to think about one."

"Dr. Raymond, we've talked about this."

I can hear her sigh. "Yes, we have. But as your psychologist, it's my job to encourage you to look toward the future."

I draw in a deep breath. "I know."

Ding-dong.

"I have to go, Dr. Raymond, someone is at the door."

"Take care, Zoey. And I'm always here if you need me."

"I know. And thank you." I hit End.

The doorbell rings again. It must be the car Nate said he was having dropped off. I rush down the stairs and swing the door open. A very well dressed woman, looking to be in her late forties, stands before me with a stack of papers in her hands.

"Hello," she announces with excitement as she steps in.

I blink and stare at the back of her chignon as she walks down the hall, past the statue, and into the living room. I trail behind her. "Nate isn't here, if you're looking for him."

She turns around. "He isn't?"

I shake my head. "No, can I help you?"

She looks at her watch. "Oh, I'm sorry to intrude. When he didn't show up for the Community Council meeting this morning, I assumed he'd be home."

"He had to go to Tampa. He said he's having issues with a deal he's working on."

She sighs. "The docks project. That bastard that owns the warehouse space is so greedy. If he gets this project off the ground, it will be a miracle. But I pray he pulls it off. It will mean so much to the prosperity of the neighborhood."

I stare at her. She's clearly affected as much as Nate by whatever is going on.

She approaches me. "Never mind my ramblings. My manners seem to have failed me today. I'm Isabella Marco. I own a boutique in town."

"I'm Zoey."

"Zoey." She smiles. "Lovely. How long have you known Nate?"

"Well, I'm not really sure how to answer that. A long time, I guess."

She looks me up and down. "You're not from here, are you?"

Her piercing gaze makes me a little uncomfortable, and I just shake my head.

"Well, be assured, my boutique is one of the trendiest in Miami Beach. If you're ever looking to shop, it's called Isabella's."

"Thank you. I'll keep that in mind. Can I help you with anything else?"

She drops the stack of papers on the kitchen counter. "Just tell Nate I stopped by with my notes on his proposal. I'd like further explanation in a few areas. I've marked where. He'll understand."

I nod and clear my throat. "Can I ask how you know Nate?"

She smiles at me with warmth, indicating that she likes him. Oliver looked the same way.

"We met a few years ago at a Wynwood fund-raiser. We both have a soft spot in our hearts for the destruction that took place there after Hurricane Andrew, and we both feel for the community's struggle to make the area whole again. It's been so long, and so little has been done. Anyway." She waves away her sadness. "Nate and I are on the panel for community development. Nate's been trying to talk me into opening a boutique over in Wynwood with a lower price point. I wanted to discuss his proposal with him."

"Really? I had no idea he was that active in the community."

"He grew up there, darling, and his father's gallery is there. His concern for the welfare of the community is admirable."

A dusting of good feelings coats me.

"I didn't know."

"And can I ask how you know Nate?"

I drop my eyes, hoping she doesn't see the intimacy I feel toward him. "He is . . ." I pause, the words catching my throat. "He was my brother's best friend."

"You're Zachary Flowers's sister. I see it now."

I raise my gaze. "I am."

Her smile becomes kind. "I'm so sorry for your loss. I met your brother a few times down in Wynwood. Very nice young man."

My heart warms. "Thank you."

She walks toward the door. "I have to run. But I want to caution you to watch yourself in Miami. The people here will eat a sweet thing like you alive if you don't."

Trailing behind her, I give a slight laugh. "I can take care of myself."

"Well, I'm sure you can, and if not, Nate will. Don't let him fool you either. Under all of that attitude is a man with a heart. And who knows, maybe you'll be just the one to help him find it."

"Oh, we're not together."

She opens the door, and then pats my out-of-control curls. "You're in his house. You must be someone special."

I fold my arms, unsure of what to say to that.

She pulls her keys from her purse. "Ciao, darling. It was a pleasure to meet you."

I watch her get into her Mercedes, and I spot a car in the driveway—a Toyota Camry. It's just like the one I have at home. It must be Nate's father's car. Was it there before Isabella even arrived? I never looked.

Nate doesn't waste time.

I close the door and walk back down the hallway. Pausing to look at the statue, I feel like she just listened to that whole conversation.

Crazy, I know.

But then again, the fact that a man told me he doesn't want to sleep with me again, and I still can't stop thinking about him, isn't any crazier.

It's time to remember what I came here for.

Yes, my brother, I think and head to the kitchen to get some coffee and something to eat before heading over to the boathouse.

On the counter near the Miele sits a note under the same set of car keys I saw earlier.

Sorry I had to run this morning. I haven't forgotten that I promised to help you figure Z out. Hopefully, Oliver will clear the way quickly. And I hope to wrap this deal up soon.

I'm not sure if I'll be back tonight, but if I am, I'll grab us dinner if it's not late.

And I want to bring you to your brother's favorite restaurant tomorrow night. I'm sure you know that just like coffeehouses, he always sought out top restaurants. Plan on 7 if we don't catch up before then.

—Nate

My heart not only skips, it trips right out of my chest. Not only because he offered to help me, lent me a car to drive, and has given me a place to stay . . . but also because he signed his name.

8
Not Again

Light from the small lamp glimmers over the polished wood of the desk. Sifting through the last of the contents of its drawers, I managed to somehow spend the day sorting through almost every piece of paper Zach had in his entire apartment. Piles of tax records, grocery receipts paid by credit card, old date books, cash receipts for art supplies, letters from Mimi, letters from me, supply lists, grocery lists, newspapers even; they are all now neatly stacked on top of the calendar blotter.

I started by cleaning out the kitchen, but then I came across a junk drawer filled with receipts. I found nothing out of the ordinary, other than the fact that from the amount of trips to the art supply store, there was no doubt Zach had been sketching. But once I moved to the desk, I found one other interesting thing. May and June's calendar pages had names written in the days about three times a week. Last names, none of which mean anything to me. The months preceding May were already torn off and were nowhere to be found.

My eyes are beginning to blur as I shut the light off before going to the glass doors to look out into the starry night. After Isabella left this morning, I texted Nate to thank him for the car and to let him know I would be moving my things over to the boathouse. He didn't respond, but then again I guess there was nothing to respond to.

Nate has been great, so I don't want to sound ungrateful in any way. Yet I feel a little more lost after our conversation this morning, more lost than I've felt in days. Being with him has allowed me to see a different side of life, a side I never knew I was missing—a more sensual side that I want to explore.

The night suddenly seems lonely, just as it had last night. I'm not sure where these feelings are coming from. I'm used to being alone.

I spin around, deciding to turn the TV on to clear my head of the thoughts that shouldn't be there. In doing so, my eyes land on the now clutter-free coffee table. A stack of magazines with names like *Vogue*, *Marie Claire*, and *Cosmopolitan* draw my attention. I sit down and pull the pile to my lap.

Odd publications for my brother to be perusing.

The *Vogue Espana* cover draws my attention. The photo features a famous soccer player, and his embrace with his girlfriend is the same exact pose as one of the naked couples I had seen yesterday in Zach's sketchpad. Upon comparing the two, there is no doubt Zach had re-created the scene. But who is the couple in Zach's sketch? It's not the same couple featured in the magazine.

My phone beeps with a text. I tear my eyes from the twin pictures and glance over to it.

Nate: I just got home. Have you eaten dinner?

My stomach rumbles at the thought of food.

Me: As a matter of fact, I haven't.

Nate: Come on over. I picked up food on my way home.

Me: Be there in a few.

My loneliness instantly evaporates.

I look down at my ragged sweatpants and tank top and shrug. At least I had showered before I changed, so I am certain I don't smell, and anything else doesn't really matter. Tonight Nate and I are two new friends eating a late-night meal together.

That's all.

I've resigned myself to that fact.

The night air feels good as I open the door and cross the grass. When I get close to the house, I can see Nate inside. He's taking food out of bags, and I giggle when I catch him eating fries between reaches into the bags to unload the food. A few seconds later, he disappears down the hall, and then suddenly I can hear the soft sounds of music playing. I watch him come back into the room, pretending to be drumming, and I'm mesmerized by the way his body moves to the beat.

Warmth swirls within me, as my eyes stay glued to his every move. Feeling a little stalkerlike, I pull on one of the doors, but it's locked. I tap lightly. When he looks up, he's got a broad smile on his face.

My toes curl at the sight.

Licking his fingers of any food crumbs, he walks my way. I have a sudden urge to lick them along with him. His hair is uncombed, and he's changed into a pair of nylon track pants and a plain white tee.

He looks incredible.

The door opens and I try to push my desires aside.

Friends. We. Can. Only. Be. Friends.

"Hey." His voice sounds warm and comforting to me. "I should have unlocked the door."

"Don't worry about it." I smile. "Something smells really good."

"I wasn't sure what you liked, so I got an assortment of burgers." He points to the counter.

It's loaded with different white wrapped packages, bags of fries, and a number of cups with straws set beside them. "I can see that, but you didn't have to go to so much trouble."

Grinning over his shoulder at me, he stops at the breakfast bar. "It was no trouble. I hope you're hungry."

"Starving."

With a jerk, he pulls out a stool. "Didn't you eat anything today?"

I look at him and try not to notice how attractive his tousled hair looks or how delicious the sight of his stubbled jaw is. "I did, but I think that was hours ago. Oh, did you get the papers Isabella left?"

"Yeah, I did. Did she talk your ear off?"

I take a seat. "No, not really."

He pushes my chair in. "Good, sometimes she gets going and never stops."

"She said she was in a hurry, so I guess I lucked out."

He chuckles as he moves to stand beside me. "She's really nice. Don't get me wrong."

I nod in agreement.

"How was your day otherwise?"

The sensation of his breath is tantalizing as it blows over my neck.

I think he notices my reaction to his close proximity.

"Interesting," I answer as he walks around the bar.

In a few short seconds he's standing in front of me with the counter as our divide. "Oh yeah? Interesting how?"

The aroma of bacon wafts through the air as he unwraps the packages and sets the burgers on a plate. I can't help but study the ease with which he moves. "You know how you said my brother hadn't sold any of his sketches in a long time?"

"Yeah, not that he ever mentioned to me anyway."

"Right. I understand that. I find it odd that he wouldn't though."

He nods in agreement before looking up. "Veggie juice, smoothie, or shake?" Liquid overflows from the lids and he pushes straws in the three Styrofoam cups.

"Veggie juice, please." I cross my legs and get comfortable. "Well, today I found receipts for a store called Art Village."

"I've heard of it. It's an art supply store beachside." He hands me a cup. "A Rabbit's Choice, just for you."

I quirk a brow.

"A blend of tomato, carrot, celery, beet, kale, and apple juices."

I can't help but scrunch my nose at the combination.

He swaps out the cups. "Take this one. The best milkshake you'll ever have."

We exchange cups. "Well, Zach was going there at least once a week for the past year."

"No shit."

I nod and take a sip. "Oh my God, this is amazing."

His grin is wide. "A French Monkey. Chocolate, banana, and vanilla yogurt."

I hand it back to him. "I don't want to take yours, though."

He rubs his chiseled abs. "No, it's fine. I have to watch my figure."

"Okay, now you better give me the juice back." I laugh.

He looks up, seriousness taking over. "You're perfect just the way you are."

I roll my eyes.

"I'm not joking around."

I smile.

He gives me the full weight of his stare. "I'm serious."

A shiver runs down my spine. The meaning of his words is clear—he likes the way I look. I wish I could be honest and tell him that I want him. That I don't want to be just friends. That I'm not looking for anything. That I just want him to fuck me.

To make me feel alive again.

But I don't; instead I take another sip. "How about we share?"

He lifts his hand. "Deal."

When I shake it, both of us hold on for longer than we should, and the electrical current that zaps through us makes me burn for him.

The plate is piled high with burgers and fries, and he sets it on the bar along with two plates, napkins, and silverware. "You were saying?"

It takes me a moment to collect my thoughts. "Can I be blunt with you?"

A smile drifts across his face. "Is there a reason you wouldn't be?"

A faint flush spreads across my body.

I delay my forthcoming admission and focus on the food by pointing to a burger with what looks to be an egg on it. "What's that one?"

"Sunny-side-up burger, I have to say it's my favorite." He goes around the plate clockwise. "BLT, veggie, tuna, turkey guacamole, sweet potato fries, and good old-fashioned french fries. Take your pick."

With a knife, I cut the sunny-side-up burger in half and scoop some sweet potato fries onto my plate.

Nate circles the corner and sits next to me, handing me a napkin. He cuts the remaining burgers in half and piles food on his plate. "Don't think I'm a pig, but I haven't eaten all day."

I laugh, easing my way into the conversation. "I hardly think that." I take a bite of my fry. "Ummm, that's seriously delicious."

His stare lingers on me and I can tell he's waiting.

"So, when I was going through Zach's things, I found some risqué sketches."

He lifts a brow and finishes chewing his food before talking. "Risqué in what way?"

"Nudes of couples."

"Okay." There is no shock in his response.

My throat feels tight and I take another sip of my shake.

"Z was an artist. He sketched and painted all types of subject matter." He takes another bite of his burger.

"These were realistic. True to life."

This gets his attention.

"The couples were having sex."

He fixes me with that steady gaze. "How do you know that?"

My shyness over the topic long gone, I respond, "Oh, if the looks on their faces didn't tell the story, the way their bodies were entwined did."

"How many like that did you find?"

"Just two. One was a replica of a magazine cover. Do you know why he might have been sketching something like that?"

Nate's hair falls down a little into his eyes. "I'm drawing a complete blank."

I finish my burger and set my napkin over my dish.

He shoves the plate of food my way. "You're not done, are you?"

"I'm so full." I lean back in my chair.

He sips from his straw. "There's still a lot more to eat."

"It's all yours, but it was delicious. Thank you."

He nods and eats the last of the fries. "Did you find anything else?"

"On his desk calendar, there were a number of names written in various dates for the months of May and June. Do you think they could have been artists from the gallery?"

"Do you remember any of the names?"

"Methot, Striker." I purse my lips and try to remember a few more.

His gaze lingers on me, and those green eyes are suddenly all I can see. "They don't ring a bell—but hang on, let me grab my phone. It's upstairs charging." He wipes his hands and drops his napkin to the bar.

A few seconds later, I call out, "Oh, Freeman, Myer," but he's already up the stairs. Without thinking, I follow him.

He's rifling through a drawer in his dresser, pulling various cords out.

"I thought of some more names."

The room is dark and as soon as I enter, his eyes are back on me. "I thought I'd get Z's phone too, but it's dead. He has a Samsung. I used to have one years ago. I thought I might still have the charger."

I walk over to where Nate's standing and glance down at his phone. Apps populate his screen. Checkmark, Google Search, Run-Keeper, Songkick, Nike, and another one called Estate.

He closes the drawer and redirects his focus to his phone. "But I can't find it."

I turn slightly so I can see the screen better and we seem to subconsciously both move closer until our hips touch.

He looks down and taps a few buttons.

My senses seem to heighten anytime he's near me.

The sound of his clicking the screen seems louder than it should be.

My nerves flare, my body tingles, my heart pounds.

"I don't see Methot or Striker in my contacts. But I wouldn't have all of the gallery's clients, just the ones I've met." His warm breath cascades down my neck and the fire within my body spreads.

I try to refocus on the task. "What about Freeman or Myer?" My finger touches his and my pulse pounds wickedly.

I don't want to just be friends with him. I want more.

He searches for the names, his breathing growing ragged.

Our bodies are now completely pressed side by side, both bent over the dresser. Standing this close to him elicits the memory of last night—all hands, and tongues, and limbs entwining. I close my eyes to suppress the memory.

"No, I don't have any of those names."

I freeze as his fingers dance over mine just before he turns the screen off. My eyes shift from his phone to him. "I'll try to find the charger for my brother's phone."

His body turns toward mine and he lifts my chin. "We'll figure this out. Don't be discouraged."

I find myself drawing even closer to him. "I appreciate your help. Thank you."

"You don't have to keep thanking me."

Neither of us focuses on what we're saying though, as the heat between us intensifies.

I swallow. My throat feels so dry. "I should probably go."

"Yeah, it's getting late," he whispers.

Moments pass in silence and yet we stay unmoving. Our mouths are inches apart. It's not as dark as last night. The dim lights of the room cast shadows over his face. "Nate?"

He exhales brokenly. "Yeah."

"Tell me why." I know I don't need to expand—he knows what I mean.

His forehead presses against mine, and a finger lightly caresses my cheek. "Zoey, just trust me. It's best if we remain friends."

I run my hand up his chest, unable to stop myself. "It just doesn't feel like it's for the best."

A sigh that could be a groan echoes in the space and then he's moving us slowly across the room. Moments later, I fall onto the bed and he hovers over me. His eyes flash over my face and even with his dark hair hanging over his forehead, I can see the reluctance they hold.

They reflect my own.

I can't stop myself. No, I just don't want to stop myself.

I'm not strong enough.

I pull him closer to me. He smells fresh, like soap, and I can't resist the overwhelming urge to breathe him in.

He feels so real.

He's what I crave.

He's what I want.

He makes me feel alive.

"Zoey—" he starts.

I look into his eyes. I'm sure that the myriad of emotions that were flickering across my face are now gone, and all that remains is pure, raw, unadulterated desire.

He drops his mouth to mine—his lips surround me, his tongue enters me, his breath is loud and audible. His hands slide down the sides of my body and his touch sears me. The heat between us consumes me. Tingles of pleasure, like magic, are all I can feel. The intimacy between us, the way our bodies react to each other—neither can be denied.

But in an unexpected reaction, he pulls away from me and the spell is broken.

The magic dissipates and tension replaces it.

Nate rolls over onto his back and throws his hand over his forehead. "Zoey, what are you doing?"

"Nate, we're two people who want each other. There's nothing wrong with that."

"You don't understand."

"I do. I want to be with you and I know you want the same. That's all there is to it."

No matter how desperate the words sound, they're the truth.

I can't help how I feel. All I want is to be with him, and to forget the lies, the mysteries, my search for the truth about Zach's life.

He rolls onto his side and his brows scrunch together. "We just can't do this again."

"Am I mistaken? You don't want me?"

"You know I do."

"Then I don't understand."

He twists and I think he's going to get up, but instead he switches on the light and dims it to the faintest setting, only allowing me to see past his shadows. Then he settles back on the pillow to face me. His fingers tangle in my messy curls. I don't even know if he realizes he's doing it.

"That's not the question you should be asking. You should be asking yourself why you'd want me to fuck you again. I'm not anyone you should be interested in, in that way."

I rest my head on my elbow and my hand caresses his thick dark hair. "Why do you think that?"

Bolting upright, he grabs my wrists and takes me with him. Like a force of nature he slaps my palms onto his face, something snapping within him. "Look at me, Zoey. I'm not the guy you've conjured up in your head. I'm not your Prince Charming coming to rescue you. I know your brother must have warned you against me."

My eyes lock on his and I can see the turbulence swirling within them like a storm. "This has nothing to do with fairy tales, or being rescued, or even my brother. I'm not looking for Prince Charming. I just want to be with you. If you don't want the same thing, just say so, but don't try to make yourself out to be some dark, messed-up asshole, because I can see through it."

His grip on me loosens and his eyes soften—desire emerges in the depths of his deep green pools. He twists back around to flick the light off, and within moments his powerful thighs are framing mine. "There's nothing to see through. Feel this." His lips skim down my neck. "This is me." He presses his body to mine. "All of me." His voice is low and seductive.

The feel of his flesh against mine eases away my thoughts but not for long. Reason soon takes over. I try to push him away, but he doesn't move. "I know who you are. Talk to me. Tell me what you're thinking."

His tongue licks around my ear. "You said you want me. Well, I'm right here. So why don't we stop all this therapy bullshit—I'm not one of your students."

His brashness, the boldness of his words, makes me go dark with anger. This time when I push him off me, I do so with force, but I don't need to; he goes willingly.

He sits up and leans against the headboard.

I pull my knees to my chest. "Talk to me. What's this about? We're talking about fucking, not getting married for Christ's sake. I'm here for a few more days and then I'll be out of your life. So why the reluctance?"

I don't usually talk like that, but I need to get through to him.

He shrugs and throws his head back. "I told you, your brother didn't want me to be with you."

I shake my head. "That makes no sense. We didn't even meet until after he died."

"No, but he told me."

"Told you what?"

"Jesus, Zoey! Not everything is meant to be discussed. Will you give it up?"

My gaze settles on his face. "No, I won't." And with that I stand up and head for the door.

"Zoey!"

I stop just before reaching the stairs and turn my head.

"Come back here." His voice is much lower.

He is right. Not everything needs to be discussed, but with

what looms over me every day, worrying that I'll die before I turn twenty-eight just like my brother, I have to know. I walk back in and sit at the foot of the bed in front of him. "Please, Nate, please tell me."

He levels his gaze at me and with a deep sigh, opens up. "On the night of Z's twenty-seventh birthday, I took him out."

My heart lurches. The day Zach turned twenty-seven. I too wish that I had given more credence to what it meant then.

"He'd gotten a text from you earlier that night and was staring at the photo."

The memory rushes back. I'd sent him a text with a picture of the chocolate birthday cake I'd made for him, even though he wasn't home. That was the first year he wasn't home on his birthday. I'd made chocolate because it's my favorite and I was going to be the one eating it. There isn't any reason to stop, but Nate pauses anyway. "Of the cake?" I ask.

He nods.

"Go on," I prompt.

"I was being a dick and harassing him about you. I asked him why you'd never come to visit in all the years he'd lived here. His answer didn't surprise me. At first he just shrugged but I pressed him and then he finally told me that Mimi was sick most of the time, so it was just easier for him to go home. But like I said, I was being a dick and pushed him to say what I already knew."

"What?" I ask, genuinely confused about what that could be.

"'To keep her away from you,' he told me."

My mouth drops. "He said that?"

Nate nods. "I already knew that."

My brows scrunch. "How?"

"The way he hated to talk about you to me unless I pushed him, I knew he wanted me far away from you."

"No, I don't believe that, Nate. You misunderstood. He was joking."

"No, Zoey, I didn't. He didn't just say it, he meant it. With his fists clenched, he all but told me he'd kill me if I ever went near you."

I reach across the bed. "Nate, he was my brother. He was always overprotective. He'd say that about any guy."

He jerks back. "No, Zoey, you're wrong. He told me once when it came to women he thought my wires were all crossed. You were the single most important person in his life. He always said you were the good for all the bad he'd ever been. He was so damn poetic. I remember him saying you were the ray of sunshine he could see through the clouds. The light at the end of the tunnel. That you believed in him when no one else had. You kept him moving forward. He felt he owed you everything. He wanted you to be happy. And he knew that wasn't going to happen with me."

Tears prick my eyes at his confession. "Oh, Nate, that's how he was. He hated the only boyfriend I ever had so much, he threatened to break his legs once."

Nate stops and looks over at me. "Zoey, you really don't get it. It goes deeper than that. I was joking with him that night and just to get under his skin I asked him, 'Do you think I'd like her? Is that what's going on here? Because I'd be happy to fly up and meet her even if she is a nice girl, I'd make an exception for you.' I used to joke with him that I never dated nice girls because they were too much work with all that love shit. It used to blow his mind."

I shift on the bed.

Nate seems to lose himself in his memory. "Zach said, 'No matter how much I'd like to trust you with her, I never could. You'd only break her heart. You're just not capable of that kind of relationship. So stay away from her.' He was pretty clear. So this"—Nate points between the two of us—"is wrong."

The words come out before I have a chance to think about them. "That was before."

He furrows his brows. "Before what?"

Now it's my turn to shut up. Opening up about the 27 Club isn't something you do. People look at you like you're crazy, and if they don't, they just pity you. I don't want either of those things from Nate.

"Nothing, never mind."

He narrows his eyes at me. "You make me spill my guts and then shut up? I don't think so."

"Before he died," I lie. The tears are now streaming down my face. I slam my eyes closed and wish things were different— different for the both of us.

The bed dips and Nate drags me closer to him. His hands rub up and down my back in a gesture of comfort. I relax into his arms and accept the warmth he has to offer. I let myself cry for all the things I can't control.

Life.

Death.

Everything in between.

When I can finally open my eyes, I look out into the night and I swear I see a shooting star.

"Did you see that?" I breathe out in short, stuttering breaths.

Nate pulls back to look at me. "See what?"

I point out the window. "A shooting star."

He shakes his head no and disengages from me altogether. "I'm going to grab some water. Do you want some?"

I look at him with a yearning I wish wasn't there. "Yes, I'll be right down. I just have to use the restroom."

Once Nate leaves the room, I walk over to the sliding glass doors and open them. The humidity is stifling, but I breathe the air in anyway. I look up into the night sky, and look at the stars— there are so many of them. And as I stare into the wonder of the sky, I can't help thinking, *Stars are born, they live, and they die—just like people.* Some shine bright, some twinkle, some are faint specks you can barely see. The lives of stars vary, their vibrancy does too—but once they burn out they extinguish, and then they fall from the sky.

Isn't that the way of life?

9

The Dinner

Miami at twilight is really something—it's like its own galaxy.

I stare out at the horizon, and not only can I see the MacArthur Causeway Bridge illuminated in neon hues of pink and purple, but also the skyscrapers of downtown Miami, and the bright white lights of Miami Beach. From the deck of the boathouse, even the bay looks like a tropical island resort with its clear turquoise water.

Looking around, I breathe in the ocean air and try not to think about never seeing anything like this again.

Do we miss things when we're gone?

If we do, what would I miss? Beautiful views, coffee, my favorite books.

God, that sounds pathetic.

My life has been so boring.

Empty.

I don't want to die before I've lived.

A cool breeze ruffles my pinned-up hair, and I feel like I'm going to fall apart.

Breathe.

Relax.

Refocus.

I shift my thoughts to what I found today.

Once the sun came out, I sat out on the deck and turned on Zach's laptop. The warmth felt good on my skin and I wanted to soak it up, but I had work to do. The checkbook I found in Zach's desk drawer yesterday told me he banked at SunTrust. I found their Web site, guessed his login would be his Social Security number, knew his password was 0515, my birthday, because all his passwords were my birthday, and just like that, I accessed his bank statements.

I was surprised at how easy it was.

Downloading the statements took some time. The Internet connection seemed to be slow, but after that, reviewing them went fast. There were very few transactions. Each month over the past year, his activity was minimal—an automatic payroll deposit that easily covered his modest bills—five hundred dollars to Nate for rent, I assume, seven hundred dollars to Ally Financial for his motorcycle, and six hundred dollars quarterly to State Farm for his vehicle insurance. In fact, State Farm contacted me just last week regarding the claim Nate had told me to make via e-mail for Zach's vehicle. Apparently, I'll be getting a check for the value of Zach's motorcycle less the amount still owed to Ally within the next month.

All of that activity seemed normal, but what didn't seem normal were the large cash deposits made weekly into his account. And even though those deposits had decreased in size over the last three months, they were still large. Following each deposit, Zach would in turn write a check to First National Bank, the bank that held Mimi's mortgage, or Grow Financial, the company I consolidated all of Mimi's medical bills with.

This wasn't anything eye-opening—it just confirmed what I

already knew. Yet, the weekly deposits give me reason to believe that Zach was legitimately earning the money in some way—it was a steady stream of income.

Or at least, I hope it was.

The laptop died shortly after I came to my conclusions. When I went in search of the cord for the computer—and while I was at it, one for his phone—I came across dozens of sketchpads under his bed and found dozens more stacked in an armoire. I flipped through a few of them, just staring at the skill and detail Zach poured into them—some of them very realistic.

Unlike yesterday though, this time I found some cartoonish sketches in one book. Those made me smile. One of a chef trying to catch a fish, one of a coffee cup overflowing with hearts, and another one of a cat marrying a dog.

In another sketchbook I found some more naked women, couples, and even a few of that dark-haired woman with the enchanting eyes. None of the ones I looked at had a title—then again, he only named his finished works.

I set those aside to look at tomorrow and charge his phone. I find none of the names on the calendar in his contacts.

How would I figure out what he did to get that money? I knew so little about my brother's life, yet I thought I knew everything. Sadness had swept through me, and I tried to force myself to be strong.

No more breakdowns.

I know Zach couldn't have been doing anything illegal. I just needed to prove this—for me and for the memory of my brother.

The sound of a large ship entering the causeway startles me out of my thoughts. My vacant gaze refocuses to my surroundings. As the familiar blue of the daytime sky begins to fade, I pace back and forth with my long black jersey dress skimming the deck of the boathouse.

Almost time to meet Nate for dinner.

Already resigned to the fact that whatever guilt Nate harbors about my brother may never be resolved, all I can do is respect his gallant behavior. Yet I know Zach. I know all he ever wanted was for me to be happy. And if he had known Nate would be the one to make me happy, he would never have forbidden us being together.

And on top of that, knowing life is short, he would have wanted me to do what makes me happy. The fact is, Nate and I never met when Zach was alive. If he was alive and saw the sparks between us, he wouldn't have spoken those words to Nate.

It's true, I know it is, but Nate doesn't see it that way.

Nate and I haven't spoken all day. When I left last night, he made sure I had the car keys and a house key, and he walked me to the boathouse door. With his hands jammed in his pockets, we said good night and he waited for me to lock up. When I went over this morning to make coffee, he was already gone. He did text me this afternoon reminding me about dinner.

The waves hitting the rocks draw my attention back to the present. When I look at my watch it appears to have stopped. Water condensation under the face tells me my trusty water-resistant Timex was not in fact water*proof.* The rain from the storm a few nights ago must have gotten into the face.

I step back inside and survey the area. I've made progress but still have a lot to do before Friday. Tomorrow I need to start packing up some things. I head to the kitchen and toss the watch into the trash can near the counter, then check the time on the stove— seven exactly.

Time to go.

I slide into my crystal-toed sandals and head downstairs. On the way, I give the thin halter straps around my neck a tug and check that the cutouts at my sides are where they should be before stepping out the old weathered door and into the backyard.

Nate is standing at the water's edge, staring out at the same view I was just gazing at a few moments ago. He looks over his shoulder, and the grin that forms when he sees me lights me up from the inside.

My resignation from earlier begins to wane.

He turns around.

I meet his eyes but regret it immediately.

My body freezes.

Every muscle tightens.

My knees weaken.

He looks so sexy—I just want to throw myself at him.

My resignation scatters.

In a light linen suit, white shirt no tie, and shoes made of a leather that looks very fine—I can't look away.

I can't move.

My heart thumps in anticipation of being close to him, even though it shouldn't.

I fight to catch my breath.

I can't pretend—I'm not going to.

I want this man.

I don't want to be empty anymore.

"Hi." I give him a small wave, feeling nervous. The twilight affords me the luxury of noticing the way he seems to drink me in, and that provides me the courage to walk toward him.

"Zoey." My name sounds warm and sensual in the way it leaves his lips.

He watches my every step as we walk toward each other.

My nerves are all aflutter—I hold my stomach in and try to move with grace.

With the sunset behind him, I have such a clear picture—he's tall, but not big, broad, all lean sinewy muscle. His hair, in the light of the yellow glow, is that perfect coffee-bean shade. And his eyes, those eyes, are greener than anything I've ever seen before.

We stop in front of each other, staring—the instant charge

between us sends sparks through the air. I can feel the burn of it to my very core.

His eyes drag up and down my body.

"You look beautiful." His words sound careful, quiet, but so real.

I look away, feeling a little shy. "Thank you. I bet you say that to all the women."

He lowers his voice. "You couldn't be more wrong."

For the first time, I wonder why he's so closed off. I wonder why a guy like him doesn't have a beautiful girlfriend, or a wife, to share his life with.

I wonder why we live our lives like we do. Never realizing some day it might be too late. My thoughts are shadowed when I feel the weight of his stare on me, and I look up, only to get lost in his eyes. All of the bravado I mustered earlier crumbles in his presence. The fresh, clean scent of this man, the way he looks, the way he moves, the sound of his voice, his kindness, the sadness he radiates that I want to turn around—I can't help but be drawn to him.

Something strikes me. If what he told me Zach thought about him is true—that he's not capable of love—we might just be the perfect match.

The thought saddens me, and I have to paint a fake smile on my face. "How was your day?"

"Not great. That deal I've been working on still hasn't closed, but I'm determined to get that property."

"Are you any closer?"

He nods. "I fucking hope so for the hours I've spent on it. Enough about me. How was your day?"

My fingers wrap around my locket. "I found the phone charger, but there was nothing on Zach's phone."

He clutches my hand holding the locket. "Can I see the photos inside?"

I nod, my fingers trembling from his touch.

He opens the silver antique oval and stares at the picture on the right. "Did Z send you this picture?"

"Yes, just before Christmas, I think."

"It was Thanksgiving, I believe, and we were picking up food at the supermarket when he stopped in the freezer section and snapped the photo. He said you'd understand."

I trace his gaze with my own. "When we were growing up, his favorite ice-cream flavor was black raspberry, but not just any black raspberry. He had to have an Abbott's."

"An Abbott's?" Nate's brow lifts.

"They were a mom-and-pop store with the absolute best ice cream. He sent me that picture in front of a pint of Ben & Jerry's Black Raspberry with a message that said he couldn't wait to come home for the real thing."

"Is that what the mural in Wynwood is about?"

"Yes, it is." My heart splits open at the memory and sorrow fills it.

He points to the other side of the locket. "She's beautiful. Is she your grandmother?"

"Yes. She was really young when this picture was taken though. It was before my grandfather died."

His fingers pinch the locket like it's precious and the gesture moves me. "What was her name? I only ever heard Z call her Mimi."

I smile. "Her name was Olivia, but everyone called her Olive because they said she looked like Olive Oyl."

"You look like her, you know."

I laugh, self-conscious. "Is that good or bad?"

My question seems to surprise him, and his hand goes to my chin to lift my face. "I've told you before—you're beautiful."

His touch sears me.

I smooth out my expression and let silence sweep between us while I try to gather my self-control.

He closes the locket. "Have I ever told you how much I admire the close relationship you and your brother had?"

My mind starts to fight a myriad of emotions.

Don't get too close.

Live.

Keep your distance.

Experience life.

"Hey." His voice is soft. "Are you okay?"

His arms pull me close to him.

It's then I realize I'm crying—again. Silent tears are streaming down my face.

I lean back and wipe them away. "I'm fine. I'm sorry; I don't know what's wrong with me. I don't usually cry so much."

He takes my trembling hands in his. "I get it. It's an emotional time. Are you sure you're up to going out tonight? I thought I'd take you to Norman's, but we can grab something to eat here. It's not a problem at all."

"Norman's?" This perks me up. "Zack told me the chef there was on *Martha Stewart* and *Top Chef.*"

Nate shrugs. "All I know is Z dragged me there at least once a week for almost a year."

"I'd love to eat there. Zach never stopped talking about Luke Nelson." My voice is even, all the sadness forcefully expelled.

Nate smirks. "Is that the chef?"

I nod.

He motions toward the driveway. "Shall we go then?"

I manage a smile and stare at him. In that moment, I decide I want Nate to breathe life into my otherwise lifeless existence, and I'm not giving up on him.

"I'm ready." I follow him with a sense of renewed vigor. I follow him up the pathway, and stare at his perfect backside, then around the house, where I can't help but gawk at his lethal stride. I follow him into the garage and watch the muscles ripple across his back when he reaches for my door. I think I'd follow him any-where, if it meant I could keep watching him move.

There is a click as he unlocks the car with his keyless remote and offers his hand.

I take it without hesitation.

With his devastatingly handsome looks, he could have been a model. But tonight that's not what attracts me to him. What I'm attracted to is the way he seems to understand me, as well as the concern he shows toward me.

I glance over at him before he closes my door. "Can I ask you something?"

"You know you can."

"Do you think people change?"

"Sure. Everything changes—people, places, technology."

"Do you think events can change people?"

He nods. "I know they can."

"Is it possible my brother might have changed in the year before he died?"

Nate looks away. "Zoey, I don't think I'm the best person to answer that."

"What do you mean?"

A pause.

"You don't have to answer that if you don't want to."

He shoves his hands in his pockets. "It's just, I wasn't around much the past year. But if you're asking me how I think he got the money—I think he earned it, somehow."

Relief overtakes me. "So do I."

He closes my door and hops in the Rover.

When he puts the car in reverse and pulls out of the garage, I look over at him. "I have another question."

"Shoot."

"Do you think my brother's opinion might have been different if he had seen us together?"

He punches the brakes and throws his head down.

I bite my lip. "Nate?"

He's silent for a few seconds and then he puts the car in park. Finally, he looks over at me. "Zoey, I just think some things are better left alone. Does that make sense?"

"No. Not really, Nate. Not when it comes to you and me."

"Look, I'm trying my best to respect your brother's wishes, but you're making it really hard on me."

I narrow my eyes at him. "I'm not trying to. That's what I'm talking about. Maybe Zach's wishes would have been different if he'd seen us together under different circumstances."

"Your brother definitely didn't want me with you. It's that simple."

"I don't think you're right. Can I be honest?"

He laughs a dry laugh. "I wouldn't expect anything else."

"My brother had a lot of opinions, but that doesn't mean he always knew what was best for me."

Nate squeezes his eyes shut. "The bottom line is, Z's wishes or not, you think you know me, but you don't. I'm not a good guy when it comes to women."

"I don't believe that."

"Come on, I know Z must have told you about me—that I never fuck the same girl twice," Nate said very matter-of-factly.

I blanch. Not at the harsh word, but at the thought of him with someone else. "Is that what this is really about?"

In all my contemplation today, I never for one minute thought his self-sacrificing need to keep his distance from me was anything more than due to my brother.

Maybe I was wrong.

He just stares at me.

I purse my lips and furrow my brows in frustration. Enough is enough. "You really don't get it. You're not even trying. If you wanted to make sure I didn't ask you to inconvenience yourself tonight—congratulations, you've succeeded." I pull on the door handle but the door is locked. "Let me out."

He grabs my arm. "Zoey, listen to me."

Rage takes hold and I search for the unlock button. "Let me out of here!"

"Listen to me. Please. I want to be with you, but I know it's wrong in so many ways."

His words stop me. "Wrong?"

"Yes, wrong."

Some of my anger recedes as I look over at the pain on his face. "It's not wrong. It couldn't be more right. We're two people who want to be together, nothing else."

"There's never nothing else."

"With me there is."

He shakes his head. "Tell me what you want from me."

"Do you want to know? Do you really want to know?"

He lifts his eyes and their focus is solely on mine. "Yes."

I stare back with certainty. "I want you to give in to this attraction between us. To push your guilt aside. I know it sounds selfish, but I have my reasons."

He throws his head back. "I can't do that. I just can't."

My heart stops.

Time to jump. "I want to tell you something, and I don't want you to think I'm crazy. So please, let me explain before you draw conclusions."

His brows knit together.

"Have you ever heard of the Twenty-Seven Club?"

Nate straightens. His shoulders go stiff as he puts his hands on the steering wheel. A few moments later, he turns toward me. "Z mentioned it once, but he was so drunk, I thought he was talking out his ass."

I twist in my seat. "My brother and I never believed we were destined to join, or that's what I thought. Then he dies at twenty-seven and leaves me taken care of, like he knew he was going to die. And now I'm not so sure of anything anymore. Did you know I turned twenty-seven a couple of weeks after he died?"

Nate swallows. "No."

"Well, I did, and I can't stop thinking I might be next."

"Zoey, Z died in a freak motorcycle accident."

"That's how everyone joins the club—tragic deaths."

Nate shakes his head vigorously. "Zoey, there is no club. It was coincidence. And just because Z died at twenty-seven, it certainly doesn't mean you will."

I shake my own head. "Is it really coincidence that my brother died while he was twenty-seven? And my grandfather, and my mother too? And many of our ancestors, whose names I don't even know? I don't think so. Zach must have believed it would happen, even though he told me he didn't. In fact, I think that's why he was doing whatever he was doing to earn money. He wanted to make sure he took care of me first. So, Nate, here's the thing—I now believe in destiny. I'm twenty-seven, and there's a very good chance my clock has already begun ticking. The timer could have started almost a month ago."

There it is—the truth.

Nate stares straight ahead and scrubs his face.

My crazy family legacy is hard for anyone to believe. But once it's digested—it's hard for anyone to deny.

When his lids lower, images tumble through my thoughts that I can't fight. Images of his hands on me, of the way he touched me, kissed me, licked me, pounded into me. But then I realize I'm throwing myself at a guy, and new emotions rivet through me.

Shame.

Embarrassment.

Disgust.

He reaches over.

I hold a hand up to stop him.

"Zoey." His voice is pained.

My heart jumps in my throat. "I shouldn't have told you. I shouldn't have thrown myself at you either. I'm sorry."

"Zoey," he repeats, but this time his voice is scratchy and seductive.

My body instantly responds. And I can't help but lean toward him.

He takes my chin in his hand, and his touch overwhelms me. "You shouldn't think that way. It's not going to happen to you."

The muted sounds of the radio replace the white noise in my ears, and all I can do is sigh. "You don't know that."

Nate pins me with his gaze. "Come here."

Pulled from my musings, I look away, feeling like such a fool for throwing myself at him.

"Come here," he demands.

I shake my head. "Why?"

"I can't stand to see you upset."

When I still don't move, he grabs my hand and drags me over the console, and my dress lifts along the way. When he settles me so that I'm straddling his thighs, I look at him, trying to read his expression, but I can't.

He wraps his arms around me and hugs me.

I lean forward and cradle his face in my hands. "I don't understand you."

"You don't have to." His hands trail up my bare thighs and the skin-to-skin contact makes my body ache for him—and not just his touch, but for so much more.

"But I want to."

His gaze turns intimate. "Take your hair down."

My thoughts scatter—nothing remains but his command, and I take the clip out of my hair. My curls fall forward just enough so that he can smooth them away with a soft gentle touch. I can't help but turn my face into it and push my mouth against his hand to kiss the skin there.

In the next moment, his mouth is on mine and his lips feel so good. His hands slide around to my ass, pushing me closer to him, close enough that the metal of his belt buckle rubs the satin of my panties and that's all it takes—arousal shoots straight through me as need takes over my entire body. I arch into him, wanting more.

I feel alive.

Nate rears back into the seat and lets out a hiss. I lean forward and put my mouth on his neck and kiss my way up it until I get to his strong jaw. Our mouths fuse; our lips meld while our tongues sweep against each other's.

When my hands roam his hard body, he jerks back, taking my lower lip with him for a few short seconds before releasing it. "We have to go or we'll be late." His voice is hoarse, but full of control.

The windows are fogged up and the sun has disappeared. I stare down at what I know I want. "I'm not hungry for food. I'm hungry for you." I whisper this low into his ear and arch into him, pressing myself against his arousal.

"Fuck." Nate throws his head back and in a rush lifts his hips in a raw, surging motion. I grasp the collar of his shirt and pull him to me. Frantic coiled energy unleashes as our mouths open to taste each other, to take what we both want so much to give. He kisses me harder and I bite down on his lip. A low sound, nearly a growl, emerges from his throat, and finally his fingertips slide between my legs. The pressure starts to build to an almost painful ache as the anticipation of his touch looms.

Beep-beep. A horn honks as a car pulls into the driveway, its headlights shining on us.

"Fuck," Nate repeats, but the sensuality in his tone is now completely gone.

I scramble to my seat, righting my dress as Oliver knocks on the driver's side window.

Nate lowers it. "Oliver." His tone is steely, almost sharp.

"Sorry, is this a bad time?"

Nate glances over toward me and the predator in his eyes is all I see. My whole body heats, and tingles radiate down my thighs.

"I was just taking Zoey out to dinner."

"That's great. There are so many good restaurants around here. Where did you decide to go?"

"Norman's," Nate responds, his composure quickly returning.

Suddenly, I remember what he must be here for. "Did you draft the documents you spoke of the other day?"

Oliver hands Nate a manila envelope. "I have the banking releases in here. This should be enough for you to access your brother's financial assets. Give me a few days to investigate the real estate holdings. My initial search shows that there are none, but I just want to pull the deed to your house and the loan agreements."

Nate takes the envelope and tucks it above his visor, then stretches out his hand. "Thank you, Oliver. I really appreciate your expediency."

Oliver gives him a warm smile. "Like I said, anytime. Hope to see you soon." Oliver's gaze shifts over to me. "And, Zoey, call me anytime if you have any questions."

"Thank you—"

"I'm sure that won't be necessary." Nate cuts me off. "I mean if I can't answer her questions, I'll be sure to call you—anytime."

I stare at Nate.

If I didn't know better, I'd say there was a bit of possessiveness in his tone.

Oliver pats the car door. "Have a great night."

"See you, man, and thank you again."

Nate closes the window and looks over at me. "What are you doing to me?"

"What do you mean?"

"We can't do this. We just can't. I shouldn't have done that. I'm sorry."

Exasperation and frustration take hold as I stare at him.

Pain fills his face. "I'm sorry, Zoey. I'm sorry," he says again.

Resignation starts to tumble through my thoughts in varying degrees of measure before I can push it away. I know he's drawn to me but he obviously needs more time to come to terms with the idea. I can give him that. I look at him and, for now, decide to agree with him. I don't want to be the cause of any pain he might be feeling. "You're right. I'm sorry too."

"Can we be friends?"

"Yes, I'd like that."

He takes a deep breath. "Good. Friends, then. Ready for dinner?"

The sexual energy is still present between us, but I can tell Nate has resigned himself to just being friends—it's evident in his body language. And although I should be done putting myself out there, I know there is something between us, and I'm not going to let it go so easily.

It's a beautiful night. I tilt my head back to stare out the sunroof at the sky. When we come to a light at the foot of the causeway I look over toward Nate, who seems deep in concentration. "I know Oliver went to all that trouble, but today I was able to get online and I went through my brother's bank statements already. I found a number of large deposits, sometimes five thousand, sometimes ten thousand dollars a week, usually made in cash, sometimes by money order. Do you have any idea how he was getting that kind of money?"

Nate's head whips in my direction, and he seems slightly rattled. "How much did you say?"

"Five to ten thousand a week, but it trailed off in the last couple of months."

"Shit. That's a lot of cash."

"I know. Are you sure you never saw him carrying around that much?"

"No. It's not like he'd be flashing it anyway. I just really have no idea where he could have been getting that amount of cash."

"Maybe I'll never know."

He grabs my hand. "We'll figure it out."

"I don't have that much time here."

"Even after you leave, it doesn't mean this ends."

I look over at him, wondering if he even knows the full extent of his words.

"What else did you find?" He catches the odd way I'm looking at him.

I compose myself once again. "Just some more sketch pads. Nothing else."

He takes a left on the causeway toward Miami Beach, again deep in concentration. When he takes a left onto Collins Avenue, he looks over at me. "I'd like to take a look at everything. I'm going to take Thursday off, and we'll go through it together. Okay?"

I smile at him. "Sure, of course."

Without even realizing it, he's inching his way into my soul. And looking over at him, I can't help but wonder if I'm doing the same to him.

10

No Strings

Atheists believe there's no God; Catholics pray to one. Buddhists believe heaven and hell are temporary places; Christians believe they are eternal.

Me, I believe in destiny.

I believe what is meant to happen will happen.

My destiny is laid out for me in the path of those before me, and there is a real chance I will die before I turn twenty-eight.

This knowledge lives in my heart, changing who I am.

I used to be a rational, normal, nonimpulsive woman who never did anything out of the ordinary in her life. But since the day I turned twenty-seven, I've felt lost, alone, adrift. But something has changed. From the moment I laid eyes on Nate I've felt different. The desire that he sparked within me has become a sexual need driving me to him.

Perhaps it's destiny telling me to let go and explore the wilder side of life. Or perhaps it's destiny that is causing Nate to pull away from me, because I have no business getting involved with him to begin with.

There's no way to know.

"Where did you go?" His voice has a hint of curiosity to it.

Pulled from my head, I look over toward him. "What do you mean?"

"I was asking you a question, and it was like you weren't even in the car with me."

I laugh. "Daydreaming, I guess. Zach always called me a day-dreamer. Once he bought me a dream catcher to wear as a necklace and told me to catch my dreams instead of wishing for them in that far off land I seemed to go to. Sorry, I thought I had outgrown that long ago."

"Don't be sorry. Dreaming is nothing to be sorry about. It makes you real."

"What do you dream about?"

He frowns. "My dreams are more like nightmares. Nothing I'd ever want to escape to."

Emotion takes hold in my chest and clutches at my heart. "Tell me about them."

He shakes his head. "I prefer to leave the past in the past. It's the best place for it." He turns up the radio and the sound of heavy metal fills the car and chases away the silence that some-times sprouts between us with thumping basses and electric guitars.

I like it—it drowns out my own thoughts.

My fingers twitch in my lap with an urge to caress the creases out of his brow, but I can't bring myself to reach across the seat. Comfort doesn't seem to be something he willingly accepts.

Instead, I look out the window at the beautiful skyline and keep replaying the conversation from his driveway through my head. But I end up at the same dead end each time. Nate isn't some-one you can press or push, but I think he is someone you can send running, and I'm not convinced he's not teetering on bolting right now. I'm not delusional in thinking he's attracted to me—I know he is, but it's his reluctance I can't break through.

He pulls in front of a restaurant with umbrella tables lit up from the underside. The restaurant is made of glass block and sits on a corner with tables lining the perimeter.

Very trendy looking.

NORMAN'S is emblazoned above the door, and the spectacular sight before me shakes away my dreary thoughts. Dinner at one of my brother's favorite restaurants is just what I need.

The valet opens my door.

"I'll come around to get you." Nate's eyes catch mine before he slides from the vehicle. Dropping the keys in the valet's hand, he moves quickly. The high slits of my dress fall to the side as I shift my legs and I can feel the weight of his stare on my exposed skin. My breath hitches and the memories of his hands on my thighs are suddenly all I can see.

He offers his hand and as I take it, every nerve in my body electrifies.

Once my feet are safely on the ground though, he lets go.

He's swift in his movements. Approaching the hostess, he stops short and turns to me. "I thought we'd eat out here. Is that okay?"

I look around at the street so full of life. "I'd love that."

He looks at the hostess. "Hi, Nathaniel Hanson. I have a reservation."

"Yes, Mr. Hanson, I have you seated at a table in the inside balcony with a view of the water."

He leans forward. "Do you think we could eat outside?"

She looks down. "Sure, I can arrange that."

Nate grins. "Thank you. I really appreciate it."

"It's no problem at all. Follow me."

Nate extends his arm in a gesture meant for me to go first. I give him a smile and as I walk, I can feel his eyes on me. I like the way I feel when I know he's looking at me—powerful.

His fingertips splay across my back, hitting the cutouts on the side of my dress. My body tingles from head to toe, as that craving that has lingered beneath the surface since I met him becomes a hunger. This is going to be an interesting friendship. I'm not sure where the lines will be drawn.

Twinkling lights, salsa music, and the bustling city streets serve as the ambiance, and it couldn't be more perfect.

We approach the table and Nate pulls out my chair.

As I take a seat, I look up at him. "I can just picture my brother sitting out here with his sketch pad in hand."

His lips curve into a smile. "Yeah, so can I. Beer in one hand, pencil in the other."

We both laugh at that.

I set my little clutch on the table. "Thank you for bringing me here."

He nods his head.

Sometimes I just don't understand him at all. He goes out of his way to make me feel important, but then he shuts me out. "I really don't understand you."

"Like I said—you don't have to." He takes his jacket off and he looks sexy as hell in that thin white button up. I swear I can see the lines of his hard body right through it, and my pulse jumps excitedly despite all my efforts to calm it.

The waiter approaches and hands Nate a wine list. "Good evening. Can I start you off with something to drink?"

"Zoey, would you care for wine?" The question makes me realize just how little we really know about each other.

"No thank you. I can't drink wine."

"Something else then?"

"I don't know." I look at the waiter. "What do you recommend?"

"Well, Madame, one of our signature cocktails is the 1988."

I look up at the waiter, my ears perked. "What's in it?"

"Absolut Ruby Red with a splash of Elderflower Cordial, ginger beer, and fresh-squeezed lime juice. Topped with Campari and garnished with a fresh ruby red grapefruit wedge. It's one of our most popular drinks on the menu."

"I'll try it. It sounds delicious."

"It is. And for you, sir?"

Nate hands the wine menu back to the waiter. "Lagavulin, neat."

"I'll get your drinks and give you time to look over the menu." The waiter disappears into the crowd before I even look up.

"Why can't you drink wine?" Nate asks.

Easy question—easy answer. "I'm sulfite-sensitive and asthmatic. The two together are not a great combination."

"But it's safe for you to drink other types of alcohol?"

I give him a slight smile. "I'm not a big drinker. Only an occasional one now and then, and so far, wine is the only alcohol that has triggered a reaction. So don't worry, chances are good you won't have to call an ambulance after our first drink together."

He studies me for a long moment. "Z talked about you all the time and never mentioned you had asthma. Tell me about it—I mean, what someone has to do if you have an attack."

I lift my small clutch off the table. "I carry an inhaler everywhere I go. If I feel like I'm being buried alive, I use it."

He winces and reaches his hand across the tabletop to cover mine. "How often do you have attacks?"

I push away my surprise at his concern. "I've only ever had one severe attack that caused me to go to the hospital, and that was when I drank almost a whole bottle of wine at my girlfriend's bachelorette party and couldn't find my purse. Trust me, that was one party none of my friends will ever forget."

He takes his hand back. "I don't think it's funny, Zoey."

"It's not, but I've lived with asthma my whole life. I know how to deal with it."

He nods solemnly.

The waiter returns with our drinks. "Are you ready to order?"

Nate looks over toward me. "Do you have any seafood allergies?"

"No. No seafood allergies. No other food allergies at all actually."

He rubs his hands together. "So, am I ordering Z-style?"

I can't help but smile. "Go for it."

"We'll have an order of the lobster pot stickers and the blackened ahi tuna, and we'll each have a grilled lettuce wedge salad, your fusion espresso-rubbed filets with parmesan fries, and the grilled asparagus."

"How would you like your meat cooked?"

Nate glances at me.

"Medium-rare," I answer.

"I'll have mine cooked the same way. Oh, and bring the lady a jalapeño margarita."

I raise a brow. "Are you trying to get me drunk?"

I laugh to myself because he must know he doesn't have to get me drunk to take advantage of me. In fact, I think I'd have to get him drunk, if I were still thinking about him that way, which I am trying really hard not to do right now.

"No, it was your brother's favorite. Anything hot and spicy."

"I know Zach would eat anything as long as he could put hot sauce on it. But no way did he eat asparagus."

Nate chuckles. "No, I like that."

"Ah, a good boy who eats his veggies." I wink at him.

"What about you? Do you have a favorite food?"

"I do. Chocolate. In fact, if I could, I would eat dessert before my meal."

Nate raises a brow. "Ah, so you're a rebel like your brother."

"That's me, a real rebel." I laugh.

"How often do you eat dessert before your meal?"

"Never."

"Why?"

"Because it's frowned upon in society, but I don't see why. I'm always too full to eat it after, so I miss out on the good stuff."

"What's your favorite dessert?"

I sip from my glass and the fresh fruity flavor is delicious, not even a tad bit of tartness. "Chocolate cake, chocolate soufflé, chocolate pie, honestly anything chocolate would do."

Nate picks up his Scotch and smells it with his mouth open. I can't help but stare. Every nerve in my body fires up as I watch his lips part. I want those lips on mine, licking down my neck, dragging down my body, and settling right . . .

I shove the thought away.

He raises his glass. "To Zachary Flowers, the man who knew how to live life to the fullest."

I raise my own glass, and for the first time think, *Nate's right, my brother did live life to the fullest.*

Unlike me.

The thought consumes me as the beautiful ocean breeze blows my hair across my face.

A few moments later, the waiter returns with my second drink, and I take a sip. "Oh my God, this is so spicy."

"Do you like it?"

I wave my hand over my mouth. "Yes, I do actually."

Nate leans back in his chair and crosses his ankle over his knee.

My eyes devour the lines of his body, his confidence, the stare that burns into me. And as he sips on his drink, I can't look away—the guy whose body I've been lusting over since I got here is so much of a man.

"So tell me about your job as a teacher." His voice is low as if he has a genuine interest in learning something about me.

"I'm not actually a teacher. I'm an associate professor."

"Teacher, professor. What's the difference? You use a blackboard or stand in front of a room of people, don't you?"

He looks so confused I have to laugh. "Yes, I do. But the word *professor* more accurately defines my role in the university setting."

He leans closer to the table, resting his hand on his glass. "But you do impart knowledge on those thirsting to learn more, right?"

I nod, thrilled by his interest in learning more about me. "Yes. I do."

"And what subject do you teach, or profess?" He smirks.

"Psychology."

His face bares shock. "Why didn't you tell me that?"

I can't help but laugh again. "Well, you never asked, and usually people feel uncomfortable when they know they're in the presence of someone who teaches the behavioral study of the human mind—you know, feelings and all that shit."

He smirks. "Yeah, feelings and all that shit," he repeats. "But now it makes sense."

"What makes sense?" I take another sip of the delicious concoction in my hand, and this time I can really taste the alcohol. It's so strong, it's raising my senses in a way that I don't need lifted right now.

"The way you're always probing for information."

"I don't probe."

"You do. I'm sure you do it without even realizing you're doing it."

"No, I don't."

"Let's agree to disagree. Now, why don't you tell me what it is that you do exactly?"

My eyes search his for insincerity, but see nothing but interest.

I turn sideways on my chair and cross my legs. The slit on the side of my dress falls open and I try to tug it closed, but it won't stay. I may not have a model figure, but I am tall, and long legs are definitely one of my assets.

"I teach Human Motivation and Emotion and He Said, She Said, which is a really fun course."

Nate raises a brow.

"Human Motivation and Emotion explores the study of motivational and emotional processes and theories that underlie both adaptive and maladaptive behavior. It can be a little dry, but that's why I've insisted my students take it in conjunction with He Said, She Said."

Whether I'm boring him or not, I can't be certain because his sharp intake of breath tells me he noticed my legs "Which is?" he asks as he averts his gaze back to my face.

I smile. "A course which relies heavily on videos to demonstrate and study how men and women talk to each other and what that means. I teach contemporary theories, and of course my students do a lot of hands-on research."

His grin is more like a smirk. "Not sure I want to know what that entails. But your brother told me you wanted to pursue your doctorate. Is that something you still plan on doing?"

Now I'm the one inhaling sharply.

I haven't been able to plan for the future.

I turn back so my body is under the tablecloth and set my glass down. "No, not anymore."

The truth is, I don't know who I am anymore or what I want to do.

A couple walks by us, arm in arm, and a sudden shot of envy jolts me.

"Zoey?"

I blink. "Sorry, what?"

"I asked why not?"

A whirling sound catches my attention and I look around.

Misting lanterns start spraying out streams of light air infused with water, and I immediately feel a gentle coolness.

Nate rubs his hands around the tulip-shaped glass. "Zoey? What is it?"

I try to refocus on him. "I don't like to talk about the future."

Saving me from further explanation, the waiter returns with our appetizers and thankfully they look amazing. I try to refocus again, this time on them.

"Would you care for another drink?" the waiter asks.

"No, we're both fine," Nate answers for the both of us.

It irritates and excites me at the same time. Something about not having to make decisions feels so freeing—I've been making them my whole life.

"But instead of salads we'd like chocolate soufflés or any similar chocolate items you have on the dessert menu."

"You'd like dessert in place of the salads or after your meal?" the waiter asks.

"In place of the salads."

"Certainly, if that's what you'd like. We offer a chocolate crêpe with raspberries." The surprise in his tone matches the size of the smile on my face.

Nate raises a brow in my direction.

I nod, beaming in glee.

"That will be fine. Thank you," he tells the waiter.

It takes all my willpower to stay in my seat and fight the urge to leap around the table and jump onto his lap. I always tell people I prefer dessert before a meal, but never has anyone taken me seriously.

As I look over at him, the need to feel the taste of his lips on mine, feel his hard body pressed to mine, to be able to lick the chocolate he ordered off his chest, and slide my tongue down his stomach, and then taste him, is one I can no longer deny.

"Are you not planning your future because you think you don't have one?"

Slamming my eyes shut, all of the erotic images disappear as I fight to breathe. Suddenly the air becomes thick in my lungs and I can't get it out. I take deep calming breaths. As the haze around me dissipates and I fight off the panic attack, I hear a fumbling in front of me. I force myself to lift my lids. Nate is attempting to open my clutch. "What are you doing?"

"Trying to get you your inhaler." Panic seems to drown out the deep green of his eyes.

I push to my feet and give him a disbelieving look. "I'm not having an asthma attack."

"You're not?" He sounds uncertain.

I shake my head and set my napkin on the table. "Excuse me, I have to use the ladies' room." I walk inside the restaurant, realizing I have no idea where I'm going. Looking around, I find the bathrooms immediately.

Just as I pull the door open, a hand covers mine. "You're upset."

I drop my head. "No, I'm fine."

"You're lying."

Summoning all of my willpower, I raise my eyes.

He lifts my chin. "You didn't let me finish. I'm trying to understand you. I want to know why, if you believe in destiny, you'd change your path. Why wouldn't you do what you had always planned on doing? Why change your course? Personally, I think destiny is bullshit. I also think not pursuing your dream is bullshit too."

Caged by his body, his scent, his presence, I look up into his burning eyes and I can see compassion there. I believe he wants what's best for me. If I think I know him through my brother, he thinks he knows me through my brother as well. And Zach wanted me to continue my education. His dream was that someday I'd be Dr. Zoey Flowers. Nate knows this.

"Zoey?" Nate's voice is questioning. Low. Maybe even slightly fearful.

"Nate"—I press my finger to his lips—"I think I need to tell you something about myself."

"What?" he asks.

In all our e-mails after my brother's death, I never mentioned the real reason for my delay in coming to Miami. I keep my eyes open even though I want to close them. "I had a breakdown shortly after Zach died. I took a leave from my job. I couldn't get out of bed. I couldn't plan one day, let alone the next. And somewhere during that time, I let any plans I had for the future fall by the wayside. I don't know what I want anymore."

"Why didn't you tell me in any of our e-mails?"

"I actually looked forward to your weekly e-mails. But I did lie to you. It wasn't work that kept me from coming to get my brother's things. It was me and my inability to cope."

He stares down at me.

"Don't think I'm crazy. I'm not. Really, I'm not."

His gaze continues to pin me in a way that makes me think he understands me.

It holds me in place. Keeps me calm.

"Zoey, God, I don't think that at all," he breathes. "I can understand how that would happen. With everything coming at you at once, and the shock of Z's death, coupled with the revelations about your family, it was just too much. I get it."

I just stare at his lips, longing to kiss him. My body is filled with so many wants and needs, and all these new urges I've never felt before. And all I want is just for him to set me free.

His gaze drops and he extends his hand. "Come on. Let's go back to the table."

I look at his outreached arm and say, "Yes, let's," and then I take his hand and he guides me through the crowd.

I feel safe with him.

Not so lost.

When we arrive at our table our chocolate soufflés are sitting beautifully before us. I clap my hands together. "They really brought them first!"

Nate settles me in my chair and then sits down. "Zoey, you need to live your life, not fear for your death."

I poke my fork in my food. "You sound like my shrink."

He looks a little full of himself. "The difference, just so you know, is that I am going to help you do just that."

"And you don't think Dr. Raymond has?"

"Nothing against Dr. Raymond, but shrinks aren't always the answer."

"And you know what is?" It sounds like a challenge, but I don't mean it to.

He drags his fork through his soufflé and reaches it across the table. I open my mouth without thought and bite down into the scrumptious chocolate. He leans closer. "I am. Starting right now I want you to tell me all the things you've never done in your life but have wanted to."

"Nate." I make a face.

"Zoey." He makes the same face.

I shake my head.

"Zoey, tell me five things you've never done that you want to do."

"What? You want me to give you my bucket list?"

He shakes his head. "No, a bucket list is things you want to do before you die. I want five things you want to do to make you feel alive."

The first thing that comes to mind is him, but I refuse to throw myself at him again. I gape at him. "I don't know—go to Paris, New York City, anywhere and everywhere I've never been."

He rolls his eyes. "Going to Paris is going to make you feel alive?"

I shrug. "I think it will."

"How's this? I'll take you there if you come up with five things you know for absolute certainty will make you feel alive. And I'm not in a hurry. You can think about it."

I think for a moment before I speak. "I'm not sure I can tell you them once I come up with them."

He tilts his head a little. "Why not?"

I raise a brow.

He laughs. "We're friends. Friends can tell friends anything."

"Well, off the top of my head one thing would be to eat dessert before dinner."

He waves his hand. "Pfff . . . that's too easy. We've already done that."

I shrug. "Dance in the moonlight."

He looks upward and then stands. "Again, too easy."

"I thought this was my list," I laugh.

He extends his hand. "Dance with me?"

My heart starts to steadily pound. "I'd love to."

Over his shoulder he says, "It is your list, but you still have five things to come up with. Not things you can simply check off a list, but rather things you feel passionate about. I'll give you until tomorrow."

"I already gave you two."

He stops and turns around. "Tonight doesn't count. Those are too easily accomplished."

"What? Something like learn to ride a bull?"

He starts walking backwards. "Sounds groovy, I've always wanted to do that, yet I can't see you mounting one. But I think you're on the right track."

We reach the end of the umbrella tables where there is a long stretch of sidewalk. He pulls me close to him and anchors his hips to mine.

"What are you doing?"

He slips his arms around my waist. "What does it look like?"

I place mine around his neck and smile up at him. "Here?"
My entire body tingles.

His feet start to move in a slow circle, and just like that we're dancing under the moonlight to the beat of the salsa music playing in the background. "Why not?"

"I don't know, there are people everywhere."

He draws me closer and then he dips me. "I don't care. Do you?"
I shake my head.

I feel alive—he makes me feel alive.

His green eyes reflect the moonlight and I can't help but think, *Kiss me*—but he doesn't.

Kiss me, I think again, as we finish our meal—but he doesn't.

Kiss me, I think, when we arrive back at his house and he opens the car door in his garage—but he doesn't.

Kiss me, I think, as we stand outside the boathouse and say good night—but he doesn't. Instead his stare lingers on my lips until the words "Good night" finally slip from them and he leaves me aching, desperate, and driven by a need I don't understand.

11

Discovery

The beauty of color, the fluidity of paint, the strokes of a brush, a blank canvas—they all collaborate together to create a story.

As I flip through one of the many sketchbooks I found in Zach's bedroom yesterday, I feel like I'm reading his journal.

Vibrant pencils bring to life the boathouse, the man in the picture at the top of the stairs between Zach and Nate, a small art gallery, the Wynwood Wall, so many places and people. Some of them are labeled, most aren't.

I toss a sketchbook to the floor and rise from the bed. The sun is just coming up over the horizon and I spent the entire night tossing and turning thinking about, for lack of a better word, the mind fuck of last night.

As a college professor, I've studied both psychology and human development. So why can't I figure Nate out? I'm trained to pick up on symbols and metaphors that are often expressed through non-verbal communication—concepts that are usually difficult to express with words. So how is it I can't decipher Nate's body language, see through his words, or get him to open up to me about himself?

He's so closed off.

Last night, I saw the way he looked at me, the way his breath caught when we were standing so close, and the way his body reacted to mine. But he had already shut me down, and when I didn't make the first move, he didn't make one at all.

Guilt is a strange thing.

Pushing Nate from my mind, I turn on Zach's laptop and decide to check his e-mails. I feel like I'm invading my brother's privacy, but I need answers. He lied to me to make my life easier. I know this. But why lie? What was he doing? I have to know.

The questions that I ask to myself bring on my own onslaught of guilt—Nate's asking me why I'm not doing what I always planned to do, why I'm not pursuing my doctorate.

His voice echoes in my mind. After all, it's part of the reason Zach felt he had to ease my debt. He wanted to make it easier for me to take on the financial burden of additional schooling. And now that that burden is gone, I don't know how to move forward . . . or even if I should.

With a sigh, I click on Internet Explorer and get back to the task at hand. G-mail is where I start. Logging in is just as easy as logging in to his bank accounts. There are e-mails from a motorcycle parts store, e-mails from his bank, e-mails from the typical solicitors—nothing out of the ordinary. Just as I'm about to log out, a ping alerts me to a new message on an alternate profile. I click the circle in the upper right corner and read the message.

From: Jordan Scott
Subject: Initial Consultation
Date: July 1 2014 06:45 EST
To: The Artist

I'd like to reschedule the initial consultation from 7 p.m. to

8 p.m. for this evening, if at all possible. And instead of meeting in the Living Room at the Estate, I'd like to meet in the bar. Here's a picture of the pose I'm interested in re-creating. My husband won't be joining us this evening, but he looks forward to experiencing your artistic abilities.

I click and open the picture, and immediately feel like bleaching my eyes. A blond bombshell is lying on a bed of fur in her underwear. Her legs are spread wide and her finger is in her mouth. It's not her leopard lingerie that grabs my attention, but the provocative *Playboy* pose this woman wants my brother to sketch of her.

I close the file and skim through the rest of the e-mails under the Artist profile. There have to be at least twenty. They all seem to be from clients. Some are upset for being stood up and others are trying to schedule an appointment.

My mind is spinning.

Is this it?

It has to be.

Zach was re-creating enticing nude scenes!

How much was he charging?

How often was he meeting with clients to make so much money?

Was he known as the Artist?

With a click, I open a new window and Google "the Estate" and "Miami." After scrolling past a bunch of real-estate links, I finally find what I'm looking for. It's stated to be a very private club—by invitation only.

Nothing else.

No address is given.

Hopefully, Nate can help me.

I hurry to get dressed, throwing on my sweatpants and a T-shirt in hopes of catching him before he goes to work. I run downstairs at warp speed, across the yard, and come to a halt—I can't just knock so early in the morning. Recovering from my little trot, I go around to the front. There's a Ford Focus under the sailcloth carport, and the garage door is open. I walk through it and right by the Range Rover, which means Nate is still home.

The thought of seeing him sends an instant surge of hormones through my veins. Those trails of want and lust mix together before I even lay eyes on him.

Just as I push open the door and yell, "Nate, it's me! Can I talk to you?" I start to think twice about asking him for help. What if my brother was doing something more illicit? Would I be betraying his memory by involving his best friend in something he obviously didn't want him to know?

Before I have time to reason with myself, a short woman with dark hair wearing a pink tracksuit comes down the hallway. "Zoey. *Hola, encantada de conocerte.*"

Her hands are waving as she picks up speed and stops in front of me. She throws her arms around me and hugs me tight. Then she pulls back to look at me. *"Usted ésta demasiada delgada."*

I point to myself. "Me no Español."

"I speak English. When I get excited, sometimes I forget." Her English is heavily accented, but I can understand her for the most part.

"You must be Rosie," I tell her, having put two and two together.

"Yes, I take care of Nate's house." She's very beautiful—dark hair, dark eyes, with a very voluptuous figure.

"Is he home?"

"He went for a run. He goes every morning."

My heart starts beating wickedly at the thought of Nate running, shirtless, sweaty, hot, and in need of a shower.

Okay, enough already.

Focus.

Maybe Zach carried some kind of card and it's in his things that Nate still has. "I'm just going to run upstairs if that's okay."

She nods. "Sure. I'm making breakfast now. Nate told me you like coffee and chocolate."

Warmth spreads through my chest. "Nate told you what I like?"

"Oh, yes. I was just putting some chocolate chip waffle mix together when you came in."

"Waffles are my favorite. How did you know?"

She drops her gaze. "Your brother loved waffles, so I hoped you would too."

My heart stops. "Well, you were right."

She claps her hands together. "Oh, good."

"I'll be right down."

I hurry up the stairs but get drawn to the doors leading to the balcony. I walk through the empty loft, but when I push them, they won't budge. It's like they've been painted shut. My guess is Nate's never gone out there to admire the view.

Shame.

I turn and walk back to Nate's room to get the bag of Zach's things in his drawer, but pause when I reach the dresser and see Nate's phone plugged into the charger. It's then I remember seeing the app on his screen. I pick it up and click on the icon that looks like a mansion with the word *Estate* below it. A reservation screen pops up. My choices include the guesthouse, the bathhouse, and the main house, but the location I'm looking for is right on the top. I select the bar, since that's where I plan on meeting Zach's client tonight. Another screen pops up with the word *Plus* and a drop-down box beside it. I click *one*. An additional screen pops up with a text box for instructions. I enter, the guest's name is Zoey, and then hit *Schedule*.

Heavy pounding alerts me that Nate is coming up the stairs, and for some reason I get out of the application and set his phone back down quickly, hoping he doesn't notice. I don't get the chance to see a confirmation, but I pray it went through and scramble away from the phone.

I'm almost to the doorway when our eyes meet. He looks incredible. He comes to a dead stop and his emerald eyes sweep my body. For a moment the world disappears and it's only him and me.

To pass the momentary silence, I picture myself sprawled out on his bed like the woman in the photo, with my legs spread wide, offering myself to him. And in my fantasy, he's already on his knees and his hot, wet mouth is licking up my thigh toward my secret flesh. Seconds later his tongue is stroking up my clit and the feel of the flesh-to-flesh contact is searing, scorching, earth-shakingly divine.

My entire body is vibrating with tension.

"Hey, did you need something?" Nate asks as he quickly slips past me in the doorway, seemingly unfazed that I'm in his room.

My fantasy dissipates as reality takes hold.

This man in front of me is not the Nate of my fantasy. That Nate couldn't keep his hands or his mouth or his tongue off me. This one, on the other hand, prefers to think of me as a friend.

Yet, this one is shirtless, his legs are bare in his running shorts, and his abdomen is almost like a six-pack, but not overly defined, so much like the one I dreamed about.

In the sunlight, his body is every bit as hard as I remember, just more spectacular.

My nipples stab through the sports bra I threw on under my thin T-shirt. Between my legs the throbbing has ramped up to unbearable.

The panther is on the move, and I can't help but stare.

A sheen of sweat covers him, but I am far from grossed out. In fact, I start to wonder what he might taste like and if he would mind if I just swiped my tongue down his chest.

I open my mouth, but close it.

Better not.

And for one brief moment something flickers across his face like he knows what I'm thinking and wants the same, but it's gone before I can identify it.

Wasn't there a question?

Yes, he asked me a question.

I have to answer, but my traitorous body can't stop thinking about Nate's body. "I was looking for"—I scurry over to the dresser and lift the dish—"this."

His look is questioning.

My heart pounds—do I tell him what I just did? No, I have to find out what it is first. But as he looks at me, I know I will tell him eventually. I have to. I owe him that for all the help he has given me.

"Okay. But don't forget this," he says as he walks next to me and opens the drawer.

Passion flares in the air as my excitement pinwheels around the room. But guilt quickly squashes it. The phone is so close, I should say something. I know I should. What I just did isn't right.

But I have to be the one to find out what my brother was doing first. I can figure out how and what to tell Nate later, I finally decide. With guilt written all over me, I reach for the bag, grab it, and take a step back, not even admiring his godlike body at close-up range, I'm so nervous.

"Zoey," he calls, just as I turn.

My heart is in my throat.

He's unplugging his phone. I swallow, knowing I should probably tell him right now before he notices.

He lifts his stare. In the mirror his eyes meet mine. "I'll be in meetings most of the day and have a dinner engagement tonight. But if you need me, feel free to call or text me."

It's on the tip of my tongue to ask him how to get to the Estate, but that might tip him off. Instead I say, "Have a great day."

"Zoey."

I try to stay calm.

"Don't forget that list. I want to discuss it later tonight."

"Yes, right. Thanks for reminding me. Can't wait."

I almost fall down the stairs in a rush to escape the web of untruths I just weaved, not to mention the sexual frustration whipping around me like a tornado.

"Oh, Zoey, you're just in time."

On the counter is a plate with two beautiful chocolate chip waffles and a perfectly made latté.

I can't help but smile at Rosie. *"Gracias."*

She beams with pride. "I'll be over later today to help you pack up your brother's things. I hope everything was okay for you when you went in. I haven't been over there since—" She pulls up her apron and pats her eyes.

I hug her. Obviously she knew my brother pretty well. "Everything was fine. Just fine."

Once we break the embrace, she leaves me to my breakfast, which I wolf down, not wanting to see Nate before he leaves for work. I can't believe my own thoughts, but tonight I'll come over and tell him everything.

Better to beg for forgiveness than ask permission—right?

Discovery is an odd kind of enlightenment.

The rain falls hard outside and lightning lights up Rosie's face as she stands next to the ladder, in what used to be Zach's bedroom.

We're packing up all of his things.

I take the last picture off the wall and hand it to her. "Did you ever see people coming over here for portrait sessions?"

The roll of brown paper is on the bed and she lays the framed sketch on it. "No, but Zachary was always at the gallery during the day when I was here."

The stepladder is wobbly as I climb down. "How well did you know my brother?"

Rosie finishes taping the paper and then hands me the packaged artwork. "I'd like to think pretty well. He ate breakfast with me every morning for almost three years. It was a habit that started the first time Milo came to stay here."

I put the sketch in the box, along with the others. "Milo, Nate's father?"

She gives me a sad smile. "Yes. He's such a wonderful man."

I drag the box into the living room and set it next to the others lined against the wall. With the marker tucked in my shorts pocket, I label it *Keep*. Staring at the row of boxes to ship home, I call through the door, "His picture is at the top of the stairs with Nate and Zach, right?"

"*Sí*. Milo thought of your brother as a second son."

I cup my elbows in my hands when I walk back in the room and see Rosie pulling clothes out of one of the drawers. "Can you tell me about them?"

With a pile of T-shirts in her hand, she looks at me. "Milo had his first stroke right before your brother came to work for him. They used to joke that Zachary turned the gallery into a number of department store windows."

I watch her as she piles Zach's clothes into the boxes. The items going into them are only things—I know this. My brother's gone, but his memory will stay in my heart, my mind, and my soul forever. He was always there for me, and I hope he felt the same about me—that's what truly matters.

Rosie must catch sight of my sorrow. "I'm sorry I didn't take care of this for you, but Nate insisted I leave everything alone. He hasn't been over here since your brother's death. He took it very hard. He and Zachary were like *hermanos*."

Her transition from English into the Spanish language doesn't hinder her message—I know what she's saying.

I paint a smile on my face; I'm getting good at it. "Go on, tell me about Milo and Zach, if you don't mind. We never knew our father and I know Zach really respected and appreciated everything Milo did for him. He told me Milo saved him from living on the street. He met him the day he had been evicted from his apartment, and he was so thankful Milo gave him a job."

She closes the drawer and opens another. "After his second stroke, Milo came to live with Nate. Zachary was already living in the boathouse. He moved in when Nate bought the place. We had it all worked out. I'd come in the morning just before Nate left for work. Zachary was taking Milo to the gallery until he was cleared to drive, so he'd join Milo for breakfast. After Milo went back home, I continued to make breakfast for Zachary. We'd eat and watch *Top Chef* or *Martha Stewart*. He loved to watch cooking shows. Then, I'd pack their lunches and Zachary would bring them to work. The two of them spent a lot of time together."

Pulling one of Zach's shirts close to me, I look at Rosie. "Why isn't Milo running the gallery now?"

She stops what she's doing. "Zachary had been running it for years. Milo never fully recovered, but Nate made sure he kept going to the gallery. It was what Milo lived for. But after his last stroke, he couldn't anymore. It affected more than just his body, it affected his *memoria*."

She points to her head but I already knew what she meant.

"And Nate, well, he—" She waves her hands. "I'm sorry."

"No, go on. It's okay," I prompt.

"He's so sad that he had to move his father into Sunshine Village."

"He couldn't live here anymore?"

She shakes her head. "He moved in more than a year ago, but then had another stroke almost two months before your brother passed. It was severe, and he had to have rehab. Nate didn't bring him home until after—"

She stops.

"My brother died." I finish for her.

She nods. "Yes, but without your brother to help, it was really hard on him. He did try though. I'd come every day to stay with Milo. It was then I noticed his memory was only getting worse. He'd leave the house to go to the store and not be able to find his car, or he'd get on the road and call Nate because he didn't know where he was. It got so bad that Nate had to take his car away. Like I said, I stayed with him during the day, but then one day after I left, Milo turned the stove on to fry an egg. He put butter in the pan and forgot about it. The fire department came before anything bad happened, but Nate knew then Mr. Milo couldn't stay here alone."

Milo must have been having episodic memory lapses as is common in all Alzheimer's patients. I had feared Mimi was suffering from Alzheimer's just before she died, so I was familiar with the disease.

"When did Nate take him to live at a facility?"

"About three weeks ago."

"I had no idea. Is the empty bedroom in the main house Nate's dad's?"

She nods and sadness fills her eyes. "He lost so much all at once, I think it was too much for him."

My heart breaks for Nate.

The storm lashes all around the boathouse and Rosie jumps higher with each thunderous boom. We finish emptying the dresser, and I decide to start on the closet. I open the door, and for the first time, look through the hanging items—suits, dress shirts, leather pants, belts, and ties.

My brother in a tie?

The leather pants I could see, but not a shirt and tie. Aside from graduation and Mimi's funeral, I don't think I'd ever seen him wear one.

I turn around to find Rosie smoothing out the wrinkles the boxes made on the comforter. "Are these Nate's clothes?"

She moves toward the closet. "No. Those are all Zachary's."

"Did he used to dress up to go to the gallery?"

She shakes her head. "He usually wore jeans. On occasion I'd see him wear a nice pair of pants, but that was rare."

The rain comes down in steady streams, and as I stare out the window in wonder, I see Rosie glance at her watch. "Do you have to go?"

"I like to pick my daughter up from summer camp when it's raining. I don't like her riding the bus in this weather."

"How old is she?"

"She's six. She'll be in first grade this fall."

I wave my hand. "Go, go get your daughter. Thank you for all your help."

"*Gracias.* Nate asked me to come back on Thursday this week, so I can help you some more then."

"Oh, I don't want you to go to any trouble."

"It's no trouble. I'd come every day if Nate needed me, but he doesn't eat here anymore, and the house isn't dirty enough for me to clean like I used to. When he called me Saturday and asked me to go grocery shopping, and put a few things to heat up in the refrigerator, I was thrilled that he had a guest."

I place a hand on her shoulder. "I appreciate it, but I hope to be done by then anyway."

"I can come back tomorrow if you like."

I look at her. "No, honestly, I think this is something I might need to finish myself."

She squeezes me tightly. "I understand." She pulls back. "I put some food in the refrigerator in the kitchen. Don't forget to eat. You're too skinny."

I laugh, thinking of all the soft spots my body bears and the dimples behind my thighs. She leaves in a rush of pink fabric, obvious affection she carried for the men who lived here warming my heart.

Getting back to work, I pull out each of the suits and stare at them—gray pinstripes, black, black pinstripes. There are five total, and I lift them out of the closet all together before laying them on the bed and removing them from their hangers. When I get to the black one, I find a small card sticking out of the inside breast pocket. I pick it up and a smile crosses my face. On creamy white heavy stock paper with gold embossing it reads:

The Estate
1212 Washington Ave
Miami Beach, Florida 33819

Nothing else.
Nothing about Zach.
That's okay, though, because everything I need is right there.

I finish folding up the suits and suddenly feel exhausted. It's three in the afternoon, so I decide to rest for a bit before embarking on tonight's excursion.

Lying on my back, I stare at the ceiling and think about what Nate asked me to do. He asked me to put a list together of things I can't live without. He said not to make a bucket list, the items shouldn't be things easily checked off—they should be things that engage emotion.

I knew my list the moment he explained what he wanted, but I couldn't tell him.

I want to have a passionate affair with someone. I want someone to think about me all the time, want to fuck me wherever we are because he can't keep his hands off me. I want someone to own me, claim me, make me his. I want someone to take away the responsibility I've shouldered over my lifetime, to make my decisions for me.

That's more than five, but it's my list.

I close my eyes and think about this list. The freedom that comes with such a bond with someone. I want that, even if it's just for a short time. I can't figure out why, or where it's coming from. It doesn't really matter.

It's how I feel.

A text message awakens me with a start, and I worry I might have missed my appointment, or Zach's. But when I look outside and it's still light, I know I haven't.

I grab my phone from the side table, seeng that it's a text from Nate. My stomach is doing somersaults before I even open it. Maybe he found out about my appointment at the Estate. Or maybe he's finally changed his mind about us, and he's texting me to tell me he misses me. To be in his bed when he gets home because he wants to do wicked things to me. In my head, I'm already stripped down waiting for him to walk in his room.

He smiles as he approaches, full of himself, as he strokes my clit, already wet for him. He puts a finger inside my pussy, then two. He lowers his head to my breasts and latches onto one. My nipples are so hard and tight the feel of his wet, hot mouth makes me shout his name. I can feel the way his lips might turn up, but then imagine he sucks harder, biting down, and the pain becomes instant pleasure. He's fucking me with his fingers, his mouth is sending small bolts of electricity through my body, and I come in a rush.

My phone beeps again, alerting me that that was just a fantasy. I sigh and close my eyes again, wishing that fantasy was my reality, and wonder where all of this is coming from at the same time.

This man has me thinking crazy thoughts. It's not just his body though; it's him—all of him.

And that's dangerous.

My phone beeps yet again, as if warning me to hurry up and read my unread message. But I know it doesn't say what I want it to and right now I'm not ready to let my fantasy go. My body is craving the release that Nate so freely gave me in my dream.

In a rush, I sit up and strip my shorts off; I don't need to be completely naked for this. Then with a slide of my palm down to my clit, I apply pressure, circling the wetness, the only thing that wasn't just a dream.

Again I imagine Nate above me, his hot breath on my neck, his scent surrounding me, and slow, sweet waves of pleasure start rippling from my belly.

I slow my pace, not wanting to climax yet, and touch myself again. Sure, I've masturbated before, used a vibrator to come quick and hard, but quick and hard isn't what I crave right now.

Over and over, I bring myself to the edge and stop until the pain of needing a release is just too much to bear, then finally I let go and crashing waves of pleasure course through me. I close my eyes and savor the sweet release that I know would be so much better if Nate were the one giving it to me.

He's my list—he's my entire list.

Thoughts of him make me forget my uncertainty, my fears of the fate that awaits me. He makes me wish I could change destiny.

The wave of euphoria passes quickly with no one to actually touch, to kiss, or to draw to my body, and I look down at my phone still beeping for attention.

Finally I open the text. It reads:

`The weather calls for another round of bad storms tonight. Stay at my house.`

I shake my head. Nate the weatherman is giving more orders and not the ones I was looking for. I text back:

`If it gets really bad, I will.`

I have to laugh out loud now. Yesterday I might have gotten excited about the prospect of him wanting me to sleep where he's sleeping, but today I can say with absolute certainty that this is more about his concern for me as his best friend's sister than any sexual attraction to me. He just won't give in to that.

He texts me back:

I wasn't asking. Stay at my house.

He's right. He didn't ask anything. He is rather controlling, and I'm so attracted to it. I want him to take his control into the bedroom. That's the first item on my list and I'm going to tell him that tonight when he gets home.

But before I do that, I have to go meet Zach's client and get the details behind this consultation.

I sit up. Time to get up, get something to eat, and take a shower. So rather than go twenty rounds with Nate, I decide appeasement is much easier and type,

Okay.

The word is simple. It's the word I want him to say when I tell him what I have in mind for my list.

Him.

12

The Good Girl

My brother was never afraid to go after what he wanted. He lived his life freely, going where he wanted to go, doing what he wanted to do. Me, I did what was expected of me—didn't smoke, didn't skip school, didn't drink. Went to college, got good grades.

I excelled at being the good girl. Zach excelled at being the bad boy. We evened each other out. But had I known what the future possibly held for me, I might not have cared so much about following the rules. I might have been more like my brother.

A woman's voice interrupts my thoughts. "Turn left at the next light."

A glance at the navigation screen tells me I'll be on Washington Avenue in a matter of seconds. As soon as I am, the traffic thickens.

I look around.

Designer stores line the streets, restaurants are everywhere, and there are dance clubs on every corner.

"Your destination is ahead on the left," GPS tells me.

I glance up and all I can see are the flashing lights of a neon sign that reads THE BALLROOM. I check the address on the business card against the one on the building's facade—it's a match, but I'm looking for the Estate, not the Ballroom.

I guess I need to ask someone.

It's dusk and I would normally self-park, but I'm not familiar with the area and have no idea how safe it is after nightfall, so I opt for valet. When I pull up to the curb, a man in a red jacket rushes over.

I lower my window. "Excuse me, I'm looking for the Estate."

"You're in the right place, providing you can get in."

"I can." I smile.

Or I think I can.

The valet opens my door and as I exit, I hand him the keys and he hands me a ticket.

The line is long for the early hour, and I only have fifteen minutes before I'm supposed to meet Jordan Scott.

Just how private is this club? You have to go through one club to get to another?

Of course I'm screwed if this place doesn't admit women. I'm in Miami, so it's probably some kind of cigar club. If it is, I hope the smoke doesn't trigger my asthma.

I really need to skip this line.

I check that my dress is secure and walk toward the door. I selected a short black dress—I thought it seemed appropriate for a private club, but now that I'm here, I wonder if it might not be a little too revealing.

I'm not even sure why I brought it. It's short with no back and a rather deep V in the front, which when you have no boobs isn't a problem. But showing too much skin in a stodgy men's club might be.

Too late now.

The bouncer is rather intimidating. As I inch toward the velvet rope, he practically roars at me, "Back of the line."

I step forward. "I'm looking to gain entry into the Estate. I have a meeting at eight and I'll be late if I wait in this line."

He gives me a hard stare. "Is that right?"

I nod, feeling a little shaky. I'm not so sure he's not actually going to bounce me out of his space.

He takes the cover charge from a group of clubbers and then diverts his gaze back to me. His eyes sweep me like I'm a piece of meat.

Creepy.

"I've never seen you before. Who are you with?"

"Jordan Scott," I blurt out. "I'm meeting Jordan Scott."

His big chunky fingers tap the screen of his phone. And then with a dry smile, he glances up. "You're not on her guest list. I hate to have to manhandle women, but if I have to"—he stands up like he's ready to lick his chops—"I will."

"Oh, silly me. I should have told you Nate Hanson made the reservation."

Skepticism crosses his face.

"You can check. He made it this morning."

The bouncer's fingers go to work again, and suddenly the man's entire disposition changes. He presses a button on his phone and speaks into it. "Get me the butler to escort Mr. Hanson's guest."

I wave a hand. "Oh, that's not necessary."

From his head bob, I interpret I'm to move to the side and wait.

I do as he says.

At least this covered area is air-conditioned. The heat and humidity are starting to get to me. Tonight's the first night that there is no breeze to cool the air.

It's hot as hell.

Within minutes, a man wearing a three-piece suit, heavily starched shirt, white tie, and stiff-brimmed hat is standing beside me. "Hello, madame. Your name would be?"

"Zoey."

He nods. "Follow me."

We enter the large space and a blue haze coats the room. Blasts of lime green spotlight areas of the dance floor. People are everywhere, but the man in front of me walks around the crowd unfazed by the drinking and partying.

Out of nowhere a guy dressed in an expensive suit steps in front of me. "How about a dance?"

His eyes seem glued to my chest, and I have to take a quick glance to make sure everything is where it should be.

It is. But it seems my nipples want to play peek-a-boo with the jersey fabric. I probably should have worn a bra, but this dress didn't accommodate one.

The man moves closer. "Come on, let's dance."

He's not bad looking; actually he's pretty good-looking.

Gazing at him, I begin to wonder if this isn't what I should be doing to satisfy this urge I can't seem to shake—casual flings and meaningless hot sex might be just the cure for the ache that won't ease. This club could very well be the answer to checking off the items on my list.

He presses his body closer to mine and begins to move. "Here is fine with me."

I stare at him and rock my hips, willing my sexual desire to flare. When it doesn't, I have my answer—no, this might not be what I'm looking for. My insistent sexual desires aren't responding to this man's close proximity. Finally I give up and flash him a slight smile to ease the rejection. "Sorry, I can't, I'm meeting someone."

He bounces his head to the beat of the music. "Sure, I understand. But I'm here if you get tired of him."

Grinding, wiggling, and bouncing bodies are everywhere. Couples moving so close together, with their hips in unison, I could almost picture them fucking. Suddenly, images of Nate flash before me—his sculpted torso, his wildly untamed hair, his green eyes, his square jawline, his full lips, the way he moves.

And just like that, it's back—that hunger that knots itself in my stomach, pulses deep within my core, and shoots straight down my legs, making my toes curl.

"Madame, follow me, please."

"Oh, sorry." I realize I'm just standing there.

The gangster-dressed man takes us through a door that requires the swipe of a key card. Once we go through the door, another bouncer greets us, and he quickly unhooks the large gold clasp attached to the plush red velvet rope.

I feel like I'm in a maze of never-ending hallways as we walk down another corridor.

This one is elaborately decorated in art deco, and the archways and design of the era make the place seem regal. We come to the end of the hallway and the man opens a set of beautifully designed double doors with a terra-cotta sunburst inlayed above them. The words on the door read WELCOME TO THE ESTATE.

I can't believe I made it.

"This way to the bar, madame." My escort takes me through a large room filled with finely dressed people sitting on leather sofas deep in conversation. Women dressed in flapper-style uniforms are serving drinks. This has to be an old speakeasy turned into a social club.

It makes sense—the difficulty of getting in, the lack of music playing overhead, and the hushed voices. I feel like I'm reliving the Prohibition era.

I wonder if the Cotton Club or Stork Club looked like this.

My gaze wanders. My curiosity spikes.

I can see how my brother would have been drawn here—it's something that fits. It's just like him. It makes sense now. Even my brother's suits now make sense.

We pass through another set of doors with the words THE BAR written above them. I glance around. It's unlike any place I've ever been. It looks like a scene from *The Great Gatsby*—a giant bar to the right, tables and booths surrounding a dance floor, and a stage directly opposite me. The stage and the tables are empty, but the bar only has a few unoccupied seats.

A woman with Marilyn Monroe hair is sitting with her purse on the seat next to her—she's the woman from the picture. I can tell from the hairstyle.

"Can I assist with anything else, madame?"

"No, thank you very much." I reach in my purse to tip him but he shakes his head.

"Not necessary. It was my pleasure."

"Thank you."

The doors close behind me and I feel like I'm in a movie. This place empowers me in a way I could get used to. I approach the woman and my high heels slide against the slick floor. I slow my pace, but still reach her before I've figured out what to say. I didn't actually think I'd find her, so I hadn't prepared a speech.

With a deep breath I lean toward the bar and look at the woman. "Are you Jordan Scott?"

Her fingers curl around her wineglass. "Yes, I am. Can I help you?"

"May I?" I pick up her purse and set it on the bar.

"Actually, I'm meeting someone here."

"Yes, the Artist."

She groans. "When I asked around, I thought I specified I was looking for a man." Her eyes look me over. "But this arrangement might just work out. The fee will need to be reduced, of course."

I blink, uncertain where this is going. Why would it matter if a man or a woman sketched her portrait? "I was hoping I could ask you a few questions."

Her lips set in a firm line. "I believe you have this turned around. I'm interviewing you."

I bite my lip. "Yes, I'm sorry. Go on."

Her heavy gaze continues to assess me and she reminds me of

Cruella De Vil hungrily eyeing the Dalmation puppies. I feel naked and uncomfortable. "I don't like to beat around the bush," she begins as she reaches into her purse and pulls out a black box of electric cigarettes. "So let's start with: What, if any, are your hard limits?"

"My hard limits?"

This isn't just a social club.

My mind shuts down.

I have no idea what to say.

"It's a simple question." Her lips pucker around the glass tip of the cartridge, and she draws the vapor into her mouth.

The bartender approaches and sets a napkin in front of me. I turn quickly to avoid her exhale. He's wearing a news cap, white shirt, vest, no tie, and baggy pants. "What can I get you to drink tonight?"

I look at him, trying to eradicate the horrified look from my face. "Whatever you recommend."

"A Lady Joy?"

I nod. "Sounds great."

He smiles at me and grabs a glass from the chiller in front of him. My eyes wander throughout the room, and before I know it, he sets a beautiful blue drink down in front of me. "Enjoy."

"Thank you."

He moves on to another customer, leaving us alone.

I turn to look at Jordan. She's leering at me with her cigarette waving in the air. She's waiting for me to answer her question about my hard limits. My mind starts to whirl with a million different reasons she could be asking me that, but only one makes sense.

BDSM.

My brother was into BDSM.

How this fits into his ability to make so much money, I have yet to determine.

Jordan's long fingernail drags a line down my arm. "You're very pretty, but I need to know your answer before we move any further. You see, my husband has certain . . . needs that I am . . . unable to fulfill—anal being one of them. So if anal is a hard limit for you, I'm afraid we'll have to end this arrangement before it begins."

My stomach lurches and I scan the bar, wondering if I have the wrong person. "I thought you were looking for portrait services."

Her laugh is only slightly bemused. "Well of course we are, my darling. As I mentioned, we're interested in purchasing the platinum package. But the fee will need to be reduced. I was looking forward to, well—a male's companionship, but I am coming around to the idea of you. Will eight thousand be sufficient?"

"Eight thousand dollars?" I stutter, trying not to fall apart in front of her, knowing I need to finish this conversation to understand the depths of what is unfolding before me.

"I can go as high as nine thousand, but no more."

My eyes widen as shock and bile work their way up my throat. I pick up my drink and gulp it—all of it.

The friendly newsboy bartender is in front of me before the glass clinks on the slick surface. "Another?"

"Yes, please."

"And I'll have a shot of Jameson," a rich, thick voice says from behind me.

My nerves go completely off kilter as I swivel on the barstool and my eyes land right on Nate's attorney. "Oliver."

"Zoey, I must say I'm surprised to see you here." He scans the area. "Where's Nate?"

I look at him blankly.

"Nate did bring you, didn't he?"

I shake my head and try to swallow the bile rising back up my throat. Then, I put a finger up then twist around to Jordan. "Can you give me a sec?"

"No, I'm sorry, Zoey, I can't." She says my actual name with a sneer.

Thank you very much, Oliver.

"Just one second," I plead.

"I have to go. I'll be in touch once I consult with my husband." She puts her wand of electric smoke back in its case and then meets my eyes. "Keep in mind for the future that should we meet again, my time is my time." Her glare practically assaults Oliver.

The bartender sets my drink and Oliver's shot on the bar. I reach for mine and take a small sip as my nerves flare up. I want to stop her and ask her my biggest question, my biggest fear—is she offering to pay me for sex, or a portrait?

The answer is clear—*both.*

I don't need to ask the question to know that.

My throat suddenly constricts and I have to forcibly make myself swallow the liquid still in my mouth. She stands up and gives me a wicked smile, her tongue licking her lips before she walks away.

"Is everything okay?" Oliver asks with a compassion I can really use right now.

Sometimes things fall apart and you can put them back together, but not this time.

I turn toward him. "No, no it's not. What is this place?"

Oliver's cool persona shifts. "Does Nate know you're here?"

With a twist, I rest my elbows on the bar and stare into the clear blue liquid of my drink.

Quid pro quo. He ignores my question, I ignore his.

Oliver throws his shot back. "Another," he tells the bartender.

My hands are shaking as I fold them on the bar. "I'll have another too."

"You haven't finished what you have."

I shrug.

His hand covers mine. "Tell me what's going on. What are you doing here?"

The alcohol flows freely through my veins and I can feel the impact. I look at him. Does he know? Does Nate know? Did they both know that my brother was selling his *skills* to make my life easier?

"Have you ever heard of the Artist?"

He shakes his head. "No, I haven't. But an educated guess tells me it has something to do with the Estate."

"What do you mean?"

"This place gives mysterious titles to the people who work here. Does this have something to do with your brother?"

I nod. "Oliver, I'm pretty sure my brother was selling himself for money."

The bartender delivers my drink and Oliver's shot.

A sudden charge of energy in the air sends a chill down my spine. I snap my neck around and see him—Nate pounding across the empty dance floor. His jacket missing, his tie loosened like he was choking and couldn't get it off fast enough, his eyes almost black, his body reminiscent of a panther out to catch his prey.

"Zoey," he hisses across the quiet room. The familiar deep voice laced with anger makes me shiver.

Oliver shrinks back—quickly. And his hand retreats, but not fast enough that sweat doesn't bloom on his brow. I can see fear swirling in his chocolate brown eyes as he loosens his tie then downs his second shot.

I wait a full thirty seconds to turn around, knowing that I can't possibly hope to delay the inevitable. When I do, Nate is already behind me, his eyes locked on Oliver, his fists clenching at his sides, his expression one of complete disapproval. He looks lethal—like an assassin who has found his target. His hand possessively flattens across the bare skin of my back.

Out of nowhere, my heart, my body, my mind empty of everything but awareness of the space he occupies. Despite everything that's happened, everything I've learned, whirlwinds of desire spin all around me.

"Oliver." Anger flares in Nate's voice. "What are you doing here—with her?"

Jealousy seems to consume him.

And it thrills me.

Oliver raises his palms. "Look, man, I just saw her sitting here. I'm not with her." He takes a step back.

When Nate's eyes shift to mine, his gaze drills into me. "What are you doing here?"

The same words directed at me, but this time his tone fills with something I can't identify. Maybe something more than anger. An ache?

"I'm going to leave you two alone." Oliver's voice sounds distant.

Nate's arms move to either side of me, caging me inside his wall of lean muscle and fresh, clean, masculine scent. I hear Oliver's words but can't respond, can't blink, can't move.

"What are you doing here?" Nate growls, the predator in him coming out.

There is no more hiding in the brush waiting—he's here, and he's here for me.

"How did you know I was here?"

A snicker, then a hoarse animalistic sound of some kind, precedes his answer. "Did you think you could come here with a reservation for two and the staff wouldn't be looking for me?"

I stare at him with a completely blank expression.

"I received a phone call at my office alerting me that my guest had arrived and wanting to know if I needed anything else for the evening. Imagine my surprise when I told her I thought there had been a mistake, and she told me a woman named Zoey was at the front door under the reservation I made early this morning."

The man standing in front of me has a dark, brooding edge to his disposition, but he doesn't frighten me.

No, in fact quite the opposite—I'm completely turned on.

His hair is tousled with imperfection, his eyes darker than the night, his cheekbones hard, his jaw slightly stubbled, and his mouth, oh his mouth with those full, velvety soft lips and the pout he's making with them—I want him, all of him.

A flash of the way he touched me, kissed me, moved inside me the night we spent together strikes, and my body hums with a new kind of excitement.

"Answer me," he demands through clenched teeth.

I stare at him, willing myself to tell him how I feel.

His warm breath blows across the sensitive skin of my neck, as his arms cage me even tighter—the fabric of his white shirt rubs the skin of my arms and sends goose bumps up and down them. "Zoey, answer me."

"I came to find out about my brother." I sit up straighter and stare into his eyes. "And now that I have, I know this is my list. This is what I want."

"I don't want you coming here again. Do you hear me?"

I quickly twist around and fumble for my drink, the full one, and gulp it down in three swallows.

"Zoey, did you hear me?" he practically growls.

I turn back, already nodding my head. "I heard you, and I can't do that. You told me my life should be about living and this is what I want. This is what I yearn for."

"That's fucking ridiculous."

His harsh tone reverberates through me and I break, I finally break.

Pieces of my life scatter in this room, and I know I'll never be the same.

My brother—why did he do this to help me?

Nate's breathing is heavy, and I helplessly lift my eyes to his.

I can't speak.

I can't think.

I can't breathe.

My airways begin to constrict. I can't get air into my lungs. I'm being buried alive. I have a heavy weight in my lungs. I can force out only shallow breaths, which is getting harder and harder to do. My heart races as panic overtakes me. It's been so long since this has happened that I almost forget to reach for my inhaler, but before I do a cool piece of metal is being slid into my palms.

Nate found it.

With the plastic to my lips and the press of a button, relief is almost instant as the Salbutamol immediately relaxes the muscles in my airway, opening them up, making it much easier for me to breathe. I release the inhaler and look into his eyes. "Thank you. Why I am always saying thank you to you?"

He stares at me in silence for the longest time, but his eyes are no longer filled with anger. Rather thick-lashed, concerned eyes shine down on me. "Are you okay? Do I need to take you to the hospital?"

"No, I'm fine now. Really, I am."

"Are you sure?"

I nod. "I think I need some water."

He raises his hand to get the bartender's attention. I'm relieved to see I hadn't attracted any attention with my attack.

"Yes, sir?" the bartender asks.

"A glass of water, and what is this drink?" He lifts my blue filled goblet.

"A Lady Joy," the bartender answers proudly. "Would you like one?"

He shakes his head. "I mean, what's in it?"

"Lemon rum, blue curaçao, and a splash of champagne."

My heart drops.

That was so stupid of me not to ask.

My nerves had caused me to take complete leave of my senses.

Just as I can't drink wine, I can't drink champagne. Even though I had no idea it would be in the drink, it was careless of me not to ask.

"Thank you," Nate says before handing me the glass of water. "The attack was caused by the champagne in your drink."

I nod and take my time sipping the water before setting it down.

"Let's go," he says.

"No, I'm not going anywhere."

"Zoey, what's going on with you?" His tone isn't harsh this time, and he resumes his stance of boxing me in, quietly assessing me as if he has powerful X-ray vision.

I take a deep breath. "This morning I read an e-mail sent to an account belonging to my brother. He was being addressed as the 'Artist.' "

Nate's lashes blink in confusion. "Are you sure?"

"Have you heard of him?"

"No, I haven't." I can tell he's telling the truth by the sheer shock that seems to cloud his eyes. "But what does any of that have to do with you using my membership to come here?"

"Everything. The client requesting a portrait session wanted to meet Zach here."

"Here? Are you sure?" I can see things starting to fall into place for him. "I don't know what to say, Zoey. I honestly had no idea."

"The client was going to pay me—*him*, I mean—eight or maybe it was ten thousand dollars. And she asked me what my hard limits were."

Anger flames in the dark flecks of his eyes. "I want you to stay away from this place. Do you hear me?"

"No, Nate. I'm not going to do that."

"Do you know what this place is?"

I lift my chin. "I have a good idea. It seems like you and your friends enjoy the benefits of it. I think my brother was somehow involved with it. And it's a place I want to understand more about. So no, Nate, I won't be staying away."

His palms grasp my upper arms. His grip is firm. "This is not a joke, Zoey. You will stay away from this place."

Feeling resolute, feeling like I have nothing to lose and everything to learn, I stand up and our bodies align in the most perfect way. "No, Nate. I won't."

"You will." The cords in his neck pulse.

"Nate, listen to me. There is a very good chance I could die within the next year. And being in Miami, being with you, has awakened something inside me that I've never felt before. I've never wanted anyone like I do you. I've never wanted to have sex with the urgency I feel when I'm around you. I've never felt the passion you make me feel. And I've never gone to the places you've taken me. It sounds ridiculous, I know, but I want to experience more of those feelings. I want to experience them with you, but you keep pulling away. If you can't be with me then—"

His eyebrows pull low over his pantherlike eyes. "Do not finish that sentence."

"I'm being honest. You asked me to make a list of things I want to do that excite me. I didn't have to think hard about it because I already knew in my heart. I want someone to want me so much it hurts. I want someone to do crazy spontaneous things with me. I want to live wild and free. My entire life I've never been anything besides responsible. I've always made the sensible decisions. I want to free my mind and let someone else call the shots. Even if only for a little while. And if you can't be that person for me, I—"

He cuts me off. "I told you not to say that. I can't stand the thought of you with anyone else. You're mine, no one else's."

I press myself against him and he locks me in with his arms, his eyes now desperate and hungry. He cups my face and fits his mouth to mine, making me feel like I belong to him. And the strange thing is, that's how I want to feel. But then, like always, he pulls away.

"I'm not though," I say softly, trying to free his hold on me.

He whispers across my lips, "Yes, you are."

I shake my head. "You won't be with me."

He leans in, and his velvety soft lips brush mine. "Yes, I will."

The butterflies in my stomach soar into flight. My voice trembles as I turn my head away. "Don't say what you don't mean just to get me out of here."

"I never say anything I don't mean," he breathes in my ear.

I lean back and assess him.

His lips part, his breath grows ragged. Desire shines bright in his eyes.

"Then I think you should know that you are my list—my entire list."

He looks at me through hooded lids, and as my pulse races, I decide I should explain.

"I don't want to be who I was before Zach died. I was boring, practical, responsible, predictable."

"You don't have to explain to me." Wisps of his hot breath blow across my neck, sending shivers down my spine.

"No, I want to. When I'm with you, I feel spontaneous . . . adventurous . . . wild and crazy."

His gaze scorches me.

My mind wanders back again to the night we spent together. The way his lips sought to please me, the way his tongue flicked out with desperation to taste me, the way his cock twitched with deep satisfaction when he came inside me.

All I want is to feel like that again.

It's the only thing that makes me forget—forget not only how lonely I was, but also what might be.

For now, he's the only thing—he's my cure.

He tips my chin toward him and rakes those predatory eyes up and down my body. The heat sizzles between us and my knees feel weak, but I can't help but think the same thing is going to happen that happened last night.

"You had your chance last night."

"Give me another," he demands.

I don't know if I should believe him. "Tell me why you've changed your mind."

"Because even though your brother practically forbade me from even looking at you, I know he'd want me to be the one to take care of your needs, not some nameless, faceless douche bag who might not have your best interests at heart."

I grab his face. "You're wrong about my brother, you know. He really respected you. He wouldn't have felt that way if knew the Twenty-Seven Club was looming over me. He would have wanted me to be happy."

He shakes his head. "No, you're wrong. He knew me too well. He knew I'd only hurt you. But, I'm going to let his position go— for you."

I rub the pads of my thumbs over his cheeks. "You won't hurt me, you know. I'm not looking for anything you can't give me. I'm not searching for love. I'm attracted to you. That's all. I leave on Friday, and who knows what will happen after that?"

He takes my hands. "Are you certain about your feelings?"

"I am."

13

A Panther

Nate, he's like a panther and I'm his prey—and that excites me, thrills me, tips me over the edge.

He doesn't respond to me at first. Instead, his eyes, the eyes of a hunter, search mine for signs of a lie.

But he won't find one.

What I told him is the truth—my only truth.

I'm not looking for love.

My destiny doesn't allow for that.

All I want from him is to let me explore this deep, burning desire I have for him—the sensuality he's unlocked, uncovered, awakened within me—it's for him only. And I want to take it further. I want to know even more—with him.

I give him a slight nod, a simple gesture reassuring him he can trust me. He has demons of his own, something besides my brother's objections holding him back. What they are, I don't know, but that's okay.

We both have baggage.

He tugs my hand, pulling me closer. "Then stay the summer with me."

My mouth drops. I'm stunned into silence.

He inches me even closer.

I shake my head slightly. "I can't," I whisper. My hesitation is clear.

His fingers splay on my hips. "You can."

I close my eyes and wage an inner battle—my want and need against my logic, against what my destiny might hold. A part of me feels like I have to go after this passion while I have the chance.

His breath sifts over my face. "Let me help you live wild and free."

I open my eyes and look into his very blue eyes. The moment I do, I know I can't stop myself from making the only decision that makes sense. I take a shaky breath. I can't believe what I'm about to say. I've never made a decision as important as this so quickly. I run my finger down his cheek. "Yes. Yes, I'll stay."

He drops his forehead to mine. "You said you have to go back to work after the summer. I want you to know, the summer's all I have to give. I'm not looking for anything else," he whispers.

"I know, and neither am I. I do have to go back to work," I whisper back.

He nods, our foreheads pressing together still.

I nod back, and just like that we reach an agreement.

And then for the first time, he kisses me without restraint. He kisses me with a hunger that makes me feel like I might explode. He kisses me deeply, his grip on my hips tightening with every passing moment of passion. When he pulls away, both of us are breathless. He takes my hand. "Come on, let's go home."

I tug him toward me and shake my head. "If you want me like you say you do, prove it. Show me what this place is."

He hesitates.

I trace the sculpted lines of his body and my heart thumps. "I want to experience it."

His gaze flickers over me. "Are you sure?"

He's nothing but lean muscle, and I swallow with the thought of what's to come. "Yes. And I want you to show me."

This time he doesn't delay his response. He stretches his arm across the bar. The bartender is in front of him in a heartbeat. "Tell the Mistress I need a room. Somewhere private."

"Who's the Mistress?" I ask.

He ignores my question and does something I'm not expecting. He pulls my body flush against his and barely brushes my lips with his. His closeness, his scent, his warm breath, his lips so close to mine that I can practically taste them, they nearly distract me from the question I asked.

Nearly.

"Who's the Mistress?" I ask again.

His tongue darts out to lick my lips, like he was thinking the same thing I was—just a taste. I need just a taste. "She manages the availability of the rooms and the clients' needs," he murmurs, his mouth remaining achingly close to mine.

"Excuse me, Mr. Hanson, but she'd like to talk to you." The bartender hands Nate the phone.

"Yeah," he says.

A pause.

"That's fine."

Another pause.

"No."

He runs his hand through his hair.

"Yes. I don't care."

A pause.

"I said it's fine."

Nate hands the phone back to the newsboy bartender and then takes my hand. "Come with me."

His grip is firm, no longer unyielding, but determined. His stride is quick, but it slows when he sees I can't keep up. He turns back to look at me and when he does, I can hardly control myself.

Desire pools in the depth of my core, triggering a flood of arousal between my thighs. He stops at the door and turns around to crash his lips to mine. The kiss might be hard, wet, and quick, but it's still enough to cause the swarm of newly hatched butterflies to race around my stomach. A wall of some kind seems to have come down tonight, and the thought of what's to come is enough to make my toes curl.

The turn of events, the catalyst behind the change, the reason I'm here—they all spin away and all that is left is just him and me. Right now, I don't want to worry about anything, I just want to be. I trail behind him as he leads us back into the room with all the sofas and the people conversing in the most normal, civilized way.

With a squeeze of my hand, I jerk him back toward me.

He twists and raises a brow.

With a giggle I demand, "Tell me where we are? What these people are doing?"

He turns around to face me and pushes a piece of hair from my eyes. "Look, Zoey, this isn't a place for you. It's not what it seems—not at all."

"I know this is a sex club, and I want to know more about it."

He steps closer and laces his fingers in mine. A haze of passion cocoons me, makes me want to give up on the talking and just get naked with him. "This room and the bar are for socializing."

"For meeting . . . partners?" I ask.

"Usually the Bar is where the single members congregate. This room is for couples."

"Swingers?" I ask, and I'm sure I must look like a doe in headlights.

He laughs and his chin dips a little in the most adorable way. "Yeah, I guess you could call them that."

"How often do you come here?"

The very first time he looked at me, I noticed how green his eyes were, but the way his gaze traces the lines of my face right now, I don't notice anything. I only feel—and I can feel his eyes on me as if they are a soft touch, a tender caress.

"I don't."

His lie stings and sucks the laughter right out of me. I jerk my hands away and try to step back, but his grip is firm. Nate kisses me again and I want to struggle to free myself, but I don't. I can't. This time his kisses are soft, light, the barest brush of his lips against mine. "It's the truth."

With my eyes closed I ask, "Then why do you have a membership?"

His sigh lingers in my ear. "That's not really what's important right now."

I keep my eyes closed. I guess there's some things guys would rather not discuss. Maybe he thought he'd like it or maybe he wanted to impress someone. Or who knows, maybe it's for business. I get gym memberships all the time and never go. Once I kept one for two years before canceling and never stepped foot inside.

"Do you know what a sex club is?" His words tingle my skin. I nod.

"You know most of the rooms here aren't as civilized as the two rooms you've been in. People walk around naked, some in towels. And they're doing it en masse, while others stand around and watch. Or rub one out. And this club also accommodates more erotic needs."

My eyes slam open, needing to erase that image from my mind. Shock makes my jaw drop, but more from his choice of words than what he just described. I try to hold my laughter in but some of it bubbles out.

He brushes his lips against the sensitive skin of my neck. "Do you find that funny?"

"It's the way you phrased it." My head tips back to allow him better access. "Are people going to be watching us?"

"Fuck no." The growl signifies his stance on that is nonnego-tiable.

I have to say—I'm relieved.

"Do you trust me to take you inside one of those rooms?"

"Yes." My voice is laced with the headiness of these erotic thoughts.

"Do you trust me to make you feel good?"

"Yes." I'm almost panting now.

"Do you trust me?" His words are dangerously husky.

The tone makes me wild, wanting.

This time there's no *Do you trust me to . . .*

Just a simple question.

My heart is skipping, jumping.

I get what he's trying to tell me. "Yes, I trust you. Yes, I be-lieve you." I grab at his hair and pull his eyes to meet mine. "Just please don't ever say 'rub one out' again."

Nate's deep voice becomes a low chuckle and the magnetic pull of his tone makes me want to be even closer to him. "I made my point."

"Mr. Hanson," a sweet, sexy voice says from behind me.

I turn to see a stunning woman with a huge smile. She must be the Mistress.

"Are you sure you don't want to go home?" Nate whispers in my ear.

Home.

Go home with him.

A feeling of safety clings to my skin and wraps around me like a warm blanket, but I push it away, shove it off.

I twist toward him. "I want to stay here. I want to experience what this place is all about."

"Curiosity killed the cat," he mutters.

"Luckily for me, I'm just a kitten."

The faint sound he makes shrills through my ears like a loud boom. Oh God, the panther's on the prowl.

"Mr. Hanson." The woman greets us face-to-face and her eyes almost devour him. "And guest," she adds coyly, addressing me with her eyes and giving me a quick once-over. I'm not offended by the title—but the way she's looking at Nate makes my vision a little green, I won't lie. The title of *guest* could be for the sake of privacy. The look, on the other hand, makes me wonder if she doesn't think we'll be asking her to join us.

We won't be.

I'm not sharing him, no matter where we are. I'm being possessive, and the only thing to back me up is a contract. Silent—yes. Binding—definitely, just not legally. Emotionally tying—absolutely.

Nate gives her a nod.

I give her a courteous yet forced smile.

"Follow me. I have the Master Bath ready."

The Master Bath?

My pulse pounds at every point. My blood rushes through my veins. I pray that I'm not visibly panting, but I fear I might be. Oh God, Nate will think I'm having another attack. I have to calm myself.

Zen.

Think Zen.

I get to bathe with him, in a huge bubble-filled tub, between his thighs, lying on his chest, with his fingers in my hair. Naked— with the lights on and maybe even candles burning.

The woman in a tight black pencil skirt and bustier top leads us down another corridor with soft, soothing music playing above us, but it's deceiving. It almost feels like I'm in a spa, but I know I'm not. I'm in a sex club about to have sex with the man who, up until about thirty minutes ago, kept pushing me away.

Pinwheels of excitement spin in my belly.

We pass a room with a sign reading THE BILLIARDS ROOM etched across it. A large glass window allows me to see in. A quick glance has my cheeks flaming—naked couples are playing pool. At least that's all I can see going on. We pass another room labeled THE MASTER BEDROOM with a DO NOT DISTURB sign on the door. I don't even want to imagine what's going on in there. My eyes appraise every nuance, every piece of art, painted trim, and glowing light of the corridor. This place is beautiful. Up ahead I see an opaque glass door with the words THE MASTER BATH scripted on it.

The Mistress comes to a stop in her very high heels and turns toward us. Her overflowing cup size takes front and center. "All of your requests have been taken care of."

Requests?

What requests?

The pinwheels I was feeling turn into pinpricks.

Oh God, what if Nate was wrong and people will be watching us? Will they be joining us—like in Roman baths? Do I want those things? All of those things? None of those things?

The only thing I'm certain about is I don't want people joining us. I've already established that. But I don't think I want others to see us either.

"Oh my," the Mistress says, looking down at her feet, "I think someone left the water running, there seems to have been a flood."

Water seeps from under the door. And with the excess water goes my bubble-filled wet-slicked sex fantasy. The Mistress starts tapping her phone, not losing her composure for even a second. "I'm so sorry, but this is easily remedied. Follow me, Mr. Hanson, and I'll show you to the Study."

Nate squeezes my hand. "Where were you a few minutes ago?"

"With you," I whisper raising my eyes.

Nate looks at me and raises a brow. "No, you weren't."

"Here we are," the Mistress says. "I'm so sorry for the inconvenience."

Nate and the Mistress exchange token words, but my mind wanders to hard and soft limits and BDSM and pain and the fact that I'm in a sex club.

A sex club that my brother worked at doing . . . well, I'm not sure yet *what* he was doing.

But I might have read a few too many books on the subject. And in those books, floggers, whips, butt plugs, handcuffs, blindfolds, and the like were always used.

Oh God, I think some of those leave marks.

"Hey," Nate lifts my chin. "Are you okay?"

I blink and my range of sight seems to refocus. When I look around I realize we're alone. The Mistress is gone and we're standing outside the room with the only thing keeping us from being alone together the heavy wooden door before us.

"Will it hurt?" I ask.

Nate raises a brow. "Do you want it to hurt?"

My heart skips around my chest. "I don't know."

He slams me against the wall. His lips part. His hands ease into my curls and he cups my scalp. "I'm going to give you whatever you want. Whatever you need to feel wild and free. I'm going to make this summer the best time in your life." His words are broken whispers punctuated by kisses.

I start to feel dizzy, completely intoxicated by him. All my thoughts of my life and its uncertainty escape my mind, and all that is left is Nate.

Tugging harder at my scalp, he kisses me deeply, our mouths colliding, heat flaming between us as our bodies ache to be closer. His feels hot and hard, mine soft and wanting—a perfect combination. He pulls harder at my hair and the pain intensifies, but his kisses become hungrier at the same time, making me melt into small pools of pleasure under his touch.

He leans back. "Is that what you want?"

Butterflies race around in my chest.

"Yes," I purr. "I want this, plus whatever else you can give me. I want it all."

"Fuck," he groans and that noise floods me like nothing I've ever felt.

Raw, savage desire is the only way I can describe it. His breath comes in short bursts of air. It takes him a few moments to focus but when his hand grazes my hip, electricity shoots through me and when his knee rubs against the inside of my thigh, heat flares under my skin. It may have taken him only moments to recover but once he straightens, I'm still left bewitched, left wobbly beneath the shadow of his long, lean body.

Our gazes lock as he finds my eyes and I get lost in his, lost in watching him, lost in wanting him. "Are you ready?" He bobs his head toward the door.

"I'm ready."

My body is filled with so many different sensations right now, I feel like I might just explode if relief doesn't come soon.

He presses a code on the keypad and when the lock clicks open, he takes my hand. With my heart doing laps in my chest, he opens the door and I step inside.

14

The Study

The stars must have aligned just right tonight, because I again feel like a character out of *The Great Gatsby* as soon as we enter the space. The erotic bathroom images that were meandering through my mind are easily replaced by visions of Nate swiping his hand across the tigerwood desk and throwing me down on it. Of Nate shoving me up against the wall of books and having his way with me. Of Nate laying me down on the Persian rug and taking me fast and hard.

This room is seductive, alluring, and intriguing with the reflective foiled wallpaper, the regal rose-colored wingback chair, and the large deco mirror beside the inlaid chrome-trimmed credenza, plus the eye-catching parquet floors.

My eyes search for anything out of the ordinary, and what I find when I turn around makes me gasp.

The space on one side of the door houses a black-pegged wall with hooks displaying whips, chains, and floggers. The space on the other side has some kind of restraining setup I can't even begin to understand. The thought of it all makes my body twitch with panic.

Nate's eyes catch mine. "I asked for the bondage gear to be removed, but that was before the sudden room change."

Relief courses through me. No matter how tough my bravado, I know I couldn't endure anything like what I'm looking at. And I'm glad Nate's on board with that plan. "Why?"

He grabs me with a laugh. The warmth of his breath sends shivers down my spine. "I could never hurt you."

"Never. Not even if I asked you to?"

Mischief glitters in his eyes. "Never, not with anything like that anyway." He bobs his head toward the wall I'm staring at and wraps his arms around me. "But my hand"—he spanks my ass— "is another story."

I jump, startled by his slap, but it's extremely arousing at the same time. "Hey!" I protest.

"You shouldn't have come here without talking to me first."

He spanks me again—this time my other ass cheek. Pricks of pain radiate over my entire behind and stream right to my sex, making it pulse with need. He reaches across the space I put between us and caresses his hand over my ass. I brace for another strike, but instead he brushes his lips to mine. At first the kiss is soft, only laced with a touch of desperation.

The intensity ratchets up though as our starving lips devour each other. Every lick, suck, and nip feels better than the last.

My mind is on a roller coaster soaring to the top and waiting for the thrill of the fall. Being in a room in a club where I know others are doing what we're about to do seems naughty, something I would have never done before coming to Miami.

There's something extremely erotic about it. Nate's hands stop wandering my body and when he grips my hips with a tug, I can feel his arousal.

His restraint makes me even hotter for him. It turns me on in the most delicious way.

I put my hand to his chest and push back. Those panther eyes go on attack, and his mouth seeks what he obviously feels belongs to him. The thought makes every nerve in my body jump with elation. "I like it when you tell me what to do," I whisper.

He grabs me hard and pulls me back to him. "Why?"

"Why do I like it when you tell me what to do?"

"Yes, Zoey. That's the question."

"Because, my whole life I've had to make decisions, be responsible, make the right choices. But with you, I don't have to. I can be free. And I like how that makes me feel. I like how you make me feel. I don't know why. I can't explain it, but I told you, it's like meeting you turned some kind of switch on inside my body that I didn't know was there."

"So you're okay if I punish you when you misbehave?"

"I'm looking forward to it."

His hand slips down the back of my dress to once again caress the spot he spanked. "Are you sure you want to play this kind of game?"

My core is on fire, and it feels so good.

"Is it a game? You're all about control. You never give it up. I'm just letting you know I like it."

His fingers snap the spaghetti straps of my dress. "I'm really upset with you for coming here without telling me. For sneaking into my room and breaking into my phone to make a reservation. For talking to other men while wearing this dress."

"That's three things," I murmur. "And only two spankings."

He laughs. "Of course you're counting."

"I'm just saying."

"You're crazy, you know."

I shrug. "I hope so."

"I think that's enough for tonight," he murmurs.

"If you say so." My voice is softer than a whisper.

My breasts are flush to his chest, yet his free hand manages to find its way past my locket and into the fabric of my dress. A hiss escapes his throat when he makes contact with my bare nipple, and his focus seems to shift. "Oh fuck, you're not wearing a bra."

I nod my head, trying to suppress my moan as his fingers tweak my nipple into what feels like a point of steel.

Singeing, surging lines of pleasure dart right from his touch to my sex. When his other hand slips down the crease of my ass with the slightest pressure, at the same time his fingers continue to pinch my nipples, I can't hold back and "Oh God, that feels so good" echoes within the room we're standing in.

His tongue drags down my neck, taking small sucks along the way, and his teeth nip me on his way back up to my lips. I open my mouth to let him in. He strokes me with his tongue, kissing me harder, deeper, rougher. "Are you sure you want to stay here?" he asks quietly between lashes to my tongue, my lips, my entire mouth.

My hands run up and down his back, itching to get beneath the fabric of his shirt, and I take my turn to lick and suck my way down his neck. "Why, you don't want to?"

"I'd rather take you home to my bed."

I bite down at the juncture between his neck and shoulder and he groans.

"I want as much as you'll give and I'll take as much as I can. I'd rather do this in my own house."

Arousal shoots through me and my sex clenches with such a need at his declaration, my head falls back and causes my mouth to lose its connection to his neck.

"What do you say?" He takes back control and licks his wet, slick tongue around the shell of my ear.

In my silence, his hand slips from my breast.

I immediately miss his hot touch.

But then his palms press into my back, pushing me against

him, locking me in place in the most deliciously tortuous way. Our bodies are fitted together so tightly, my locket presses into my skin deep enough that I'm positive if I were naked, it would leave a mark. "Is this your way of getting out of being with me?"

With a swivel of his surging hips, I can feel his erection already tented in his slacks. "Does it feel like that's what I'm doing?"

I turn and then look over my shoulder to smile at him. Considering my options, I walk toward the silver domed tray. It's set on the table next to the wingbacked chair. I'm feeling parched and assume there must be some kind of food and drink beneath it.

When I take hold of the fancy silver stem to lift it Nate yells, "Don't!"

He rushes toward me.

It's too late.

Underneath the lid there is no water, no bowls of fruit, no whipped cream, but rather a pair of chrome handcuffs and a black silk blindfold.

The dome flickers and tiny sparkles of light radiate around the room. I look down at the shiny chrome rings. Do I want my freedom to touch him taken away?

I need to think about this.

My eyes flicker to the blindfold—soft, smooth, solid. Do I want my sense of sight hindered? Blindfolded I won't be able to see anything—there'll be no watching, no seeing the look on his face. My other senses will have to compensate for the loss of sight. My sense of touch should become more sensitive, and I'll feel him with more intensity. My hearing will become more acute and his groans and heavy breaths that seem to drive me to the brink will sound louder. And taste, will it . . .

"Zoey." He slams the lid down. "That's not for us. It's standard in all the rooms."

I look up at him. "Have you ever used either before?"

His gaze drops and anxiety spreads like fire through my body.

No lies.

We said no lies.

He runs his hand through his hair and then moves closer to me.

I take a step back.

He moves closer still and again I step back.

When he does it again, my back is flush against the pegged wall and I'm not sure the answer is really important.

But then, he puts a hand on the wall behind me and jingles one of the shackles attached to it. "Do you really want me to answer that?"

I swallow, my mouth dry. "Yes."

His breath stirs the strands of my hair. "Yes."

My pulse beats rapidly in every hollow of my body. I think I already knew that. "What if I want you to use them on me? Would you?"

He looks down at me, and although I don't raise my gaze, I can feel the weight of his stare surrounding me. "Is that . . . what you want?"

His other arm extends toward the wall, and my entire body vibrates as I press my palms against the open holes. "Honestly, I don't know."

His hands slide to my hips and he pulls me close. "We don't have to decide tonight." The gruff, sexy tone of his voice sends electricity through me in bolts. He presses me to the wall and crashes his lips to mine. He kisses me with a passion that makes a kiss not just a kiss. He's all tongue, teeth, and hands; and his kiss makes me feel drunk, dizzy, lost in the moment. His mouth glides down the soft skin of my shoulder and I breathe in his scent as he kisses his way back up my neck, alternating between licking and sucking.

I don't think a man has ever licked me before, nor have I ever licked a man, but I want him to slurp me up—and I want to do the same to him.

He melds his lips back to mine with a starvation that can only be pure desire.

No longer able to control myself, my hands flit across his chest. I feel the smoothness of his skin while I trace the lines of his muscles, feeling all his sculpted leanness.

His hands grab mine. "Do you have any idea how much I want to be inside you right now?" he growls.

"I want that too," I respond, hungrily eating up his kisses like they are the finest pieces of chocolate I just can't get enough of. I take his face in my hands. "If I leave here with you now, will there be other nights?"

He pushes his hard cock against my thigh. "Does this answer your question?"

Another wave of desire shoots through me.

Thoughts of many more nights with him have me doing cartwheels while standing still.

His hands glide up my back and they tug at my hair, pulling the handful down so tight his hand rests on the top of my ass.

I love the way he likes to play with my curls.

His long, lean body presses against mine as his hands roam every curve, every inch of me.

"I really wish there was a fucking bed in here," he murmurs.

And I laugh. I'm offering myself to him any way he wants me; I'm vulnerable, I'm his to do with what he wants and he wants to fuck me—on a bed. It's then that I decide yes. Yes, I want him to take me home. I also make another decision. I want to know what it's like to submit to his control. I know I can trust him. With a steady breath I say, "Take me home. But I want you to know, I want to use them—the blindfold and the handcuffs both—just not tonight."

His lips part and form an incredible smile that makes my heart go pitter-patter. With his brute strength, he clenches my hips and grinds into me with his hard cock, and everything in the world as

I know it is gone—I have all I want, all I need, right here pressing into me.

His lips are at my ear and his tongue slides around it. "You drive a hard bargain," he whispers, and I can still feel his naughty smile as his lips brush my ear. "Lucky for you, I'm in the negotiating kind of mood tonight. And I accept the deal on the table."

His whisper floats into the air and shivers run down my spine. I want this so much, this time with him, this summer of sex with him. And for a moment, I can't believe this is my life.

But just for a moment because then his hand presses to the small of my back and I know . . .

This is real.

15
Let Go

Every day could be my last.

Faith, love, and hope.

Spells, fortune-tellers, and horoscopes.

Full moons, shooting stars, and wishes made.

Nothing will change my path.

I know, in the back of my mind.

Over my shoulder.

Behind my eyes.

Lurking around every corner.

My destiny is there. The path is already laid out.

I have no expectations that I can change it; one cannot reverse the course of destiny.

Can they?

So when Nate asked me to spend the summer with him, I didn't hesitate for long. That voice inside told me to stop living for dying and start living like each day is my last—to make the most of the time I might have left.

Pretty much what Nate told me last night.

Sure, I have things I want to do.

Paris in the spring.

London in the summer.

New York City in the fall.

Colorado in the winter.

But Nate, he is first and last on my list. And yes, I have a life left to live. I know I do. But my job and things back home can wait. Death might still loom over me, but I'm going to try to shove away its whispers for as long as I can and concentrate on the here and now.

Starting right now.

For the first time I notice the black soot over the stove as I pull my head from my dark thoughts and my gaze lands on the sexy way Nate moves around the kitchen making sandwiches at midnight. Although the bedroom was first on my list, I could tell Nate wanted to take things slow, so I concurred with him that we should eat when he got home.

"I can't believe you've never had a Cuban sandwich before." Nate opens the refrigerator and takes out a number of clear bags with the name Publix Deli printed on them in green.

I laugh and point to the paper teepeed on the counter next to the old tarnished waffle maker that seems out of place with everything in the shiny kitchen. "From the instructions Rosie left you, I'd wager a bet that you've never *made* a Cuban sandwich before."

He tosses the meats and cheese on the counter then shakes his head in that adorable way that's almost indescribable. From right to left, his head turns, his chin dips, his eyes close for only a moment, but the sexiest part is that smirk that accompanies it. "I wouldn't do that if I were you. You'd only lose. I grew up on sandwiches, mostly Cubans. I just don't make them the same way Rosie does."

"They're good?"

He rubs his stomach and looks over at me. "The best."

I can't help but grin at him. "Can't wait, then. How can I help?"

Nate picks up the recipe Rosie had written out for him. "I think I got this. Just have a seat."

I lean against the counter next to him to watch the show. "I'm good here."

His eyes scan my body as if I somehow might distract him from his task, but then he shrugs. "Suit yourself."

I laugh. "Do I make you nervous being this close? Afraid you won't get the job done correctly?"

"I always get the job done correctly," he says with a wink.

He's teasing, but heat still flows through me like fire. Impulsively, I lean over to kiss him. "I bet you do."

He shakes his head in that adorable way again, and I capture the moment in my mind for posterity.

Feeling a little too emotional over some silly banter, I decide to change the topic. "Tell me what you know about the Artist," I ask.

The cutting board is tucked behind the waffle maker as if Rosie left it there for him. He grabs for it and sets it on the counter before opening a drawer. "I really don't know anything."

"Oliver said it sounded like something that would be associated with the Estate. What did he mean?"

Removing a serrated knife, he reaches for the loaf of long, skinny bread in a brown paper bag beside the waffle maker.

Rosie did put everything together for him. It's kind of cute in a maybe-he's-helpless kind of way. But I know he's anything but.

"Oliver shouldn't be talking to you about anything to do with that." I hear his irritated exhalation of breath even as he crinkles the paper to take the loaf of bread from its wrapper. Once he's done, he sets it on the cutting board and turns toward me. "What I know is that every title has many nameless faces behind it. The Mistress isn't just the woman you met tonight; there are others like her who fill that same role. There is also the Butler, the Bartender, the Cigar Girl, they're all the same—those positions all have more than one person filling them and the Estate employs them all. In addition, there are positions that are contracted."

"Contracted?"

"Yes, those people arrange their own contracts with their clients and pay a fee to the Estate."

He turns back toward the loaf of bread and slices two hunks about eight inches long.

"And the Artist would be one of those contracted professionals? Are they allowed access to the club in return for their fee?"

"I assume so." He slices open each piece down the middle. His hands seem a little shaky.

I hop up on the counter to steady my own trembling legs. "What other occupations are allowed in . . . to service clients' needs?"

He opens the refrigerator again and this time removes a jar of pickles, a yellow bottle of French's mustard, and a stick of butter. When he puts them on the counter beside me his eyes shift up to mine. "I know there's the Photographer, the Masseuse, the Hairdresser, the Stylist. I'll ask around."

"Do you know anyone who might have known what he did?"

"Look, Zoey, I'm really not feeling this conversation. I said I'd look into it. Let's change the subject."

The noise of the yellow squeeze bottle is the only sound in the room as he coats each hunk of bread with mustard. When he sets the plastic bottle down and starts to loosen the pickle jar's lid, I place my hand over his. "Nate, please tell me. I just want to understand what my brother was doing to get the amount of money he did."

With a jerk, he pulls his hand away and the jar with it and glares at me. "Isn't that what you figured out tonight? What else do you need to know?"

"Everything. Anything. It might not make sense to you, but I want to understand this more. I want to know what he was involved in. How he got involved in it. Who he worked with. What exactly he did."

"Jesus, Zoey, I think you're smart enough that it doesn't have to be spelled out." He drops his gaze and practically hammers pickles on top of the mustard until hardly any yellow shows.

"I'm not talking about the sex. I'm talking about the rest of it."

His phone rings before he can respond. He wipes his hands on a towel and pulls it from his pocket. "Give me a sec. I need to take this."

"Okay, sure." I hop off the counter.

"Hello, is everything okay?" he says and walks down the hall toward his office.

I listen, even though I know I shouldn't.

"Yeah, something came up and I couldn't make it tonight."

A pause.

"Tell him I'm sorry that I didn't call."

A sigh.

"Sure, of course."

Another pause.

"Hey, Dad, I'm fine. No, the weather is fine, that's not why I didn't come. Something came up. Something I had to take care of."

Another sigh.

"Listen, what do you say I bring you one of Rosie's Cubans in the morning? You can have the nurses heat it up for you for lunch."

A steady thumping noise like he's tapping his heel against the wall.

"Yeah, promise I'll call next time."

More thumping.

"Good night, Dad."

Another pause.

"Yeah, I love you too."

Nate comes back into the kitchen a few minutes later just as I'm slicing another hunk of bread.

He looks at me questioningly.

"Sorry, I didn't mean to eavesdrop, but I heard you say you'd bring your father a sandwich."

He shrugs and bobs his head for me to move over. "Thanks. And don't worry about it."

"Rosie told me your dad used to live here before he went into a nursing home."

With quick work Nate starts to doctor up the third hunk of bread like the other two. "He did. On and off for the past few years. But the last time, I realized I couldn't take care of him. He needed twenty-four-hour care. I knew his Alzheimer's had started to take its toll and he couldn't stay here anymore—it wasn't safe for him. I had to find a place where he could be supervised."

"I'm so sorry."

Nate opens the bag of Swiss cheese and places slices on top of the pickles. "Shit happens. He's in a really nice place. Some days I go there and he doesn't know who I am. But most days, like today, he looks forward to my visits."

The sadness in his voice tells me what his words don't. And guilt strikes. I'm the reason he didn't make it to see his father. "I'm sorry you didn't get to see him today."

"I'll go in the morning."

"I'll have extra on mine," I say before he closes the bag of cheese.

He looks up and grins. "You like cheese?"

I nod. "Chocolate and cheese—my favorite foods. In fact, I think they should both have their own food groups."

He rolls a slice of the cheese and reaches toward my mouth. I open my lips as he feeds it to me, and that familiar hunger surfaces immediately.

"I'm not sure chocolate meets the nutritional guidelines," he jokes.

I gasp in mock horror. "I'll have you know dark chocolate is loaded with minerals and soluble fiber as well."

He looks at me for the longest time and then he grabs me and crashes his lips to mine. The sudden movement is unexpected. He pulls back from me, gazing with heavy lids at my swollen lips. "If you're spending the summer in Miami, I want you to stay over here, and sleep in my bed with me."

Little tiny thrills prickle my skin.

He releases me, and stares down at me as if waiting for an answer.

I didn't think I had to give one, but I do. "Sure, okay, if you're sure that's what you want."

He turns back to the sandwiches and starts folding ham slices in half and laying them on the other side of the bread. "Yeah, it is."

I wait for him to turn and meet my eyes, but he stays focused on finishing his task. "Can I meet your dad sometime? Zach talked about him a lot. He said your father really helped him when he first got to Miami."

On top of the ham, he places slices of pork, though less than the ham, and then he closes the two halves of bread. "Yeah, I think he'd really like that." I hear the smile in his voice even though he still hasn't looked at me. Instead, he plugs the waffle maker in and cuts a few dabs of butter off the stick.

"What about your mother?"

This time his stare swings to mine. "What about her?"

"Does she help with your father?"

He drops his gaze and puts the butter pads on top of two of the bread slices and then points to the drawer where I'm standing. "Do you think you could wrap this up for me?"

"Sure." I open the drawer and remove the Saran Wrap.

"No, use the tin foil."

"Oh, sorry." I reach for the Reynolds Wrap.

"It's easier to press that way."

I nod, even though he can't see me.

A few moments later he says, "She left us when I was seven."

I stop wrapping the sandwich. "I'm sorry. I didn't know."

"Don't be." The sorrow in his voice is too much and I reach for him. He shrugs my hand off his arm in a lame gesture of transferring the sandwiches to the waffle maker. Once they're on it, he smashes the lid down and presses on it. I must be staring at the tarnished metal because when he finally looks up he says, "My father used this waffle maker all the time to press the sandwiches he made for us to eat after she left. I know I sound callous about my mother, but what she did, the way she left, it was unforgivable."

Golden brown, crispy delights emerge as Nate lifts the lid and quickly removes the sandwiches. He sets them on plates and slices each diagonally.

I set the wrapped sandwich down and just stare. "Those look delicious."

He nods his head toward the refrigerator. "Stick that in there and grab us some waters."

God, something about his body language, the way he uses it to communicate, elicits an urge to kiss him every time he makes one of those gestures. Somehow, I manage to suppress the need as he saunters through the living room, out the sliding glass door, and over to the glass table beneath the covered roof of the lanai. But once he sets the plates and napkins down, I can't suppress the urge any longer.

When he pulls out my chair, I throw my arms around him and press my mouth to his. The taste of his lips, the feel of his tongue, the way he nips at my bottom lip just before he ends a kiss—everything about his mouth is already so familiar, and I relish the idea of getting to spend two more months like this.

He nips my lip right on cue before pulling back. "We better eat these while they're still hot." His chin dips toward the table and the yearning, the urge, the need—it all feels overwhelming.

I sit down and look at my plate, anywhere but at Nate.

Finally, the pulse between my legs starts to wane as the smell of the melted cheese consumes my senses. And for now anyway, one hunger replaces the other.

It's hard to eat while laughing, but somehow I manage. Nate is telling me story after story of the things he and my brother had done over the years. I know some of them are exaggerated for effect, because I had already heard them, but I don't care. I love to hear about the crazy things my brother did.

It makes me feel like he lived his life.

"So what about you?" Nate asks, sipping the last of his water.

I push my plate away. "What about me?"

"What kept you on the straight and narrow?"

I make a face, trying not to roll my eyes at his terminology.

He studies me. "What?"

I shrug. "Straight and narrow?"

He grins. "Are you denying it?"

"No."

His grin widens. "At least I didn't call you what your brother always did—a good girl."

"A good girl." I roll my eyes. "Just the mold I want to break."

"Is that what I'm about? The guy that you want to corrupt you?"

I lean across the table. "Do you have a problem with that?"

His tongue sneaks out to wet his lips. "As a matter of fact, I don't."

I lean back and give him my most seductive stare. "Then we have an exciting summer ahead of us."

Nate pushes his chair back and tugs me between his legs. "Tell me when you're ready to start."

Every fiber in my body ignites.

I look down at him. "I think you know I've been ready, but if you're asking me what I want you to do next, my answer is everything."

His hands slide under my dress, and in a quick swoop, he

stands up and brings me with him. "Good. Let's start with fucking in my bed."

My arms and legs wrap around him. "You're really excited about your bed," I purr.

He steps in the house from the lanai and laughs. "What, you don't think it will be exciting?"

"I didn't say that."

He nips my lip—hard. "Don't worry, it will be. In fact, I plan to make every time even more exciting than the last."

I gasp in delight.

He takes the stairs quickly and our mouths remain fused in wild need for each other.

No one has ever carried me in the heat of passion.

It thrills me.

He's strong, virile, all man. And I'm so incredibly turned on.

Nate sets me on the floor. "Get undressed."

He's already ripping off his clothes and I hurry to catch up.

The room is dark, lit only by the light of the hall, but even in the darkness, I know he's tracking my every move. I feel like his prey, and I love it.

The minute my dress hits the floor, his arms are around my waist. The next thing I know I'm on the bed on my knees.

Ripples of excitement tear through me.

Chest to chest, we both kneel before each other. Our heavy breathing is the only sound in the room. And this time when our lips collide, there's nothing gentle about it. Licking and stroking, both in equal amounts of desperation.

I can taste his hunger for me—it's there in the way his lips move, attacking mine with a vigor I've never felt from anyone before, the way his hand molds to my back, holding me in place, and the way he gasps when I press my body against his.

Those mesmerizing eyes meet mine. "Tell me what you want."

A need to give myself up to him bubbles to the surface. I want him to lead the way. I want to make sure he knows this. "I want you to own me. I want you to take me to places I've never gone."

With a groan, he drags his tongue down my neck at the same time his hand travels up my body and they both meet at my breast. He lifts his head. "Watch me, watch the way I devour your nipples."

My gaze greedily drops.

He doesn't waste any time tugging my nipple into his mouth, teasing me with his strokes. Both of my nipples immediately tighten at the contact. They are hard and aching and when his thumb passes over my other one, I suck in a breath.

His small bites are sharp jabs of pain relieved by his tongue lapping around my nipple and sucking it into his mouth.

I throw my head back and moan.

"You like that?"

A quiet "Yes" is all I can manage.

"Good." He moves to the other side where he starts with the teasing all over again.

My knees weaken as pleasure skates through my veins. I have to place my hands on his shoulders to stop from teetering.

Those luscious lips make their way to my neck, alternating between nips and sucks.

The slight pain followed by pleasure makes my whole body tremble.

His hand shifts lower and slips between my thighs. I am already soaking wet. I can feel it. And I know as soon as he does when I hear the noise of satisfaction that escapes his throat. His fingertips circle my clit.

Burning heat consumes me. Soft, light touches make me desperate for more.

As if he can read my mind, he dips his finger inside me. "This?"

"Yes," I breathe.

His touch is magic.

My fingers trace the length of his cock and I swear I feel his pulse leap at the contact.

There are no barriers between us as my fingers follow the angle of his erection and the freedom I feel is unyielding. I stroke with a power I can't suppress. He groans loudly in my ear when I circle his moist tip and hundreds of tiny darts of arousal shoot right to my sex.

In the next beat, he presses his chest to mine, pushing us both to the bed. He growls and moves closer. Pinning me with his arms, his tongue slips inside my mouth. As his mouth locks onto mine, I writhe beneath him in need.

My head is toward the footboard and he raises my wrists with just one hand, as the other moves my curls from my face.

Then his lips are gone, moving down my body, only stopping at my navel to circle my belly button before drifting farther down.

"Keep your hands over your head."

I want to touch him, to feel the stubble of his jawline, to run my fingers through his hair. Held like this, I can't do any of that. It makes me feel vulnerable, exposed, naked, but at the same time I'm filled with anticipation, excitement, and so turned on.

His descent is slow and torturous, but feels so good. His breath gusts over my clit and my body tenses in anticipation of what's to come. When his fingers open my pussy and he drives his tongue inside me, I forget all about my need to touch him.

My body unravels, uncoils—he's like doses of a sexual stimulant that I can't get enough of.

He slides his hands under my ass and lifts me right to his mouth, eating me with that hunger I've craved from a man. The way he drives his tongue into me with such force, makes me feel like I might explode.

He stops long enough to look up at me. "I want you to watch everything. Feel it with your mind and your body."

All I can do is nod. Before I have time to think too much about it, his mouth covers my clit again.

I don't watch for long.

My back arches and my thighs spread wider out of some sort of desperation to have him as far inside me as he can be. Suddenly, his fingers enter me, but his mouth stays on my clit, and the combination of the two push me to a place I've never been—one where pleasure almost makes you forget your own name.

Never have I felt this way before.

Intoxicated by sex.

I grab onto the polished wood of the footboard, slapping at it, pulling so hard I can hear it squeak.

"Let go." His tone is hoarse and guttural.

A cry leaks from my throat as everything I am disappears.

My body strains and I bite down on my lip to stop the sounds I can't control—the pain in no way a distraction from the pleasure coursing through me. If I thought I had ever come before in my life, I was wrong.

This feeling is sublime.

Something to never forget.

Something to live for.

Something that makes a person want to feel it over and over again. I can see now why people lock themselves into a room for days just to fornicate. And I'm feeling greedy like that too. I want more. I want to feel him fill me, stretch me, come inside me.

I reach for his cock.

"I told you to keep your hands in place. Zoey, you have to learn control."

The sound of his voice is domineering and if I thought it might be funny to disobey him before, I don't think so now. "I'm sorry."

"Never use those words when I'm fucking you. If you can't do as I ask, I want you to make up for it."

I swallow, secretly thrilled. "How do I do that?"

"I'll show you when the time is right. No more talking. I need to be inside you, now." His voice is hoarse and muffled as he works his way up my body with his lips. "I'm going to make you come again, but this time with my cock. Do you want that?"

"I do."

He rises off the bed and his eyes lock on mine for the briefest of seconds. The momentary softness, the shyness I see in them, makes my stomach flutter.

"Come over here."

I do as he says, already knowing he'll be there to guide me. As soon as I lower my feet to the floor his arms are around me and his lips are on mine.

"You wanted to touch me, do it now," he orders before drawing my lower lip into his mouth.

I flatten my palms to his chest and glide them down his torso, tracing his perfect definition along the way. I move lower still and with trembling fingers, I draw a line down his erection and then back up before gripping onto his cock. Once I do, I pump him. It's the most natural feeling in the world and the groan that he whispers into my mouth makes me wonder if he'll come in my hand. But I don't wonder for long.

"Turn around."

I don't think. I just do what he says.

The telltale sign of tearing alerts me he's putting a condom on. In the next moment, his hand lifts my hair off my neck and replaces it with his lips.

I lean into him, wrapping my arms around his neck and listening to his heavy breathing.

He's the air I need to breathe.

"Drop to your palms and crawl down the bed."

When I'm on all fours, his hands grip my hips, pulling me back toward him before he slides into me, fills me, makes me feel even more alive. Another cry, even louder than before, comes out of my mouth in a rush. He feels so good. This feels so good.

He thrusts in and out at a rapid pace.

I've been fucked in this position before, but never has it felt like this. My body is absorbing his cock—it's like we fit together in a way I've never fit with anyone.

"Are you okay with the bed now?" His tone is arrogant.

"Oh, yes," I answer, my voice quivering as flashes of joy, flickers of pleasure, sparks of bliss all radiate from my core and spread throughout my body, making my toes curl.

On the brink of my orgasm, I'm not ready for this to end. I want to ride out this feeling of ecstasy. Without thinking, I push myself back and his thrusts go deeper. His thick groan is music to my ears and only for a moment does his rhythm falter. I do it again and this time his groan is a sexy exhale, a spill of lust, and it unleashes his own need.

He clutches at my hips harder, his thrusts growing wilder.

A moment later his hand comes around and rubs my already swollen clit—pure elation is all I can feel. I close my eyes and fireworks flash where I used to see only fear. Desire consumes me, and raw need eats me up as my orgasm takes me to the brink of incoherency.

Nate stills and lets out a loud guttural groan, while at the same time color explodes behind my eyelids. He pulses inside me and we come together in a burst—pieces of my mind, body, and soul shatter and come back together over and over.

It's pure elation—a feeling of soaring high above the clouds with no landing in sight.

It's the way I've always wanted to feel.

16

Stood Up

Flames are licking at my skin as a burst of heat scorches through my body. I wake up with a jolt and look around. It's not a fire; it's the blazing rays of bright sunshine coming through the glass windows in Nate's bedroom. I reach across the bed and grab my phone to check the time—six twenty in the morning.

Nate's an early riser.

I look around—our clothes in small piles where they landed last night. His running shoes and shorts have also joined the heaps. He must have gone for a run and I missed him stripping out of his clothes.

Smiling at the thought, I stretch my tight limbs and grin even wider when I hear the pounding pressure of the water in the shower.

He's still here.

I'm suspended in the moment as the same flickering images I've had of him wet and in the shower shuffle through my mind. I stand and grab his white shirt off the ground to wrap myself in.

Then I patter in the bathroom and with the sight of Nate in the shower—I can barely breathe.

The clear glass is fogged and water drips down the smooth surface of the shower wall, blocking my full view—allowing me to only catch sight of the curves and contours of his beautiful silhouette.

He runs his hands through his hair, rinsing his shampoo.

I move closer and watch as the muscles in his arms tighten with every movement. Every inch of his naked body looks powerful. Every surface looks smooth and inviting.

When his eyes catch sight of me, he cracks a grin so wide, so amused, it makes my heart stop. "Do you want to stand there and watch, or are you going to join me?"

My water fantasy turning into reality takes away every single breath I have, and I'm momentarily left stunned.

"Zoey." He says my name like it amuses him. "Are you coming in?"

I nod and with deep calming breaths, I slip his shirt off then walk toward him. "Good morning. You're up early. Do you get up this early every morning?"

Soft lips touch my shoulder as I enter through one of the two open archways into the large marble-tiled shower.

Shivers run up my body at the sight of him up close, naked, gloriously wet, and hotter than ever.

"I have to stop and see my dad before going to work."

"So we have to be quick?"

He nods. "I'm going to fuck you hard and fast right here in the shower. Unless you're not a morning person?"

I take his lip between my teeth and bite down on it, not hard enough to bleed, but hard enough, and at the same time I reach down and stroke his already hard cock. "I am if I can wake up like this every morning."

"I think that can be arranged."

I smile at him but then he disappears, and so does my smile. It returns moments later when he does, with a condom already opened in hand.

His hands go right between my thighs and soon after his cock follows.

He's hard already.

Really hard.

His thrusts are quick and when he urges me to wrap my legs around his waist, he buries himself deeper than anything I've ever felt.

So deep.

My orgasm hits without warning. My muscles clench around his cock as I come—every part of me shattering into a thousand pieces.

"Oh fuck, Zoey, you feel so good." He tucks his face in my neck. His groan, his sexy voice, they reverberate through my body, the pleasure spreading through my veins, the feeling so absolute I can't breathe, I can't think—all I can do is feel.

Just what I want.

I run my fingers through his wet hair.

He lifts his head and finds my mouth. His kiss is soft and gentle.

I know I'll never forget this time with him.

"I have to go," he murmurs over my lips.

"Will you bring me back to the club tonight?"

He pulls me tight to him, tighter than when we were joined. His laugh tickles my ear. "Not tonight—tonight I'm taking you someplace else."

"But I'd like to go back to the club." I nip at his lip.

"Not tonight." He nips me back harder.

"Okay. Are you taking me to meet your father then?"

He shakes his head and steps out of the shower. Grabbing two fluffy white towels, he hands one to me. "You're full of questions this morning."

He wraps the towel around his waist and vacates the bathroom. "Nate?"

"Zoey, I have to go."

I dry myself off and wrap the towel around my head before slipping my arms through his shirt that I left on the floor earlier. The soft fabric feels good against my naked skin, and I can't help but breathe in his scent that's so familiar, so fresh, so clean. It smells like something else I can't identify.

"I have to run," he calls from the bedroom and I can hear his feet pounding down the stairs.

And just like that he's gone—no "Good-bye, honey," no kiss on the cheek, no "Have a great day," no "I'll miss you" or "See you tonight." But then again, I shouldn't expect anything more. This is an agreed-upon summer fling. Anything else, any other emotions, weren't negotiated and aren't wanted by either party anyway.

The pitter-patter of rain on the glass is soothing, and I sit on the side of the bed to watch it for a bit.

It's then I realize my foreboding isn't about Nate. It's remnants of my family legacy that won't stop haunting me. Those dark thoughts keep bleeding through the shield I've been building. I didn't wake up thinking today might be my last day on earth, so my subconscious must be trying to cast its shadow on me.

I try to push it aside, try to embrace the hope that has bloomed within me. Some kind of wish that if something is going to happen to me, it won't happen until the summer is over.

I desperately want this time with Nate to get to experience a different side of life—one where touch overrules emotion.

Glancing back at the mussed-up pillows and tangled sheets that Nate and I created last night, I can't hold back my smile. I drag a pillow to my chest and smell it. It smells like him, like summer rain. That's it. That's what he smells like.

A sharp intake of breath has me turning at the sound.

There he stands, leaning against the doorframe in a black suit, gray shirt, no tie and holding a latté in his hand. With his eyes wide, watching, wandering, he strides toward me, the smell of summer rain drifting through the air.

He sets the cup down and I stare up at him in surprise. "I thought you left. I heard the door—"

My back is on the bed and he's prowling up my body before I can finish.

Mischief glitters in his eyes as he brushes his mouth against mine. "I forgot something."

My towel falls off my head, and his hands are in my hair. "My coffee?" I laugh.

He licks my lips to part them, then strokes his tongue against mine. "No, not that. I told you, I'm really not good at this shit. I forgot to say good-bye properly."

I loop my arms around his neck and squeeze him to me as our mouths fuse in a good-bye kiss that's as good as anything I've ever seen in the movies. When he nips at my lip, I know our time is up. He rises onto his forearms and just looks at me, stares at me for what seems like the longest time. Then he swipes a piece of hair from my face. "You really are beautiful."

I let my head fall to the side in wonder.

He makes me feel like the sexiest thing he's ever seen.

He turns my chin back to face him. "I mean it."

"I believe you," I answer breathlessly.

He dips down and licks my top lip then sucks on it. He does the same to my bottom lip before locking his mouth on mine one final time. Soft, smooth, and gentle—a kiss to join the other one I'll never forget. "I think you should know something. I've never had a girlfriend."

His confession shocks me both with what he said and the fact that he told me. "Never?"

He shakes his head, and I see a little bit of that shyness I've caught glimpses of. "Honestly, I've just always seen women as a lot of work and even more heartache. I don't believe in love and marriage. And I always thought that's why women wanted relationships... until I met you."

His hair falls forward, and I push it from his face. "You know love is a lot of work. I'd say that's probably a pretty accurate assessment."

His laugh is dry. "You're not going to try to get into my head with all your psychology talk?"

I stroke my hands through his soft, silky hair some more. "Once upon a time, I would have jumped all over a statement like that. But no matter how much we try to change things, we'll end up where we're supposed to be. So if you're meant to be with someone, you will be."

He shakes his head. "Destiny."

I nod. "Yes—destiny."

He sits up. "Let's agree to disagree. I don't believe anyone's fate is laid out for them like you think it is."

"But you understand that I do?"

"I do," he whispers.

At an impasse that won't ever be resolved, I reach for my mug.

He rises off the bed and strides across the room. This time he turns around. "I'll be home by seven."

Murphy's Law is if something can go wrong, it will. I've always put credence in the philosophy, and it sits right up there in my mind with *Nothing is as easy as it looks*, and Heinlein's *It is impossible to make anything foolproof, because fools are so ingenious.*

Later that day, with a quick look at the clock, I'm surprised to see it's seven forty-five in the evening.

Now that's not super late by any means, but I'm surprised Nate hasn't called. I grab my phone and check for a text or a message—none.

With a deep breath, I decide to call him. It goes right to voice mail.

"This is Nathaniel Hanson. Leave a message."

"Hey, Nate, it's me. Just checking on you to make sure everything is okay or that I didn't get the time wrong."

I hang up.

Dressed in a deep V neckline, cherry-red chiffon dress that cinches at the waist and hits mid thigh, I sit at the kitchen bar and toss my snakeskin pumps off.

Anger and fear.

Two emotions I've carried inside me since the day I turned twenty-seven—no, since the day my brother died. Yet, the anger I feel right now is different. It isn't laced with fear. I have to be watchful to not let it get a hold of me. Nate doesn't owe me anything—except the same courtesy he'd extend to anyone else.

I stare at the blank computer screen of my brother's laptop for fifteen minutes, and then his e-mail pings. I click on Gmail and wait for it to load.

I moved my things back to Nate's this morning and spent the day going through all of Zach's e-mails. The only thing I found to help shed any light on what the Artist's role at the club is all about was an e-mail Zach sent to someone named the Photographer almost a year ago. He was asking to meet with him. The Photographer responded that he'd be happy to, and they set up a meeting at a coffee shop in Wynwood.

Not knowing what else to do, I e-mailed the Photographer from Zach's account and explained who I was. I told him I'd like to talk to him, but kept it at that so as not to scare him away. As Gmail loads and I click to the alternate identity, I can't believe it's the Photographer's response. The message reads.

From: The Photographer
Subject: Meeting
Date: July 2 2014 19:19 EST
To: The Artist

I would be happy to meet with you anytime. I'm usually at the Ballroom every weeknight between eight and ten. Just ask the bartender for Leo, the Photographer. He'll point you in my direction.

I reread the message over and over as my fingers tap on the countertop.

At ten after eight, I call Nate one last time and get his voice mail again. Something must have come up at work.

I stare at the screen a few more minutes and when I start to feel a little flustered that he couldn't at least call me, I decide to make a trip to the Ballroom.

With the prospect of learning a little more about my brother, I stand up, grab my purse, and head out the door to meet the Photographer.

17

Confessions

In the car, I keep the radio turned off, my mind replaying that meeting with Jordan Scott last night. She was a bit snooty. I can't see Zach putting up with that for long.

When my phone rings, I assume it must be Nate and answer it without even looking at the screen.

"Hello, Zoey." Dr. Raymond's voice crosses the line with a cheerful greeting.

"Hi, Dr. Raymond."

"How are you? I'm sorry I couldn't take your call earlier. My schedule today has been a killer."

As I drive over the bridge, I can't help but notice how the high winds seem to make the sturdy signs flap a little.

"Oh, don't worry about it. Look, I was just calling to tell you I've decided to stay in Miami for the summer."

"You have? Can I ask what influenced your decision?"

"A number of things."

"Do you think this is wise?"

"Yes. Nate asked me to stay, and I want to stay."

"What prompted his request?"

"I'm not really sure, but once I told him about my fears concerning the Twenty-Seven Club, things started to change. And I know you must think it's pity, but it's not. He's the first person who hasn't looked at me like I am crazy. Instead, he told me to make a list of things I wanted to do in my life. You know, he even told me it wasn't a bucket list, that I should look at my situation a little differently."

"And?"

"He's right."

"Bravo, then! Such a big step for you."

"Don't get too excited. I'm not sure what it means."

"That's okay. At least you're willing to explore your feelings outside the narrow spectrum you had created for yourself before you left."

"Well, not really. Like me, he's not interested in having a relationship, but is willing to help me accomplish some things I'd like to experience in my life."

"I'm glad to hear you've thought about this. Would you like to share them with me?"

My cheeks start to flame. "I'm not sure I can tell you over the phone."

Her laugh is low, but I can still hear it. "Pretend you're lying on my chaise."

I blurt out. "I want to have unconventional sex."

The line is quiet for a bit. Then she clears her throat. "I'm not going to ask you to go into detail. But I want to warn you to tread carefully. You know that I am completely on your side. And I think a change of scenery and a change of pace is just what you need. But remember, temporary means temporary."

I slow down as I turn onto Ocean Drive and hit the bumper-to-bumper traffic. "I know that. I'm not looking for anything more."

"Zoey, I'd like to tell you it all sounds fabulous but again I'd like to advise you to proceed with caution. You are still in a fragile state, and you don't need any more heartbreak in your life."

"I get what you're saying, Dr. Raymond, but I know what I'm doing."

"I hope you do." Her tone is more one of concern than condescension.

The neon sign reading THE BALLROOM comes into view. "I do. I promise."

"Did you find someone there to talk to? If not I could ask around and send you a recommended list."

"No, I haven't. But I was hoping to keep my sessions with you. Can I call you at my scheduled visit times?"

"Yes, we can do that. But think about finding someone there. It will be more beneficial for you."

"I will."

"Take care, Zoey," she says, and the line goes dead.

The light ahead turns red, and for a moment I close my eyes, thinking about everything Dr. Raymond just said. But this thing I arranged with Nate is for me—it's just fun and sex, nothing else. I won't end up even more broken when I go home. My eyes fly open as soon as my thoughts register—I'm actually thinking about the future and not the dread of the 27 Club.

Beep-beep.

Horns honk from behind me and I press the gas. A few minutes later, I pull up and leave the car with the valet and then come to a dead stop when the line is just as long, if not longer, than last night. Okay, I have a choice to make—wait in the line or drop Nate's name with the bouncer. Since I don't have a reservation, there would be no reason for anyone to call Nate.

I opt not to wait.

The night is breezy and my chiffon dress is blowing all over the place, causing catcalls from onlookers. I hold the skirt as tight to my legs as I can and approach the bouncer. It's not the same guy, but just like the one sitting in the chair last night, his eyes rake my body from head to toe.

"Can I help you?" He extends his palm, stopping the clubbers in the entry line.

They are not happy with me.

"Hi." I push my hair from my face and my dress gives a little show.

Great.

I leave my hair alone and tug the ends of my hem. "I'm here to meet the Photographer."

His eyes narrow in on me. "Do you have a membership card?"

"I'm Nate Hanson's guest."

Technically I am—at his house anyway.

He stares at me for what seems like forever and then finally unlatches the velvet rope and allows me entry.

Nate's name seems quite recognizable.

Nate told me he didn't frequent the Estate, but we never discussed the Ballroom. Yet, somehow images of Nate pulling a John Travolta under the disco ball don't quite seem like him.

I doubt that if he comes here it's for the dancing.

The sound of a dance beat to a popular techno song I can't quite place thumps loudly in my ears. Watching all the people who came here to let loose and have fun puts a smile on my face.

It's early, so the crowd is just filling in. I make my way to the bar and take a seat on one of the funky-shaped barstools. I spend a little more time inspecting the club than I did last night. It's a mix of art deco and techno—the combination is sensual and appealing. Neon colors in sunburst shapes with inlays and mirrors are everywhere. It reminds me of what a real disco might have looked like in the seventies, just more modern—Studio 54 meets the Jetsons.

"What can I get you?"

I twist around, and a cool sensation whispers up my legs.

This dress is a little shorter and has a lot less stretch than I'm used to.

At Nate's I didn't realize just how much thigh was showing when I sat down, but now I feel a little uncomfortable. I lean forward, tugging my hem down again, and my locket clinks on the bar when my sheer sleeves hit the slick surface.

The bartender's eyes go right to the low V of my dress and I'm sure, by the way his eyes flare, he can see my flesh-toned lace bra.

Not good.

"I'll have a cranberry juice."

"Cran-vodka?"

"No, just the juice."

His grin is tight. "Working tonight?"

"No," I gasp.

He laughs. "I don't mean what you think. It's just most people who come in here and aren't drinking usually have to go back to work. That's all."

Compared to most of the women in here, I am dressed more skimpily in some ways, but overdressed in others. My dress is short, but has sleeves. As I look around, the majority of the women are wearing some kind of suit and their jackets are removed, revealing sexy lingerielike tops—pencil skirts with spaghetti strap camisoles, short loose-fitting skirts with tight white blouses, and pants with sheer tops.

Demure but sexy—like a naughty librarian.

I actually like the way they're dressed.

I'll have to keep it in mind the next time I go shopping.

Out of nowhere, I start to wonder if Nate's assistant looks like these women.

My heart drums loudly in my ears at the thought, and an image I can't erase burns in my mind—Nate's eyes are closed, his head is thrown back, and his assistant, or his secretary, whatever she's called, is on her knees in front of him with his cock lodged firmly in her mouth—the same look of pleasure on his face as I saw last night.

"Here you go. One strong cranberry. Don't sip it too fast."

I shake the stomach-wrenching image away and sit back, crossing my legs.

What's wrong with me?

"Thank you."

"Can I get you anything else? Maybe a chaser to go along with your juice?"

I laugh and lean forward again. "Can you point me in the direction of the Photographer?"

The bartender's dark hair flops in his face and his blue eyes narrow on me. "I knew you looked familiar. You've been here before."

I sip my drink and stare back at him. "Nope. First time, but I'm meeting Leo. Can you point him out to me?"

His blue-eyed gaze roams over me and then settles on my eyes. "He's sitting in a booth near the dance floor. Blond hair, horn-rimmed glasses. He's wearing a checked scarf."

"Thank you." I twist to the side and reach in my purse to pay for my drink.

He flicks his hand. "Don't worry about it. It's on the house. And I'm here all night, if you change your mind about him."

I start to say *It's not what you think*, but does it really matter what he thinks?

I walk away and then turn back to see that he's staring at me, so I give him a quick wave. He winks back, and I have to laugh. I've never been one for the club scene, never had the time and was never really interested, but this feels somewhat liberating to walk into a bar and have attention diverted in my direction. Whether the cute young bartender is paid to act like that or not, it felt good for those few moments to have someone flirt with me.

Finding the Photographer is easy.

He's just where cute bartender boy said he'd be, and he's alone. I approach the booth and for once, my nerves aren't jumping.

"Hi," I say loudly over the music.

His gaze lifts from his phone and rises to his feet. "Hi, I'm Leo. You must be Z's sister."

"Zoey." I shake his offered hand. "Nice to meet you."

"Sit." He motions his head toward one side of the U-shaped bench.

I set my drink down and take a seat.

His grin is slow, but once it plasters across his face, he points to my glass. "Can I buy you another?"

"No, I'm good. I haven't finished this one."

He leans closer. "Zoey, how can I help you? Are you looking to get your photo taken?"

I shake my head no.

"Pity, I was already framing the pictures in my mind."

I shrug. "Sorry."

"How I can help you then?"

"I was hoping you could tell me a little about your business? How it works?"

"So . . ." He pauses as if thinking and then moves closer to me. "Sorry, it's loud in here. Are you interested in taking your brother's business over? Is that what this is about?"

"No."

He pauses again, waiting for me to say more, but I don't. I feel like he's not going to tell me what I want unless I play this game of cat and mouse with him.

He takes a sip of his beer, and my eyes flash to it. The label reads Wynwood Brewing Company. The bottle is black and the label purple and white—eye-catching. He makes a humming noise as he sets his bottle down. "You have to give me a little more, sweetheart. I can't just tell you all about my business without knowing why. Hell, I can't even be sure you're who you say you are. For all I know, you could be the feds looking to shut me down."

My eyes meet his and I make sure to sit up straight so my dress stays put. "I work at a college and until recently, I'd never even heard of this place. So I can promise you that I'm not here to take you down."

He laughs and runs his fingers up my thigh. "A schoolteacher. Oh, the pictures I could take of you."

I brush his hand away. "Can I be honest?"

"Is there any other way?"

I squirm a little in my seat. "Leo, I'm here to figure out what my brother did at the Estate, not for any other reason." My tone is stern. This man's flirting isn't in the least appealing to me. Cute bartender boy's harmless flirting was one thing, but this man has an endgame in mind, and I'm not interested.

He settles back in the booth and his earring glimmers in the light. "If you haven't figured that out yet, sweetheart, I'm not sure you want to know any more."

I fumble through my purse and pull my brother's business card out. I slide it across the table. "How does the business work? That's what I want to know. Can you help me or not?"

Nobody can hear us, nobody knows what we're discussing, yet he inches even closer and rests an elbow on the table turning in my direction. "I liked your brother, so I'll help you out. But in the future, you don't show up at someone's office hours unless you're looking to do real business."

Office hours?

"Great, I'd appreciate as much information as you can give me."

His lips tilt further and I wonder if his smile will split his face. "How about I tell you a little about my own business? You can extrapolate anyway you like. I don't feel comfortable talking about someone else's business."

"Can I get you another drink?" a girl in short shorts and a cropped top asks us.

"I'm good." I smile at her.

"We'll both have another of these." He raises his bottle.

"I'll bring them right over." She walks away and Leo's eyes follow her ass, cheeks showing and all.

It makes my skin crawl.

"I did that for your benefit. That's what you think of me, right? That I'm some horny motherfucker who can't get enough ass."

"No, I don't. You're acting like an asshole, but I'm not really sure why. I'm not a threat to you."

His gaze brightens. "Boom! You're Z's sister, that's for certain. I just had to make sure."

I blink, realization dawning that he was testing me, and I passed.

"Here you go, two Wynwood Brews. Enjoy." The waitress slides the bottles on the table and turns away.

He slides mine closer.

I give him a smile.

"I saw you staring at my bottle. You seemed interested in trying it."

I lift the beer. "Thank you." I sip it. "Um, it's good."

"The best." He clinks my bottle. "Liked that brother of yours. I'm sorry about what happened to him."

"So you knew him?"

"I did. I helped him set up his business. He was extremely anxious. Said he might not have a lot of time. That was a little less than a year ago, but it's not like we kept in touch."

Not much time—so he did *believe.*

I must have made a face, because Leo says, "It's not what you think."

Feeling guilty and defeated, I slouch in my seat. "Honestly, I don't know what to think."

He places his hand over mine. "Listen, honey, let me put your mind at ease. We don't do this kind of work for the sex. It's for the art of it. You see this—" He waves his arms around the club. "This is for the sex." Then he points to the entrance for the Estate. "Being inside there isn't about the sex for us. It's about the craft. It's a way to utilize what we love and couldn't succeed in with our day jobs. At night we're kings, whereas during the days, we're just part of the court. Make sense?"

"It does." He's shed a new light on things, and I can understand my brother's work in a different way. All this time I thought my brother had turned onto a different road, but maybe there was never a road to turn off of. He was who he was. He painted a picture for me and I saw what he wanted me to see. Perhaps the real Zach, the one who did this for a living, was just as happy with his job, his work, and with his life as the picture he painted for me.

They were just different.

After I learned the house wasn't his, I thought he lied to me. But now, after talking to Leo, I think he knew me, knew I wouldn't be able to accept his money if he had been honest with me.

And because he knew me so well, he lied so that I would accept his money.

Leo peels the label from his bottle and then looks up. "I take pictures. I take pictures of women naked, sometimes alone, sometimes with their husbands, sometimes with other women—pictures women want to give their husbands. I take pictures of couples posing seductively for each other, having sex, eating strawberries, whatever they want. To them it is something they want to look at and remember forever. And sometimes the couple needs more. Sometimes they want me to join them, sometimes watch, sometimes the husband wants me to fuck his wife so he can get off. But everything I do, I do at the couple's request. I don't judge. I understand every relationship needs something to keep it alive and if my craft, my photos help—all the better. It's a win-win. I get to do what I love, have a little fun, and make a lot of money. No one gets hurt."

"So my brother did the same thing, except instead of photographing, he sketched?"

Leo shakes his head. "I'm not sure what he did. Your brother was a lot more private than I am. No one around here really knew him. But he was close to one girl though. You could ask her about him."

"Do you know her name?"

"Sorry, I'm really bad with names."

Zach never mentioned a special girl or a girlfriend and he was always one to tell me when he was crushing on a girl.

My spine begins to tingle at the very moment Leo's eyes flash up. He springs to his feet. "Mr. Hanson, how can I help you?"

My heart literally stops. My head snaps to see Nate, hands on his hips, and a furrow in his brow that is anything but confusion.

"Zoey," he bites out through his clenched teeth.

I rise to my feet and look at Leo. "Thank you for meeting with me. I appreciate your time."

Leo nods, but his gaze is still on Nate.

Nate isn't looking at Leo though. I know where his gaze is—I can feel it burning right through me. Purposely not looking at Nate as my anger builds, I say, "I'll leave you two to your business."

His hand wraps around my upper arm and he pulls me toward him. "I'm not here to see Leo, and you know it."

"Do I?" My sarcasm isn't really me, and I reel it in.

"Look, I fucked up, but that doesn't give you the right to do something I strictly forbade you from doing."

"Forbade?" I hiss.

"You know what I mean," he sneers.

"No, tell me."

"I don't want to do this here. Let's go home."

Home.

Emotions begin to shift inside me.

My anger dissipates as quickly as it rose up—toward him and my brother.

Relief takes its place.

I feel relieved. I'm okay with the life my brother led. I have to believe he was doing what he wanted, and the money was an added benefit for him.

But with that relief, fear also rises.

Death doesn't care about happiness—it strikes when it's ready.

The air in the club feels suffocating, and I have to get out of here. I shrug out of Nate's hold and walk toward the exit. My pulse is racing and my vision seems a little blurry, but I realize it's just the strobe lights.

With each step, that old nagging worry rises beneath my feet.

What am I even doing here?

Destiny's out there and it's coming for me. Happiness won't stop it.

"Zoey!" he yells.

I don't stop.

I can't.

I just keep walking.

Finally, I'm breathing the fresh air that I so desperately need.

Joining the 27 Club isn't something you get to decide.

Trying to fight off the looming darkness, I start running.

I need to escape my own thoughts.

My heels clack along the concrete.

I run faster, passing people on the street.

Beep-beep! Beep-beep!

As my body goes on alert, I snap my head to the right.

Beep-beep! Beep-beep!

The noise is coming from a car speeding through the intersection. Its headlights blind me. I hear people screaming. I look around and then I realize I'm in the middle of the street.

Beep-Beep! Beep-beep!

My breath leaves me in a gasp. All I can see is the sleek black surface headed for me.

This is it. My time has come.

I hadn't imagined dying being hit by a car, but it makes sense—the tragedy of it all.

I'm not ready.

The car skids before me.

Suddenly, an arm is scooping me up. I'm off the ground in one moment and being set onto the sidewalk in the next.

The car had already screeched to a stop.

"Hey, is she all right?"

I turn around to see the man from behind the wheel getting out of the car.

"Yeah, I got her. Sorry about that, man."

"She came out of nowhere. Is she okay?" The driver sounds upset.

"She's fine. She didn't get hit."

The man nods and gets back in his car.

Nate's eyes narrow at me. "Are you out of your fucking mind?"

My body is trembling. "I think I am."

I almost died.

I could be dead right now.

"What's going on with you?" Nate's voice sounds stern and concerned at the same time.

I look up at him. "I just realized whether you're happy or sad is irrelevant if it's your time to die."

He scrunches his brows. "What are you talking about?"

"Nate, don't you get it? I thought that maybe my brother's destiny had been bestowed on him because he was unhappy. I don't think he was anymore. And somewhere in the back of my mind, I thought that if I could, for once in my life, be happy, I wouldn't die. But, I was wrong."

Nate shakes me. "Zoey, I want you to stop all this. Your brother would not want you dwelling on shit you can't control. Fuck, take each day that you have and live it. Stop this bullshit about dying."

My legs are wobbly and I use the building for support. Before I can manage to trace a brick or two with my fingers, his big hands clutch my arms and those green eyes stare into mine. I freeze. The pain in his face is so unexpected. "You're right. I can't control my fate."

His grip tightens, sinking into my flesh. "I don't want you to appease me. I want you to stop thinking that way."

I twist my head from side to side. "I can't."

He shakes me again. "You can. You can do what we discussed and live for the moment. Stop dwelling on your brother's death, and stop thinking about your own. It isn't healthy."

I nod, agreeing that it isn't in the least bit healthy.

But I can't stop it from happening.

Silence.

A long silence.

Then Nate takes my hand. "Come on, let's go for a walk."

We stroll for a long while, up the busy street, past shops, restaurants, and bars. I'd almost forgotten to ask him about the girl Leo mentioned. But then I turn to him, noticing his profile is just as beautiful as the rest of him. "Nate, do you know if my brother had a girlfriend?"

He turns to stare at me. "He dated a lot of girls. But as far as I know, there wasn't anyone in particular. Why do you ask?"

"Leo mentioned a girl he had seen Zach with."

"Your brother was always with girls."

"Yeah, I guess you're right."

He comes to a stop in front of a gray concrete building with a brown and red sign that reads, Segafredo Espresso. "It's not Las Olas Cafe, but it's pretty close."

I look up at him. "I'll take it."

The coffee shop has upholstered sofas scattered throughout, and I take a seat at one of them. Melding into the cushion, I feel my anxiety ease.

"A latté?" Nate asks.

"Surprise me."

He walks up to the counter and my break from reality seems like a distant memory. He's right. I know he is. I need to stop dwelling. When it happens, I can't control it. That begs the question—do I stay for the summer or go home? Is it fair to Nate to bring him into my life and rip myself from his when my time arrives? My mind wanders, evaluating my two options. In the end, I can't see myself leaving Nate before the summer's end. After all he knows, just like me, what to expect at the end of this fling—an already agreed-upon parting of ways.

A black mug sitting on a red napkin is set in front of me. On top of the froth is the most perfect heart-shaped latté art. And beside the cup is a chocolate.

It has to be an invitation to stay.

Nate bends at the waist. "An espresso macchiato just for you."

"You're the best," I tell him with a huge grin.

He sits down across from me. The tension is gone from his face. With an espresso shot in his hand he says, "Look, Zoey. I'm sorry for talking to you like that, but you have to stop this."

"I know."

He narrows his eyes at me.

"I do. I don't know what that was about. Too much focus on my brother's death, I think. You're right; I just need to leave it alone. And I'm in no place to judge."

"What does that mean?" He sets his cup down.

"What we're doing makes me happy. Maybe that was what he was doing, going after what made him happy."

"Let's talk about what we're doing."

"What is there to talk about?"

"How about I start with I'm sorry I was late. We signed the deal I was working on tonight and the final details kept me occupied."

I put my hand up. "You don't need to explain. I'm not your girlfriend."

His mouth thins. "What if I want you to be?"

"I thought we talked about this." I look down. My espresso is hot and I blow on it, trying not to ruin the heart.

"No, I told you I'd never had a girlfriend."

"I assumed that meant you weren't interested in one."

"And you're okay with that?"

I sip my drink and let the warm liquid slide down my throat. "Nate, I am. We decided I'd stay for the summer. I don't need to label our relationship."

"You weren't pissed when I didn't show up tonight?"

I study him. "I was a little upset."

"So you took off and went somewhere I told you not to go?"

"Not because I was mad at you."

"I want you to be more than a little upset about that. I want you to be fucking pissed at me." Nate voice is low but harsh.

"I don't understand."

He sets his cup down and comes to sit next to me. "You want me to do things with you you've never done. I want to do those things with you more than you know. But, I've gone from woman to woman, engaged in consensual arrangements with no ties for as long as I can remember. I can't be like that with you."

"Why not? We said no strings."

"Look, I can't explain it. It just doesn't feel right. I don't believe in love, that's never going to change, but that doesn't mean I can't be with a woman for a couple of months and do more than fuck her."

I stare at him, not sure what to say.

"You think you're going to die, right?"

I swallow, my eyes stinging from holding back the tears.

"For the sake of this conversation, let's just say I don't disagree with you. Let me make these next couple months everything you've wanted. What do you have to lose?"

Nate is right that I have nothing to lose.

I lean over and kiss him. "Yes."

"Yes, what?"

"Yes, I'll be your girlfriend, but you do realize that makes you my boyfriend."

His flinches, subconsciously I'm sure, and I let it go and kiss him again.

"We should go," he whispers. "And just so you know, I'm still pissed as hell at you for going there tonight."

I try to apologize, but before I can say anything he's striding toward the door.

We walk in silence back to the club. The wind has picked up again and when my dress flies up, his hands quickly move to hold it down.

I press my palms to the sides of my thighs. "I've got it."

When we turn the corner, I see the Range Rover is being held in front of the valet stand.

I point to it. "Why is your car parked there still and why does everyone at the club know who you are?"

His body stiffens, but his response comes quickly. "Because I own it."

My mouth drops open. Closes without a sound. Opens again but the only word to escape my lips is, "What?"

"I own it."

"Oh my God! How could you not have told me that?"

Face now tight, frustration seeps into his expression. "When exactly should I have mentioned it—before or after you demanded I fuck you in one of the rooms to prove to you I'm interested in you?"

My hand flies to my mouth and my dress goes up with it.

"You said you'd never lie..." I let my words trail off, feeling like an idiot for believing him.

"I know what you're thinking and you're wrong."

I shake my head, willing any tears to vanish. I don't need to cry again.

"I didn't lie. I've never been with anyone in one of those rooms. I've never blindfolded, handcuffed, flogged, or whipped anyone inside that club."

The words would have been funny in any other context, but not here, not now. "So why do you own a sex club if you're not interested in using it?"

"Do you know what I do, Zoey? What my business does?"

"You deal in real estate."

Shaking his head, the lines on his face remain strained. "Not just real estate. I buy businesses in Miami that are faltering and put them back together then sell them for a profit. I bought this club last year when the owner wanted out quick."

"You're like a Robin Hood?"

He seems to cringe a little at the description. "No, not at all. I don't steal from the rich and give to the poor. I just see potential in every business and put the right people in place to run it, turn it around, and sell it for a profit."

"Oh, like Richard Gere in *Pretty Woman*?"

His brows furrow. "What the fuck are you talking about?"

Obviously he's never seen the movie, so I drop it.

Examining his expression for any sign of deceit, I see none. But curiosity does bubble up in me. "If you don't go to the club, how do you know the Photographer?"

"If you're talking about Leo, he owns a photography studio near the gallery and that's how I know him. I had no idea he contracted with the club."

I cross my arms over my chest, trying to absorb all of this. "And you didn't know what my brother was doing here?"

Irritated now, Nate glares at me. "No. I already told you I didn't. I'm not involved in the day-to-day operations."

I look up at him. "I want to believe you."

Nate takes his jacket off and wraps it around me. "You have no reason not to."

"I know."

"Now let's get off the street and finish talking in private."

I search his troubled face. "Is there more?"

He takes my hand without answering, but then looks down at me. "Later."

With my palm firmly in his, he leads me the rest of the way to his car. We cover the short distance quickly.

Once inside, I take his jacket off since I'm feeling extremely hot.

He goes around to his side and when he gets in, he starts the car and floors the accelerator, pushing out into the oncoming traffic. At lightning speed he does a U-turn.

I look over. "What about your dad's car?"

His expression is neutral. "I'll have someone drop it off at the house."

"Are you sure? I can drive home. I only had a sip of beer."

The noise he makes is almost a growl. "If you didn't come here tonight because you were mad at me, why did you come when I asked you not to? Why didn't you wait for me?"

"You told me not to go to the Estate without you. I went to the club." My stomach does a strange sort of twist as I know what just came out of my mouth is only a play on words.

Nate grits his jaw, and his fists tighten around the steering wheel. "Come on, Zoey, I know you're smarter than that. Tell me—is what's really going on here the fact that you want to be with other men? Is this new awakening of yours more than about me? Because I'll tell you right now—I don't share."

I freeze where I sit.

My muscles stiffen as I stare over at him in astonishment. "No!

I just wanted to find out about my brother and okay, so maybe when you didn't show up, I might have known it would piss you off that I went there. I'm sorry."

He runs a hand through his hair and it just makes him even more handsome to me. "I told you not to say *I'm sorry.*"

I drop my gaze. "You said not to say that when we were in bed."

"No, you're not to say that for anything other than something like breaking my coffeemaker."

I laugh and lift my eyes. "I'd be sorry for sure if I did."

"Or, I'm sorry I backed into your car pulling out of the driveway."

I wince at that. "I get it. I get it."

His serious gaze locks on me.

He is so damn sexy.

I hate how much I want him right now.

"So, how do I apologize then?"

"I'll teach you." The look on his face sends sparks skipping down my spine. With intensity gleaming in his eyes, he reaches over and pulls my lips to his.

My entire lower body pulsates in need.

The kiss is quick but the point he's making is clear: I want to be with him and he wants to be with me. We are both going to mess up and that's okay. We have two months together and I want to spend it tasting his lips on mine, with his breath on me, and wrapped in his arms. Not arguing and fighting and worrying about things that, once I'm gone, won't really be important anyway.

He surprises me when he reaches in the back seat and drops a bag on my lap. "I was also late because I wanted to stop and buy you something."

I stare down at the beautifully wrapped gift.

"Aren't you going to open it?" he asks.

The bright orange bag in my lap with the words HERMÈS PARIS printed on the front makes me a little nervous.

I've never owned anything from a store like that.

With trembling fingers, I reach inside and pull out two tissue-wrapped packages. I open the first one and my heart crashes right into my rib cage as it does wheelies around my chest.

It's a large turquoise-printed scarf with pictures of birds all over it. I open it to see the entire scenic screen-print. It's one big square with two lovebirds on branches, repeated in various locations. "It's exquisite," I say out loud, my throat clenching as I clutch the beautiful silk fabric.

I don't dare look over at Nate, for fear I won't be able to turn my attention back to the other package in my lap. This one is smaller, and I open it faster. It's a solid turquoise matching silk scarf, but this one is long and narrow.

My pulse joins in the fun, and it's now chasing after my heart.

I can't control my excitement the moment I figure out just what these are for.

A blush covers my cheeks and I turn toward him. "Oh my God, you're a naughty boy."

18
Naughty Boy

Nate remains quiet the rest of the drive until he pulls into a local Chinese takeout restaurant. When he puts the car in park, he turns toward me and says, "I'll be right back."

I sit in the car and wait on pins and needles for what seems like forever.

Ever since I opened the scarves, or *bindings*, he hasn't so much as glanced over at me. I think he's still brooding about me going to the club.

The door opens and he sets a bag on the floor in the back seat. The next ten minutes are also driven in complete silence. We pull into the garage and get out of the car, go into the house, and he sets the bag on the kitchen counter.

I hold the shopping bag in my hands.

"Are you hungry?" He glances at me and then removes the small white containers from the bag.

"Not really."

He shrugs and throws a few sets of chopsticks on the counter.

"Are you going to talk to me?"

His gaze flicks down as he sets the spring rolls next to the takeout. In the very next moment, he yanks me close, crunching the orange bag between us. One hand presses flat against my back, while the other one quickly swoops under the short hemline of my dress, sneaking right into my panties. His eyes summon mine in the most hypnotic way. "I'd rather fuck you right now, if you want to know the truth."

Shock pings through me, and I gasp as my arousal coats his fingers when he slides one inside me. It feels like sparks flicker across the folds of my sex as he rubs his palm over it, sliding just that one single finger in and out—teasing me.

Then just as quickly, too quickly, he removes his hand.

His eyes still burning into mine, he puts his finger in his mouth, the one that was inside me, and sucks on it.

Holy hell.

Blazing heat consumes me.

Nate holds my stare for a beat, a pause, forever, until I crack. "I'm . . . good with that."

He pulls back, still no sign of a smile, but his gaze burns bright.

Hungry.

Savage even.

He takes me by the hand, fingers laced together, and leads me up the stairs.

I clutch hard at the bag in my fingers, as my pulse races to escape its frantic pace in every hollow of my body—my stomach, my throat, my wrists, between my thighs.

Once we get up the stairs, he stops beside the bed and pulls me to him—one hand behind my head, the other just below my breast.

The heat I feel from his palms brands me.

Before I know what's happening, his hands clutch the V of my dress and he rips it open, right down the middle, and shoves it off my shoulders.

The orange bag falls to the ground with it.

"I liked that dress." My words come out in short, harsh pants.

I know my eyes must look wild—my body even wilder.

"I'll buy you another. I didn't like everyone seeing what you were wearing beneath it," he growls and then crashes his lips to mine, kissing me with an intensity that makes me weak at the knees. He nips my lip and steps back, his gaze flickering over me, heating my core to a boiling point. "You don't want anyone else? This is about you and me, right?"

My breath hitches. "I only want you."

"You're sure?" His voice is rough.

I nod, swallowing at the intensity of his stare. "Only you."

He toes off his shoes, takes off his socks, puts his hands on his belt, slides his pants and boxers off then removes his shirt—naked, completely, gloriously naked, he stands in front of me.

I lick my lips and then follow suit, removing my bra and panties, joining him in his nakedness.

The current that flows between us is electrifying.

I want to touch him—I'm close enough to—but I wait for him.

Thank God I don't have to wait long.

"Get on the bed, on your knees. Face the headboard. Put your hands on the iron rails and leave them there."

The command almost makes me stumble—almost.

But the adrenaline that soars within me gives me the stability I need to move, and I quickly do as he says.

Once I'm in place, I look toward him.

His eyes meet mine and they flutter, his long lashes brushing his cheeks. When he bends down, he retrieves the orange bag and removes the scarves, then tosses the bag to the floor.

The look on his face steals all the air from my lungs.

The mattress shifts and I can feel him behind me on his knees, just like I am. "Ready?" His words echo in my ear.

No time to think.

I just act.

I suck in a thin breath—a little bit scared and a lot thrilled.

I close my eyes and grip the iron rails. A flush crawls up my face and my lungs constrict, as impatience seems to take hold of me.

What is he doing?

While I wait, the sound of his voice replays in my ear over and over—almost tortured when he asked me if I wanted him.

Why would he think I wouldn't?

All thoughts leave my mind though when his warm breath cascades down my neck and the familiar silky turquoise printed cloth covers my eyes—rolled up more than a few times. As he ties it snuggly in place, my heart pounds, my blood races in my veins, and within moments, darkness is all I can see.

Then out of nowhere, there's a tingling slap to my behind. You wouldn't think so, but the pleasure of the sting expands all the way to my core.

Before I can catch my breath, his hands cover mine, his mouth is on my ear, and his body is so close I can feel the warmth of it. "Zoey, do you have any idea how insane you made me, going to that club alone?"

Arousal makes my voice breathy. "I do now."

His body shifts, and his blanket of warmth is gone.

Even though I'm kneeling in place, it's still disorienting, makes me feel vulnerable, and maybe it's just a little terrifying as I wait for what's next.

Another sting to the other side strikes my skin.

I have to will myself to stay calm as second thoughts speed through my mind, but then Nate begins to spread wet open-mouthed kisses over the surely reddened flesh, and a feeling of pure intimacy covers up any negativity.

My desire soars.

"Expect three more," he whispers.

I nod, more excited than anything else. Something about his need to punish me thrills me.

"Consider them all your *I'm sorry*s."

I will, I think. *Keep talking*, I wish. I just love the way his breath seeps between my thighs when he speaks.

But he doesn't. Instead, his lips glide up my back and his hands follow from my belly up to my chest.

I love that just as much.

"I want to give you something no man's ever given you. I want to take you higher than you've ever gone," he confesses.

My nipples feel like hard candies when his palms skim them. "I want that too." My words sound like raspy squeals as my entire body comes to life—head to toe, I feel electrified.

His lips are on my neck, his hands too. His grip is firm, not choking though. "Good, because I can't wait to fuck you. And trust me when I say, I can't wait."

The promise of what's to come hits me as a rush, a high, and suddenly a new door opens in my mind. This is exciting, different, just what I needed in my life at just the right time. This man came into my life when I had nothing but ordinary. This is anything but, and I think he feels the same way too.

Something about the two of us together—not oil and water; no, more like gasoline and a match—with one strike, we're on fire.

His hands trail down my back and his lips follow.

My desire soars high above any clouds. Higher than the heavens. So high the world is no longer visible—and that means everything.

Another spanking, this time even lower. The sensation of pain is as much a turn-on as the feeling of helpless submission—and I thought I didn't want to submit.

I want to scream *Take me*.

All of me.

Whip me.

Fuck me hard.

I want it all.

Nate's natural personality—controlling and maybe slightly cocky—seems to manifest itself instinctively between the sheets—and God, what a turn-on.

Couple that with the tender way he pushes my hair off my shoulder to kiss my neck, and I can't help but love the way he makes me feel. He makes me feel so sexy, so wanted, so desired.

The smell of him, fresh and clean, is enough to spark a flame but the feel of his lips sets my skin on fire. Each kiss feels hotter, as I wait in anticipation of what's next, and the ache between my legs starts to throb.

With another agreement made—that tonight is about pushing limits—Nate seems to get back to business, and I'm pulled from our lustful trance. Once again his hands cover mine. "Can you see?"

I twist my head to the right, to the left.

Nothing.

"No." I feel like a kid playing Pin the Tail on the Donkey. Nate takes the next step—silk wraps around one wrist and there's a tugging. Silk wraps around my other wrist and another tugging. No more Pin the Tail on the Donkey. I swallow nervously. I don't have much range of motion, and the thought evokes a twinge of panic. I can feel the tightening of my lungs as the panic sets in.

No.

Stay calm.

Stay calm.

"Is it too tight?" The gravelly, sex-infused sound of his voice eases my nerves.

"No."

A breeze, a rush of air, greets me, and I feel so much better.

No, not air, it's Nate's hungry mouth lowering to mine. His kiss is demanding and every muscle in my body tenses once again. "You good?"

His whisper is hot over my lips.

Drawing in a bracing breath, I nod. Darkness is all I can see, but exchanging sight for the feel of Nate's body on mine is more than fair.

"One more after this." An open-handed slap to my rear. It is closer to my middle and the pleasure only expands further and triggers my need for release.

Wetness drenches me between my thighs.

My heart pounds as blood rushes to my ass, my pussy.

His fingers trail up my spine, urging me to lean forward.

I do, hoping his hand will slip between my legs and rub my needy clit.

But instead, his hand caresses my ass and finally, with the lightest of touches, he draws his finger down between my thighs to my sex.

Pleasure and anticipation expand in unison as I wait.

"Relax, Zoey." His voice has the most sensual undertone, and it does relax me.

At least until he takes his hand away, and all of a sudden I feel powerless with my hands tied. I want him to touch my clit, or at least I want to be able to if he won't.

My need is rising higher and higher and I'm not sure I can take much more—the pleasure that seeks release is building way too fast.

The last spanking comes and this time, immediately after the slight strike, his hands grip my hips and his body blankets mine. The feel of his erection against me sends goose bumps up my spine and a whole new wave of sensations takes over.

I exhale a ragged breath. "Please make me come."

"Not yet."

"When?" I cry out, my orgasm hovering at the fringes, waiting to be released.

His laugh is wicked. "When I feel like all atonement has been made."

"When will you feel that?" I practically squeal.

"You'll know. But I promise you, the longer I wait, the more pleasure you'll feel."

What if I can't hold out?

His palms slide down the backs of my thighs, past my knees, and down to my toes. The sensation takes me to a new dimension. His fingers circle my ankles and they become cuffs, anchoring me in place. His breath whispers across my skin and his soft-as-velvet lips trail up the path his hands just roamed. He pauses and his teeth nip at the sensitive spot inside my knee, first one side then the other.

Oh my God. Electricity flashes through me as little sparks of pleasure flicker against my skin beneath his mouth.

His tongue continues its delicious path up my legs and his hands join back in the fun, caressing my breasts. My nipples spike at the contact, and his thumbs circle my tips.

This is sensation overload—his hands and mouth are everywhere, and pleasure percolates from my very depths. The feel of his skin, his body against mine, is tantalizing and an instant dose of arousal goes right to my core.

Suddenly heat and wetness surround me and I cry out as he sucks somewhere between my thighs. His fingers pinch my nipples at the same time and the hard pressure spurs on my desire.

Pain and pleasure rocket through me in equal measure.

His mouth slides from my sex back up. "Does this feel good?"

"Yes!" I shout. The world is already gone, I'm floating somewhere out in space, the feeling of gravity sublime.

I'm so close—almost there.

"You're so wet," he groans.

Tension coils in my belly and the sound of his breathing covers me. I feel myself orbiting around the sun, heat rushing to my core. Suddenly, Nate's mouth eases off me.

And then it's gone.

The next thing I feel is him pushing my hair to the side and his mouth finding that spot behind my ear that drives me wild.

Under a gasping breath he whispers, "Don't come yet."

My hands grip the bars tighter as little bites on my shoulder give me tremors of delight. His hands spread my legs wider. His erection rests between my ass and his arms wrap around me while his fingers work their way inside me.

My body starts to tremble with need, with want. "Why?" I call out.

"Why do you think?"

"Please," I beg.

He eases off. "Not yet. Next time you do something I specifically ask you not to, I'll put you over my knee."

"Nate, please. I won't do anything like that again."

I can't take any more of these sensations; I can't take another minute without a release.

His chest is flush to my back. Flesh to flesh—it feels so good.

But then his fingers leave the welcoming depths of my sex completely and I feel lost.

Everything is heightened—more sound, more touch, more need, more want.

"You want me inside you?"

"Yes!"

I hear the telltale sound of foil ripping and I know we must be close. One hand goes to my hip but the other . . . Where's his other hand? There it is. The crown of his penis hits me right where I need him and the feeling is incredible as he guides his cock into me.

I bite down so hard on my lip that the searing pain is a good match to the pleasure brewing inside me. Anticipation grips me as he slowly eases into me.

"Please, faster," I say again, wanting him to just take me over the edge.

Inch my inch, he eases in and then back out. Once he's all the way in, I feel myself start to teeter, but then he pulls out.

"Nate!" I yell. "What are you doing to me?"

"Do you want to come?"

"Yes, yes!" I shout.

"Are you going to behave again like you did today? When I tell you not to do something, are you going to do it anyway?"

Oh my God, he's keeping my orgasm hostage to prove a point.

The problem is I have no leverage.

I can't take another minute of this madness. "No, I already told you no." My cry is strangled.

He pounds into me all the way. His fingers tease my clit, but then he eases off again.

"Nate, please, I promise I'll talk to you first."

His lips take mine. "That's all I ask, Zoey. All I want."

And then I get him—all of him.

Hard and fast, he thrusts in and out of me.

His groans in my ear tingle all the way to my sex. His fingers grip me as his thrusting turns to pounding.

So good—just so good.

If he's a panther, I'm his mate out in the wild as we both turn into animals.

His grip is tight, his groans low and steady, and with each one I'm soaring higher and higher, riding the brink of pleasure and pain, so close to orgasm I can taste the joy of it. The relentless pounding offers the biggest source of pleasure, but his fingers gripping me add to the sensation.

This is rough sex. Sex like I've never had before, but it's the sex I begged for, and the sex he's giving me.

"I want you to come now."

His voice is so thick, so hoarse, so sexy I can't deny him his wish, and just like that, everything goes away.

There's nothing but shooting stars, crashing waves, and flashes of bright colors.

He must have come too because I can feel his pulsing cock inside me and the warmth of his body as he collapses on top of me. "What is it about you that makes me want to do crazy things to you?"

Words that are easily said in the dark. Words like a boomerang reflecting my feelings exactly.

"I don't know, but don't stop."

In the dark my senses are so much keener. Heavy breathing and the smell of sex are everywhere.

A tug from around my head and the blindfold drops. His fingers easily undo my bindings at each wrist and in one swoop he pulls me down onto the bed with him and draws me into his arms. We're lying in the wrong direction—our heads are at the footboard but neither of us cares.

It takes me a few moments to focus.

When I do, I look at Nate.

His stare is locked on mine with some kind of emotion flickering through it that I can't identify.

"Wow," I say around his mouth as the aftereffects of my orgasm continue to tailspin around me.

He rubs his thumb over my lips and repeats my word. "Wow."

I laugh and push at his chest. "Hey, I said it first."

He pulls me back. "It only seems appropriate."

With a tug he pulls the covers over us and claims my mouth with a possessiveness that I both need and crave—both of which also scare me.

Feelings stir that I know shouldn't be there, but I can't hold them back.

19
Teeny Bikini

"I have to go." First I hear his soft warm words and then, an even softer, hotter kiss floats over my lips.

My eyes flutter open to the bright sunshine of the early morning light and focus on the figure leaning over me—tall, dark, and handsome.

He's dressed in another gray suit that accentuates the leanness of his body, a thin white shirt that allows just a glimpse of what lies beneath, and a grin that makes my heart jump start to life this morning.

My arms loop around his neck and I pull him down to me, not caring that I haven't brushed my teeth or what my hair might look like.

All I seek is his warmth, his scent, his touch.

He doesn't hesitate to open his mouth. In fact, he even deepens the kiss. It's not long enough, but maybe forever wouldn't be long enough. I want so much for Nate to slip beside me under the rumpled sheets. He nips at my lip, but his mouth lingers over mine for the longest time.

Surprisingly, he doesn't pull back, but rather he kisses me again and I feel the velvety brush of his tongue and yet another kiss.

But then it comes—a breathy good-bye sigh.

The gentle caress of his skilled hands roaming my body only makes me crave him more. And his soft, teasing kisses only serve to leave me feeling wanton as he rises to his full height.

I smile up at him. "I wish you could stay."

He closes his eyes for a minute. When he reopens them he leans down. "I know I said I'd take today off, but I want to wrap up the deal I signed yesterday. It's Fourth of July weekend and I'm taking Friday through Monday off. After I take you to meet my father in the morning, I'm taking you to the Keys for a long weekend."

A weekend alone with Nate—it can only be a sex-filled fantasy come to life.

My skin erupts with tingling pleasure.

My body flares as heat engulfs me.

"I left my credit card on the dresser. Go shopping today and get what you need."

I blink the image away. "Nate, I can't take your—" I start to protest.

He's almost near the door, but he turns quickly, his hand going up to stop me. "But you should know—we're taking the boat, so buy accordingly." Then he winks at me. He actually winks at me, and any of my protests fly out the window with my soaring pulse and the butterflies that freed themselves from my stomach.

He's gone, and I look around the room with a smile.

He's messy.

It must be Rosie's biweekly visits that keep the place clean because Nate certainly doesn't—although he has been a bit distracted, I'll admit, and the place was clean when I arrived.

I scan the room, noticing the heaps of clothes where they lie from yesterday and the day before and of course, mine have joined his. The Chinese takeout containers that we ate from last night cover the nightstand. But my inquisitive eye stops when the vanilla envelope catches it—the one that Oliver gave Nate. I never opened it because I had already gained access to his accounts, but I probably should.

I hop out of bed and snag it off the dresser.

Crawling back in to open it, I pull out a stack of papers—death certificate, a letter confirming my next of kinship, a copy of the deed for Mimi's house bearing my name only, debt payoff print-outs, bank statements with wire-transfer forms attached for me to fill in my account number, and a complete summary of his estate.

My stomach drops at the words printed across the top and the sadness of it all—once the debt is settled there will be a little less than five thousand dollars left in my brother's estate. He paid off more than two hundred thousand dollars' worth of debt to better my life, but he didn't seem to save any for himself. Tears leak from my eyes as I clutch the papers to me. Was he happy?

Zach, tell me you were.

I don't see any accident report so I flip through the papers again—none. So I reach for my purse and Oliver's card lying on the bed next to the envelope. My phone comes to life as I press the center button and tap the ten digits.

"Oliver Martinez's office. How can I help you?"

"Hi, this is Zoey Flowers. Is Oliver available?"

"One moment please." Soft elevator music plays as I flip through the documents and grab for a pen in my purse to sign those requiring a signature.

"Zoey, good morning. How can I help you?"

"Hi, Oliver. I'm good. I have the documents that needed signature ready for you."

"Excellent. I'll send a courier by to pick them up. You're still at Nate's?"

I pull the sheet tighter to my chest. "Yes, I am, and I was hoping you could do me a favor."

"I can try. What is it?"

"Would you be able to get me a copy of Zach's accident report?"

"Yes, but it won't be until next week with the holiday. But Zoey, I have to tell you that I read the autopsy report. It states your brother was going way too fast without wearing a helmet; head injury is cited as cause of death."

Sadness creeps into me. He never wore a helmet. That was the rebel in him. "I'd still like to see it, if you don't mind."

"Not a problem, I'll send the courier in about an hour to pick up your paperwork and will call you next week when I get it."

"Thanks, Oliver."

"No problem. Have a good day."

"Wait! Oliver, are you still there?"

"Yeah, I am. Did you need something else?"

"Your fee. I didn't see your fee itemized on my brother's statement or a bill attached either."

"Don't worry about it, Zoey. Nate's business is covered on retainer by my firm."

"No, I want to pay for this myself. This doesn't have anything to do with Nate's business."

He chuckles. "Not going to happen. It's all wrapped up anyway."

"Oliver, it can't be that hard to bill me separately."

"Look, Zoey. Nate and I have been friends for a long time, a really long time, and deep down, under all his brooding, I-don't-give-a-shit bravado is a big heart. Don't break it by rejecting what he wants to do for your brother. Z meant a lot to him. Let him do this for him, if not for you."

My throat closes up. There's so much emotion in his words. I draw in a breath before answering. "You know what, Oliver? I can do that. Thank you . . . for everything. Have a great day."

"You too," he says and then hangs up.

I press End and stare down at the papers for a long while before filling out the rest of the information. Once I'm finished, I push everything back into the envelope. In a rush, it happens, and I can't stop the images of the life I led with my brother from flashing before me. My mother had Zach when she was seventeen, and I was born six weeks early, just nine months after Zach. Since we weren't even a year apart in age, we were in the same grade throughout school. Everyone thought we were twins. We never knew if we had the same father—yet it wouldn't have mattered.

We were in the crazy, messed-up life my mother led, together. Luckily, we had Mimi. And for all the neglect my mother dampened our lives with, Mimi showered us with love.

When we were five, we went to live with her, and my mother visited us. It happened after our first day of kindergarten. We were left stranded at the bus stop with no one there to pick us up, and Zach had to find our way home. I was no help. I was crying and scared and he told me he'd always find our way home. And he always did. He found our house that day and when we couldn't get in, he took me to the neighbors and asked them to call Mimi.

Tears slide like heavy rain down my cheek.

My destiny—I can't change it.

My mother died of a drug overdose a few years later. She was twenty-seven. I didn't believe my aunt the day she told me about the club, but I do now.

I've cried enough for two lifetimes thinking about it, and I refuse to shed any more tears over it. I'm living more of a life right now than I ever have, and I want to embrace what time I have left.

My destiny—I might not be able to change it.

But maybe I can skate around it for as long as possible.

I set my phone down and decide it's time to clean up—both the Chinese leftovers and myself. I make quick work of the bedroom, bringing the trash downstairs and stuffing the laundry down the chute, jotting down a mental note to ask where the dry cleaning goes. Then I hop in and out of the shower. The weather is hot and sunny, so I select a white tank dress with colorful palm leaves on it. I'm just sliding into my sandals when the doorbell rings. My shoes *click-clack* as I hurry down the stairs, drop the envelope on the counter, and scurry down the hallway where I open the door to find Skater Boy standing in front of me.

His grin is more like a smirk. "Z's sister, you're still around."

I open the door wide for him to enter. "I am, Speedy."

He looks around. "My real name is Andrés."

"Andrés—I like it. Please come in, and I'll get you the envelope."

He drops his eyes, embarrassed. "Speedy sounds much more badass."

I walk down the hallway toward the kitchen and he follows. "Badass, huh?" I laugh.

"Yeah, too bad Oliver won't let me use it when I'm on the job."

We cross the living room toward the kitchen, and I glance back at Skater Boy. "Personally, I think Andrés is a pretty badass name."

Under his cap, I'm pretty sure Skater Boy is blushing.

"What do you do for Oliver?"

Skater Boy sits on one of the barstools. "Whatever odd jobs he needs done."

With a raised brow, I look over at him as I circle the kitchen counter.

"Nothing bad," he laughs. "I make copies, deliver documents, file, get lunch, boring odds-and-ends-type stuff. But I only work in the summer, so it's not that bad and it gives me enough spending money while I'm in school. Oliver and Nate won't let me work during the school year, except Christmas break."

The keys to Nate's dad's car are lying beside the coffeemaker. He must have come back while I was in the shower. With a slight dreamy sigh, I turn the Miele on and wait for it to warm up. "Oliver and Nate won't let you?"

He steeples his fingers and taps them together. "Yeah, they pay for me to go to UM and have this preoccupation with my grades. It can be really annoying. And Santiago is always more than happy to report any of my missteps to them as well. Again, really annoying."

I laugh, my heart expanding in my chest at the act of kindness. "Do you live with Santiago?"

"Yeah, he's my brother. Our mother died in Hurricane Andrew the year I was born and my dad's job takes him on the road all the time. So it's been just us."

"Oh my God. I'm so sorry. Was anyone else hurt?"

"No, just her. She was alone. She worked beachside and was taking the bridge back over to Wynwood when she lost control of her car and hit an oncoming tractor-trailer.

My hand flies to my mouth. "That's terrible."

He shrugs. "I don't even remember her. For me being without her has always been a way of life."

The button turns green on the Miele with a beep. I nod at Skater Boy, guessing he's probably right—you can't miss what you never really had. I was almost ten when my mother overdosed, and not having her around most of the time before that had also become a way of life.

Different situations entirely—but still both really sad.

"Anyway ever since, Nate, Oliver, and Santiago have acted like they're all my mothers—sometimes it's a huge pain in the ass. But if you promise not to tell, I'll let you in on a little secret—I can't imagine my life without them."

"That's really sweet, and my lips are sealed."

"Yeah, I guess the story goes that we were all together at Oliver's house riding out the storm when she died, and ever since, they've felt like they have some lifelong bond to me."

"I can understand that."

He checks the time on his wrist.

"Can I make you a latté, cappuccino, or espresso?"

"Nah, I don't drink coffee. Santiago says I'm hyped up enough without the added jolt of caffeine."

I shake my head at him. He's cute. "How about something else?"

He hops off the stool. "I can get it."

"Okay." I open the refrigerator to get the milk and set the carton on the counter. The cups are in the little drawer under the coffeemaker and when I slide it open my heart skyrockets out of my chest. There's a note in there. I grab it with a mug and set them both down. The note reads:

> Looking forward to what tonight brings. The car should be in the driveway. I asked Santiago to drop it off with Rosie and to leave the keys on the counter in case you weren't up yet. I'll call you this afternoon to see what you'd like to do for dinner.
>
> —Your boyfriend, Nate

My mind jumps to last night, and not just the spankings but every single part of it makes me smile. I wonder if I should misbehave again. I rather liked what came later—well, more than liked it. But no, I'd better not.

The sound of Andrés's sneakers squeaking on the kitchen tile has me spinning around. When I come face-to-face with him, I have to wipe clean the dirty thoughts swirling in my head.

He glances at me, and I quickly flip the note over.

He ignores the note and opens the refrigerator. "Cool, Rosie cooked. Do you mind?"

I shake my head. "No, not at all."

He pulls out a container labeled *empanadas* and opens it. "Have you tried these?"

"No, are they good?"

He takes a bite and hands me the Tupperware, nodding his head. "The best," he mumbles, covering his mouth.

"No, thank you. I haven't had my coffee yet." My mind is whirling and my stomach is flipping with excitement way too much to eat food.

Skater Boy's expression is full of contentment as he finishes chewing. "You don't know what you're missing."

"I'll try them later, promise." The milk pours easily without concentration, and I put the little silver-handled pot under the steamer spout and then slide my coffee cup under the dispenser.

Andrés grabs a bottle of water, obviously feeling at home here. "You being here is a good thing. You know that?"

I pour the steamed froth into the dark liquid, and with my cup in hand, I turn to him. "Why do you think that?"

He shrugs. "Ever since Nate's dad went in the home, he's kind of gone off grid. We never see him anymore. He even told Rosie she didn't need to come every day. He's been paying her the same, but she doesn't feel right taking it. He hadn't asked her to cook or anything until last Saturday. I guess right after you came. It's nice to see him out and doing things, I guess is what I'm trying to say."

"You know Rosie?"

"Yeah, I live with her," he laughs. "She's married to my brother."

"I had no idea."

"Well, Nate's not exactly an open book. But me——" He smiles pointing to himself. "You can ask me anything."

For a moment I consider asking him about Nate's mom but decide against it. If Nate wants me to know anything about her, he'll tell me himself.

He scurries around the counter, pressing a palm to it to lift himself higher. "I gotta jet before Oliver docks my pay."

His smirk is full of mischief.

"Well, thanks . . . for everything." I smile at him.

Once I walk him to the door and he leaves, I sit down with my latté and phone and send Nate a text.

> I'm looking forward to tonight as well. I'm headed out to do some shopping and I'll stop at the grocery store while I'm at it. I want to cook dinner, so don't worry about making plans. And, don't laugh, I've never been on a boat . . . anything in particular I need?

His response is immediate.

> Dinner in sounds great. If you cook anything like your brother I'm already looking forward to it. As for boat gear—a pair of sneakers, a two-piece suit, and a long-sleeve shirt in case the sun is too much. The resort is very private and casual. See you tonight.

Private. I like the sound of that.

> Me: Ha! Bikini? Will any bathing suit suffice?

> Nate: No. In order to board, you must be wearing a VERY teeny bikini. Isabella's is between Collins Ave and Ocean Drive on Eighth Street. There are a number of other stores there as well. They should have everything you need. And use my credit card. I mean it.

I have to laugh. Teeny? I've never even worn a bikini. My trusty black one-piece has always been sufficient. But for Nate, I want to look sexy.

My eyes wander out to the ocean. It's so beautiful out there, and an entire weekend with nothing but the wind, water, sun, and Nate is better than any dream. It's heaven—palms swaying with the gentle breezes of the Atlantic Ocean, gracefully silhouetted by a breathtaking sunset, soft white sand and bright sunshine, me and Nate naked—heaven.

My mind doesn't even conjure up images because I know the real thing will be so much more than I can even fantasize about.

I rinse my cup and grab the keys, heading off in search of a teeny bikini.

I find a place to park and walk to Eighth Street. Isabella's is a beautifully decorated white-tiled store. It has pink orchids in various locations on tables with all kinds of clothes and accessories.

"Can I help you?" a beautiful woman in a fitted orange dress and funky heels asks.

"Yes, is Isabella in?"

"No, but I'm her daughter, Gabriella, and I'd be happy to help you."

"Sure. I need to find a two-piece bathing suit."

She smiles. "You're in the right place. What style would you like?"

Now, I could say teeny, but I don't. "I'm not sure."

"Okay, let's start with the top. Do you want bandeau, flouncy, triangle, sport?"

I take a deep breath. I like shopping well enough, but I'm usually a quick trip into Macy's, get what I need, and get out kind of girl. "I'll be on a boat, and I'd like it to be a little skimpy."

There, I said it.

Her eyes size me up from head to toe. "I have one that just arrived I think would be perfect. Come with me."

I dutifully follow as she hands me something unlike anything I've ever worn.

"This is a bralette-style top with adjustable straps, so it's practical for boating, but the keyhole detail and unusual ties in the back along with the hipster-style bottom add an air of sexiness to it."

"It's beautiful." I marvel at the lavender straps, the printed pattern, and the mint green band around the waistband that matches the ties at the back of the top.

"I have a number of cover-up options and matching jewelry as well. A pink palette-shelled necklace would go beautifully with the suit."

I stare at her in awe. "Pick out whatever you think would go the best. I love the suit."

She claps her hands together. "I love clients like you. Give me a few minutes."

The bathing suit fits perfectly, and the sales associate adds a white sheer tunic with an exposed back, the necklace, a white canvas beach bag, and a pair of white Keds-like sneakers with a platform sole.

"Where are you going?"

"The Keys," I say with a smile.

"With your boyfriend?"

It takes me an actual five seconds to answer. "Well, yes and no. He's not really my boyfriend."

"Oh," she says in a scandalous manner.

"Well, we just met and—" I stop. What am I going to say—we just met and we are having the best sex of my life, and I'm not looking for anything else because chances are I'm going to die sometime within the next year?

Yet, as the words sink in, the thought of Nate as my boyfriend does funny things to my heart.

I push that feeling aside, even though that's what he said we were. I can't think that way—summer of fun, that's all this can be.

"Key West is beautiful. Have you ever been?"

I shake my head no.

"You'll love it. Do you need any other clothing options? We

have some comfortable T-shirt dresses and casual maxi dresses that would be perfect for the Keys."

Feeling a little deflated for some reason, I decide to let her finish my shopping for me. "Yes, those things would be great. Oh, and I need a long-sleeve shirt."

She laughs. "For what? It will be over one hundred degrees in the Keys."

"Nate said in case the sun gets to be too much on the boat."

She leans back against the counter and puts a pencil tip in her mouth. "Nate? Would that be Nate Hanson by chance?"

"Yes. Do you know him?"

"We've met . . . a few times."

"Oh." That's about all I can say, because obviously something took place in those few times.

It's written all over her face.

"Anyway that's nice that he's taking you on his boat all the way to the Keys. I've never known him to bring a girl anywhere. I guess the long-sleeve shirt must mean he's concerned about you. But, he's not your boyfriend, you said?"

Concerned?

I shrug off the feeling that she thinks he's acting like my big brother. "It's complicated," I shoot back.

"Isn't it always?" She smiles.

I let it go. I can't very well tell her we have an agreement—sex only. It fits his needs and mine too. It works—for now.

"Give me a few minutes and I'll pull everything together for you. And here, take these." She hands me a few samples. "These are the most popular perfume and body sprays. They both smell amazing."

I take them and shove them in my purse.

She stops and turns back around. "And I didn't mean to pry. It really isn't any of my business."

I leave the store laden down with questions about her and Nate, along with everything she initially pulled together plus a few maxi dresses, flip-flops, and one long-sleeve white sun-repellent tee—one thousand five hundred and eighty-five dollars' worth of clothes to be exact.

I've never spent that much on clothing at one time in my life.

Yelp tells me Victoria's Secret is around the block, and I do need some underwear. These though I'm buying myself. I'm in and out quickly and feeling extremely hot and thirsty.

There's a Starbucks on the corner, so I decide to hit it up before heading home. While I'm sipping on my iced latté, I receive a text from Nate.

I Googled asthma and WebMD states people with asthma are able to run or jog. Is this correct?

I actually laugh out loud and answer:

Me: No! It's not. I absolutely cannot run. Nothing to do with my asthma though. ;)

Nate: Pick up some Asics and running shorts while you're out. You're coming with me in the mornings.

Me: Nate—I'm not a morning person, and running isn't my thing.

Nate: I thought we discussed listening and the repercussions of not doing so?

Me: We did. I'd be happy to pick some up, but if I forget, it might just be on purpose.

Nate: Don't be a tease.

Me: I wouldn't think of it. ☺

Nate: How's your day going?

Me: Good. Interesting.

Nate: Glad your day is going well. See you tonight.

I don't bother to mention Isabella's daughter—there's no reason.

Couples walk by me holding hands, and I wonder what kind of relationships they have—committed or casual?

Nate and I could be one of those couples. I wonder what people would think about us when they see us together.

I sip on the last of my drink and squeeze my eyes shut.

Is this getting too personal between us?

Are things getting too complicated?

I'm already becoming attached.

Attachments aren't for you, that inner voice that I thought I buried says in my ear.

I close my eyes and for some reason, I wonder what dying feels like. Will I know it is happening?

Anger balls inside me.

The darkness starts to consume me.

I can't let it.

I'm stronger than this.

I am.

I'm getting stronger and stronger every day. I refocus on Nate. He's helping me. Maybe I can help him.

His protective shell is softening. This could be a good thing for him. Perhaps, once I'm gone, he'll be open to letting someone else in, like Isabella's daughter.

I ignore the burn in my throat and tap a few keys on my screen. Once I'm done, I put Isabella's daughter aside and switch back to my messages.

Me: One more thing. Will Nike do? There's one a few blocks down.

Nate: Yes.

Short and simple—perfect. Just the way I like it, I think. I tuck my phone away and head out to finish up. By the time I've gotten everything I need, it's almost three o'clock. A quick stop at the grocery store and then I'm finally home, back to Nate's, I mean.

I'm shocked when I open the garage and the Range Rover is parked inside. I park behind him, because maneuvering the car beside Nate's is way too scary. Parallel parking scares the crap out of me, but squeezing between Nate's car and a concrete wall really terrifies me.

I'll move it whenever he needs to get out.

I gather up the first of the shopping bags and set them just inside the garage door entrance. Then I get most of the groceries and head to the kitchen. "Nate!" I call.

No answer.

"Nate?"

I set the plastic bags on the counter and when I look up, I see movement down at the boathouse. The bay doors are open and the cherry red boat and the rickety old fishing boat have swapped places. Nate's on the bow of the Scarab doing something with one of the lines. In his low-slung faded jeans and black T-shirt, his hard, lean, muscled frame moves with ease as he tugs the ropes tighter with complete competence.

I rest my elbows on the counter and just stare—I could watch the way he moves all day.

Seconds turn into minutes.

With a sigh, I turn to make dinner. After all, I did tell Nate I'd cook.

The light from the windows is bright, and when I head back to the garage to get the other bags, the gilded frames in Nate's office sparkle like sea glass when it washes up on the beach.

Something draws me to them.

I step in the office and study the landscape scenes done in magnificent watercolors that look out of place with the rest of the house.

They're signed *Milo Hanson.* Nate's dad painted these.

His work is extraordinarily detailed and very eye-catching. I wonder why Nate has never mentioned his father was an artist.

I guess it just hasn't come up.

I'll add it to my growing list of things to ask him about. At least now they make sense in the house—another waffle maker, so to say.

Once I've placed my purchases on the stairs, I steal another look outside. Nate is standing on the concrete pad with his hands on his hips, just staring at the boat. His stance, even from the back, is breathtakingly beautiful.

I quickly turn away, my heart pounding at the sight of him, and I have to force myself to focus on dinner.

I've decided to make fettuccini with creamy red pepper sauce. Pasta is the one thing I learned how to cook from Mimi, and if I do say so myself—learned to cook it well. When money is tight, experimenting with pasta adds flair to an otherwise ordinary dinner, and Mimi did a spectacular job at creating delicious meals.

Once I've prepped the ingredients and started the sauce, I turn the heat to simmer and wipe my hands on a towel. With the pot filled with water, fresh bread sliced and covered, and the lettuce chopped and put in the refrigerator, I pour two freshly made lemonades and set out to find Nate.

Even though I'm soaking up the Florida sunshine, the walk seems farther because I'm anxious to see Nate.

He's no longer in the bay, but I catch sight of him as soon as I cross the open threshold. He's sitting on the second to last step with his head bowed, his elbows on his knees, and his hands on his head. He has the same clothes on, but his hair is slightly damp and his feet are bare. He smells like the Irish Spring soap that was in Zach's shower.

"Nate?" I hurry over toward him, lemonade spilling.

He looks up. "Zoey, hey, I didn't hear you come in. Did you get everything you needed today?"

The lemonade is sticky in my hands, but I hand him one anyway. "Yes, I did—and a few extras too."

He smiles at me and takes the glass. "Thanks, looks good."

"Scoot over. What you're doing out here?"

"Just getting the boat ready for the trip."

I put my free hand on his knee. "You came home early."

He looks over at me. "Yeah, I haven't been out here in so long. I needed to get everything together while it was still light."

Even with the fringe of his hair still wet and falling into his eyes, I can see he's wearing a look of complete vulnerability on his face. I have an urge to run—run fast, and run far—because if I don't, I feel like another door might open, and the more that open the harder they are to close.

But I can't go anywhere.

He looks like he needs me.

I swipe his hair from his eyes and set my glass down to cup his face. "Nate, tell me what you were thinking about when I came in."

He shakes his head. "Nothing. It's nothing."

"That's not true." I look at the wall of boxes I saw him staring at earlier. "Tell me why you emptied out your house. Tell me why you haven't been over here since my brother died. Everyone handles grief in his or her own way. But sometimes it helps to talk about it."

He sets his glass down and rises, grabbing for my hand. "Come on, let's go inside. I'm done out here."

With a gentle shrug, I stay where I am. "Nate." My voice is low, calming. "You can talk to me."

He runs a hand through his hair then down to cup the back of his neck. He stands tall before me—all long, lean strength, his shirt pulling from his waistband, but it's not his body I'm looking at, it's his face, so full of despair. "Come on. I want to close up before it gets dark."

I sit back on the step. "It's only five o'clock. We have time. Why did you empty that bedroom out after your dad went to live at Sunshine Village?"

His gaze burns me, but I don't cower. He needs someone to talk to; I can see it in his eyes.

"Nate, talk to me. Why haven't you gone upstairs until today?"

Nate walks over to the wall of boxes. With his back to me he says, "You see all of this?"

"Yes."

I hope I'm making the right choice by pushing.

He turns toward me and I can see the storm brewing in his eyes "This is my father's life! It's in boxes! Everything from his whole life is right here, except for that shitty waffle maker of his that sits inside." He points up the stairs. "And what you're doing up there, same thing. Everything of Z's will sit in boxes until you decide what to do with it. And more than likely, all of those boxes will end up at some secondhand store for someone else to use in their life, just like all of these will. You see, Zoey, I didn't empty a room—I condensed my dad's life into boxes."

"No, he lived his life, he still lives his life. You just tidied up some of his things."

He turns back around. "Is that what this is—tidying up? Because it feels more like tearing apart to me."

The sun starts to beat on us inside as it lowers in the sky. I push to my feet. "Nate, look at me."

He doesn't.

I don't back off though. Instead I circle him and put my hands on his arms.

He pushes me away and turns to face the boat.

My voice is strong. "Nate, listen to me. Your dad's life is not what is in those boxes." With my chest to his back, I put my chin on his shoulder and wrap my arms around him. My palm finds his heart. "It lives here, in your heart. Sure, you can't keep everything of someone else's, but you keep the things that matter, the things that remind you of that person, the things that make you smile when you look at them. That's one of the reasons I came here—to bring some small piece of my brother home that will make me smile, to bring home my version of your dad's waffle maker."

Nate places his hand over mine and tears well in my eyes when he squeezes it. "I just couldn't box Z's life up so close to my dad's. Not another person's, I thought, and I even asked Rosie to leave everything the way it was. And then today, something occurred to me, that I left it for you to handle and I felt like an asshole about it. So I went up there to do what? I have no fucking clue because as soon as I saw the boxes, I couldn't move. I even took a shower to try to snap out of it. I didn't want you to see me like this."

My arms squeeze him even tighter. "To see you like what, see that you're human? That you care about people? I like this side of you."

He turns around and pulls my body to his, holding me for the longest time. Like statues, we stay in the embrace. Once we've both seemed to recover, he takes my face in his hands. "Watch what you say. I might think you want more from me than just my body, that this isn't just your innate need to probe."

My heart falls right from my chest. And then, before I have to pick it up off the floor, I try to shove it back in place. I try to push my feelings away, but they're there growing stronger with each beat of my heart. I need to get control over them, and Nate's body is the only thing that can help me do that.

Running a hand down his chest, I mutter, "I can't help myself. Probing is what I do."

Then, sliding further down to the front of his jeans, I smile up at him and eye the cherry red Scarab. "You know, I've never done it on a boat."

20

Dr. Seuss

And so it started. We did it on a boat, in a bed, on a beach, in a pool, everywhere and anywhere in Key West that we could have sex, we did. The no-strings romance developed its own kind of ties over the weekend.

He blindfolded me.

Tied me up.

Did me from behind.

Chest to chest.

And head to toe.

He had me every which way, in every way he could.

I opened myself up to him, and he took as much as I would give. Each time pushing me higher and higher, making me feel more and more alive. I felt like I was actually living my life—enough for two lifetimes—and that was just what I wanted.

The bed in the hotel suite had a mirror above it, and it was one of my favorite parts of the trip.

"Look in the mirror," he told me.

I was on his lap facing away from him and when I looked up, the bird's-eye view made me realize just what the Photographer and my brother did for couples at the Estate. I wanted to capture the way we looked together forever. My hair was wild, my face flushed, my body owned by his—his hands competently anchored my hips, his cock moved in and out of me at a painfully slow pace, his face was buried in my neck.

I swear I could even see the hisses of pleasure radiating from our union—everything about it was painfully beautiful.

It was a picture I wanted to remember—always.

The sex-filled getaway was magical, but somehow another door had opened.

We were creating memories, taking photos to capture them, and we trusted each other more and more with each step we took. I knew we shouldn't be doing that, but somehow the baby steps had turned into giant leaps. And I just didn't want to close any doors—not yet.

I could feel Nate shedding a little more of his protective shell, with each passing moment, which is good for him. And with him, I am someone I've never been.

I feel young, wild, and free. Life, for the first time, feels more than worth living—it feels amazing.

But with that comes my fear. And it makes me feel more lost than ever at times.

We got home late last night and once we had secured the boat in the boathouse with me backing the truck down the ramp—terrified, I might add—he opened a few of the boxes and showed me some of the things in them. We even brought some photos of him with his dad inside and set them on the fireplace mantel.

Two pictures did not a home make, but it was a start.

Today I spent the day with Rosie packing Zach's things that I never finished last week. Rosie told me about a shelter over near Wynwood that provided hurricane relief to those in need, and I decided to donate his things to people who have lost a bit of their own life. It makes the circle of life feel a little more whole in some small way. So I took a carload over after Rosie left and plan to take the rest there tomorrow.

When I pull in the driveway, I'm surprised to see Nate's car in the garage. It's only six. The fact that he's home early makes me smile. He left this morning before the sun came up. A quick kiss on the forehead and he was gone. I'm not sure if he even went running. When I heard Rosie downstairs a few hours later I got up and got ready quickly, leaving the room without looking at our piles of clothing on the floor.

As soon as I turn the car off, the door opens and the doorway fills with the most beautiful sight. Nate, having changed out of his suit, is in his trademark sexy-as-hell low-slung jeans and a plain white T-shirt. Hair still damp from a shower, the ends look more like espresso beans than coffee beans when wet.

I want to pounce on him right now. I can't help my thoughts.

He leans against the jamb and crosses his arms, looking rather amused.

I fix him with a steely gaze as I close my door. "What?"

He bobs his head to the open spot beside his car in the garage. "I'm going to get you to park there, you know I am."

Feeling all kinds of empowered and naughty, I sway my hips while walking toward him. "Lessons in a car. I'm ready if you are."

He doesn't move to let me pass, but rather presses me against the jamb, his hands going to my hips, his mouth seeking mine. "Not right now."

"Are you sure?" I shift my knee between his legs and press a little. "Because I think you just might be ready too."

An evil laugh in my ear tells me he likes my kind of naughty. "We're going out first."

I press myself against his crotch. "You sure?"

He's practically panting in my ear while pushing against me.

I so wish I hadn't worn shorts today. A dress would have been much easier for him to get around in a car.

Then, out of nowhere he grabs the keys from my hand. "I'll move the damn car. Get in mine."

Breathless, I stare at him. "You suck."

He turns back to look at me while striding out of the garage with that walk I could watch all day. "I'll do whatever you want—later."

I twirl a piece of hair around my finger. "I'll hold you to that. Tonight I'm taking control. Can you handle that?"

He's opening the Camry's door while I'm talking, but he can hear me. I know he can when he licks his lips and then his mouth twists into a sly smile. "You'd be surprised what I can handle."

I shake my head, knowing I might not have gotten my way with the car sex, but the tradeoff is more than worth it.

Tonight he is all mine.

Images flash through my head of Nate naked, erect, and tied to the bed, while I drizzle chocolate syrup on him and lick it up, teasing him to the edge and back over and over.

I wonder if he'd let me.

I wonder if we have Hershey's chocolate syrup anywhere.

"Hey, where are you?" His hot mouth is in my ear.

I blink and a blush paints my cheeks. "Should I change?"

"Nah. What were you just thinking about?"

"Nothing," I squeak out. "Where are we going?"

He moves closer, pinning me to the door. "What were you thinking about?"

"Food, I was thinking about food."

It's the truth.

He grabs my hand with a chuckle. "We won't be long, and Rosie left chicken enchiladas with some new sauce she's dying for us to try."

"Yum, sounds good."

I get in the car with damp panties and tight nipples, hoping neither is noticeable and that both will be gone by the time we get to wherever we're going.

Sunshine Village is my guess.

Maybe Nate stopped by before he came home to check on his father and his disposition was good.

When Nate had taken me last Thursday morning, his father couldn't quite place him. I think he thought Nate was someone else and kept asking where Marisa was. Nate hurried me out to wait in the hall and went back in alone. Milo looked recognizable as the man in the pictures in the stairwell of the boathouse, but his health was nowhere near what it had been when those photos were taken.

His Alzheimer's seems to be progressing quickly.

Once we left Sunshine Village and were in the car, I turned to Nate. "Are you okay?"

He nodded.

"Nate, who is Marisa?" I asked.

He looked at me with flat eyes. "My mother."

After that, he was quiet for a long time. I understand loss when the loss hadn't occurred yet. And whether his grief was for his father who was dying, or his mother who wasn't in his life, I couldn't be sure, but it didn't matter—it was there and I understood it enough to give him the space he needed.

Grief and I know each other all too well—I'm familiar with all its shapes and forms. Relatives lost, some I've never met, a father I've never known, the deaths of my mother and brother. My grief isn't only for those who have died—it's for the living too.

I grieve for myself and the fate that might await me. I grieved for my grandmother before she passed, when cancer took away who she was, and little by little her body started to deteriorate. When sleep was the only comfort she found. She was living with me, she was alive, but she wasn't living any kind of life.

I left Nate alone to his own thoughts, as mine swept me away for those first few silent hours when we first boarded the boat. It was the first time that I doubted the hold destiny had over me. It made me stronger. Made me want to fight not to lose my life to it.

Nate tucks a loose piece of hair that's escaped my elastic from my face and returns me to the present.

I look over at him.

"Hey, what's going on with you today?"

I grab my locket and squeeze it tightly. "Nothing. Just dying to know where we're going."

The driveway backs out onto the main road, so he does a fancy K-turn, turning the car around. Before he puts it in drive, he pulls his sunglasses down from the visor. I pull the pink pair he bought me out of my purse.

"It's not a surprise or anything."

I look over at him a little confused.

"Where I'm taking you. It's not a surprise."

"Okay." I smile at him. "Then where are we going?"

"To the gallery. I know you wanted to see where your brother worked."

"Wanderlust?"

He looks at me with his lips in a firm line.

"What is it?"

"Fuck," he mutters and throws his head back.

"Nate?"

"I hate that name."

Shocked, I twist my whole body in his direction. "Why?"

This goes deeper than a name. I can see it in his body language. But I've learned a lot about Nate in the short time I've been here, and I know not to push. If I push, he'll just sink deeper into his own thoughts. Instead, I sit quietly and wait.

He doesn't answer for the longest time. Then, just as he turns off Fountain Street and onto the bridge heading west, he points straight ahead. "Do you see that?"

I look where he's pointing. The sun is low and orbits of yellow and orange color surround it. "The sun?"

"I mean the colors around it."

"I see them."

"They look like something my father might have painted."

"Yes, they do. I saw the watercolors in your office."

He runs a hand through his hair. "Yeah. Those were all done before he met my mother."

I open my mouth to speak but decide to wait for Nate instead.

He takes a right on Biscayne Boulevard and stops at a light. "The gallery was called Hanson's when my father first opened it. I wasn't born yet, but I heard the story from my father and a few different ones from his friends—they aren't exactly the same but they do all have the same ending."

The light turns green and his scuffed-up black work boot jams on the gas.

"He opened it to showcase his paintings. Buildings were really cheap back then, and it functioned as his studio as well as a store-front. He also sold art supplies and gave lessons to make some extra money. But everything changed for him the day my mother walked in his studio. She was a college student, had just turned twenty-one, and she wanted my father to display her sculptures."

The statue in the house must be his mother's. I don't have to ask.

Nate turns onto Second Avenue, and I know we are close to the gallery. "And according to my father, it was love at first sight. He asked her to marry him within a month of meeting her and instead of going back to college, she helped him run the gallery. But she wanted a real art gallery, not a shop. She somehow convinced him to stop giving lessons, to stop selling supplies, and told him pieces done in color weren't edgy enough to draw the in-crowd. Black-and-whites were what people wanted. She later proposed a name change to Wanderlust. Do you know what *wanderlust* means?"

My gaze travels over his face, filled with so many emotions that any one is hard to pinpoint. "Something about traveling."

He turns his blinker on and very easily parallel parks the Rover. Then he puts the car in park and turns to me. "You're close. It's a strong, innate desire to rove or travel about."

I nod, understanding the definition but having no idea what he's getting at.

He swallows and then draws in a deep breath. "She was pregnant with me within a year of meeting my father. She was twenty-two. He was forty and had never been married. He'd lived to paint and then she came in his life and became his world. He did everything for her. I'll give it to her—the gallery did well under her guidance. She made connections, consigned only from the latest new, up-and-coming artists. She sculpted, my father managed, she networked, my father took care of me. To him, it was a dream come true—from what I'm told, for her, it was her worst nightmare." He shakes his head. "I even changed my alarm code to the gallery name because it was the one thing he could always remember."

I stretch my hand to take his but he pulls it away and turns off the ignition. "This is it." He points to a storefront across from us: a large window with the name WANDERLUST scripted across it in black and below it AN ART GALLERY in red.

Simple, yet eye-catching.

It's sandwiched between a coffee shop and a closed-down vintage clothing store.

I look over at him. "Do you want to finish talking?"

He throws his head back and pulls the door handle. "Let's go."

"Wait a minute."

He turns back to me.

"We don't have to go in."

He sighs. "It's not like I can avoid it forever. Let's go."

He comes around and takes my hand to help me down, but he drops it as soon as my feet hit the sidewalk.

When we cross the street, I grab it back and hold on tightly.

Pedestrians roam the sidewalks, but not that many. Most of the stores look closed, and the restaurants with outdoor patios seem to be filling up.

I stare at the red color in the logo on the window, and Nate catches my gaze.

"Your brother added that." He smiles.

That makes me smile too. Both are smiles of sadness, but smiles nonetheless.

Nate looks grim as he unlocks the door.

"Hey, we don't have to do this. Really we don't."

He presses his head to the glass of the door. "I haven't been here since Z died. It's time."

I wrap my arms around him and press my cheek against his before giving him a gentle kiss. "We'll do it together."

He leans into my embrace and turns his cheek to place a chaste kiss on my lips, which surprises me.

The moment is gone quickly though and with a twist of the lock, Nate pushes the handle and we walk in. We're standing side by side in a room with black walls and a black floor and bells chiming. "I hate those fucking things," he says, but the tone of his voice isn't one of anger; it's more of amusement.

I look up to see a string of tarnished bells tied to the hinge of the door. I raise a brow. "Security alarm?"

He chuckles. "I guess you could call it that."

I purse my lips. "What do you mean?"

He looks at the security panel behind the door. "You don't want to know."

"Oh, but you're wrong. I do. I so do."

He presses a few buttons on the pad. "Strange the alarm isn't set, but it's working fine."

"Who was the last one in here?"

"The Realtor. I put it on the market a couple of weeks ago."

"It must have been an oversight."

"Yeah, I'll call her when we get in the car."

"You were saying?" I remind him as I glance around.

The studio is laid out like department store windows, with each piece spotlit in its own space. Various statues, like the one at Nate's house, decorate the space, but they don't appear to be for sale. They are all smooth plaster—some black in color, some white. And they are all of women with different looks on their faces doing various tasks. The sculpture closest to me is of a woman running, and her face looks to be in distress. The statue seems to communicate the benefits of hard work and determination, or the harsh consequences of demanding physical activity—the interpretation could go either way.

I find it fascinating.

There are about a dozen more like that one, and they are all so true to life and all magnificently sculpted.

Nate pulls me to him, breaking me from my concentration. "Thanks for coming with me."

I nip at his lip, happy to be here with him. "You can thank me by telling me about the bells."

He drops his gaze, and the shy boy that I've seen more than a few glimpses of is back. "Let's just say that when I met your brother, it was in a very compromising way."

I look up at the bells. "You didn't!"

He nods. "I did."

"Was he having sex with someone in here?"

Nate's grin is wide as he points to a door in the back. "Not exactly, but close. You should have seen the look on his face when I opened that door. Needless to say, those fucking bells went up shortly after."

The laughter rolls out of me. "Sounds like Zach," I say through muffled hysteria. Not that any of it was really that funny, but it eased the moment at the most perfect time.

Suddenly, the door Nate had been pointing at opens, and two women, both dressed professionally—one in black, and the other in navy—walk into the gallery.

"Oh, Mr. Hanson. I didn't expect to see you here," the one in navy says, placing her hand on her heart, as if we frightened her. "I was just showing the gallery to—"

"I know who she is."

Nate's entire body goes stiff. Something isn't right—I can tell right away.

Dead silence spans a moment, and then another, as Nate's eyes rake over the woman in black standing next to the woman I assume is the real estate agent.

"Oh, I'm sorry. I hadn't realized you'd met. Well, since you're here, Mrs. Winchester is going to be making an offer," the real estate agent announces excitedly.

Nate's eyes turn dark, his jaw stone. "I'm not interested."

The Realtor's eyes widen.

"Perhaps you could give us a moment, Mona," the lady in black says to the real estate agent.

"Of course. I'll just be next door at the coffee shop." She passes us and Nate's stare doesn't leave the woman in black.

The bells start jingling again and my heart pounds this time.

What is going on?

"Nate, you're being unreasonable," the woman says, stepping closer to us.

"Unreasonable? Are you fucking kidding me?"

"Nate, please don't speak to me that way."

A dry laugh escapes his throat. "I haven't wanted to talk to you at all since you came back. But, you can't seem to get that through your head."

"Natey, I want to talk to you. I want you to talk to me. What do I have to do to make that happen?"

Nate's fists clutch at his sides. "Don't call me that!"

Suddenly, I know who this is—her green eyes tell me all I need to know.

This is Marisa, Nate's mother.

"Nate." I grab for his hand. "Maybe we should go."

He waves off my attempt to hold his hand and pulls the car keys from his pocket. "Zoey, can you wait in the car for me?"

"You're Zachary's sister?" The woman attempts to shake my hand, but Nate pushes me behind him.

"Zoey," he hisses.

I look at the woman. "You knew my brother?"

"Only for a very short time, but he spoke of you with such adoration." Her smile is genuine.

"You shouldn't have been coming here, and you know it," Nate says through clenched teeth.

Her smile drops. "It was the only way I could get you to contact me."

Nate shoves the keys in my palms. "Go."

I take the keys.

"You know what? Never mind. We'll both go."

"Nate, don't walk away."

"You're the one who taught me how."

"Nate, that's unfair. I explained to you I wasn't well."

"You were well enough to start a new life."

"It's not like that."

He looks at me, motioning for the door.

"No," she says. "It's okay, I'll go. But Nate, please think about my offer. If you sell it to me, the gallery will stay open. If you sell it to anyone else, the likelihood of that is very slim. My offer will be fair."

"I don't want your money."

Her eyes drop. "I know that. I know you don't want anything from me. But I won't stop hoping that changes someday."

Silence follows her comment.

She walks past us and looks at me. "Zoey, I was so very sorry to hear about your brother."

I squeeze the keys tight in my hand. Nate's mother opens the door and when the bells ring again, I want to scream. The door closes and I turn my head as Marisa walks past the window, and then just like that, she's gone.

Nate's inhale is deep and although I can't see his eyes, I imagine they are closed. A few seconds later, he reaches back and takes the keys and my hand at the same time. "Let's go."

The past doesn't change, no matter how much you want it to. Whatever happened between Nate's mother, Nate's father, and Nate can't be remedied.

I should know.

I had a mother who forgot her children almost everywhere she went. And every day I used to wish that wasn't my life, but it never changed.

I can't help but wonder if my mother stood before me now, sober, cleaned up, and with her act together, if I would forgive her. I'd like to think I would.

Yet I'll never know.

The bells chiming help me drive my dark thoughts away.

Nate is quiet and his stride is quick as we cross the street. Once he closes my door, he moves even faster to get to his side, like he's worried his mother might come after him.

I glance at the coffee shop directly across from me and see Nate's mother standing just inside the door, wiping tears from her eyes.

Tears prick the back of my throat, but I swallow them down as Nate slams his foot on the accelerator. There are no cars, so accelerating to slide into traffic isn't necessary. More than likely it's a reflex.

That run-fast-run-far thing I've seen glimpses of.

He passes car after car.

I stay quiet until we reach the bridge. But once we do, I can't wait any longer.

The anguish on his face is almost too much to bear, and the anger seething from his grip on the steering wheel, mixed with the stiffness of his shoulders, makes him look like a wild animal in a cage right now. If I don't say anything, I know he's going to drop me off and bolt.

I also know I have to approach this with caution. "Nate," I say softly.

His eyes flash to mine. "I can't talk right now."

"Nate, tell me what happened when your mother left."

He slams the steering wheel and I jump.

I'm not scared, just startled. "Nate, you can talk to me about it." Silence.

"She didn't leave. She disappeared," he says faintly.

I can barely hear him.

"You think that woman you just met is a nice lady, who deserves a second chance, don't you?" He looks at me again before redirecting his gaze out the window.

My mind turns slowly and steadily as I ponder the question he just asked me.

My thoughts start to whirl when I see how torn apart he is right now.

And then, as the merry-go-round turns in my head, I begin to think about why he has never had a real relationship with a woman.

It has to have something to do with the way his mother left. It must have broken him in a way that's never been repaired.

I look over at him. "No, Nate, I don't. I don't know her well enough to think that. The question is: do you think she does?"

The car jerks off to the side of the road, and he parks in the emergency lane.

It's almost dark, and the lights of the bridge are turned on. But dusk seems to shadow everything. He gets out of the car.

I follow him, trying not to look down at the water beneath us. "Nate, get back in the car."

His hands grip the safety rails and he bows his head. Over the wind he yells, "No, she doesn't deserve shit from me!"

I slide under his arms and place my hands on his chest. "Let's get in the car and talk about it. Not out here, okay?"

He looks at me, his eyes seemingly lost to the past. "Hurricane Andrew struck harder than anyone imagined. No one was prepared. Schools were dismissed early and I waited and waited and waited for my mother to pick me up, but she never came. My dad was closing the gallery and Mrs. Martinez had to come back to get me. My father came hours later and when we went home, my mother wasn't there. Her car was gone and so was she. My father filed a missing persons report. He thought she died. A piece of him died that day. Three months passed with no sign of her and no body either. He never even realized she had emptied out their savings account. Then, one night there was a knock on the door and a man in a suit delivered an official court document—a petition for divorce."

I gasp and cover my mouth, unable to hold the tears back.

He shakes his head. "Don't pity me."

"Nate, I don't. My heart breaks for the small boy you were and for your father, but that's not pity."

He rubs my tears away as cars go flying by and headlights shine on us. "She never came back. We never heard from her again, until about the time I had to bring my father to Sunshine Village, when she moved back to town—husband and two kids in tow and wanting me in her life."

This time I keep my gasp to myself but move my hands to cup his face. "That had to be so hard."

Nate closes his eyes and leans his forehead against mine. "She abandoned us like an unwanted dog. She didn't want us. She broke my father's heart. Ruined his life. I can't accept her back in my life, no matter what lame excuses she gives. I just can't."

The psych teacher in me wants to dig deeper and help him work toward a possible reconciliation of some kind, but the woman in me that cares for this man and sees what this has done to him, wants her to stay as far away from him as humanly possible. I kiss him softly. "I understand. I do."

He pulls me to him and holds me. Just holds me, on the bridge spanning two completely different worlds and I feel like he and I, we have a bridge too—and it's my brother. "Come on. I shouldn't have pulled over here. Let's get home."

We get in the car and ride in silence to the house. When we get inside, he turns to me. "Do you mind if we just make a plate and sit and watch TV? I don't want to think about anything right now."

"That sounds really great. I'll change then be right down."

When I get up the stairs, I close the door and fall to the bed. Emotions zigzag through me. I want to ask him all kinds of questions. I want to help him. I want to dig deeper, to uncover his hurt.

But I shouldn't.

I can't.

I have to get myself back to the only mind-set I should be in right now—that this is a summer fling. I can't get involved in all of this. He's pulling me in, and the more I let him, the harder it will be for me to leave. I can't fix Nate, just like he can't fix me. But the problem is that I understand him now. He's no longer just a guy I want to have sex with. He's a guy who's protecting himself the only way he knows how.

I get it.

I'm doing it too.

The easel, sketchbooks, and paints I brought over from Zach's place earlier today sit in the corner—my version of Nate's waffle iron.

I look at it, and that voice whispers in my ear, *Don't forget your destiny.*

Like I could.

With a clear head and even clearer direction, I change into the running shorts and T-shirt I bought to wear last weekend but never did. Turned out, Nate didn't want to get out of bed in the morning either, although sleeping in wasn't his main reason—sex was.

That's right, Zoey, think sex.

I keep telling myself this.

Don't dig too deep; you'll only open another door.

The lights in the kitchen guide my way down the stairs. Nate is sitting in the dark living room on the couch with his feet up on the coffee table, along with two plates of food and two lemonades.

I try to shove his boots from the table. "Reruns of *Breaking Bad*—I love that show."

"A former teacher turns to a life of crime and recruits his former student, and you love this show—classic."

I shrug and decide to just step over his extended legs. "Don't judge."

He grabs my waist, pulling me to him and kissing me abruptly. "I wouldn't think of it."

With my hands on his chest, I push up and look at him. I can feel my clearer direction fading fast the minute I look into his eyes. I force myself to refocus. "I watched the first few seasons, but never finished it."

"Sounds like a marathon night."

"I had those with Zach all the time."

"Funny, we did too a long time ago."

"What changed?"

He shrugs his shoulders. "You know, I'm not sure anymore. We both just got busy and even though he lived right behind me, I didn't see him that much over the last year. I never thought about that until you got here."

"I guess sometimes everyone tends to get self-involved."

"Maybe." He runs his fingers through my hair, taking the time to twist them around a few curls. "I've never known anyone with hair like yours."

I roll off him and reach for the plates, handing his to him. "When I was in school, everyone called me Shirley Temple."

"Shirley Temple, I can see that."

We take a few bites and watch the TV. I turn to him. "I hated it. I hated the name and hated my hair."

He laughs and pokes his fork into one of the enchiladas. "Do you sing and dance like her? Because that's something I'd love to see."

I take another bite of my food and swallow. Then once I set my plate down, I turn my head toward him, pucker my lips, and clap my hands under my chin. "You gotta S-M-I-L-E to be H-A-double-P-Y."

He sets his plate down next to mine, and with one quick move closes the distance between us. "Do that again."

Puckering my lips, and clapping my hands under my chin I sing, "You gotta S-M-I-L-E to be H-A-double-P-Y."

This time he's not smiling when I look at him, but rather heavy-lidded eyes are gazing back at me.

My eyes go to his pants and he notices. My breathing picks up and I'm pretty sure he notices that too.

"My friends called me Handsome in high school and I hated it. I never would have embraced it and made fun of it like you did." His voice is rough, gravelly. It sounds like sex.

I shrug; all the while my pulse beats rapidly with an urge to touch him. I move closer, close enough to kiss him and even to put my hand right where my eyes had been, but I don't do either.

"When you can't beat them, join them. But I still hated it. And your friends still call you Handsome by the way."

His tongue sneaks out and draws a line around my mouth. "Only when they want to yank my chain," he mutters quietly between licks. "I've learned to ignore it and that bugs the shit out of them."

"That strategy works too." My tone is breathy.

He looks at me, then down.

My lips part as my fingers tickle up his leg, and when I get close, he presses my hand on his cock and moves it up and down the denim.

The moan that escapes my mouth is much louder than it should be as my arousal plows through me in a burst. With sudden haste, I unzip his pants and move even closer. "Take your pants off," I whisper in his ear.

He stares at me, maybe a little shocked, maybe a little turned on.

My chocolate syrup fantasy gets taken over by another. "You said tonight was mine. I'm taking you up on that. I want to watch you touch yourself."

The breath rushes out of him. "You take *your* pants off. I want to watch you touch yourself."

I move my hand faster up and down his erection. "I will after you."

"Fuck," he hisses and throws his head back.

The excitement that pinwheels through me isn't containable on any level.

If anyone could orgasm without manipulation, I think I just might have.

I'm the first to stand and strip out of my clothes.

His eyes drink me in until I'm fully naked and then he stands and takes his boots off followed by his clothes. I would have done it for him but it just would have taken too long. He sits back down completely naked. The glass doors behind us let the moonlight and darkness spill in, but the water is his only close neighbor, so no one can see us. His cock is fully erect and he leans back on the couch cushion and lays his arms at his sides with legs spread at an even width with his shoulders.

He looks sexy as hell.

His gaze flickers down and I know he's waiting for me.

I move closer and he takes my hand and puts it on his cock again. My fingers grip beneath his and he curls his fingers around them and starts to move. With my free hand, I reach for the back of his neck and pull his lips to mine.

We meet right over our hands.

He moves my hand faster and I give the hair on the back of his neck a little tug. He grits his teeth and lets out a strangled, raspy noise that makes me move even faster, but then I let go—of his cock and his hair. "Your turn. I want to watch you. I want to watch you come."

I almost think he might say no as his own hands lay limp beside him.

"Please," I add. "Please let me see you how you look when you come. When we're together, the moment is so wild, I can't concentrate." There's something so erotic about the possibility of watching him touch himself for me. I've seen Nate finish in me, and in my mouth, but I've never been able to give him my undivided attention. He might be touching his own sex, but he's doing it for me, and that turns up the hotness scale to scalding, if you ask me.

His hand runs down his abs and when he finds his cock, he grips it, stroking slowly from the very tip all the way down to the base.

His eyes meet mine.

My nipples tighten and warmth floods between my legs.

Holy hell!

I've never watched porn or seen a man masturbate, but this is an image I'll never forget.

Up and down he strokes—he's in no hurry, no orgasm seems to be chasing him. Me, on the other hand, I can't control myself.

My hands grab my own breasts and I think of how his hands feel on me there.

His dark eyes gleam and his mouth twists up into a smile as I pinch my own nipples. He slides further down the leather of the cushion, arching his back and thrusting his hips upward.

I rise to my knees right beside him for a bird's-eye view, allowing my kneecaps to touch the side of his thigh for that flesh-to-flesh contact I crave.

He tips his head back. Then he takes his free palm and places it over my lips. On instinct, I lick up and down it. The world outside fades as I watch with such intent when he puts the hand I licked on his cock and grips it tight.

His other hand reaches across to one of mine and urges it downward.

I comply.

Finding myself already wet, I don't waste any time as I slide a finger inside myself and look down at his hands. He strokes faster, thrusting his hips up in rhythm with his hand movement and I do the same with my hand.

The image is clear—his fist is my pussy and my finger is his cock.

Then out of nowhere, his hand is on my nipple, circling it, twisting it.

Oh God, my knees feel weak and tingling spreads all through me. I'm trying to focus on him, on the beauty of the way his cock lengthens with each stroke, on the way his face contorts as he grips harder, on the way his hips rise from the leather beneath him, but I can't.

I fall back, losing my connection with him and move back toward the armrest. Once my head is supported, I let my thighs drift open.

Now he's the one with the bird's-eye view, but I can still see him.

His hand sinks beneath his cock and I have to bite back a moan.

I close my eyes as I add another finger to join the one already inside me and pretend my fingers are his cock. Before I open them to look at him again, the couch shifts and he's on his knees between my legs.

I look up.

"Don't stop."

His words resurrect an aching need in me, but this time, it's to make myself come and show him just how much he turns me on. My hips thrust up of their own accord to absorb the pleasure.

His palm moves faster and faster around his cock and I can see his desire reach higher and higher. The pleasure builds and my breaths come in short bursts. His groans become louder, wilder. Our eyes meet and a connection draws tight between us. And then, as he reaches his hand to rub my clit and I reach my fingers to stroke the underside of his cock, we both lose ourselves.

I cry out as I let myself go.

I arch my back as the exquisite sensations overcome me.

Rock me.

Take me to another dimension.

My head falls but I quickly snap it back up.

I have to watch him—I want to so much.

In this moment of ecstasy, my eyes on him, his on me, my body trembles as it comes alive and I cry out even louder in pure pleasure. "Oh Nate. Oh Nate."

"Fuck," he cries. "Zoey."

Saying a person's name when you orgasm is so personal, and yet we both seem to be doing it more and more.

Hot wetness spills onto my chest. I watch as it happens and it's a beautiful thing. After a few spurts his hand shields himself, and the rest leaks from beneath his palm.

When it's over, he collapses on top of me, using the armrest to support himself and his scent fills me as his body covers me. Tingles linger throughout my body and the warmth of his skin electrifies me. He bestows a soft and gentle kiss on me.

Kiss after kiss, our lips stay melded to each other until he pulls back and grabs his T-shirt off the floor to clean us up. When he's done, he shifts me so he can lie against the back of the sofa and I flip around to spoon him.

The sound from the TV attracts my attention, and when I look over, the closing credits are rolling. "You missed your show."

Teeth circle my ear and a tongue jets inside it. "No, I didn't."

21

The Statue

Sunlight filters through the clouds and spills into the bedroom. My eyes squeeze shut, and I'm definitely not ready to wake. A hand runs up my thigh and I'm surprised to feel Nate's body behind mine. His skin is warm and soft and his fingers leave a tantalizing trail of desire in their wake. The pitter-patter on the window makes me smile.

Rain?

Is that all it takes to keep Nate in bed in the morning?

If so, I might just have to figure out how to do a rain dance.

A gentle touch swipes my hair to the side and his soft lips kiss my shoulder. I snuggle further into his body and clench his fingers, pulling them up to my lips. With his warm legs tangling around mine, his smooth chest flush against my back, and his arms circled around me, there is nowhere I want to go and nothing I want to do except what we're doing right now. His velvet lips work their way up my neck and my pulse races faster and faster with each added touch, pushing me to that place I never want to leave.

That place where there is no destiny.

"Good morning," he whispers in my ear.

I flip around and wrap my arms around his neck. "Good morning. What, you don't go running when it's raining? Afraid you might get wet?"

He chuckles, dipping down to nip my lip. "I do—all the time. I just didn't feel like getting up today."

All of sudden he smacks my ass. "Ouch," I call out.

"I'll go tonight and you'll come with me, smartass."

With a groan I think, *Screw the rain dance.* "Can't wait." I roll my eyes.

"Sarcasm turns me on."

My eyes run up and down his face—his stubbled jaw, his sculpted nose, the chiseled cheekbones, deep green eyes, and that hair, tousled, messy, but somehow perfect. "I thought *I* turned you on?"

His mouth is hungry when it attacks mine. "You do. I think I've proven that to you more than a few times."

In a blink, he's on top of me.

Our eyes pin each other and his grin is sly—full of promise.

I like it—a lot.

He skims my naked flesh with his fingertips, sending shivers down my spine. The desire that's never far away starts pulsing between my legs and my hands are on him as soon as his lips find mine.

My fingers find their way down the sinewy muscle of his chest and then over the ridges of his ribs.

God, I love his body.

Just as his lips trail down my neck, his phone rings. He reaches for it, but I grab his wrist. "Let it ring."

He glances at his phone, then at me. "I can't; it could be about my dad." He sits up and after glancing at the caller ID answers it. "Hello." There's a sleepiness in his voice that is sexy as hell.

A long pause has me concerned, and I sit up. I try to catch his eye to ask him if it's his father, but he's already moving out of bed—his back is to me and his feet are on the floor.

"Sure, no, it's fine. I can do that."

It must be his office. His tone is different than it is when he's talking to his dad or the staff at Sunshine. As the conversation continues, I begin to think how strange it is that I know the different tones of his voice.

I know when he's upset, angry, turned on, intrigued, amused, complacent, and even happy.

The bond we've forged on so many levels has afforded me that knowledge, and the recognition terrifies me. Every day another door opens, and with each one I can feel my heart doing the same.

It feels good.

It feels right.

But yet, it's wrong.

I throw myself back down on the bed and look at him, at his sexy back, and even now that the mood has changed and sex is off the table, my stomach still flutters with anticipation of the next time.

This fling has become an addiction, and that's dangerous.

Addictions are hard to break, and this ends in exactly seven weeks from today.

But what if I stay in Miami, get my own place, and go back to school here? Does it have to end?

Suddenly, that damn destiny cloud starts to rain in my mind. My life isn't mine to command—my inner voice reminds me: *your destiny is already written for you, like those before you.*

Maybe I could be different?

Maybe once I get back home, I can find a way to beat it, cheat it, escape it, and then I could come back.

No, I shouldn't think that way.

I look over at him, so self-contained, controlled, and wonder if he'd even want me to consider living here. When he turns his head and runs his hand through his hair, I think no, probably not. And besides, he has too many demons to conquer before he can think about anything with anyone.

But I can help him—I can.

I know last night, in this very bed, I told myself I needed to avoid getting too heavily involved, but today in the light of day, I need to help him.

The phone call ends and he sets his phone down with his head hanging low. "I have to get ready to go. A friend needs—"

"Nate?" I ask, my mind whirling with things I probably should leave alone, but can't. "Is that statue at the bottom of the stairs your mother's?"

His head snaps in my direction. Fierce, cold eyes hold mine. "You already know it is. So why ask?"

"Why did you bring that one here?"

"What does it matter? And what's with the fifty questions about a fucking statue anyway?"

"I want to know why you're using it to torture yourself."

His stare narrows. "You don't know what you're talking about."

But he's wrong. I do. I saw the other statues in the gallery last night and none of them invoked loneliness and despair like the one downstairs. "Is the statue to remind you of you or her?"

He clamps his jaw shut and strides to the bathroom, slamming the door.

I scurry off the bed and go to the door. When I turn the knob it's locked. So I knock. "Nate, I'm not trying to hurt you. You have to know that. I just want to help."

The water turns on and silence is my only response. I throw some clothes on and wait. When the water shuts off, I knock again. "Have you talked to her, let her explain why she left? It might help bring you some closure."

The door swings wide and Nate practically stomps by me and into his closet.

I follow him. "Nate, talk to me."

He pulls on a pair of boxers and lets the towel fall as he slips into them. He takes a pair of slacks from a hanger and slips into those as well. Then he removes a white shirt from a row of white shirts and puts it on. Only when he's done does he look at me. "Yeah, as a matter of fact, it was the first question I asked her when she showed up at my door, and it was the last one too. Her reason was pretty simple really—she was unhappy and it was making her mentally unstable. Same bullshit story you hear every day—got married too young, felt suffocated, didn't want to be tied down. Her story *isn't* the same though, because she was a coward. She didn't want to see the pain on my father's face, so she just decided to leave. The storm only helped her disappear easily. She even fucking told me she would have let everyone think she was dead, but she needed money and needed to work, so she couldn't stay anonymous. As for me—she thought I was better off with my father." The closet is large, but feels very small when he breezes past me with his shoes in hand like I'm not even standing there.

I pivot around just as he takes a pair of black socks from the drawer.

The rumpled sheets don't seem to bother him as he sits on the bed and pulls his socks on and then shoves his feet into his shoes. Before he stands back up, he finally looks up at me. His eyes are filled with anguish. "What? Cat got your tongue?"

I swallow and try to keep my tears at bay. "No, it's just I know what it's like—to feel abandoned. My mother was a drug addict and either lost or forgot Zach and me almost everywhere she took us. But then she died and some days I wish she were still here—that's all." My hands are trembling as I use the doorjamb of the closet for support.

"I don't share those same feelings—at all! The statue reminds me what she was really like and why she left. It erases the mirage of the *Leave It to Beaver* life I conjured up in my head because, let me tell you—she was never a June Cleaver." His jaw takes a harsh shape and his tone is drenched in anger.

"I understand that, Nate, but maybe she's different now. People make mistakes, and she wants you in her life. Maybe you should give her a chance—if not for her, for you."

I can feel him shooting daggers in my direction as he stands. "This shrink visit is over. I'll be home late tonight."

His stride is quick as he passes me without a second glance and slams the door behind him. A few moments later, I hear something shattering.

My stomach falls.

That didn't go so well.

Tears fall in streams from my eyes.

What I'm crying over, I have no idea—Nate, his mother, me, my brother. I bury myself back between the warm, comfortable sheets and stare out the window at the rain. My eyes close and I burrow my head further into the pillows seeking comfort in his scent and wanting to shut out the world, if even just for a little while.

When I wake again, I reach for my phone, but there are no messages. It's close to ten so I leap out of bed and go to the bathroom, shower, and dress for the day. It's still raining and I wish I had packed a pair of comfortable jeans to slip into. But I didn't, so I settle on a T-shirt dress and the platform sneakers I got at Isabella's last week, then grab my raincoat. I'm going to go to Nate's office after I drop off another load at the hurricane shelter and apologize to him. At least there he can't hang up on me, ignore me, or slam a door in my face. I shouldn't have pushed it as far as I did, but regardless of how mad he might have been at me, I think it might have helped. At least he talked about his feelings and got them out. Not a miracle cure by any means, but maybe a start on the road to the closure he so desperately needs.

My phone rings.

"Hello?"

"Zoey, it's Oliver. How are you?"

"Good. And you?"

"I can't complain. Look, I'm about to run into a meeting, but I wanted you to know I received the accident report. I can send it over this afternoon."

"Do you mind if I pick it up? I'm going to be out for a bit and I can get it then."

"Sure, not a problem. I'll leave it with my secretary."

"Thank you, Oliver."

"I have to run, but call me if you need anything else."

We hang up and I come to an abrupt stop at the top of the stairs.

The statue is in pieces—shattered all over the floor.

Guilt strikes me in my chest and my heart weighs heavy. I didn't mean to push him that far. But maybe it being gone will be the first step in moving on, because no matter what Nate says, he's still stuck somewhere between when his mother left and when she came back.

A memory flickers in my mind—the night Nate and I turned the corner of our relationship and he agreed to spend the summer with me. He asked me, "Are you sure you want me?"

Sadness creeps into my bones.

We aren't so different—he and I—both putting a shield around us to protect what was damaged long ago, to protect ourselves from ever feeling unwanted again.

I've done it all my life, made excuses of never having time for a relationship, but isn't that what they were—just excuses?

When I get down to the bottom of the stairs, I sit on the second to last step and cradle my head in my hands. After a few minutes, I fumble for my phone in my purse, pull up my contacts list, find the name I'm looking for, and hit the office number.

"Hello, Dr. Julia Raymond."

"Dr. Raymond, it's Zoey."

"Zoey, today isn't your scheduled time."

"I know. Do you have a minute to talk or are you busy?"

"Hold on, let me just switch extensions."

I can picture her moving from the small reception desk out-side her office to the secure confines of her soothing blue walls to sit behind her large, intimidating desk. Dr. Raymond's secretary, Kate, isn't there in the summer, so she works alone.

"I'm back. What's going on?"

I get right to the point. "I was hoping for your professional opinion."

"Of course. Is this about you or this new man in your life?"

"Both, neither— Oh, I don't know." Tears coat my eyes as I try to blink them away, but the burn in my throat from forcing them back is too much. "Dr. Raymond, I don't know what I'm doing. I feel like one walking contradiction after another, and this time, I think I might have gone too far."

Telling Dr. Raymond everything that's going on between Nate and me without discussing the insane sexual chemistry isn't easy, but for purposes of this conversation it seems irrelevant and also a break in trust—like what we have now is somehow more intimate than when I first told her about us.

I'm not sure why.

She listens—a few questions, a few sighs, and a lot of under-standing. Finally she says, "Zoey, you aren't wrong in your assess-ment. Abandonment fears do typically stem from a loss in childhood, such as the loss of a parent through death or divorce, but they can also result from inadequate physical or emotional care, as in you and your brother's case. Seeing you want to be with someone is a big step. But in both of your cases, these are issues that are complex and not fixed by a single conversation, and sometimes not fixed in a lifetime. In adulthood, those early childhood experiences result in fear of being abandoned by those you bring into your circle. While some degree of abandonment fear is a normal part of being human, traumatic experiences most definitely impact the development of healthy relationships. Having never met with Nate, I can't render an opinion on him. But as for you, Zoey, you do know what you're doing, and you're not a contradiction. The bigger question is: are you willing to see it for what it really means?"

I picture Dr. Raymond turning toward the window in her chair and looking out into the tree line like she always does when she's waiting for a response.

"Dr. Raymond, you know I'm not looking for anything but a fun time."

She sighs.

I lean back on one of the steps, sighing myself.

A buzz sounds loudly through the line.

"I think someone's here, can you hold on a moment?"

"Sure."

About thirty seconds elapse before she comes back on the line. "My patient just arrived. Can I call you back this evening?"

"Of course. And Dr. Raymond, thank you for listening."

"Zoey, listen to me, think about what you're feeling and be open to those feelings. Don't lock them away. Can you do that for me?"

My shoulders sag dramatically as I sit back up. "You know I can't. That won't be good for him or me. And besides, he'd just run."

"I'm not so sure about that. At least think about it and let's talk some more later, shall we?"

"Yes, Dr. Raymond. Good-bye."

I press End and look out at the beautiful view. The rain is still coming down and it looks like a beaded curtain as it hits the pool. I stare at it for the longest time, thinking about everything Dr.

Raymond just said, thinking about how I feel, and thinking about how Nate must be feeling right now. The bottom line is that it wasn't my place to push him like that.

I gather my things and follow the planks of hardwood surrounding the tiled living room to the hallway leading to the garage. I pass the fireplace and look at the two photos of Nate with his dad. They look happy. His dad has salt-and-pepper hair and brown eyes, but other than that, they look very much alike—both handsome.

Our plates are still on the coffee table, and I stop to pick them up along with the empty glasses of lemonade. Once I've tidied the kitchen and loaded the dishwasher, I make a quick cup of coffee, opting for cream instead of frothing my milk to save time, and I bring it with me.

Yesterday, Rosie and I put all the boxes in the garage so I'd be able to load the car easily. I really didn't want to have to back it down the ramp, and now that it's raining, I appreciate the foresight even more. When I step out into the garage, the boxes aren't against the wall where we left them. A quick glance in my car tells me Nate loaded them for me.

My heart squeezes in my chest at the kindness.

Mad at me or not, he still wanted to help me.

I have to see him, apologize for pushing.

And I have to stop treading in areas where I shouldn't be.

22
Slugger

The Southeast Financial Center is no more than fifteen minutes away from the shelter, but in heavy traffic it takes me thirty minutes to get there. The building is tall enough to be seen from the beach, so finding it is easy. Nate's pointed it out a few times and because I seem to make so many *Miami Vice* jokes, he told me that his office building appeared in several episodes of the 1980s TV show and was also featured at the end of the movie's opening credits.

I found it extremely cool.

Nate on the other hand was far less impressed by the status that the building where his company is housed holds.

When I turn off Thirteenth Street and merge onto Biscayne Boulevard, the underground parking garage is on my left. Once I've parked, I make my way to the lobby. Two electric blue escalators lead up to the main floor. The white tiles are huge, and plants are everywhere. There is also a map on the wall of the city of Miami, illuminated in neon pink.

The tenant listing tells me Skyline Holdings is on the forty-fifth floor. There's no visitor desk or anyone to call up for access, so I ride the glass elevator overlooking the Miami skyline. The view goes on for miles and miles.

The doors *ping* and open.

Ahead is a long glossy black reception desk with a beautiful blond woman wearing a headset. Above her head is the insignia for Nate's company—an outline of the Miami skyline with the letters that spell Skyline Holdings cut out of it.

"Can I help you?"

"Yes, I'm here to see Nate—I mean Nathaniel Hanson."

She looks toward the computer screen. "Do you have an appointment?"

"No, but tell him Zoey is here."

She glances up in mock smile. "I'm sorry, but Mr. Hanson doesn't see anyone without a scheduled meeting."

I lean over the desk. "Could you please just tell him Zoey Flowers is here? I'm sure he'll see me."

Well, I'm not so sure, but I know he wouldn't expect me to make an appointment.

The phone rings and she holds up a finger. "Skyline Holdings, how may I direct your call?"

Pause.

"Certainly, hold please."

She hits a few numbers on her phone.

"Claudia, Mr. Elliot for Mr. Hanson. It's about the pending sale."

Another pause.

"I'll put him through to you."

She hits a button on the phone and then gives me her attention again. "I'm sorry. Mr. Hanson is out for the afternoon. May I leave him a message?"

I look at her, uncertain if she's telling me the truth or not. But other than causing a scene, there isn't much more I can do. "No, that's okay."

My locket swings as I hurry toward the metal doors, and I clutch it the entire ride down as the elevator glides slowly to the lobby. Once there, I sit in one of the black leather chairs and pull out my phone.

I call Nate.

"You've reached Nathaniel Hanson. Leave a message."

"Nate, it's me, Zoey. Do you think you could call me? I'd really like to talk to you."

With a tap, I end the call. When I put my phone away, I pull out Oliver's card and make my way to his office. It isn't far.

Oliver's office is in Wynwood, in one of the storefronts close to the gallery. His secretary hands me a white envelope, and I take it to the coffee shop I saw next door to Wanderlust.

After the girl behind the counter hands me my coffee, I take a seat on one of the wooden benches and reach for the white envelope in my purse. Opening it, I read the short personal note attached from Oliver.

> Zoey,
>
> This is the 6-page report you asked for. I didn't include any of the photos from the accident. Should you need anything else you know you can call me.
>
> Best,
> Oliver

I feel anxious as I unfold the report. But I've been feeling extremely anxious lately whenever I'm not with Nate. I think I need to schedule a video session with Dr. Raymond. I know I need to find other ways to deal with the darkness that lingers around the corners of my life, other than finding solace in the passion I feel whenever Nate and I are together.

I set the report on the table. The pages are covered in black ink. My eyes quickly scan the title at the top where it reads *Florida Traffic Report Long Form* in the upper left-hand corner. The first section beneath it says *TIME & LOCATION: Date of Crash: 5 May 2014. Time of Crash: 01:31 AM.*

The boxes are endless: *Time Officer Notified, Time Officer Arrived, Report Number.* The page is filled with more boxes and numbers: *Type of Vehicle, Insurance, Address,* etc. I scan it, then flip to the next page. Dozens of boxes with check boxes for road conditions, sight location, traffic characteristics. I flip again.

This page is labeled *Florida Traffic Crash Report Narrative/ Diagram.*

I suck in a breath.

It reads: *Vehicle one was traveling in a northeasterly direction while exiting the Douglas MacArthur Causeway and continued to travel northeasterly. Vehicle one crossed over the roadway (Lemon Street) and the concrete curb onto the grass median where it struck a tree.*

I close my eyes when I come to the final sentences: *Vehicle one came to a final rest facing southbound.* I open my eyes and force myself to finish reading: *The driver of the vehicle was dead on arrival. The passenger received extensive injuries and was airlifted to . . .*

I steady myself on the table.

Passenger?

There was someone with him?

I quickly turn the page, looking for more information. It's an illustration of the crash site, and at the bottom it lists:

Passenger Name: Gisele Guzman Address: 6831 Bear Ave Apt 2 City: Miami Beach

Oh my God!

I blink rapidly at the words on the report, my vision fading in and out.

My heart clenches.

Could this be the same woman Leo told me about?

I have to talk to her.

Grabbing my purse, I hurry back to the car. With a deep breath and trembling fingers, I enter her address into the GPS system and hit the gas.

I pick up speed and soar onto the causeway.

My heartbeat kicks up in anticipation of meeting this woman.

The General Douglas MacArthur Causeway is a six-lane highway, and I feel like I know all three and a half miles of it very well. Once I pass the entrance to Palm Island, as well as the traffic light and bus stop, it's another two miles and then I'm beachside. Large cruise ships pass me, and their ship horns sound as they enter the ocean.

I find myself trying to remember the phone call that came the night Zach died, but once the police officer told me Zach had been killed, I pretty much blacked out. I can't believe there was someone with him.

With my mind somewhere else, GPS guides the way and I'm there before I realize it. The yellow two-story apartment building is north of the beach on the corner of Bear Avenue and Indian Creek Drive. Street parking seems to be my only option, as the parking lot is for residents only. Parallel parking into a spot isn't easy, but I manage after a few attempts. The white gate surrounding the building isn't locked, so I easily walk up the brick-paved sidewalk and find the apartment. I probably should have called first, but there was no phone number on the report, and I really want to talk to her

Walking up to the apartment, I see the door is slightly ajar, and I can hear people inside.

I start to panic.

What am I going to say?

Something like, *So you were on my brother's motorcycle with him. He died. You didn't.*

No. That sounds bitter.

Maybe, *Are you the girl from the club my brother used to wait for?* That sounds better.

But what if she isn't the same girl?

Never mind.

I'm working myself into a frenzy. It's best to just let this play out.

With a deep, calming breath, I press the doorbell. The door opens quickly, and a small boy wearing a Marlins jersey and holding a giant bag of M&M's smiles at me. "You're not Grandma," the cute toddler says with chocolate rimming his lips.

"Mateo! No! You never answer the door without asking who it is first."

A woman's voice echoes from somewhere inside. I glance around, but I can't see her. The place is small. Stairs are directly behind the child and there's a hallway leading to a bigger room beside them, with a breakfast bar on the left.

"I got it," a velvety smooth voice I know all too well calls before Nate turns the corner, rolling up his white sleeves.

My breath leaves me in a rush. Completely blindsided by his presence, I have no idea what to say. I can't even think, let alone form words.

Shaking, I grip my arms above my elbows. "Nate."

"Zoey." He blinks in utter confusion. "What are you doing here?"

What am I doing here? What is he doing here?

"Oliver gave me the accident report and I wanted to talk to the woman who was with my brother when he died."

The words come out but I don't even hear them—my pulse is beating in my ears so loudly.

Nate's expression must look just as shocked as mine. "She was?"

It's obviously news to him.

The little boy pushes on the screen door and I manage to move my legs to step aside and it opens. "Do you want to color with me? I also have Play-Doh. Oh and finger paints too."

"Mateo! Come here."

It's her!

The woman in the archway is the exotic-looking woman from my brother's sketches. She has the same dark hair, enchanting dark eyes, and olive complexion.

I stare at her.

A ping of sympathy hits me in a wave. Her arm is in a sling and the skin on her face and hands seems pigmented—new skin mixes with her own flesh, and I can tell it must have been grafted.

She must be still recovering.

She walks slowly down the hall.

My heart stalls.

"Can I help you?" she asks. She takes a few more steps closer and then slaps her hand over her mouth.

Nate's confusion only seems to multiply as he looks from Gisele to me.

My eyes dart to hers, and a wave of sorrow engulfs me, but I hold my tears back.

My brother obviously meant a lot to her.

The small child is demanding my attention, and causes my focus to drift. "Come on. I got a lot of new toys and I want to play."

I crouch down and look at the toddler tugging on my dress. He smells like chocolate and Play-Doh. He has warm brown eyes with dark ruffled hair—he looks like his mother. "Mateo, right?" I extend my hand. "I'm Zoey and I'd love to play with you, but can I talk with your mommy for just a few minutes first?"

The wind blows his bangs off his face even under his baseball hat and he smiles at me. "I know who you are. Zach showed me your pictures. You're his sister. I wish I had a sister."

He puts his small palm in mine and shakes it.

His words touch me, and tears well in my eyes.

Rising back to my full height, I catch Nate's stare.

He's guarded, hesitant, and stunned.

Suddenly, he's in my head and I can't dispel my thoughts—raw, crashing emotion making it all the more painful to meet his eyes.

Why wouldn't he have told me about this woman? What is he doing here?

Oh God, does he have a child?

"Zoey." Gisele's voice breaks, and tears flow freely from her eyes.

Before I know it, one arm is around me and she's clutching me to her, hugging me fiercely. "I'm so sorry. I'm so sorry."

I pull back, moved to tears that I can no longer contain. "Shhh . . . it's not your fault."

"But it is," she cries.

I look at her and shake my head.

"What's the matter, Mommy?"

"Come on, slugger, let's go upstairs and play." Nate's voice is gentle as he speaks to the little boy, and they definitely know each other. He takes Mateo's hand and looks at me. His eyes fill with something I can't identify—understanding, realization, comprehension, or maybe it's just guilt.

I shake it off and concentrate on the woman breaking down before me. "Can we go sit down and talk?"

She looks at me with her dark eyes fringed in long lashes, now swimming in tears. I recognize something familiar in them.

Heartbreak.

She nods her head.

"Race you to my room!" the little boy yells and starts up the stairs.

"You're on." Nate follows behind, his eyes still on me.

Once they disappear, Gisele and I walk down the hall past a small kitchen with bags of groceries sitting on the counter.

Packages of unopened toys litter the family room carpet, but what catches my attention are the three sketches on the wall behind the red sofa. They're Zach's work. One is of the child. One is of the woman whose arm is in a sling. And the other is of the mother and child laughing on the playground. They are sketches that capture the essence of the people in them.

My brother created them.

Gisele sits on the sofa and rubs the sling holding her arm. In the light, I can really see her true beauty. She's simply dressed in a thin T-shirt and slender jeans. And with the many silver bangles around her wrist and the large hoops in her ears, she looks like Natalie Wood, or maybe even Elizabeth Taylor.

A woman I could see my brother being attracted to.

"You knew my brother." I sit down in the chair next to the sofa.

She nods.

"Fairly well," I add, pointing to the sketches behind her.

Torment whips across her face. "Oh, Zoey, you're why I called Nate today."

"I don't understand."

"Your brother and I loved each other so much."

I feel like I've been punched in the stomach.

I sink back in the chair.

The thought overwhelms me with both happiness and sorrow. My brother, the romantic—did he get the girl of his dreams after all? Did he fall in love and then lose his life before he had a chance to experience what I know he would have been great at?

I feel my emotions start to spin out of control.

Breathe.

Her soft voice reels me in. "Are you okay?"

That far-off voice echoes again in my ear. *What happened to your brother is going to happen to you.*

This is not my inner voice. This is my fear manifesting itself. It's the first time I realize it. For the first time, I can distinguish between my own voice and the darker ones harboring within me—

the ones that drove me to Dr. Raymond to begin with. She taught me how to deal with them.

Deep calming breaths.

Breathe.

I shake my head, willing the voice away, then sit up straight and look at Gisele. "Yes, I'm fine. I'm sorry. I'm just trying to understand this. Why wouldn't he have told me, and what does Nate have to do with this?"

She moves closer and puts her free hand on my knee. "Your brother was going to tell you. But he was insistent that he wanted to wait until the time was right. We both had a mountain of debt to pay off, and the path we had chosen wasn't conventional."

"I know about the Estate and what he did there."

She looks relieved. "Then maybe you can understand why we both wanted to start a new chapter in our lives, one that included making a respectable living, before we told anyone."

The room around me spins and I grab the chair. "How long were you together?"

She swipes at her tears with her hand. "We met at the Ballroom last year. We clicked and became friends. Zach asked me what I did for a living and I told him I worked for the Estate. He was looking for a way to make a lot of money and before I knew it, I was helping him create the Artist. Somewhere in the process we fell in love."

My mouth drops open. I'm stunned into silence.

Does she know what he was doing there?

"Zoey, I know what you must be thinking. How could we be together and do what we were doing? But when we first met, we really were just friends. And it was a job. I wasn't ready to be in a relationship when I met your brother. I had my own baggage to take care of. But then, the more time we spent together, my feelings for him intensified. When I was finally ready to commit, he told me he had loved me since he first met me. And we both stopped including anything of a sexual nature in the services he offered."

"I don't understand. Then how did you both still work?"

"Everything at the Estate isn't about having sex. It's about giving the client the high they're looking for. We just found other ways to do that. Your brother was an artist, so he'd paint his clients, sometimes on paper, sometimes on canvas, sometimes on their bodies. He'd sketch them however they wanted to be sketched. At times that meant watching a couple have sex, but that never bothered either of us. We understood it was part of the job."

More rocked by the love in her voice than by her confession, I'm still struggling with the anger that festers beneath my skin—not at her but at my brother.

Why would he think I wouldn't have accepted her?

But it wasn't about accepting Gisele and Mateo, was it?

It was about accepting the money.

His need to take care of me overrode his own happiness.

Goddamn you, Zach!

Tears fall freely, and I swipe them as fast as they come.

"He loved what he did, Zoey, just like he loved you. Making women feel good about themselves, by sketching their inner and outer beauty, made him so happy."

Her voice sounds small but I'm riveted by her words and I'm already apologizing to him in my mind when my eyes refocus on Gisele.

"It was my fault he died, not that damn family legacy he warned me about."

"What are you talking about?"

"It was my fault he was driving so fast."

We're staring at each other, but I feel like we're not even in the same room. "Gisele, Zach always drove fast."

"He wouldn't have even been out that night if it weren't for me. My mother called me at work and said Mateo was sick. My car wouldn't start, so I called Zach and he came to get me. He knew I was worried about Mateo, so he was driving fast. He made me wear his helmet since he didn't have a spare. We never rode on his bike because we always had Mateo with us. Zach was rushing to get me home when he drove over some debris in the road and lost control of his bike."

Zach—she calls him Zach just like me. The room is a decent size but suddenly seems so small as the walls start to close in on me.

In a rush, I grab her and pull her to me—not as gently as I should. "Don't think that way. He did what he did because that's who he was. His dying is not your fault."

It's no one's fault except destiny's, maybe.

It's easy for me to beseech her not blame herself because I truly believe she shouldn't. You can't blame anyone for someone else's death. You just can't, unless they were killed—shot by a bullet, stabbed by a knife, a club to the head.

Her crying turns to sobbing and I just hold her in my arms. Time passes slowly as we come together over the loss of someone we both loved.

When she leans back, she stares at me and pushes one of my stray curls from my face. "You look like him, you know."

I smooth my out-of-control curls that frizzed in the rain. "Everyone thought we were twins when we were little."

"Do you think his child will have curly hair too?"

Light from the window cuts across her body, and I can't see it through the sunshine peeking in.

My eyes go to her flat stomach. "Are you . . . pregnant?"

She nods her head, her eyes overflowing again—or maybe still. "That's why I called Nate this morning. Santiago told me you were staying with him, and I wanted to ask him to bring you over."

"Oh my God!"

I clutch my locket as an unfamiliar happiness floats around me. "Did he know?"

She frowns. "No. I didn't know until I was taken in to the hospital. It's early still, and with the trauma I've suffered, the doctors say I'm at risk for a miscarriage."

From elsewhere in the house, I can hear the patter of little feet. "Mommy, I'm hungry. Can we have lunch?"

Whispers float down to where we sit. "Never mind. Nate says I can have ice cream if I wait until you call me down."

"Slugger, you're not supposed to tell." The sound of Nate's voice and the way he interacts with Mateo do something to my heart.

Gisele presses her hands to her eyes to wipe her tears. "I haven't told anyone yet, not even my mother. You're the first. It just doesn't seem real."

"What doesn't seem real? That out of tragedy comes light?"

"I never looked at it like that."

"That's how I see it. It's the only way this makes any sense."

"I wasn't sure how you'd feel since we never met. Zach and I were planning on telling you we were together before anyone else. Mateo and I were going to come to New York with him when he came for his birthday next month. He thought by then, he'd have talked to Nate and everything would be in place for us."

"Have talked to Nate about what?"

"Oh, our plans. Zach wanted to buy the gallery and turn it back to what it used to be like when Milo first opened it. Milo had talked to Zach for hours about how to make it work—offering lessons in the evening hours to drive traffic into the shop when it would otherwise be closed. They had discussed commissioning some of the artists who left their mark on the Wynwood Walls and calling out their works as exclusive to the gallery. They even discussed changing the name back to Hanson's."

"Did Nate know any of this?"

"No. Zach was waiting for the right time to approach him. He said Nate hadn't seemed ready to accept the fact that his father wouldn't be going back yet."

"But he knew about you and Zach?"

"No. Like I said, no one knew. He still doesn't even know why I asked him to bring me home from my mother's today. I was going to talk to him once I got Mateo settled."

"Then how do you know Nate?"

She gives a small, lopsided smile. "We grew up together. Him, Oliver, Santiago, and I all lived on the same street. My mother and Oliver's parents are still there."

"That's really nice."

"It is. I had lost contact with the guys after high school, but then last year, I went to Oliver for help with my divorce. We ended up staying in touch and shortly after that Oliver, Santiago, Nate, and I all met for a drink in our old neighborhood."

"So did you meet Zach through Oliver?"

She shakes her head. "No, Nate kind of introduced us."

I raise my brow. "Kind of?"

She sinks back in the couch. The look on her face is reminiscent. "I knew the owner of the Estate was looking to get out, and I knew that Nate liked to invest in small, profitable businesses, so I invited him to the club to meet the owner. It turned out to be a really bad night for me, until I met Zach. My ex was threatening to take Mateo away from me, just because he could. I was crushed and had been drinking pretty heavily before Zach arrived. I saw him and introduced myself before I even knew he was Nate's friend. It was his birthday and we celebrated together. He too was feeling down. And that's how I met your brother. Everyone was already helping me out with Mateo, so no one questioned when he came over. They just thought he was helping too."

"Helping how?"

"All the guys took turns watching Mateo for me on Saturdays so I could go back to school and take the last classes I needed to finish my fashion merchandising degree. My ex-husband made me quit college when I got pregnant. Then once I had the baby, he didn't want anything to do with him, which was probably for the best. He didn't have any patience—for either of us. My mother watched Mateo during the week so I hated to have to bother her on the weekends too. And besides, she doesn't drive, and the weekend bus schedule isn't very convenient."

Warmth like honey spreads through me. This girl seems so full of life, and even in the depths of sorrow, she has hope. "Will you let me be a part of the baby's life?"

She moves quickly and surprises me with a hug. "Oh, Zoey, nothing would make me happier—nothing."

"Mommy, Mommy." Mateo's little voice is gleeful coming down the stairs. "Nate told me he'd take me to a baseball game. A real baseball game."

Nate sidetracks him on the stairs and scoops him up sideways, causing his hat to fall off his head. "You're supposed to stay upstairs."

"It's okay." Gisele pulls back and looks at me. "Stay for lunch?"

I nod. "I'll do more than stay; I'll make it. What's on the menu?"

She looks at Nate. "Nate did the shopping before he picked us up from my mother's. Mateo was ready to come home, and I thought it was time."

My eyes shift to Nate.

His smile is genuine.

He rubs his hands together. "I got everything we need to make grilled cheese and tomato soup."

"I don't like the way you make tom-two soup."

"Mateo, it's tomato, and that's not nice."

Nate lowers to his knees and swipes his hand over Mateo's head. "You always used to eat it. What changed?"

"I like the way Zach makes it."

Nate's eyes shift to Gisele's.

She lifts her shoulders.

I crouch down next to Nate, our thighs touching, electricity shooting through me like a wildfire. "I know just the trick."

Nate looks at me. "You do?"

I nod. "Milk instead of water."

"Ah, gourmet style," Nate says and we all laugh.

Mateo laughs along and then puts his little hand on my face. "Will you be my sister too?"

I take his palm and kiss it. "I can't be your sister, but I can be your friend."

Those little arms wrap themselves around me and I melt. "I'd really like that."

Nate and I make lunch and spend more time accidentally running into each other than actually cooking. He brushes up against me as I wash out the cans at the sink, I lean across him when I reach for the utensils in the drawer next to him, we come chest to chest when I move to put the milk away and he goes to get the glasses down from the cupboard.

At that, his lips part.

A sigh escapes me.

I want to kiss him, but I don't.

I don't know if he's still mad at me. I don't know if I'm still mad at him. I just really don't know anything.

More of those doors keep opening for us.

Every day I see a new side of him.

But I know I can't get any more attached.

I just can't.

After lunch, Nate settles Mateo with a movie and Gisele tells him everything she told me.

He is shocked.

He is upset for not being told.

But most of all, he is happy that Gisele and I have met.

By then Gisele is exhausted and as soon as she lies next to Mateo on the couch, she's asleep within minutes.

Nate and I clean up and just as we finish putting everything away, Gisele's mother, Carmen, arrives. She's going to stay with them for a few days.

Gisele is still asleep, so I leave my number on the table with a note for her to call me tomorrow. Then I kiss Mateo on the head and promise to come by and take him to the playground, and Nate promises ice cream. Mateo is so caught up in his movie, he just smiles and waves good-bye. Carmen walks us to the door and hugs each of us.

When I set foot outside, the rain has stopped but the muggy heat assaults me. The waning sun is butter yellow and is close to setting for the day.

I feel exhausted—not just physically, but emotionally too.

I have so much to think about.

To consider.

"Where did you park?" Nate asks as Carmen closes the door.

I point across the street, and we both walk that way.

"I'm sorry." His words are soft but certain.

I look at him. "For which part?"

He scratches his head. "You know, I'm a little confused here, so you could give me a break." His snicker is adorable. "But I'm sorry for the way I acted this morning. I wasn't expecting to see my mother when I took you to the gallery. Then when you started probing me, I just didn't want to deal with it. I've made it my mission for so long to ignore the fact that I even have a mother."

His sincerity tugs at my heart. I take his hand. "I get it, I really do."

He squeezes my hand. "Do I have more I'm supposed to be sorry for?"

Okay, that was even more adorable.

We cross the street in quick strides and once we reach the sidewalk, I stop and lean against the car. "Why didn't you tell me about Gisele?"

He puts his hands on his hips. "Honestly, I didn't think it was important. She was a friend who had gotten in an accident, which was all I knew. I found out she was in an accident last Saturday when I took you to Wynwood Walls. Santiago told me then that Gisele had been in the hospital and was staying with her mother. I never knew she was with your brother. We were all messed up after Zach's death, so not hearing from her didn't seem odd at all. I swear none of us knew she was with him."

"She told me that."

"So, are we good?"

I laugh.

He raises a brow.

"Yes, we're good."

The problem is we're too good.

This is getting dangerous. On my part anyway. I feel pulled between wanting to stay here to be with Gisele—and if I'm being honest, to be with Nate. But I know he's not looking for anything long term. A summer of fun is a fling, and flings don't get emotionally connected.

He presses his forehead to mine. "Are you okay?"

My body eases into his and the contact sends my thigh muscles into spasms.

"There's something else." He looks hesitant.

My lustful thoughts quickly dissipate and I take his face in my hands. "Tell me."

His eyes squeeze shut. "You know I don't really believe in destiny."

I sigh. "Yes, I do."

"Did Gisele tell you how she and Zach met?"

"She said you sort of introduced them."

He squeezes my hands with his own. "I brought him to the Ballroom when I was looking to close the deal with Jeremy Mc-Queen on the property. He met Gisele that night. Do you think if I hadn't taken him there, he'd still be alive?"

My thumbs caress his cheeks. "No. Don't you get it? That's the thing about destiny, you can't change it, borrow from it, cheat it, or beat it. If destiny is meant to be, it will be. He was meant to die when he was twenty-seven and anything you did or didn't do wouldn't have changed it."

He shakes his head in a disbelieving way.

"Nate, don't you see? It's just like me. It doesn't matter what I do. If I'm meant to join the Twenty-Seven Club, there's nothing I can do to change that."

He takes my hands and kisses each of my fingers. "Don't talk that way."

I nod, suddenly understanding why my brother rarely spoke about our destiny or legacy as he called it. It wasn't because it was too hard for him to accept, but rather because it was too hard for others to accept.

I understand that now, as I look into Nate's eyes and whisper a reassuring, "Okay, I won't."

23
Hot to Hotter

The sound of shattering glass wakes me.

When Nate and I got back from Gisele's last night, we were both unusually quiet. We lay together on his bed and the last thing I remember is the soothing feel of his fingers caressing my back.

Sitting up, I realize I'm still dressed in my clothes from yesterday. And I can't stop the onslaught of feelings that rush through me.

Uncertain.

Alone.

Scared about my future.

I want to be around to see my niece or nephew born. I want to embrace my relationship with Nate, even if neither of us has acknowledged it. It's there, and I want to see where it takes us.

But the future is too uncertain.

Another sound of shattering glass has me jumping out of bed and racing to the top of the stairs. The branches of the palm trees hinder my view of the beautiful early morning sky. But looking down, the view is equally as stunning.

Nate.

Strong and powerful.

My compass to remind me there's more than a dismal future for me.

So I focus on him.

Take refuge in him even if he doesn't know it.

He stands tall, lost in his own world. When he bends over again with a broom and dustpan in hand, I realize he's cleaning up and a sadness sweeps through me, this time for him. I survey the area. The larger pieces of the statue are nowhere in sight, but he is sweeping the smaller pieces into a pile and emptying them into the trashcan beside him.

I tiptoe down the steps and stop halfway, taking a seat so I can compose myself before talking to him.

He looks up. Shadows dance across his face, but my pulse still races at the sight of him. Sleepy, unshaven, and wearing the same clothes he wore yesterday, he's still sexy as hell.

I tuck a piece of hair behind my ear. "Good morning."

He nods and drops his eyes. "I want to say thank you."

"For what? You cleaned up, not me."

He shakes his head. "For making me face what I never have. You're right. When it comes to my mother, I'm stuck somewhere between the day she left and the day she returned. I don't know how to work those feelings out, but I do know it's time I tried. I think I should talk to someone about it. And then whatever happens, happens."

An ache creeps into my chest. There's a lot of heartache that comes from trying to figure parents out. I understand that all too well. I spent years in therapy seeking answers I never found. My eyes search him in a cautious manner. "I think that's all anyone can do. None of us know what the future holds, but if you try to move forward, that's a great first step."

His eyes dart to mine and he studies me. "Are you okay?"

I nod, my curls bouncing in chaos around my face. "I am."

He narrows his eyes at me. "Are you sure?"

I nod again and change the subject. "I can finish that for you. Aren't you going to be late for work?"

He smiles at me. "I'm not going to work today."

I wrap my arms around my knees, finding an odd comfort in his voice. "Oh, really. Are you allowed to take sick days?"

"I'm allowed to do whatever I want, and today I want to spend the day with you."

Excitement surges through me, my earlier sullen mood dissipating quickly in Nate's presence. "And what exactly do you plan to do with me?"

He sets the broom and pan down and crawls up the stairs.

A panther on the prowl.

I have to actually restrain myself from launching at him.

When he reaches me, he hovers over me. "We're going to take today on a need-to-know basis. And right now, the only thing you need to know is that we are going to take a shower."

I swallow, desire pooling between my legs.

He scoops me up and tosses me over his shoulder. "But I'm not responsible for how cold the first sprays of water are."

"You wouldn't dare."

"Wouldn't I?"

He has my legs firmly in his grasp and all I can do is swat him a few times.

"I wouldn't do that if I were you," he warns.

Lust makes my entire body tingle.

I laugh, giddy, high on emotion, happy to be with him. "I'm not afraid of you."

"Is that right? What do I have to do then to get you to talk? Spank you?"

"I like it when you spank me," I purr.

In the shower, he turns the lever all the way to the left and then with his clothes still on and mine too, he walks right under the frigid water. "Well, I need to have a better reason to spank you, but I do know how to get you to talk."

I scream, squeal, and protest until he turns the water to hot and slides me down the front of his wet body.

He takes my face in his hands. "Now, tell me what's wrong or I'll do it again."

The moment turns serious as I look at him. "I'm afraid."

His thumbs caress his cheeks. "We talked about this yesterday."

I run my hands up his chest. "I know, but I can't help it. I want so much to be a part of Gisele and Zach's baby's life."

"You will be. I know you will."

I take the leap. Jump off the cliff. "What about us? What do you know about us?"

He stiffens under my touch.

"Nate?"

His focus seems to have shifted elsewhere as he stares at me for the longest time. "I know I missed being inside you last night. I know I'm going to fuck you in the shower, fuck you this afternoon, and again tonight. And I know that I'm going to make you come more times than that."

My own body trembling, I let him wash away the real meaning behind my words with sex because really, what kind of answer was I looking for anyway? We made an agreement and I plan to stick to it.

"Now, back to those slaps you gave me on the way in here. I think there's restitution to be paid."

His voice draws me away from my thoughts and my heart pitter-patters at the thought of what he might have in mind. Both my hands travel down to the zipper of his wet pants. "I'm not sure I agree."

He catches my game and turns the water off. "Luckily for you then, that's not what I have in mind."

Since I still long to touch him, my fingers fumble for the button on his fly. "But that's what I want. What I need. No, I take that back, what I really want is to taste you."

He shakes his head. "Step back and get undressed."

I blink, both crushed and thrilled by his command.

"Control is something I don't give up easily, and even if you were pushing me this way, I was already headed here."

His grin is smug; in fact, I'd say it borders on egotistical.

It turns me on.

Then again, everything about this man turns me on.

"I thought we were taking a shower?" I ask.

"We will, in due time."

His voice is smooth, like caramel, and my stomach twinges as if the butterflies are getting ready to take flight.

I feel nervous.

I step back and begin to lift my dress. The lights are on and there is no hiding. Nerves begin to prickle my legs.

This time feels different.

So much has happened. We have grown emotionally closer— even if neither of us will admit it.

He prowls across the room to the counter and leans back against it, crossing his arms over his chest. Now the butterflies are definitely in formation. "Turn toward me," he orders.

He wants me to strip in front of him?

Those pricks of nerves hammer into me, and my legs feel wooden. I pull the dress over my head.

He lifts his chin, urging me to continue.

I remove my bra and my small breasts spring free. I tug my panties down until I'm completely exposed.

His lips part. He grips the counter. His half-lidded eyes sweep me with a burning gaze of appreciation of every inch of my bare skin. "You really are beautiful," he whispers.

And that bit of shyness comes across in his voice.

It's very endearing.

I have to drop my gaze at his scrutiny.

But then he exhales a long, slow breath, and the sound is almost that of a purr as it echoes through the room. "You're perfect."

My eyes lift to meet his, uncertain if his words are sincere.

"You. Are. Perfect," he repeats in a voice that is only slightly higher than a whisper. It breaks with a guttural huskiness that is definitely animalistic, definitely Nate.

An indefinable emotion creeps into his eyes, and as I stare into them the moment passes quickly when they glaze over.

He stands there, long and lean, all male, and stares at me from across the room. After a few moments he crooks his finger and I glide across the cool tile floor—all my burdens disappearing and making me feel light as a feather.

I stop in front of him on the intricately designed tile floor, feeling empowered and strangely nervous at the same time.

We've been together so many times already, but this feels different.

This is both need and want rolled together—it's a dizzying combination.

"Drop to your knees," he commands.

Suddenly, my nervousness fades and all I feel is elation.

He puts his hands in my hair and combs through it before resting his fingers on my head. Impulsively, I lean in, and with trembling fingers I unbutton his pants. His hips push forward in a surging motion and I take a moment to stroke the cloth-covered erection that I can't wait to hold.

As I continue undoing his pants, the sound he makes is more like a mew and it causes my whole body to quake in need.

He breathes out, "Tell me this is what you want."

I lift my eyes and in my most reassuring voice I say, "I really want this—with you."

Nate always seems hesitant about giving directives during sex but once I reassure him that's the way I like it, his hesitation quickly dissipates.

I can tell he likes it this way too.

"Tell me what you want right now then."

"I want your cock in my mouth. I want to taste you. I want to swallow you whole." The naughty, filthy words fly from my throat and a shot of pleasure goes right to my sex.

He lets go of my hair and grips the counter. "Do it. Put my cock in your mouth."

I bite down on my bottom lip to stop from pulling him out and licking him right away. Instead, I give him a few more strokes through the fabric to draw out his pleasure as he does to me so often. Yet, when he arches his back at the contact, my reserve dissolves and I can't help but move faster.

Nate coming undone at my hands, at my feet, is something I love to see.

With steady hands, I ease his pants down without much effort.

Nate makes quick work of toeing his shoes off and pulling his socks off. Obviously he knew better than to clean up broken glass without them.

Good boy.

I take that time to stare at him in his delicious-looking black boxer briefs that ride low on his hips, at the jut of his hip bones, at the faint trail of hair on his otherwise hairless body, at the lines and definition that fade into the waistband of his boxers, but mostly at the impressive bulge standing up for attention.

Then I can't wait any longer.

As he unbuttons his shirt, I slide my fingers into the waistband of his boxers and glide them down, first over his hips, then his thighs, letting them fall to the ground, not caring where they go from there. The tip of his penis is already moist, glistening in the lights of the room. I lean down and lick the pre-cum.

The taste sends an arrow straight to my sex.

With a shift of my eyes to the mirror, I try to catch a glimpse of the look on Nate's face. The image is clear—the sheer pleasure on his face is enough for me to remember this moment forever.

Oral sex has never really been my thing. I've given blowjobs to men before, but never with the driving need to want to please them, to rock their world. But with Nate it's been different. I've had all those urges. And right now, I want to turn Nate's world upside down and inside out at the same time. The very thought sends chills down my spine. Unable to wait another moment, I take his cock in my hand and put my lips around him.

Lapping my tongue against the crown of his penis and moving my hand up and down his shaft at the same time makes his body tense. He groans and within moments his fingers move back into my curls and he combs through them in a rhythmic motion. Without looking up, I take him further into my mouth, enjoying the sounds he makes as well as the feel of hands on me at the same time.

His cock in my mouth feels so good, so right.

I lick every inch of him, savoring the feel of him against my lips. Another groan has me twisting up to look at him, and when I catch his gaze on me, I want more, even more of him. So with my fist, I tightly grip his base and push my mouth all the way down.

His eyes flutter.

When my lips meet my fist, I move in the same rhythmic motion of his hands in my hair. After a few strokes down his length, I notice his fingers stop their stroking and grip my head as a loud groan escapes his lips.

With a quick glance in the mirror, I find his eyes are heavy lidded and his lips parted—the erotic image makes me squirm. Wanting to take him as deep as I can, I glide my lips down his length in its entirety. When his head hits the back of my throat, he lets out a shuddering sigh. "Zoey . . ."

My name from his mouth in the heat of passion thrills me.

Pulling back, I then take him all the way again and his hands on my head guide me as he thrusts into my mouth over and over. My mouth sucks, my fingers stroke, and my lips move in all the ways I think he'll like. Soon, his muscles start to shake. And when my tongue finds his tip again and I trace a path around the moistness beaded there, he shudders and murmurs my name again. "Zoey."

I can tell he's approaching orgasm, and the rush of euphoria coursing through my veins is the biggest high I've ever experienced in my life.

"Zoey, stop."

I don't.

I can't.

"Zoey, stop. I'm going to come."

I shake my head no and even though my own sex aches to have him inside me, I want this more right now. I pull back slightly. "I want you to come in my mouth."

"Fuck." The gasp is the loudest vocalization of pleasure I've heard from him yet.

Empowered by the hope of rocking his world, I drag my teeth down his shaft, trailing it with my tongue, and I swear I feel the pulse of his cock beneath it.

The sounds he makes tell me just how much he's enjoying this.

Like a lightning strike, he pushes into my mouth harder, faster and then he comes—the liquid going straight down my throat. I'm not sure I've swallowed a man before, and Nate's never allowed himself to come in my mouth, but I find pleasure in doing it—pleasure in the act, pleasure in pleasing him, and pleasure in the moans of his satisfaction.

Without warning Nate pulls me to my feet and in the next moment my behind is planted on the marble countertop with Nate standing between my thighs.

His mouth finds mine in an instant and I know he must taste himself on me. We kiss each other as if we can't get enough of one another.

When I surface for air, I strip his shirt from his shoulders.

"I want you," I tell him.

"I'm right here," he says, dipping his mouth to my neck. "But first, I need a taste of you."

His lips course their way down my body and I start to quiver. When his wet mouth moves over my sex, I can feel his hot breath on me and I shake harder. His hands grip my legs and pull me closer to the edge of the counter. In a flash, he drops down and spreads my legs as far apart as he can. When his tongue circles my clit, it starts throbbing.

His touch is hot.

His breath is warm.

His lips are wet.

And I'm pulsating everywhere.

His fingers trace patterns around my slick flesh and when his tongue follows the same path, I nearly lose my mind. I throw my head back and try to quiet the sounds leaving my mouth.

"Watch me." His voice his authoritative.

And I feel myself growing even wetter as I follow his instructions. I'm shocked when a soft ripple tumbles through my core so quickly. I can't take my eyes off him. I lean back and grip the counter harder, watching intently as he thrusts his tongue in and out.

Oh God, it feels so good.

So right.

I arch my back and call out for more. "Don't stop! Don't stop. Please don't stop."

I can feel the upward tilt of his lips, his own satisfaction in pleasing me, and my body throbs for him—the other parts neglected by his touch growing envious.

I want to feel him everywhere.

I want him to feel me everywhere.

Suddenly, I am overcome with that same worry I've been feeling lately. That one summer won't be enough time for everything

I want to do with this man. But then his tongue finds its way deep inside of me and my orgasm roars to life like the engine of new car. I start to tremble, my face tenses in ecstasy, and everything in the room becomes shades of gray.

"Let go, Zoey." He lifts his mouth for just a moment and I have an urge to push his head back down, but he does it all on his own.

This time when his lips touch my sex again, I let myself go.

Let him rid me of everything I don't want to remember, everything I don't want to think about, and everything only he can help me forget.

My head falls and I arch my back as he licks, sucks, and kisses all of me, until I feel boneless. My toes curl as the most exquisite sensation rivets through me, rocks me unlike anything I've ever felt before in my life. And I cry out louder than I ever have.

He stands back up with his lips glistening. Panting, naked, and oh-so-beautiful, he grabs my waist and pulls me close. Although I feel spent and I'm sure he does too, I want more.

I'm greedy for more.

I want his cock in me.

I missed it last night.

I want to feel him move against me.

I want him to come again, this time inside me.

His lips lower to mine and I can taste myself. When I can feel his lips turn up, I know he must be thinking the same thing.

"I saw you watching us . . . in the mirror." His voice is gravelly.

I spin around. "I like the way you look."

I can feel his eyes follow me. "I like the way you look too."

I'm so hot for him. I moan at the thought of him inside me and writhe against him with my own savage need.

He cups my sex with one of his strong hands and grabs my breast with the other.

I wrap my fingers in his soft, silky hair and tug on it with my own form of dominance.

"Fuck," he hisses.

I lick my mouth at how delicious the word sounds leaving his lips. Breathless and wanting, I ask, "What is it?"

He throws his head back. "I want to be inside you without a condom."

I look up at him. My hair moves with me, and a few locks fall in my face.

He reaches to push the strands, tickling my cheek.

His touch sears me, shoots me back to the world of passion that I'm never far away from when I'm near him.

Heat swells between my legs and there is no way I can deny him. "Are you clean?" I ask, my voice raspy—but already know he is. He'd never ask this if he wasn't.

"Yes. I've never had unprotected sex and I get tested regularly."

"I'm clean too. I haven't had unprotected sex since I broke up with my boyfriend. And that was years ago. And I take the pill religiously."

Okay, that sounded like a checklist.

A hiss, a wince, a sound as if he's been stabbed, ricochets through the air and has his body propelling toward me.

In a flash, I'm pinned to the shower wall.

He's hard again and I'm more than ready. He glides into me and takes me fast right here, against the wall, with my arms pinned in his hands.

It feels so good.

He feels so good.

It doesn't take me long.

It doesn't take him long.

I come hard with a strangled shout—one that mimics his own.

"That was —" He stops, as if considering what to say.

I finish for him. "Amazing."

At the same time he says, "Fucking hot."

"That works too." I can't keep my smile at bay. Nobody's ever told me that before.

"I mean it. You felt amazing."

My grin only grows wider and we proceed to shower together in that comfortable silence that always surrounds us. When we're both clean, he reaches out his hand and a different kind of joy rocks me. "Come on, let's get ready. We have a full day and I'm starving."

Just as he walks into the bedroom, he turns back to look at me. "Wear a dress today and leave your panties in your purse."

My mouth falls open. "Why?"

From his closet door, he gives me a wicked grin. "Let's just say I have a very special way to say I'm sorry. And you're going to be feeling much better by the end of today."

I smile, wondering what exactly he has in mind but not having to think too hard. This could be fun. Then I catch sight of myself in the mirror, swollen lips, rosy cheeks, and a glow I've never seen—something is happening between us, something more than, as Nate put it, fucking-hot sex. Some kind of connection is growing, one I need to be watchful of.

With the future so uncertain, I can't allow any ties to bind me to someone else.

Nate has been relentless. He checked for my panties before we left this morning and made me come right in the doorway to the garage. He followed me into the bathroom at Las Olas Cafe, the coffee shop Nate had promised to take me to more than a week ago, and brought me to orgasm so fast, no one even knocked on the door. His hands wandered my form whenever the opportunity presented itself when we stopped by Gisele's and took Mateo to the beach for an ice cream. And most recently, his fingers snuck under the hem of my dress in his Range Rover and he plunged in and out of me, bringing me to the brink and then stopping at least twice before he let me ride out the wave of pleasure.

I throw my head back. "Oh my God, is it possible for a woman to have this many orgasms in a day?"

He stops at a light and leans over to kiss me. "I've heard of women having more than one hundred in a single day."

"You're lying."

He grins. "No, it's true."

I raise a brow. "Where would you hear something like that?"

"Your brother insisted on listening to Howard Stern whenever we were in the car for an extended amount of time. I learned a lot from him."

I laugh. "Zach worshipped that man."

Nate accelerates and we turn onto the causeway. "That man is full of knowledge."

"Please, school me on women," I laugh.

"Is that sarcasm I sense?"

"Well, maybe, but honestly I have to say my curiosity is piqued."

He taps the steering wheel and looks out the window.

"I said please," I add.

The look I receive is priceless. "Okay, but it's true, so you don't need to look so doubtful. He said a woman not only has a G-spot but an erogenous zone too. And if a man can find that spot in a woman, the pleasure he can give her is boundless."

I gawk at him. "Have you done this before?"

He narrows his eyes at me. "Are you jealous?"

I shrug.

He smirks. "It's not that easy to find. I've spent enough time with you that after this morning, I was pretty sure I'd found it. After today, I know I have. So to answer your question—you are the first woman I've attempted to bring to orgasm as many times as possible in a single day. Are you complaining?"

"No," I sigh with a smile. "But what are you sorry about anyway?" I never did ask earlier.

He passes the turnoff from the bridge to his house. "For yesterday."

"You already said you were sorry about that."

"I know. But you seemed sad this morning and since I am your list and all, I wanted to do something to make you feel better."

He laughs a little at the end.

Maybe even blushes.

He has never mentioned the list since I told him. The way he said it was . . .

Adorable.

Sincere.

Heart-wrenchingly special.

Crazy too.

I know I wanted a sex-only relationship, but I find myself craving more. I have to curb my appetite—for both our sakes.

I tug my dress down. "Where are we going?"

He turns right at the end of the bridge. "To see my father," he says matter-of-factly.

I grab his leg. "Oh my God, I can't see your father like this."

He gazes over me. "Like what?"

"Like I just came over and over."

"You did," he chuckles.

"I know. And I'm sure I smell like sex."

He pulls into the parking lot of the shopping plaza. He reaches across and gathers my hair in his hand. "You do not smell like sex, and at least I told you to bring your panties."

I rummage through my purse and pull out the small triangle of black lace. "This is what I brought. I didn't know why you wanted me to bring them, so I brought a sexy pair."

His gaze is fixed on me, calm, unflappable. "Put them on. You can show them off to me later."

I gape at him.

"I already told him we'd be by before dinner, so hurry up."

"You're evil, pure evil."

His grin is beyond charming.

I do as he says. Then I dump the contents of my purse on the Range Rover floor and hurriedly look for the small perfume sample I got when I was at Isabella's last week. And miracle of all miracles, I find it and spritz some on—everywhere.

When we pull into the parking lot of the resort-looking facility Nate's father lives in, I notice him wiping his palms on his shorts. "Ready to do this again?"

"Are you nervous?"

"No, I just hope this visit goes better than the last."

"Please stop in the men's room and wash your hands before we find your father."

That sly, wicked smirk of his presents itself. "If you're saying I smell like sex, it doesn't bother me at all. I think it's hotter than fuck."

I shove his shoulder. "Nate!"

He leans over and kisses me. "I will if it makes you feel better. But we do have time for another before we go in."

He fingers dance up my thigh.

I push his hand away. "No, not here."

He shrugs. "I figured. Just thought it was worth a shot."

He opens his door and comes around to help me out. "What if he hates me?"

When my feet are on the ground, he pulls me to him. "No one could hate you. Don't be nervous. My father loved your brother, and he'll love you."

I'm no longer nervous. I put a smile on my face. I was nervous thinking that Nate was introducing his girlfriend to his father, but now that he's introducing his best friend's sister to him, the pricks of nervousness are gone. I push the sense of rejection aside and focus on the positive. Milo Hanson knew my brother very well, enough that he thought of him as a son. I can't wait to meet him.

This luxury assisted-living facility is the most lavish I've ever seen. Mimi had been in and out of various ALF's, but none were like Sunshine Village. When Nate and I were here last week, he showed me the putting greens, the computer labs, and the lecture room. I guess university professors come to speak on topics of interest to those who reside here.

Nate and I walk up the path to the grand front entrance. Walking paths, ponds, and gardens surround the building. The giant fountain in the lobby makes me think of a resort rather than a *facility*. I thought the same thing the last time I was here.

We take the corridor into the Memory Care unit and once we check in, Nate, as promised, stops in the rest room to wash up.

I do the same.

We meet back in the hallway, and Nate rubs his hands together. "Let's go find him."

He doesn't take my hand as we walk down to his father's room.

The door is open and the TV on. I can hear a sports announcer, so I assume it's ESPN or something like that.

Nate taps on the door and peeks in. "Dad, you awake?"

"Nate, my boy, come in. I'm just catching the football drafts. Did you hear Mike Warren got traded?"

Nate's smile is bright. "No, Dad, I didn't. But you can tell me all about it after I introduce you to someone."

I step into the lovely furnished room, planked with hardwood floors, not linoleum like traditional nursing homes I've been in. This room is meant to look like home, and my heart swells that Nate wanted this for his father.

The large hospital bed concealed to look otherwise is on one end and the living space on the other. There's even a fireplace. Milo Hanson is sitting in a comfortable chair with the remote to his large TV in his hand. He mutes the TV and stands, motioning me toward him.

That nervousness I was feeling earlier is back and I walk

slowly toward him. Once I reach him, I extend my hand. "Mr. Hanson, it's so nice to meet you."

"Nonsense," he says, brushing my hand away.

I start to worry that maybe he's not as cognizant as Nate thought.

But before I can glance at Nate, Mr. Hanson pulls me to him and kisses me on the cheek. "Zoey, my girl, I'm so happy to finally meet you. I've heard so much about you. Sit down, please."

He points to the chair beside him and I take a seat.

Nate rumples his hair and shoves his hands in his pockets, obviously preferring to stand rather than sit on the sofa.

He looks nervous.

But even so, he still looks sexy as hell in his worn shorts, frayed at the hems, black polo shirt, and pair of Adidas.

Yum.

Mr. Hanson takes my hand in his, and I refocus on him. I notice tears shimmering in his eyes. "I thought of Zachary more like a son than an employee. He was so young when I first met him, but he had come a long way over the years."

"Mr. Hanson, my brother really appreciated all you did to help him. He said he'd have been back home on Mimi's couch if it wasn't for you."

He puts his other hand over the one that's already squeezing mine. "Call me Milo. And Zoey, you have to know, Zachary was a rare find. He just needed someone to help him believe in himself."

I nod, swallowing hard and holding back my own tears that threaten to spill.

"Enough of the sadness. Tell me about you and my boy here. You two have been spending a lot of time together."

"Dad," Nate warns.

Eyes sharper than I would have imagined dart to Nate. "Sit down, and stop looking so nervous. I'm not going to embarrass you by bringing out photos of you when you were twelve. I just want to know what you two have been up to this summer."

Nate must have told his father about me.

My cheeks blaze.

What did he tell him, and why didn't he warn me?

Milo shifts his gaze back to me and my own nervousness causes me to speak without thinking. "I saw the gallery. It was lovely."

Out of the corner of my eye, I see Nate take a seat, rubbing his hands once again on his worn khakis.

"Yes, your brother helped me keep it open as long as it was."

"I know he loved working there."

"He did. We planned for him to take it over. I really wanted to keep it open. The neighborhood needs the culture."

Gisele had already told Nate about Zach's plans, so this wasn't news to him.

Milo drops my hand and abruptly rises to take a seat next to Nate on the couch. "Your mother was here yesterday. She told me what happened."

Nate's eyes blaze in anger. "Why is she still coming here? I told her not to."

Milo takes his son's hand. "I want you to sell her the gallery."

"No, Dad, I can't do that."

I stand and clear my throat. "I'll leave the two of you to talk."

Milo's voice is strong. "Stay, Zoey, please. You're the first person in a long time that Nate has spent time with. I think it's important for you to hear this too."

"Dad," Nate warns again.

"Nate, I don't know how much time I have left or even if I'll know who you are the next time you come. So please, let me get this out."

Nate nods.

"Your mother loved you. She loved me too. I know you've heard all kinds of stories, but the only one that matters is the truth and the truth is, even if I wasn't too old for her, we weren't a perfect match. She needed someone more free-spirited, like herself.

She was an artist and artists live by their own set of rules. I was always more businessman than artist. She didn't mean to hurt you; she only wanted to protect you from the need she felt to find herself again. She knew she wasn't good for us and needed to leave. I understand that now, and I forgave her a long time ago. My hope is that someday, you will too."

"Never," Nate spits out.

Milo pats Nate's hand. "Never is a long time, son. I've never asked anything of you before, but I'm going to ask this one thing of you. Try. Try for me. Try for you."

"I can't promise you that."

"Nate." His name slips from my mouth accidentally.

His eyes meet mine.

I look at him and will him to tell his father what he told me this morning

Nate stands and scrubs his jaw. "Dad, I'm going to talk to someone about Marisa. But that's all I can promise you right now."

Milo rises and hugs his son, whispering something to him I can't hear. Then after a few moments he turns around. "What do you say I show you two the new game room that just opened. Bingo every day at noon and six. And I want to hear all about what you've been up to."

My cheeks flame at the thought of what we've been up to.

The three of us spend another hour with Milo in the cafeteria, drinking coffee and talking about my brother. He told me all about when he first met him and the things Zach told Milo he dreamed about doing. His future did look bright. Now I know that although there may have been days he wanted to give in to the idea that he wouldn't live long, he pressed on and lived his life.

Nate holds my hand tight in his as we walk back down the path toward his car and when I look back, I decide it's time I do the same.

24

Involved, Not Entwined

Three weeks later . . .

The steamy summer evening doesn't dissuade me from sitting on the balcony off Nate's bedroom and admiring the beautiful view. It's strange how everything in my life seems more alive, brighter, bolder, full of color. The grass is greener, the flowers prettier, and the sky looks bluer. Sunsets and sunrises have suddenly become so important.

I've decided to make the most of my life.

Some days I forget what I promised myself.

But most days I don't.

My weekly calls to Dr. Raymond help with that.

Nate and I run to the sun rising in the morning and eat dinner to the sun setting at night. My heart seems to beat slower between the rise and the fall of that giant ball in the sky, which marks Nate's leaving and coming home. The weekends, though, make my heart race constantly. We're together most of the time then, either on the boat or bumming around Miami, filled with lust and always ending our outings with sex. We've gotten to twenty orgasms in a day, even without factoring in multiples.

Nate's body, his touch, and the pleasure he brings me—it's what keeps me from plunging into the darkness as time creeps by.

Life is becoming so familiar here.

I try not to dwell on what my destiny holds for me. I've even started to believe I won't die—but then reality hits when I'm alone, the memory of all those people in my family who have succumbed to destiny before me, and I know I shouldn't be thinking that far ahead.

When my thoughts tend to wander, I rein them in. The truth that Zach is gone from my life because of our destiny is the driving force behind my reserve. It's the one thing that keeps reminding me that I could be next. Yet, as the departure date to return home quickly approaches, I want to believe in fate less and less. However, no matter how hard I wish or pray, in my heart I know my future is uncertain.

That's what makes everything so hard.

There are people who have come to rely on me, and I know I shouldn't have allowed that. But it was the only way I could convince Gisele to go back to school full-time and finish up her degree before the baby comes. Gisele was hesitant at first because she hadn't worked since the accident and money was tight.

Also, going to school full-time meant she'd have to quit the Estate. I talked to Nate and asked him if he could arrange some kind of paid leave. Turns out, Nate had sold the Estate, so there was nothing he could do. But that's his business, buying and selling small businesses. And besides, I really didn't want Gisele to have to go back there to work. Instead, I gave her the insurance check I received from the totaling of Zach's motorcycle, which should be enough to help her through until she graduates and finds a job.

She didn't want to take it, just as she had refused any financial help from Nate. But I convinced her it was for her and my brother's child and that's what Zach would have wanted.

That got through to her.

She told everyone about the baby and they were all thrilled. No one more so than me though, because with that baby, a small part of my brother will live on even though he's gone.

I've been keeping myself busy. While Nate goes to work, I watch Mateo either at Nate's house or Gisele's. When I'm at Nate's, Rosie brings her daughter over to play with Mateo. I've even temporarily converted Nate's empty bedroom into a playroom.

I pray every day I'll be around for the birth of Gisele and Zach's baby, although I never say it out loud to anyone.

I've also stopped thinking of Nate and me as a couple past the summer. It's more than just my fear of what the future holds. It's Nate's refusal to talk about a relationship. When I think about it, it might make things easier for both of us to pretend there are no attachments.

The ringing of the phone pulls me back. "Hello?"

"Hello, is this Zoey Flowers?"

I look at the caller ID, but I don't recognize the number. "Yes, it is."

"Hi, I'm Julian Sanders, director of the Watermark Haus. I'm not sure you've heard of us, but we have a gallery in South Beach and dedicate our time to connecting artists with buyers."

"Oh, I think there's been a mistake, I'm not an artist."

"No, but your brother was."

Was—she knows he died.

"Yes, he was."

"I'll get right to it. I came across some of your brother's sketches at a flea market a few weeks ago and hung them in the lobby of my gallery. Since then, I have had many inquiries about them. I was able to track you down through Andrés, a friend of my son, and I was wondering if you'd consider selling his collection."

My hands and my voice are shaky. "Which sketches are you referring to?"

"They are cartoonish in nature, but the undertone breathes realism. My clientele has found them extremely appealing."

This was my brother's dream—to sell his works.

"I'd love to discuss it with you." I try not to sound too excited, but I'm jumping up and down on the inside.

"Perfect. Tomorrow at my office?"

"Yes, what time?"

"Does ten work for you? I'm on Ocean Drive right next to the Flamingo. You shouldn't have a problem finding me."

"I'll see you then."

"Oh, and if you could catalogue his work, that would be most helpful in determining the sales price."

"Of course."

"See you then." She hangs up.

Oh my God. Sell his collection. I wish so much Zach were alive for this. He'd be beyond thrilled.

I dial Nate. He has to work late but I'm dying to tell someone and I shouldn't tell Gisele until I know the sale is certain. I get his voice mail and decide not to leave him a message; I want to tell him in person.

I'll surprise him by bringing dinner to him.

I'm in the car and stuck in five o'clock traffic before I can process what that call means. His whole life, my brother dreamed of being an artist, selling his works—and in the end he sold himself and portraits to make my life easier.

I haven't judged his actions.

I've even accepted that it made him happy. But this would have been his big break. And even if he's not here, it could be his child's big break.

The thought brings tears to my eyes.

The Southeast Financial Center rises from the sky as I turn the corner. The garage is full and I'm surprised it hasn't emptied out by now because it's nearly six. I find an alternate garage and walk down the sidewalk of Biscayne Boulevard with my bag of Chinese food in hand. Inside the lobby it looks just as I remember, neon pink map and all.

I haven't been back here since the day I came to apologize.

No one is waiting for the elevator. The place is eerily quiet despite the full parking garage. I ride the glass elevator overlooking the Miami skyline to the forty-fifth floor alone and admire the view that goes on for miles and miles.

The doors *ping* and open.

The same beautiful blond woman wearing a headset sits behind the glossy reception desk. When I approach, I realize I never got her name.

"Can I help you?" she asks, obviously not remembering me.

"Yes, I'm here to see Nathaniel Hanson."

"Do you have an appointment?"

It feels like déjà vu.

"No, but could you tell him Zoey is here?"

She looks toward the computer screen and taps a few keys and then she glances up in mock smile. "I'm sorry, but Mr. Hanson is gone for the evening."

I lean over the desk. "Are you sure?"

She stares at me. "Yes, I'm very sure."

Just as I'm considering how to find out where he is, the elevator dings and a man holding a large floral bouquet steps out. The girl from behind the desk holds up a finger and addresses the man. "Are those for the fund-raiser?"

The man fumbles with the delivery slip. "Yes, for the Imagine Annual Charity Gala."

"That should have already been delivered to the annex building next door, fifteenth floor."

"I'll take it right now," the deliveryman says and steps back into the elevator.

"What is the Imagine Annual Charity Gala?" I ask Blondie.

She narrows her eyes at me.

I shrug. "I'm just curious."

"Well, if you must know, it's a fund-raiser hosted by Isabella and Gabriella Marco to raise money for the Wynwood Community improvement projects."

"Is that where Nate is?"

"I'm not at liberty to say where Mr. Hanson is, but I can leave him a message."

I give her a fake smile. "No, that's okay. I'll catch him later. Thank you."

My stomach lurches. *Why didn't he tell me?*

I ride down the elevator, dump the food in the nearest garbage can, and walk back to the garage I parked in down the road, obviously because a gala at the Southwest Financial Center caused the garage to be full.

The fact is, no matter how close I think Nate and I are, we aren't close enough that he wants to entwine me in his social life. My thoughts turn bitter as I drive home.

How many nights has he said he's working late when he was actually socializing?

Everything we do, we do just the two of us, or with Gisele and Mateo. But the evolution of Gisele and Mateo into our lives came from my inquiry, not Nate introducing us.

When I get home, I go over to the boathouse and begin to photograph Zach's pieces. They're all packed in boxes, so it will be easy to do. I'll stop somewhere in the morning and have the photos printed on glossy paper. I'll e-mail her the catalogue of the items in the next few days, but for now I'm exhausted.

When I get back to the house, my phone is beeping. Nate's left me a couple of voice mails and a text.

`Are you hungry? I can stop and get you something on my way home.`

I reply quickly.

No. Tired. Going to bed.

It's close to nine when I slip into bed and hear Nate come in downstairs. A few minutes later he's in the bedroom. I know I shouldn't be mad at him, but when he slips into bed and wraps his arms around me, I feign sleep. Even when he kisses my shoulder, I pretend not to stir.

I'm not mad at him.

I shouldn't be mad.

I can't be mad.

So why am I?

After all, he's with me because of me. He's doing this thing between us for me.

Giving me the summer I asked him for.

The one with no strings.

And as I allow myself to fade off into darkness, that fact has never been clearer than it is right now.

Last night, I not only feigned sleep when Nate came home but when he woke me in the morning to run, I told him I didn't feel well.

I can't avoid him forever, I know.

But I needed time to think. And I did. I decided I'm not going to say anything. There is no reason I should be upset that he didn't invite me to last night's fund-raiser.

I've talked myself out of being upset.

After all, no strings means no strings.

Dr. Montgomery slides the ultrasound probe over Gisele's stomach, and the image on the screen brings me out of my thoughts and tears to my eyes at the same time.

Bleep, bleep, bleep.

It's the sound of the baby's heartbeat.

"The baby is fine, right?" Gisele asks nervously.

"Let me take a few more measurements, and I'll be better able to answer your question."

"She's beautiful." I can't help but choke up. The baby's legs, arms, and head are visible, but the tiny fists are what cause my tears to shed.

"She?" Gisele says.

I shrug.

The doctor clicks and then clicks again, calling out numbers that the nurse records—the circumference of the baby's head, the length of the baby's leg, the number of chambers in the heart, and size of the baby's brain.

He clicks a button and hands Gisele the photo before turning off the machine. "The baby is progressing as he or she should. My estimate is that you're further along than your records indicate. I will see you back here in six weeks and if you'd like, we should then be able to identify the sex of the baby."

"I want to see it, Mommy," Mateo says from the chair he's sitting at with his coloring book.

Gisele nods at him and looks at the doctor. "Can I come back sooner?" She grabs my hand. "I want"—she looks at me—"my sister-in-law to be here, and she has to fly back to New York before then."

The shock of her words almost rattles me, but then she winks at me and I laugh.

"I don't see that as a problem, but I have to warn you, identifying the sex might not be possible much earlier," the doctor replies.

"But it might be?"

He nods.

"Okay then," she says and then smiles at me.

Gisele wants me to stay here, in Miami, but I've told her my life is in New York. Although that might not be totally true. At

least my home and my job are there. The life part I'm still trying
to figure out.

I take the picture from her to show Mateo and bring him to
the waiting room while Gisele dresses.

Her classes end in four weeks, so at least I'll get to see her
receive her degree before I leave. Mateo also starts kindergarten
in September, so he'll be taken care of during the day once Gisele
finds a job.

Before I leave—those words are getting harder and harder
to say.

But I know my leaving is for the best—for everyone's sake.

I tell them I have to get back to my job, but that's not the real
reason.

The real reason is something that's harder to say.

Something I've decided not to allow myself to think about.

I am thinking about making sure the baby is taken care of, in
case I'm unable to do so. Financially, with the money I will receive
from the sale of Zach's art collection, Gisele shouldn't have to
worry. But money isn't the only thing to worry about. I want to
make sure the baby has a father figure in his or her life. I'm going
to talk with Nate about whether he's willing to be that person.

My brother and I never had anyone like that in our life and I
don't want my brother's child to grow up the same way.

It's important to me that he or she has more support than we did.

My phone rings. It's Nate. "Hi," I answer.

"Hi, are you feeling any better?"

I take a deep breath. "I am."

"Good, because I have somewhere I want to take you tonight."

"Really, where?"

"You know that new restaurant that opens tonight, the one
that hired Jack Breakers as their chef?"

"Yes, I know about *Top Chef* Jack. The question is, how do you
know about him and how did you get a reservation?"

"I'll try not to be insulted by that."

"I didn't mean it that way."

"Zoey, I know what you like and I have my ways."

I try to contain my glee. "Nate, I can't wait."

"Me either. Be ready at seven."

"I will."

"Oh, and you know what not to wear."

"Nate!" I look around as if someone could hear him.

"Yes, Zoey."

With flaming cheeks and Mateo at my side, I decide a response isn't necessary. "I almost forgot. I have some exciting news to share with you too."

"Are you wet already?"

I cup my hand over my phone. "You're being naughty and Mateo is sitting right next to me. Let's talk later."

"No. Tell me now. I'm curious."

I look over to Mateo, who is back to coloring, and turn my head a little. "I think I sold my brother's art collection."

"You're kidding. That's fantastic. To who? I didn't even know you were trying to sell it."

"I wasn't. It's crazy."

I tell him the whole story, except for my detour to his office yesterday. His excitement seems just as palpable as mine.

When I look up, Gisele is at the desk making her next appointment. "Hey look, I have to go but, Nate, I can't wait to see you."

"Same here. I missed you last night."

"Me too," I whisper.

And that is the honest-to-goodness truth.

25

Like a Hurricane

Three weeks later . . .

Janis Joplin. Kurt Cobain. Amy Winehouse. Zachary Flowers. I always knew my brilliant brother would one day be listed among the great artistic minds of his time. His artwork graces the cover of *Ocean Drive*, a local magazine, and I couldn't be prouder.

He was wild and crazy and lived his life his own way. Me, I was always the calm one, the perfect foil to his freewheeling wild spirit. Even with Nate in my life, that hasn't really changed.

I'm just better at hiding it.

Nate, though, seems different from when I first met him—more open, more willing to talk to me about just about anything. Yet, he still refuses to talk about my leaving or about destiny. Maybe it's because he sees it as being inevitable. Or it could be because he knows it's time for both our lives to move past this bubble we've formed around ourselves.

I'm not sure which.

Besides, real life can't be like this fantasy we've been living—

where you find someone you feel close enough to talk to about everything and also have the absolute most amazing sex with.

After all, what we conjured up—we conjured up knowing it was always going to be temporary.

"Zoey, can I watch another one please? Please?" Mateo sits up, and his hands go under his chin in the cutest way.

My gaze swings toward the small child who woke up this morning with a slight temperature. I'm afraid he got my cold. I've been coughing all week.

I rub his head. "Sure, one more and then you need to close your eyes and take a nap."

"But I'm not tired!" he squeals.

"One more, that's all." I look into his eyes.

"Okay," he grunts and throws his head back down on my lap.

I feel his forehead for signs of his temperature spiking.

He sits back up. "Can I take my shoes off?"

"Sure, we're not going anywhere. In fact, I'll grab your Spider-man jammies and we'll put those on so you can stay cozy."

"Really? Jammies in the middle of the day?"

I nod.

"That's so cool."

I can't help but smile.

I get him changed and turn another episode of *Dora the Explorer* on, then turn back toward the small sliding glass door that looks out on the tiny patio.

I've become very familiar with the heavy rainstorms. It rains almost daily. Sometimes just a sun shower, sometimes torrential downpours. My raincoat has become my best friend during the daylight hours, whereas Nate's body has become my best friend in the late hours of night.

Both protect me from the storms—both keep me warm.

This afternoon is one of those days where you can't even see out the window, it's raining so hard.

My phone rings and I reach over to the coffee table to answer it. I smile when I see it's Nate.

"Hi." My voice is rattling from my cough.

"Hey, not feeling any better?"

"I thought I was."

"Well, tomorrow if you're still coughing, I think you should go to the doctor."

"It's summer. I'll be fine."

"Zoey."

"Okay, Nate, let's see what tomorrow brings."

"Thank you. Have you been watching the weather reports?"

I give a slight laugh. "No, just the rain out the window. Mateo isn't feeling well, so I let him watch TV all morning."

"Lucinda has been upgraded to a hurricane. Seventy-five-mile-an-hour winds are pounding Cuba."

"Yesterday when it was over Jamaica, forecasters said it was headed toward the panhandle, so I didn't think we had to worry about it."

Frustration ekes out in his voice. "Those same forecasters are now worried, with it being so early in the season, that the predictability of Lucinda's path is uncertain."

"Nate, we've gone through A to K with you telling me the same thing. It will be fine."

"Zoey, I'd feel better if you and Mateo packed up and went to my house now."

I look at my watch. "Gisele should be home soon. Let me get her settled and I'll head home. There are no evacuation mandates and the bridges are open. Chances are the weather will clear up before I even get home."

He sighs in frustration. "If it gets worse, I'm coming to get you both. I'm headed out to get some supplies now."

"Nate, don't overreact."

"I'm not, Zoey. I'll call you soon."

We hang up and I continue my vigilance out the window. When I look down at Mateo, he's fallen asleep. Feeling tired too, I turn my phone to vibrate and close my eyes, letting the pounding of the rain lull me to sleep.

"Zoey, we have to go. I've been calling you."

My eyes open in an instant to see Gisele throwing some things into a bag. "What are you talking about?"

"Beachside evacuation has been suggested. It's not mandatory yet, but probably safer if we leave now before everyone else."

I try to sit up, but Mateo is like a dead weight on my lap. I feel his forehead. "He's burning up. It hasn't even been six hours since I gave him the medicine."

My worry seems much greater than Gisele's over Mateo's fever. He wasn't awake when Gisele left, so I had to call her and ask her where to find everything.

She grabs a bottle of Motrin from the cupboard and some crackers and juice. "He'll be fine. I've been through this many times. I'll give him some Motrin in the car. Can you put his socks and shoes on? I'm just going to grab us some clothes. I'll spend the night at my mother's."

Gisele hurries up the stairs while I grab Mateo's socks and shoes from beside the couch and put them on him.

He still doesn't wake up.

I feel his forehead again, and this time when I touch him he does wake up.

His little eyes look at me and he rubs his tummy. "I don't feel so good."

"Do you feel like you might be sick?"

He nods and before I have a chance to bring him to the bathroom, he projectile vomits all over the place, me included.

I scream and that scares him, causing him to cry.

Gisele hurries down the stairs. "Oh no!" she says, tossing everything in her hands to the ground and grabbing a kitchen towel. She cleans Mateo up in no time, easing his tears as she does.

Not panicking must take practice.

Once she's done, she lifts him in her arms. "I'll finish packing quickly. Why don't you go ahead?"

I shake my head. "Let me drive you both over to your mother's."

"No, no. You go home."

"What if he gets sick again and you're driving?"

She stares at me, thinking about what I've just said.

"It's only rain."

She looks out the window. "Okay, but let's hurry. Grab a few bags from the kitchen while I change his shirt."

She fumbles for one out of the duffle and says calm, soothing words to him while she changes his shirt.

I get the bags, which I can only assume are for puke purposes, and wipe my own puke-covered top as clean as I can. Then I turn to her while grabbing my purse off the counter. "I'll put everything in the car."

Gisele is right behind me. Once we're all in the car, I pull out into the heavy falling rain and weave down the small side streets. When I come to the light just before the bridge, I reach for my purse to fumble for my phone.

I need to call Nate.

Crap!

I left it on Gisele's table.

"Gisele, can I borrow your phone to call Nate?"

"Sure."

I glance in the rearview mirror and see her searching among the bags we threw in the backseat.

The light turns green and I begin the journey over the bridge.

"Zoey, I must have left it in my car. I kept calling you, and when I got home I just ran in thinking I'd be coming right back out with Mateo."

Taillights in front of me guide my direction as I clutch the wheel. "That's okay, I'll call Nate when we get to your mother's."

The sound of water pelting the window keeps me focused. But the winds gusting and pulling at the car cause me to clench my teeth. The three-and-one-half-mile drive takes more than thirty minutes. But as soon as I hit the mainland, the drive is much quicker.

The rain is lighter.

The storm is not as fierce.

Once I arrive at Carmen's, I quickly help Gisele and Mateo inside. He slept the whole drive and thankfully didn't throw up again.

While the two of them get Mateo settled on the couch, I pick up the cordless on the desk in the family room. "The line is dead."

Carmen looks up once she's covered Mateo with a blanket. "Terrible service. It happens during every storm."

"Mom, get Zoey your cell phone."

Carmen rifles in her purse and hands me her cell.

I look at the screen and press a few buttons. "It's dead."

"Oh, Mom, you need to keep that charged."

"Gisele, honey, you know I never use it."

"Let me find her charger. It won't take long to charge."

I look at the old-style flip phone and doubt its ability to even charge. "I'm going to get on the road. I want to get to Nate's before it gets dark. Can you just call him for me?"

"You should stay here in case the roads get any worse," Carmen suggests.

"No, I should get back. The hurricane isn't supposed to hit land until later tonight, and Nate has a thing about storms. I think I should go back. I'll be fine."

Gisele looks at me knowingly. "Be careful and go slow."

"I will."

Quick hugs and promises to call Carmen's cell when I get to Nate's, and I am out the door.

The weather becomes increasingly worse on my drive back.

My hands are shaking so much because I can barely see two feet in front of me. The sky darkens and the rain comes down even harder. Again, I find myself clenching the wheel. I even turn the radio off so I can have complete concentration. It takes me much longer than it should to get back because so many cars have pulled off to the side of the road, causing traffic to slow.

When I pull in the driveway, the garage door is open and Nate is standing at the edge of it with his head down, his hands on his hips. He's still dressed in his work clothes but his feet are bare. He's so close to the blowing rain, he's getting wet.

Something seems wrong.

I hurry out of the car and rush over to him.

He raises his head and his face—it looks tormented.

"What's the matter? Are Gisele and Mateo okay?"

"They're fine." His voice is even, devoid of emotion.

"Then what's the matter?"

"Let's go inside." He takes my hand and even his skin is wet.

When we reach the dark kitchen, I look around.

Cases of water, candles, and flashlights cover the counter and my phone is on the breakfast bar.

He must have gone to Gisele's to pick us up like he threatened.

My stomach lurches. I feel really bad that he was concerned.

"Hey." I grab his hand. "I'm fine."

Nate gives a heavy sigh.

I pull him closer to me and take a deep, relieved breath to be home.

Home.

No, not home—at Nate's.

My fingers creep up his slightly damp shirt and I toy with his buttons. "Talk to me?"

He shoves my hands away.

I reach for him, but this time he grabs my shoulders, keeping us at an arm's length. "Not right now."

I pause.

"Nate, don't be upset."

"I said, not now." Dark, cold eyes meet mine.

"I'm sorry if I worried you. It was so chaotic; I left my phone there. Mateo got sick, and Gisele—"

"I know that," he interrupts. "Gisele called me just after I left her house."

"Then what's the matter?" I try to brush his wet hair from his eyes, but his grasp is firm.

"I said not now."

"Nate, please."

"You couldn't have left her house when I asked you to earlier? Would it have been that hard to listen to me, to follow my instructions?"

I flinch and try to calm myself but I can't. "Follow your instructions? I'm not your employee. I'm not Blondie behind the desk. I did what I thought was best for Mateo and Gisele."

He pulls me so close I have to tip my head to look at him. "And what about you? What's best for you—for you to die out there so then your fucking destiny will be fulfilled faster?"

We're breathing hard; him from anger, me from shock.

I take his face in my hands. "No. No. I don't want to kill myself. I don't want to die at all."

He shrugs away from me and walks toward the sliding glass doors. "I'm not so sure about that. Or about anything anymore."

I wait patiently for him to explain.

He presses his palms and his forehead to the glass. "You say you don't work for me, but you see, you do. We have an agreement, right? Fuck buddies, friends with benefits, or whatever the hell you want to call it. You're like one of my summer interns but instead of making copies, your job is to fuck me."

My jaw tightens with anger and my fists clench. "That's not true."

"Isn't it?" he mutters.

"That's not how either of us feels, and you know it's not."

He pounds the glass with his fists and then turns toward me.

I'm standing where the statue used to be, and I can see his eyes blazing with fire.

"You want to know what I know?"

I open my mouth to speak, but he doesn't wait for me to reply.

"I know you came to Miami, found me desirable in some warped way, wanted to add some fun into your otherwise boring life, so you crawled into my bed and fucked me good. So good that you made me fall in love with you, all the while knowing you were leaving here and leaving me. That's what I know."

I freeze right where I stand, any anger I may have been feeling quickly retreating.

His words stun me.

He loves me?

I start coughing.

My hand flies to my mouth and my fingers tremble over it. "This wasn't supposed to be about love."

"No, it wasn't. But you made it about more than it was supposed to be. You made me fall in love with you, with your *I'm so fragile, I have no one, we're so much alike, you can talk to me, I understand you* bullshit."

"Nate, that's not fair. You can't just change the rules and then be mad at me for it. You haven't even included me in your life really, just your bed."

His hands fly behind his head. "Rules! Are you fucking kidding me? Do I look like someone who follows the rules?"

"No, but that's what made you safe."

"Safe! What? Do you think I'm not capable of falling in love? Is that what they taught you in school? That those damaged beyond repair can't feel? Because I wish to hell it were true right now. I really do."

"No!" I cry. "That's what you told me."

I'm not even sure he's listening to me as he continues. "And what the hell do you mean, you weren't included in my life? You've been my life."

My voice is small. "The charity gala. You went without me and didn't even tell me."

"Are you for fucking real? I went after work to talk to the committee and then left. I never attend events like that—they're pretentious and not me."

Emotion wells deep in my heart. Issues aside, he loves me and I know without a doubt that I feel the same way about him. I've known it for a long time. Small pieces here and there have turned into a whole, and it was hard to ignore.

But I can't do this.

I can't stay here and worry about being ripped from this life.

I just can't do that to him.

Maybe later if . . . if that's the biggest barrier.

I want to go over and throw myself at him, tell him I'm his for as long as he wants me. Forever I hope.

But I can't, because in the end, if I don't live to twenty-eight, it will only be harder for him.

Tears fall like rain down my cheeks, over my chin, down my T-shirt.

I don't try to hold them back.

I couldn't even if I wanted to.

Instead, with tears in my eyes, I stand straight and meet his stare. "You can't say things like that to me, and you can't be mad at me. We talked about this and it wasn't about love. You agreed."

It's the hardest thing I've ever had to say.

He just narrows his eyes at me.

My breath catches on a small squeak. "You did."

His hands fly to his hips as I watch everything about him go hard—his jaw, his shoulders, his stance. The fire in his eyes is gone, the flame extinguished. Hatred fills him as he looks at me now and says, "Fuck you, Zoey, and fuck your destiny bullshit!"

Words catch in my throat, whip my mouth raw trying to get out, but nothing comes.

Just tears.

That's all I have.

Just tears and a sudden feeling of emptiness.

He stalks away and grabs something off the counter. I watch the way his muscles ripple through his wet shirt as he walks down the hall.

He doesn't turn.

I wait. Then I hear the jingling of keys and the door slam.

An increasingly tight sensation builds in my chest and my coughing won't quit. Torn between wanting to run after Nate and knowing I shouldn't, I decide to pack my stuff, call a cab, and be gone before he returns.

It's for the best.

But I need a glass of water from the kitchen first.

When I try to swallow it, I can't.

Suddenly, I can't get any air into my lungs.

It feels like I'm being buried alive with dirt blocking my airway.

My lungs are heavy weights, and they're stopping my breath from expelling. Shallow breaths are all I can manage. But those are getting even harder and harder to force.

My heart races.

My purse. Where's my purse?

Panic sets in, but before it completely overtakes me, I remind myself that it's on the front seat of my car.

Now, almost completely unable to get oxygen in or out of my lungs, I'm gasping as I fumble for my keys, Nate's dad's keys, but they're gone.

Nate must have taken them when he left.

With my phone in my hand, I dial 911 and stumble to the door with a slight hope that Nate hasn't left yet.

"Nine-one-one. What is your emergency?"

"I . . . can't . . . breathe."

"Where is your location, ma'am?"

I manage to step outside and into the garage. The air smells of the storm. The smothering humidity is like a gas that my lungs won't allow in. I try to suck in a deep breath but nothing will fill my mouth.

My hands fly to my throat.

Small gasps vibrate in my ears. No, not small gasps, someone's voice. "Where is your location, ma'am?"

I can't answer no matter how hard I try.

This is it.

This is my destiny.

It's my time to join the 27 Club.

Someone is crying? No, not someone. That's me.

The sky darkens and the wind picks up. I lean into it, and it holds me there. I feel like I'm flying. The rain is cold and hard and it stings my face. I try to move back but suddenly I'm falling down, blinded, and all I see is the blackness as it approaches thick and close.

My eyes flutter back open and the sky is a brilliant shade of blue, not black at all. The rain has cleared and the sun is shining bright. The air is cool, not steamy hot, and a gentle breeze blows by.

"Come on, Zoey. Hurry up."

I sit up and look at my palms. Leaves are stuck to them and my clothes too.

"Zach, is that you?"

Hurrying to my feet, I look behind me—two angels carved out of a pile of leaves. I turn back and shield my eyes. Up ahead I can see my brother and he's running toward the playground near Mimi's house as fast as he can.

He turns and yells, "Zoey! Why are you being such a slow-poke?"

I reach my hand out. "Wait, wait for me."

He jumps on a swing and starts pumping his legs as fast as he can.

"Why didn't you wait?" I cry when I reach him.

"I'm mad at you!"

I put my hands on my hips. "Why? What did I do? You're the one that left me."

The chain kinks and his body flies higher and higher.

"Answer me!" I stomp my foot.

He jumps off the swing and turns toward me. "I can't believe you can't figure this out."

"What do you mean?"

He shakes his head at me. "Our paths were never the same, you know that. How many times do I have to tell you to quit following me? You and me, we were never going to end up the same, that's not the way it works. It's only one."

"I don't understand."

"You don't have to. Zoey, destiny is determined by the path you choose to take. How can you not see that?"

"I still don't understand."

"Like I said, you don't have to. You just have to go before it's too late."

I turn around and cross my arms. "I'm going to tell Mimi that you won't let me play with you."

"Zoey, look at me."

I turn around.

"You shouldn't be here. You don't belong here."

I wrap my arms around myself. "But I miss you."

He reaches out his hand. "Come on, one more time and then you have to go. You have to hurry. You have to take care of something for me. You know you do."

"What do I have to take care of?"

He pulls me toward the swing. "You know what it is, and I know you'll be great at it."

We both hop on the swings and move our legs as fast as we can, soaring through the sky like birds.

"Hey, Zoey, do me a favor!" he yells over the wind blowing in our faces.

"Anything, you know that."

"Tell Nate I was wrong."

"Nate?"

"Yeah, you'll know who I mean when you go home."

"I am home."

"No. No, you're not. Stop saying that."

"You're scaring me. Stop yelling at me."

"I'm sorry. You know I love you. Take my hand."

I reach for his hand. "Close your eyes."

"Already am. Ready?"

"Yes!" I yell.

"One, two, three—jump!" he calls.

I do.

My feet touch the ground and my eyes flutter open. The sky is dark again and I feel a little drunk, groggy.

I can't keep my eyes open.

As awareness hits me, I can feel someone's mouth on mine. They're blowing into it and squeezing my nose at the same time.

Those lips, I know those lips.

Wait, they're gone.

Those hands, those fingers—they're so familiar.

"Don't leave me." The voice is distant. "Please don't leave me. I'm sorry."

Is it Nate?

"Nate, I'm here," I try to say, but I can't get my mouth to open.

I hear bells in the distance.

No, it's sirens.

The familiar mouth and hands are gone, replaced by an unfamiliar touch.

A heavy gust of air, and the weight is being lifted from my lungs.

Shuffling.

I'm being moved.

I'm lying on something firm—definitely not the grass, more rubber like. Cool metal touches my skin—someone is listening to my heart, my chest. I can hear murmurs of sound—voices, adult male voices.

"Any longer with a restricted airway and her heart could have stopped." It's an unfamiliar voice.

Is he talking about me?

I try to speak, but something is over my face—a mask.

"What is that machine?"

Nate's voice.

It's Nate.

That was him!

"It's a nebulizer. I'm attaching it to her mask. The drug should quickly relax the constricted muscles in her airway and make it easier for her to breathe. It sounds like she has an upper respiratory infection."

"She has been coughing a lot."

I'm moving.

Being lifted.

Rolled into something dark.

My lungs seem to be working again. I feel myself breathing as I inhale and exhale like normal.

An echo of words I don't understand rings in my ears—*destiny is determined by the path you choose to take.*

I finally manage to open my eyes, and when I do, they land right on Nate's beautiful green ones.

He's wet, soaking wet.

I reach my hand out and he takes it.

I squeeze his and give it a tug, hoping he'll come with me.

"Can I ride with her?" His voice is low, grim.

"Normally we don't allow passengers but in weather like this, it's probably safer for you to ride along with us than in the car, so I'll make an exception."

I'm rolled inside even further and when I hear the doors slam I look around.

Nate is sitting on a built-in bench and he grips the metal bar when the ambulance starts moving. The paramedics are going to work, hooking me up to monitors.

Time passes and when I open my eyes again, Nate leans forward and his handsome face comes into view. "Hey, you scared me."

His smile is gentle.

I fumble to lift my mask but he stops me. "Come closer," I manage before he puts the plastic back in place.

Nate leans down. "We'll talk later."

I shake my head and lift my mask again. "I love you."

He takes my hand and kisses each of my fingers and then the inside of my palm. "I love you," he whispers. Then he leans over again and his warm, hot breath is in my ear. "And that's how I should have told you in the first place."

My head spins, and little hearts spiral all around me.

There's a sweet ache in my chest—it's a feeling of utter bliss settling into it.

It's like we are the only two people here; and for the first time in a long time, maybe forever, I see happiness in my future.

His lips linger on my skin and I twist my head, wanting that tingling sensation on more of me.

"Kiss me," I mumble from under my mask.

He doesn't laugh or ignore me. Instead his lips trail down my nose and right on top of the plastic barrier, just as I asked. There may not be real physical contact but my pulse still races, and one of the monitors starts beeping wildly.

"You have to sit back, man," the paramedic says to Nate.

Nate does as he's told, but holds my hand tightly.

The paramedic presses some buttons on a machine and I close my eyes. Visions of a life with Nate imprint themselves behind my lids. It's something I never would have allowed to happen when fear lived there, but for some reason that fear is gone.

I can see Nate and me driving down the highway in a convertible with the wind blowing in my hair and the palm trees swaying back and forth. I can see him and me in a house and it's not just a house; it's a home, our home. I also see kids, our kids and others, swimming in a pool, jumping and having fun. And sunrises and sunsets—lots of them.

I see a future filled with happiness and Nate.

In what seems like mere moments later, a whirling wind blows inside the ambulance and then I'm being rolled, lowered, lifted, and I'm moving again. I open my eyes and see the words JACKSON MEMORIAL HOSPITAL EMERGENCY UNIT above me.

Everything that occurs next happens in a blur.

More wheeling.

I'm in a room with a curtain. I can hear Nate's voice somewhere, talking to someone. I'm being hooked up to what the doctor tells me is a magnesium drip and given another nebulizer treatment.

With no idea how much time has passed, I'm in a hospital room with an intravenous antibiotic drip hooked up to an IV in my arm.

The lab coat disappears.

The lights dim.

The door closes.

"Nate!" I call out, afraid that I'm alone.

One hand takes mine, and the other presses against the pillow near my head—his long, lean body hovering over me. "I'm right here."

"I'm sorry."

His mouth dips low near my ear. "Shh, stop saying that. Just close your eyes and rest."

My eyes meet his gentle-looking ones. "No, I have to say this. I'm sorry I acted like I did. I shouldn't have driven Gisele home without letting you know first. I should have thought about how you might be worried."

"Zoey, everything happens for a reason. If you hadn't done that and scared the ever-living shit out of me, I may have just let you go back to New York. And that would have been the real tragedy."

My heart plays patty-cake with my chest, and I'm surprised the monitor doesn't go crazy. "You know, I'm not sure I would have been able to leave when the time came even if you pushed me out the door."

His thumb brushes over my cheek. "I'm sorry this has been so difficult—you and me."

"I'm not."

Nate just shakes his head and laughs at me. "Why is that?"

"Because it means we were meant to be."

He leans back, and utter seriousness overtakes him. "Please, no more destiny philosophy. Promise me."

"Promise."

Nate stands straight like he's going to leave.

"Will you stay with me?"

He presses his lips to mine and with his soft, gentle kiss comes an outpouring of emotion, almost as if I asked him to stay with me for eternity. "I'm not going anywhere."

26

Like Cinderella

I'd been unconscious for seven minutes—seven whole minutes.

Had I died?

It's impossible to say.

But that dream—I can't forget that dream. It was so real.

Nate had been sitting in his dad's car when he saw me collapse. He tried to dose me with my inhaler, and when I didn't respond and he couldn't feel a pulse, he'd started to administer CPR. The ambulance arrived and quickly took over. They revived me and gave me oxygen. I remember bits and pieces, yet nothing but that dream between the time I blacked out and the time I regained consciousness

I spent the last three days in the hospital with oral and inhalant steroids added to my daily regimen of the antibiotic cocktail I'm being given. Nate, just as promised, has been by my side the entire time, only leaving to go home and shower, get us food, and check on Gisele and Mateo.

It's only been three days but a lot seems to have changed in those three days. Nate arranged to move Gisele out of her apartment beachside and into his father's house in Wynwood. He didn't want me to worry about them evacuating every time a storm hit. In addition, the doctors changed my medication and now I'll control my asthma with not one, but two inhalers. One I'll use every morning to prevent attacks, and one will stay on standby to relieve an attack, should I have one.

But what has changed the most is me.

I feel free.

I feel free to live my life.

I've had that dream about my brother and me swinging many times in my life.

Maybe that's because of the picture Mimi had on her mantel of Zach and me on swings at the playground.

Maybe it's because it was one of my favorite things to do with my brother when we were little.

Maybe it's because I needed his guidance.

I don't know.

But this time, the dream seemed like so much more than a dream—it seemed so real.

I've spent a lot of time thinking about destiny while lying here and if my destiny was to die, did I cheat it?

I didn't think it was possible.

I open one of my brother's sketchbooks that I asked Nate to bring back when he went home yesterday, along with some other things. After we leave here today, I have a stop I want to make.

I flip page after page, trying to find a blank one.

I stop on a drawing of a family tree.

It's my family tree.

Seven generations back, names fill the space by generation. Each generation has one giant red X on it. Each time the X is over an ancestor that died at the age of twenty-seven.

I gasp when I get to the bottom. Only two people remain in

this generation that have already surpassed twenty-seven. The names read Zachary Flowers and Zoey Flowers. There are no red X's on those spots, but rather a question mark next to each.

My eyes lift to the title. It reads: *It's Only One.*

I squint my eyes to see what's erased beneath the title. It reads: *Let it be me.*

My heart aches. My tears flow as the pieces come together.

My dream—that's what my brother was trying to tell me. The family legacy only takes one per generation.

He figured that out.

He knew it would be him or me, but couldn't tell me.

I wouldn't have told him either, had I known.

I raise my eyes to the heavens. "I love you, Zach."

I wipe my tears away.

I've shed too many tears.

I take in big lungfuls of air.

Things feel different. The darkness within me is gone.

Sure, life isn't fair. It was always one or the other. But it wasn't ever our choice. I'm glad I didn't know. I'd like to think that if it were my brother lying here right now, and not me, he'd feel the same. He'd decide it's time to live. Take a chance on what's out there. And that's what I'm going to do—live each day like it's my last.

"Hey, you're awake and dressed." Nate's voice is soft and gentle and his smile makes me feel invincible.

I can't stop marveling at him.

Maybe my destiny wasn't to die; maybe it was to find Nate.

I have to believe Nate and I were drawn to each other by more than just sexual chemistry. Like maybe I was empty and he was meant to fill me, and he was empty and I was meant to fill him. A little over the top, but it's better than saying he's my Prince Charming, or that I'm wearing glass slippers, or even that we are living a fairy tale—but the truth is we are.

So why can't we have a happily ever after?

I hop off the bed and run toward him, throwing my arms around him, kissing him the way I always wanted to whenever I saw him, but my fear always held me back.

His grin is sly. "What's this for?"

I let my thigh press against the inside of his. "No reason. Just because I want to."

"You're crazy. You know that, right?"

I nip at his lip and slap his ass.

"Watch yourself. Just because you've been in the hospital doesn't mean I won't spank you back when we get home."

"Maybe that's what I want." I lean back and wink.

He shakes his head and mutters, "Certifiably crazy."

I take a deep breath and go for it while I still have the *I've been in the hospital* thing going for me. "Speaking of crazy, somewhere between the time I passed out and the time the paramedics arrived—"

He cringes.

"Just listen, okay?"

He nods.

"Somewhere between the time I passed out and when the paramedics revived me, I had this dream about my brother and he told me to tell you he was wrong."

He squeezes his eyes shut and pulls me to him. "That's not crazy at all."

I try to pull back to look at him, to see those eyes of his, but he won't let me. "You don't think I'm crazy?"

He shakes his head no.

"Do you know what it means?"

"Yeah, yeah, I do," he whispers into my ear and just holds me. "I think I do."

I'm pretty sure I know too, but there are some things not meant for discussion, and this is one of them.

"Ready to go home?" he asks.

"Yes, but first I have a stop I'd like to make."

He eyes me wearily.

"It won't take long—I promise."

Jackson Memorial Hospital isn't far from Wynwood Wall and even though Nate thinks I should go home and rest, I feel the need to do this.

He parks the car right under the colorful mural of the man in a cowboy hat and tie with his hands held up in delight.

"Do you remember where the mural was that Zack painted of him and me?"

"Yeah." He looks at me with a raised brow.

"Can you grab us a latté and meet me there in twenty minutes?"

"Zoey."

"Nate, please. This is important to me."

He opens his door and looks over at me.

I pout my lips.

He grins and shakes his head. "Okay, but I'll be there in less than twenty minutes."

I wait for him to open my door.

Once he does, I plant a kiss on his lips, grab the things I asked Nate to bring from home, and quickly cross under the blue metal sign that says Wynwood Walls.

The painted images are everywhere, and I smile at each and every one of them as I weave my way back to the painting that my brother sketched of us with the ice-cream cones.

I sit on the ground in a pair of jeans and get to work drawing on a blank space on the wall. When I'm finished, I stand up and look at his image and mine, side by side.

The next thing I know Nate's arms wrap around me and I lean into him. "You and your brother swinging. It goes perfectly next to the other one of the two of you."

I twist to kiss him. "I thought it would. Just one more thing."

I take the thin paintbrush and in red write above it, *My favorite memory*.

I stare at them both for the longest time, letting my tears fall.

Grief doesn't always need to be suppressed; sometimes letting it out is how you heal.

Once I feel ready, I pick up my supplies and take Nate's hand. "Come on, take me home."

And this time when I say the word *home*, I mean it.

We walk to the car, both lost in our own thoughts.

Once we get in and Nate drives away, I turn to him and say, "So I was thinking maybe you could come to New York with me next week and help me pack."

His head snaps toward mine. "Pack?"

"Yes, I thought I'd put the house up for sale and apply for the doctorate program at the University of Miami. Of course, I'll need a place to stay."

He pulls the car into the nearest parking lot.

The panther in him is on the prowl as he leans over to me. "I would love to be able to help you out with that but you see, there's this hot sexy thing that's been sleeping in my bed all summer and I'm not sure she'll approve of this kind of longer-term commitment."

I watch the way he breathes—the familiar in-and-out movement of his muscled chest I've come to love. "Oh, she'll approve. I guarantee it."

He brushes his thumb over my cheek. "You know you don't have to sell your grandmother's house."

I look at him, generosity bleeding through his charm, as he brings his hand to my lips. "I know. I actually thought I'd use that money to set up a trust for the baby and donate the rest to the community center. Who knows, maybe it will be enough to help reopen it."

He leans back into his seat and starts to drive, quiet for a long time. Then he looks over at me. "You know, let's make sure it is enough money. I'll get with the community's committee and see what we have to do."

There's so much culture here, so much heart. The neighborhood where Nate grew up, the place Gisele and Mateo will soon be living.

I turn toward Nate. "Can I ask you something?"

"Sure."

"Do you ever think about moving back here?"

"To Wynwood?"

I nod.

"Sometimes. Why, would you like to live here?"

"I don't know. It just seems like a place someone could easily call home."

He looks out the window. "Yeah, it does."

"You know it's Zach's birthday next week. Do you think we could fly Mateo and Gisele up to New York while we're there, so I can show them where Zach and I grew up?"

"Yeah, I think that would be great."

Nate seems to fall back in time to some distant memory, and I let him have this time to reflect.

The rest of the drive passes in that comfortable silence. When Nate pulls into the driveway, everything looks the same but somehow different.

I remember when I first came here and tried to see a house that fit my brother. But now, the green bricks beneath us no longer show a funky edge, but rather provide a hard surface for which to walk on. The sailcloth carport no longer looks like an abstract sculpture, but rather a place to seek shelter. And the house's tropical-modern design with its Spanish-style roof looks like what it is—a house.

Nate pulls the Rover into the garage next to the Camry. I sink back in the leather and just smile as he opens my door.

"What?"

"Nothing."

"What?"

"The car. You put it in the garage."

He shakes his head. "Come with me. There's something I need to tell you."

My heart stops.

Is he going to tell me to go home without him?

That he can't do this after all?

We haven't really talked about us since we both said I love you in the ambulance—it wasn't exactly a hospital conversation.

I follow him down the hall, past the kitchen, and into the living room. The whole time my mind is wandering to ways he's going to let me go.

Maybe something easy like, *I'm sorry, Zoey, but I think you misunderstood me.*

Or maybe something harsh like, *You had your chance and you blew it.*

"Sit down," he says, pulling me from my reverie.

Now I really start to worry, but I do as he instructs.

He sits next to me and pushes my hair to one side and then plants the most delicious openmouthed kiss right on my bare skin.

I'm wearing a tube-style maxi dress with no bra, and I can feel my nipples tighten into little peaks at the contact.

Okay, so if he's letting me go, this is one way I never thought of.

He kisses up my throat to my ear. "I want you, Zoey Flowers."

I draw in a breath as desire overshadows my fear.

He nips at the soft spot behind my ear. "Whenever you walk into the room, all I see is you."

I close my eyes and listen to the rhythmic sounds of his breathing.

"I need you, Zoey Flowers. I need you next to me when I wake up in the morning and lying beside me when I fall asleep at night. I need you like the air I breathe."

My belly jumps from the sheer tone of his voice alone.

His lips seek mine, but he keeps them a breath away. "I want you, Zoey Flowers. Every single time I see you—I want you."

Stars imprint beneath my lids as I keep them squeezed shut just to listen to the tone of his voice, to the echo of the words I once said to him in a completely different context—the sound is like no other.

"I wasn't looking for love, never expected to ever feel it, but then you came into my life and it just happened—I love you, Zoey."

My eyes widen and when I look at him, I can't help smiling and tearing up at the same time.

Relief.

Love.

Lust.

Want.

Need.

They all spill out from me in a rush.

He's right—it did just happen.

There was no single moment I can point to and say I fell in love with him.

I just did.

We just did.

Piece by piece.

Until we were whole.

I caress his cheek. "You saved my life, you know."

He tries to smile. "It wasn't me, it was the paramedics."

My hands snake around his neck. "That's not what I mean. I was ready to give up. But then I met you. You gave me something to fight for. A reason to want to live."

He bites his lip. "That's not true."

"It is."

"Let's agree to disagree. But I want you to know, you were full of life from the moment I met you. Don't doubt it."

With a smirk, I pull him down on the couch with me. "I love you."

My mouth reaches for his and he complies, easily parting his lips for me, kissing me. My tongue sneaks into his mouth and he meets me with his. But when I thrust my hips into his, he pushes himself up.

His green eyes stare down at me. "Zoey, what are you doing?"

I take his face in my hands. "You asked me that the first night we spent together."

"I remember." His grin is wide.

My lips move on their own to take his between my teeth—just a little nip. "Do you remember what I said?"

He pushes himself up a little more. The smirk on his face tells me this is going to be good. "It went something like this, *'Oh, Nate, I need you. I don't want to think about anything. I just want to feel. Can you help me do that?'*"

He is almost mocking me with his tone, but I don't care.

I rise to my elbows and run my tongue around his lips for just a little taste.

He groans, and the sound is sexy as hell.

His lips are still melded to mine and I can feel his erection growing with each passing moment.

"Well, can you?" I ask. "Can you forget I was in the hospital and focus on right now?"

"Zoey, I'm not sure we should, so soon after your release." His lips trail across my forehead, stopping to plant a long, lingering kiss there.

"Yes . . . we . . . should."

I pronounce each word clearly to make sure he gets the point, yet all he does is continue to stare down at me with those mesmerizing green eyes.

Doesn't he know when he looks at me that way that all he's doing in revving me up?

Threads of pleasure are already beginning to seize me. I take his face in my hands and pull him back down with me. "Nate, I didn't wear any panties. I want you to make love to me right now."

His groan is guttural as he shoves my dress down and my breasts spring free.

The sight causes the wild animal that lives within him to overtake any restraint he might have had. "God, no bra either. I fucking love you, all of you."

He rolls us over, and his hard body sinks into my soft one in such a way that we fit together perfectly. He takes my nipple in his mouth and I throw my head back as his tongue laps it. When he tugs it between his lips, I moan, "God, I love you too."

Love, it comes in all shapes and sizes. Sometimes it's patient, sometimes it's kind, but sometimes it emerges from the depths of something dark. Nate and I found each other in the arms of grief—at a time when we both needed someone. And in the aftermath of the death of the man who will forever be twenty-seven, there emerged a love that will last a lifetime—no matter how long or short that lifetime is.

EPILOGUE
Happy 28th Birthday to Zoey

Nate Hanson | Nine months later . . .

There are times in life when vanilla just won't do, and this is one of them.

I searched the ends of the earth for the right cake recipe—couldn't fucking find what I was looking for. Then, I mention to Rosie that I'm making the birthday cake myself and right off the top of her head she tells me she saw Martha Stewart make a chocolate-coffee double layer cake one day when Z was hanging around and watching TV.

Brilliant! Fucking brilliant.

Chocolate and coffee—her two favorite things.

Google, I fucking love you!

Once I gather all the ingredients, I put them on the counter.

With the glass bowl in one hand and the cookbook beside it, I dump in everything as instructed on each step. Martha Stewart could make her recipes a little simpler, but it's not like I can't handle it.

Actually it's pretty easy.

Just two minutes on medium speed with the mixer, stir in the coffee and melted chocolate, and the batter is ready.

The two round pans sit side by side on the cherry red counter-top in our new kitchen that just so happens to be inside our new house.

Yes, we moved to Wynwood.

We have a huge backyard that Zoey has filled with toys and tables and chairs. The pool sits safely inside the perimeter of an iron gate and is equipped with a slide and a diving board.

It's her mission to paint every room in the house with a splash of color. So far, she's painted one wall in the family room lime green with palm leaves and the dining room is a shocking pink with some kind of flower on it.

Like her brother, Zoey has a penchant for color.

She painted our bedroom this week. It's the only room where I had to lay down the law and forbid anything too girly like pink or yellow. She actually went with a dark purple. I don't mind the color at all. In fact, I helped her when I got home the first night she started painting, but she looked so crazy hot dabbed in speckles of amethyst, I think she might have been more productive when I wasn't around.

The playroom, and no we're not expecting a baby or planning on having one soon, is a red-and-white-striped combo with circus animals painted everywhere and even a big top in the center of the ceiling.

Zoey wants the kids we do have in our life to want to come here and have fun. I think it's a missing piece of her childhood that she wants to relive with Mateo and Olivia. Gisele had a baby girl and named her after Zoey and Zachary's grandmother.

I never thought I'd care about any of this domestic shit. But Zoey has turned this house into our home—yes, our home. With photos of everyone we know and love displayed on the walls and the fireplace mantels, we have reminders of all we have to be thankful for all around us. But most of all, I have her to come home to.

Turns out, photography was a hobby Zoey had long ago abandoned. But now, with the lighter class load she took this semester to help Gisele with the baby, she's gotten back into it.

I have to say it's benefited us both.

At first, when she told me she wanted to photograph me, I was like, sure—cheese. But then she became so authoritative using words like unzip, sit, take it off, closer, touch it, show me how you feel that I found myself completely turned on.

One giant hand clamps on my shoulder, pulling me out of my erotic thoughts. "Hey, son, I hate to rain on your parade, but I'm pretty sure you should have greased those pans before you poured the batter into them."

"Fuck," I mutter and dump the brown liquid back into the bowl.

My dad grabs the pans from me and takes them to the sink to wash. "I don't think I've ever seen you make more than a sandwich. I'm impressed."

My dad has his good days and bad days, and I've decided to take advantage of the good ones. Whenever I can, I bring him over, even if it's just for an hour or two.

He hands me the pans and I dry them. "I figured, how hard could it be to make a cake?"

My dad laughs. "Don't be nervous, Nate. She's going to say yes."

"I'm not nervous."

"Oh yeah, then why did you just pour the batter back in the pans without greasing them?"

"Fuck!"

"Let me finish this. Why don't you grab us a beer and have a seat?"

"You can't drink, Dad. You know that."

"I can watch you and pretend."

I shake my head at him. "You're the best."

And he is.

I started seeing a therapist. Now I can admit that my mom did make the right choice to leave me with him—I never really doubted it. He raised me to admire what I don't have and not be jealous of it, be generous when possible, care for those who need it and above all else—respect others and myself. I hope I've made him proud, because he's made me proud.

My father started the community center the year my mother left us. I grew up there, taking jiujitsu from a man who had lost his house and was just grateful his family was okay. That center and its people became our family, and now Zoey and I are doing what we can to keep it open. So far so good, but we have a long way to go in raising the funding necessary for the longevity it deserves.

I grab that beer my dad suggested and watch him.

Today he seems so much like himself. It's days like these I know I have to remember, because soon enough the bad ones present themselves.

Forty-five minutes later, a bowl of frosting in hand, and two beers in me to calm my nerves, I move on to the more difficult part of making a cake—icing it. I put my dad in front of a baseball game and just stare at the two chocolate circles and read the directions again: *Bake 35 minutes in preheated oven. Cool in pans for 10 minutes. Then remove to a wire rack to cool completely.*

What the fuck, Martha?

Could you not tell me how to get them out of the pan or what the hell a wire rack is?

Fuck it.

I turn them both upside and when I lift the pan off of the first one, it sits beautifully on top of the counter. The second one has a little trouble. Half of the cake gets stuck in the pan. I leave it there for now and put the unbroken one on a plate, then take the half not broken and set it on top of the first layer. With a knife I scrape out the broken half and set it beside its mate. Next I take the frosting that turned out pretty good, I must say, and scoop a heap on the cake.

I want to save some of the frosting for later—if you know what I mean.

With a butter knife, I start spreading the frosting and fuck me if the pieces of cake don't seem to be easing their way around in the frosting. I stop for a minute and look back at the directions. It says nothing about what to do if that happens.

"Hello, I'm here. The enchiladas just need to go in the oven."

I turn around to see Rosie holding a huge tray in her hand.

Thank fuck.

"Here, let me get that for you."

"There's more in the car." Her eyes jet to the counter and then back to me.

"Hey now, don't look at me like that."

"Like what?"

I shove the pan in the oven. "Like you're afraid you might lose your job."

"Oh, that's not what I was thinking at all."

She turns the Miele on.

That's the one thing that thrilled Zoey when we first looked at this house. Although it was the driveway that sold her—its expanse is the length of the house with double garages on each side, his and hers, she calls them, and so she no longer has to worry about hitting anything when she pulls in or out. I suggested using one for the boat, but she nixed that idea.

Now it stays at the marina.

I ignore Rosie's attempted wit. "How about I empty your car and you finish frosting the cake?"

"Is that what that is?"

I look over at the sad chocolate heap on a plate. "Maybe I should run to the store?"

Rosie gives me an unexpected hug. "No, it's perfect. I can fix it up, no worries. Where is the other present you bought her? I want to wrap it."

"I hid it in the office, but it's already wrapped."

She waves her hand. "Nonsense. They always wrap everything in black. Zoey loves color. I bought the perfect wrapping paper."

"You're the best."

"I know. Now go."

If anyone can make what I made look like a cake, I know Rosie can. And if anyone can wrap a present, it's her as well. I had Santana, a jeweler near the gallery, make Zoey a platinum and gemstone dream catcher necklace to remind her to always keep dreaming.

God, I sound like a fucking sap.

Squaring off my shoulders and feeling more masculine already, I glance into the family room and find my dad sitting on the couch with his head fallen back and snoring. I stop for a minute to look at him and wish he were like this all the time. But then my eyes shift to the easel in the corner of the room displaying the picture Zoey had transferred to canvas of the two kids eating ice-cream cones, and I'm thankful for the time I have left with him instead.

The car is parked close to the front door with the trunk open, and I grab what I can. "You have enough food here to feed an army," I tell Rosie, dumping the first load on the kitchen table.

"You can never have too much to eat, and besides the lot of you boys is like feeding an army." She laughs and starts to pull everything from the bags.

After my third trip, I glance toward the island and sitting beautifully right in the middle of the cherry red counter on some cake stand thing is Zoey's birthday cake—a genuine-looking chocolate confection that I hope she likes. "Great job."

"I found some extra icing in the refrigerator, so it was easy."

Damn!

"Oliver is on his way with the flowers."

I buff my nails on my button down. "Everything is going as planned. Who would have thought surprise parties would be so easy?"

"Well, not everything," she squeaks.

I narrow my eyes at her. "What?"

"Gisele just texted me that Zoey and the kids picked her up early."

"How? The store doesn't close until five."

"I guess your mother popped over and told her she'd close up for her."

Fuck!

I can only shake my head—good intentions, I guess.

Not only did I end up buying the closed-down store next to the gallery, and not only did I finally convince Isabella to open another clothing shop there, I also recommended the perfect manager for the place—Gisele.

Isabella's Wynwood is right next door to the gallery—the same gallery I ended up selling to my mother.

As for my relationship with my mother—let's just say it's a work in progress.

I look down at Rosie and rub my palms together. "Okay then, let's get this show on the road."

She claps her hands under her chin as if in anticipation.

With Rosie's eyes on me, I shakily pull the two-carat cushion-shaped yellow diamond ring from my pocket and stare at it. The light in the kitchen plays off the cut of the stone and reflects a spectrum of color onto the white cabinets. The way the prisms sparkle, move, almost dance around me reminds me of the first time I laid eyes on Zoey.

The moonlight was streaming into my room and I thought it was playing havoc with my mind. Light and shadow painted a picture that made me stop on a dime. "Z, is that you?" I asked into the darkness. The facial features on my pillow were so familiar, but I knew it couldn't be him—he was dead.

As I moved closer, the figure began to take shape—it was a woman.

At first I thought I was hallucinating—but I hadn't had anything to drink that night. Then I thought maybe sleep deprivation was the cause.

She stirred without waking and I crept closer still, realizing it wasn't my imagination—someone was sleeping in my bed.

Moving cautiously, I only stopped when I was standing over her. With the twist of a knob on the bedside lamp, I could see her more clearly. I stared down for the longest time as the light reflected off the red in her hair. I'd seen her photo, talked to her on the phone, and communicated with her via e-mail, but even if I hadn't, I'd have known who she was.

Her profile was softer than Z's but very similar. Her hair was a mess of curls that haloed around her sun-burnished skin, nothing like Z's skater cut, but her hair color—the unique red and brown tone—was exactly the same as Z's.

My eyes traveled downward and I quickly twisted my head to avoid looking at her. She wasn't dressed and it was wrong to stare at her like I was, but it was too late, I'd already had a glimpse and fuck, she was exquisite beyond belief. Her flesh-toned bra showed off her slight curves and the delicateness of her rib cage made me think her bones were made of porcelain. Her matching panties were small but just enough to cover what I had no right to see anyway. Thank fuck, at least I stopped looking before I got that far.

Z's sister, Zoey Flowers, was without a doubt the most beautiful thing I had ever seen.

"It's beautiful." Rosie's voice boomerangs me back.

"Yeah, it is, just like her."

"She's going to love it."

"I hope so." A slow smile drifts across my face, because I think she will too.

I selected the yellow stone because Zoey loves color and a clear diamond just didn't seem like her. And it's two carats, no bigger, because like my father, Zoey doesn't like anything too flashy.

I learned that the hard way.

When I traded in my father's Camry, I brought her home a Mercedes SUV. Let's just say she suggested we take it back and use the money for something else, like feeding a third world country. On the way back to the dealership, she told me she fantasized once about driving a convertible.

That was easy—one Mercedes SUV for a Volkswagen convertible.

Done!

The doorbell rings. "I'll get it!" Rosie beams with excitement.

I nod at her and with one last look at the ring I take a deep breath.

God, I love Zoey.

She changed my life.

I never thought relationships and domestic shit were for me. Never wanted anything to do with them. Never cared about any of it.

My father's life had been torn apart when my mother left during that storm. With the dark hazy blur that sped in and out of Miami, a piece of him went with it. But the minute Zoey ran through that fucking rain the first night she was here, I knew something deep inside me had changed.

Sure, I have always needed control in my life—it is how I live. But until that moment I had never felt the need to commit to any one woman. *Zoey was different.*

When I looked at her I wanted to own every piece of her. Wanted to know her in ways I'd never known another. I wanted to right her wrongs—to take her pain away in any way possible.

But she was my best friend's sister and I knew I shouldn't be feeling that way—that was for fucking sure. He hadn't wanted it—had warned me away from her.

The struggle was harder than I could have imagined, because the line wasn't so defined. Sure, I was the sadistic motherfucker who had just broken her heart, but I was also a man with a God complex who wanted to figure out a way to put it back together.

I knew I should walk away, but when I saw the way she looked around for pieces of her brother that weren't anywhere, I couldn't leave her there alone. Her eyes were scanning, searching, wanting, seeking—I had to stop them, put an end to her pain. And I did. After that, no matter how hard I tried, I couldn't stay away from her.

Once she said she was staying, I let my need to take care of her overcome my guilt—it was the only way for me to survive. I made my own peace with Z, telling him what I was doing was for her, and I really thought it was.

I had every intention of letting her go after the summer. I thought about keeping in touch, but nothing past that. I'd never had a real girlfriend and I liked having her around, but just because I'd never been in a relationship didn't mean I didn't understand what we had wasn't real—it seemed too good to be true. I thought what we had was a result of both of us knowing we were temporary.

And besides, love wasn't something I knew, had never wanted to.

But the day I thought I might have lost her, the day she was missing in the storm and I couldn't find her—everything changed. I didn't understand what it was until she pulled in the driveway and I knew she was okay. I was so mad. I was so happy. I was so relieved. I knew then that although I never meant to, I loved her.

I really loved her.

Rosie grabs a towel and wipes her hands.

I thought she'd left.

The doorbell rings again. "I'm coming!" she yells and then looks back. "You better hurry if you want to eat the cake before dinner. *Dios mío.*"

I laugh.

Of course I do.

One of Zoey's checklist items was to eat dessert before dinner, so once in a while I indulge her. And of course, tonight has to be one of those nights.

With one last look at the ring, I take a deep breath and plunge the ring into the cake, smooth over the messed-up frosting, and mark the spot with a single tall candle.

That's her piece.

Now some people might be concerned that she'll actually take a bite and chip a tooth, or worse choke on the ring, but I won't let it go that far.

If she doesn't see it first, I'll point it out.

Yet, if anyone knows Zoey like I know Zoey, they'd know today marks the first day of the rest of her life. At twenty-eight she isn't worried about dying anymore. No longer twenty-seven, in her eyes she's already beat the odds of joining the club like her ancestors before her.

The sound of voices murmuring from the other room pulls me out of my head—the guests are arriving.

Time to get ready.

The minutes tick by so slowly; but soon enough, she's pulling in the driveway. We all hide and when the door opens we yell, "Surprise!"

She stands in the doorway with a look of shock on her face—startled eyes and her mouth half-open. She drops her purse to the floor, pats her hair, and straightens her clothes.

God, I love her.

All I can do is gawk.

I can't help but think what a lucky bastard I am.

"What are you waiting for, son?" My dad nudges me forward.

She's searching for me among the crowd. I emerge feeling like a triumphant warrior. When she catches my stare, and I'm close enough to see the rise and fall of her chest as her breathing steadies, I extend my hand. "Come with me."

She looks around at the house full of people and then back at Gisele. "Will you be okay?"

Rosie rushes forward. "I got this, now go."

She walks my way and I study every line, every curve of her figure. When she's close enough, she puts her hand in mine. "I had no idea."

I lean over and whisper in her ear, "Are you sure?"

She nods, still catching her breath. "You did this?"

My pride shines. "I did."

I lead her into the kitchen. Small votive candles are lit all around us, and soft music plays in the background. I stop in front of the counter and light the candle before looking at her. "Happy birthday, Zoey."

She looks around, her hands now trembling. "Are we doing this alone?"

"Yep." I smile. "Go for it."

Her tension eases as she looks at me.

And I can't help but kiss her.

When the kiss deepens and starts to drive my body where it should not be headed with a houseful of people, I nip at her lip and pull back, then point to the cake.

She blows out the candle.

The knife is next to the stand. I cut a slice—*the* slice—and just as I'm handing it to her, the ring clinks to the plate.

That's my cue.

She pinches it between her fingers and stares. "Nate?"

I press my finger to her lips. "Shh."

I didn't think I'd be nervous, but I am.

She gazes at me adoringly and I melt on the spot. My nervousness gone, my feelings pour out in a rush of words.

"You changed my life. I never thought relationships were for me. Never wanted anything to do with them. Never cared about them. But the minute you ran through that fucking rain, that first night, I knew something deep inside me had changed."

"I felt it too," she whispers.

I push the hair from her face. "No matter how much I tried, I just couldn't leave you alone."

"I'm glad you didn't."

"How could I have? I didn't know it then, but we were made for each other."

Tears stream down her face.

I take the chocolate-covered ring from her hand and drop to my knee on shaky legs. Then I take her hand in mine and hover the ring over the tip of her finger. "Zoey Flowers, you are everything I could want in this lifetime and the next. Let me be the one to hold you, love you, take you to Paris, to the end of the earth, anywhere you want to go. Just say you'll marry me."

She slaps her hand over her mouth and drops to her knees.

Moments pass.

Seconds fly by as she stares at me in shock, not saying a word.

Finally, she clenches my face. "Nate, you've filled my heart with shooting stars and my mind with full moons. Yes, yes, yes, I'll marry you."

Relief.

More relief

That's how I feel.

Love.

Lust.

Want.

Need.

And a lifetime of happiness.

That's what reflects back when I look into her eyes.

My heart grows just a little bigger in this one moment.

I love the way she looks with a smile on her face and tears of happiness streaming down it. I smile back at her, the biggest, brightest smile I have ever worn.

And then I slide the ring on her finger.

"It's full of frosting," she cries.

"I can fix that." I drop my head to lick it clean and she joins me, our mouths connecting in such a way that I know can only mean a lifetime of joy and happiness.

And when I look up and our eyes meet, I have to say that even though I never bought into her fate-is-what-it-is-and-the-stars-have-it-all-laid-out-for-me talk, tonight when the moon rises in the sky, I'm going to howl my new motto as loud as I can—FUCK DESTINY!

Dear Reader,

Thank you so much for reading. I hope you enjoyed *The 27 Club* and would consider sharing your thoughts by writing a review on the retailer Web site or Goodreads.

For the latest news, book details, and other information, visit my official Web site at authorkimkarr.com or follow me on Twitter @authorkimkarr or Facebook at Author Kim Karr.

ACKNOWLEDGMENTS

My infinite thanks go to:

Amy Tannenbaum of the Jane Rotrosen Agency, who always has my best interests at heart and is more than willing to talk to me anytime, about anything. Amy, you are such an amazing person and I couldn't be more grateful to have you as my literary agent.

Kerry Donovan of Penguin for always finding ways to make what I write so much better. I couldn't respect your outlook on romance any more than I do.

Penguin and the team at New American Library, for so eagerly and enthusiastically taking on each book as if it is my first and for your willingness to work with me on even the smallest of details. I really appreciate all of you.

Mary Tarter, Jody O Fraleigh, and Laura Hansen. Thank you for all your help and for your friendships—both of which I truly value.

In addition, I would also like to thank everyone who read this book and provided me with their feedback.

All of the bloggers who have become my friends—you're all so amazing and I cannot possibly put into words the amount of gratitude I have for each and every one of you!

And finally, my love and gratitude to my family—to my husband of twenty years who became Mr. Mom while continuing to go to work every day, to my children who not only took on roles that I for many years had always done—laundry, grocery shopping, cleaning—but always asked how the book was coming and actually beamed to their friends when telling them their mom wrote a book.

And finally—a giant thank-you to all of you.

PROLOGUE
Crazy

August 1999

This was the best place on earth. Music roared through the speakers, electricity filled the air, and crowds of people rushed to find their seats. My father and I stopped quickly to purchase our concert T-shirts. Clutching our tickets tightly, we made our way through the crowd.

The excitement around us was almost indescribable. We sat down, mesmerized by our surroundings. It was impossible to take everything in. Being so close to the stage was intoxicating. I was frozen with shock, and my eyes flickered through the rays of the spotlights as they made their way up the stairs.

Bono encouraged thousands of fans to wave their hands and nod their heads. Eventually, I began to absorb my surroundings as U2 began to play "Beautiful Day." Slipping into an almost hypnotic state, I closed my eyes and swayed to the pulse of the beat as the vibrations of the music penetrated my body. I remained in this state throughout most of the concert, just as I had many times before.

Going to the Greek Theatre, or the Greek, was an experience like no other. It was the largest outdoor amphitheater in the area. Celebrities, unknown bands, known singers, groupies, and concertgoers gathered here from miles around, but they had all come for the same reason: to listen to the best music ever.

My father was the general manager of the Greek. He loved music, mostly rock, from the eighties and nineties. He'd been going to concerts since he was thirteen and always bought a T-shirt. To say that he had a few concert T-shirts was putting it mildly. He started working at the Greek at a young age and never left because he loved his job. He always knew the inside scoop about bands and lived for sharing his stories with me. I was even lucky enough to have one of the Wear Purple ticket stubs from Prince's sold-out Purple Rain concert in my possession.

But there is one concert that will forever hold a place in my heart. It was the Nirvana benefit concert for Bosnian rape victims. They opened with "Rape Me," and the emotion in that song made me fall even more in love with music than I already had. After I left the concert that night, the Greek was not only my father's favorite place to be, but mine, too.

My mom was not into music; she preferred clothes to concerts. She taught me to sew, and together we made a quilt with the concert T-shirts I outgrew. Between my father and me, we collected over two hundred pieces of music history.

Trying to figure out what I wanted to be when I grew up was always hard. I was torn between my father's love for music, my mother's love for fashion, and my love for photography. I thought maybe I'd have a music career or go to the New York School of Fashion and Design like my mother had. But whichever career path I chose needed to provide me with the freedom to take pictures.

CHAPTER 1
Out of My Head

October 2006

Walking through the Greek-lettered doors of Kappa Sigma, I felt like I'd just stepped onto a movie set. It was Halloween, everyone was wearing costumes, holding red Solo cups, and dancing . . . well, not everyone.

I looked twice to be certain, but sure as shit, there was a large dark blue ice luge in the center of the living room. The guy at the bottom of the channel was my boyfriend, Ben, and the person in line behind him was my best friend, Aerie. I didn't go to a lot of fraternity parties, and looking at the two of them now, I knew why.

Frowning at the two drunken idiots on the receiving end of the ice luge, I headed toward the kitchen to grab a beer. As I crossed back into the living room, I saw Ben sucking on a lime and squinting his eyes with his nose scrunched as he moved his head from side to side. While shaking my head, I passed by a couple playing beer pong and laughed. Clearly she'd had a few too many drinks.

Noticing me, Ben shot a wicked smirk in my direction and

crooked his index finger, gesturing me toward him. He strode a few steps closer, his gaze holding mine as the crowd cleared the way.

Standing face-to-face, I could see that his forget-me-not blue eyes were slightly hooded, allowing me only a glimpse of his dilated pupils. But his sly grin was still present, meaning he was in a somewhat coherent state of mind.

Raising an eyebrow, I pointed to the dark blue ice sculpture. "Hey, how many times did you hit that?"

Feigning confusion, he raised his hands palms up. "Not sure," he said as he cocked his head to one side while shrugging his shoulders.

Ben took the cup out of my hand and set it on the table beside us. He snaked his arms around my waist and pulled me to him. "Hey, Dahl. What took so long?" he asked as he placed his strong hands on my behind.

Wrapping my arms around his neck, I rested my forehead on his chin and let out a slow sigh. "Photo shoot took longer than expected. Drake had a meltdown when the models' outfits weren't the shade of purple he'd asked for."

Ben groaned and dipped his head to kiss me. "Drake's a fuckin' pansy-ass. He'd better hope you find a new internship for next semester because he's really starting to piss me off."

Flinching a little at his words, I leaned back to place my hands on his hard chest before looking into his slightly glazed eyes. "Ben, promise me you'll stay away from him."

"Will do. Promise, Dahl." He chuckled, the smell of alcohol strong on his breath.

I sighed and ran my hands up to his hair, combing my fingers through it.

Looking at me with concern, he whispered, "You okay?"

"Of course. The wrong color purple isn't really the end of the world."

He studied me and hesitated before responding. "Dahl, you know that's not what I mean."

I stiffened. I knew what he meant, but I didn't want to talk about the anniversary of my parents' death.

"Ben, I'm cool. Let's have a good time," I muttered. I broke our embrace, grabbed my beer, and looked around the room for Aerie.

Ben nodded, his sly grin returning while he watched me chug the entire contents of the Solo cup before chewing on the ice cubes. Beckoning me to the center of the room, he pointed to the luge. "This way, gorgeous."

Having refilled our drinks, we stood at the liquor-filled ice dispenser. The party was in full swing, and I watched Ben hit the luge yet again. When I excused myself to use the restroom, I glanced around at the crowd and pushed through the chaos. There were wall-to-wall people in every room. I stumbled into a tall guy with red hair, and I knew he was beyond drunk when he tried to kiss me. I shoved him and giggled when he tripped over his own feet and fell on his ass. I continued making my way to the stairs. They were filled with students drinking, making out, or doing way more than I ever needed to see.

The room smelled like alcohol mixed with sweat, and I suddenly felt like I couldn't get out of there soon enough. Weaving around the crowd on the stairs I was thankful to finally make it to the bathroom.

After splashing my face with water, I headed to Ben's room for a much-needed mental break. This particular day was the hardest one of the year for me, but being around friends always seemed to help me through it. As I headed toward his bed, I noticed the tickets he had given me this morning. I knew he meant well by buying us Greek tickets to see one of my favorite bands, Maroon 5. He thought he would brighten an otherwise dark day, but I couldn't go back there.

Sighing, I threw myself on the bed. Yes, he meant well and he really wanted to be the one to take me there, but he knew I would never go back. I've told him this. The U2 performance was the last concert I went to with my family before my mother, my aunt, and my father died in a small plane crash coming home from Mexico.

I'm not sure how long I stayed in his room thinking about my parents until I finally decided to rejoin the party. I first stopped in the kitchen to grab a third beer, and then headed back into the living room. All the lights had been turned off and orange candles glowed everywhere as the sound of haunting music filled the room.

I felt a strong arm wrap around my waist and Ben nibble on my ear. "Where you been, Dahl?"

"Just grabbing a beer," I answered, holding my Solo cup up in the air and twisting around in his arms.

Loud screams pulled my attention back to the ice luge where Aerie was jumping up and down, grabbing her throat, and squealing in pain. Motioning my head toward her, I set my cup down on the banister. "What's she drinking?"

Clutching his arms tighter around my hips, he pulled me closer. As he slipped his long fingers inside the waistband of my black leggings, he fingered the lace of my panties and whispered in my ear, "Don't know." Then he placed one of his legs between mine and asked, "Want some?"

I shook my head no but was nearly panting as I responded. "I promised Aerie I'd go with her to the bar and listen to some new band. One of us should stay somewhat lucid—at least until we get there."

He trailed his hands across the top of my panties; the fingertips of his one hand grazed from my backside across to my hip bone. Before I knew what was happening, his fingers started drifting down into the front of my pants.

"I didn't mean the luge," he said coyly before plunging his tongue into my ear and grinding his hips into mine.

I pulled back from him and removed his hands from inside my

leggings. I needed to stop this very public display of affection before I couldn't. I brushed his blond hair away from his seductive blue eyes and asked, "You coming?"

Grinning fiendishly, he answered, "I hope to be soon, gorgeous!"

I laughed and shook my head. "Ben Covington, you're impossible."

I reached around his neck and tugged his head down to mine, connecting my mouth to his.

Ben pulled his soft lips from mine and groaned in my ear. "My room now. I need to fuck you."

I leaned back and stared at his incredibly irresistible grin. Summoning all of my willpower, I tried to decide what to do.

Before I could respond, Aerie tugged my ponytail. She swayed slightly and slurred, "There you are, girlfriend! You ready?"

Separating myself from him, I shrugged my shoulders and mouthed, "Sorry. Rain check?"

He exhaled and muttered under his breath to Aerie, "Nice fucking timing."

Aerie, being Aerie, thumped him in the forehead. "Watch the language, asshole," she quipped as she reached for my arm.

Leaning back toward Ben, I gave him a swift kiss. With Aerie forcefully tugging me toward the door, I managed to say, "Meet you back here later." Walking backward and giggling, I blew Ben a kiss and waved goodbye.

Rocking back on his heels, he stood with both hands in his pockets while biting his lip and shaking his head at me.

The cool night helped to settle the heat Ben had ignited. Sounds of Halloween echoed from every direction as we walked down fraternity row. We only took a taxi part of the way; then we walked the rest. Once we got out of the taxi, I glanced at Aerie, or more specifically, at her devil costume. She must have been plastered when she got ready because it wasn't something I could have ever imagined her wearing: a very short red sequin dress, a devil tail, high heels, and all the accessories to match. It could barely pass as an acceptable red-light-district ensemble—let alone a Halloween costume.

As we walked toward the bar, I grabbed a stumbling Aerie by the arm before she landed on her ass. "Have a nice trip?" I laughed, knowing full well she didn't like to be made fun of but not really caring.

Aerie shrugged, pulling her beautiful wavy blond hair back and fastening it with the clip she had been fishing out of her purse when she missed her step. "Be nice," she quipped, stopping me so she could readjust her shoe. "At least you can't call me a noncon-formist!"

I never told Aerie that Halloween was the anniversary of my parents' death. Ben was the only one who knew I never wanted to camouflage my feelings with a costume.

I sighed and wrapped my arm around her shoulder and put on my very best Vincent Price voice from "Thriller." "Ahhhahhahaaa-haaa, you know I never conform. It's against my religion."

We continued walking—Aerie in red high-heel vixen pumps, me in black Converse sneakers—and she tripped again, leaving her shoe behind her. "Aerie, really, I think your outfit could have done without those shoes. They're too big, you dumbass." I turned around and picked up her shoe. "What size are these?" I asked, squinting to see inside.

"Don't worry about it; it's not like you'd ever wear them any-way, Miss I-Always-Have-to-Wear-Comfortable-Shoes. It was the only pair of red shoes left, and one size too big is hardly an issue when they match your outfit perfectly," she announced, yanking the shoe out of my hand. "You know it's all about the look. I'd sacrifice comfort for style any day. Ahem . . ." She cleared her throat while looking down at my shoes.

Shaking my head at her, I couldn't help but roll my eyes. "Whatever."

I walked a little slower so she could keep her shoes on. Aerie said in a much sweeter voice, "Thanks for taking me out. Now, come on. Let's get moving and have some fun. It's girls' night out after all, and I have a broken heart to mend."

I gave her a little smile as I squeezed her arm. "Sweetheart, I think you started the mending process hours ago!"

Aerie shuffled down the sidewalk to hold her shoes in place, and I knew this was going to be an interesting night. Aerie, my best friend since freshman year, broke up with her boyfriends like I changed the flavor of my coffee creamer—often.

Aerie was type A, even though you would never have known it from her drunken state. She strove for perfection—not just with herself—but with her boyfriends. Which explains why she broke up with her last boyfriend yesterday. Tonight she was looking forward to new options, and I was looking forward to hearing a new band.

Kim Karr lives in Florida with her husband and four kids. She's always had a love for books and recently decided to embrace one of her biggest passions—writing.

CONNECT ONLINE

authorkimkarr.com
facebook.com/authorkimkarr
twitter.com/authorkimkarr